Also by Rilla Askew

Strange Business

The Mercy Seat

Fire in Beulah

Harpsong

Kind of Kin

Most American: Notes from a Wounded Place

Prize for the Fire

a novel

Rilla Askew

UNIVERSITY OF OKLAHOMA PRESS : NORMAN

Financial support was provided from the Office of the Vice President for Research and the Office of the Provost, University of Oklahoma.

Library of Congress Cataloging-in-Publication Data

Names: Askew, Rilla, author.
Title: Prize for the fire : a novel / Rilla Askew.
Description: First. | Norman, OK : University of Oklahoma Press, [2022] | Summary: "Draws on The Examinations of Anne Askew and other historical documents to re-create in novel form the life of Anne Askew, who was tried, convicted, and burned at the stake in 1546. Follows Askew from a rebellious girlhood in Lincolnshire, through an abusive marriage in the Fenlands from which she escapes, to an underground network of evangelical Reformists in London, where her public interpretations of Scripture bring her to the attention of the authorities"—Provided by publisher.
Identifiers: LCCN 2022003338 | ISBN 978-0-8061-9072-3 (hardcover)
Subjects: LCGFT: Novels.
Classification: LCC PS3551.S545 P75 2022 | DDC 813/.54—dc23
LC record available at https://lccn.loc.gov/2022003338

The paper in this book meets the guidelines for permanence and durability of the Committee on Production Guidelines for Book Longevity of the Council on Library Resources, Inc. ∞

1 2 3 4 5 6 7 8 9 10

For Ruth

So be it. O Lorde so be it.

—By me Anne Askewe

Contents

Book Four
London
1544

Book Five
London and Lincolnshire
1546

Prologue

Anne and Henry

In their final months, their lives brushed, as one's sleeve may glance another's in a crowded hall and transfer contagion, silk on silk, the barest whisper—a faint exhalation of the grave's breath. It is not known for certain if they ever met. Anne claimed once to have seen him—at Hampton Court, it is said, when he came petulantly to the queen's closet as she stood disguised among the queen's ladies, her Testament quickly hidden in a fold of her gown. Or was it an evening hour as the king and queen strolled in the privy garden at Whitehall? No matter. In the end, Henry was forced to acknowledge her, and worse, to acknowledge what his bishop and lord chancellor had done to her—though he would not acknowledge, would never acknowledge, what he had charged them to do. The king's anger at this affront burned in him, still, upon his deathbed.

That tortured hour found him groaning with terror, for he who had believed his own theological arguments, erratic, contradictory, self-serving, saw then with the sight of the dying. In his bloated and poisoned fever, he saw that which he had never witnessed with living eyes: the beheaded wives, slaughtered servants, traitors drawn and quartered who had never been traitors at all. The aged countess screaming and bloodied at her botched execution. The young heretic tied to a wooden chair praying aloud to Christ the Bridegroom as the flames licked her breasts. He hated her perfect faith, hated all he had been told of the grace of her dying. Henry clutched the archbishop's hand, begging him with silent grip to perform the old rituals that he might be guaranteed entry to the Heaven he had always believed in, though he could not, even in dying, confess his true sins to avoid the Hell he knew he deserved.

But this is not that great glutton's story, though he remains always on the periphery. Anne's life was shadowed by Henry's, as the lives of all the king's subjects were shaped and shadowed by His

Majesty's will. Anne Askew believed, as all England believed, that the Almighty had bequeathed unto Henry the power to reign. She believed, as Henry believed, that the king's will and the Lord's will were one and the same. In her young years she believed this. She did not die believing it. She died with her eyes lifted to a glowering heaven, seeing what only the dying may see, knowing what they know.

Book One

Lincolnshire and the Fenlands

1537

I

They Live Meanly Here

Friskney

Winter into Spring

1537

– Chapter 1 –

They live meanly here, Maddie, and demand of me that I do the same. It is not poverty of purse but meanness of spirit which causes them to crimp their mouths if one but ask for a bit of beef for one's supper. Oh, my dear sister, you cannot imagine! I say this daily, hourly, and then I think, but she does know! She must know everything, see everything, from her place on High.

Do you, Maddie? Can you see all, know all?

Or are you in that other place where the priests say we must suffer until we are burned pure enough to enter Heaven, our souls scoured by fire to be made fit for God's presence? I cannot bear to think of you in Purgatory, suffering penance for sins which I know to be no more vile than a butterfly may sin when she lights upon the primrose to steal its nectar! You are good and pure and pious beyond measure—why would God not take you directly to His bosom the very instant the breath left your body? I tell myself it must be so!

Yet my heart will not settle. My thoughts turn to no good purpose. The urgings in my limbs cause me to walk and walk, though there is no comforting place where I may walk in the whole of this fetid country! And no person to turn to, no friend or brother to ask, and I dare not read thy secret book, which I carried with me from South Kelsey, for *he* would discover me, and tell the vicar, and the vicar would accuse me; he would say it is this reading of Scripture which causes my heart to doubt. Not so!

At least, I think it is not so.

He conspires with the Kymes daily, you know, this dour and wolfish priest, Thomas Jordan. Oh, I would a thousand times prefer our old piggy Father Sebastian to this cold-eyed vicar who comes skulking about in the evenings to advise and direct *him*, my so-called *husband*, and his bald-pated father, and most especially his mother, the old mistress, Margaret Kyme, who is round and puffed as a mother hen, though she watches the comings-in and goings-out of goods in this household with the ravening eyes of a hawk.

It was she who discovered the missing sweetmeats I had taken from the larder, for the which I am banished to this airless tomb until my so-called husband returns from Lincoln—banished! Like a child! To sit and ponder my iniquities, as the old mistress tells me, and I am not even allowed to have my maid to attend me—and where does she think she is given that right? I shall send a letter to Father to tell him how she treats me! I told her this. She seemed in no manner concerned.

And yet, if it were not for how I must sit here for hours on end in daylight, or what passes for daylight in this cursed fen country, I should be glad for the nights of peace, when I am able to sleep in my cold marriage bed alone. Though I do not sleep. I am up at all hours, wandering this cramped room, wall to wall to wall. Oh, what would I give to be in that large, sweet room of our childhood. Our own oaken bed with its velvet curtains and pale pillow beres the colour of clotted cream, sewn by your own hands in those months before—

Oh, Maddie, if you had not died, I would not now be here!

I know. I must consider: if you had not died, you would be the one here suffering beneath that man's harsh thumb and the greedy eyes of his mother. Small penance, in this lifetime, that I have taken your place. And then my selfish soul will whisper: *but perhaps Maddie should not have minded so very much.*

Oh, see. See! I am even now, this day, the same selfish girl I have ever been. I remember your hurt eyes that last morning we spoke. I see again your sweet smile, feel again how your smile caused such rage in me, and then my foul words fly back to my ears, and I—oh, I cannot bear it! I must walk.

If you had not died. I murmur the words beneath my breath like a novena, whisper them at morning prayer. I cry them in silence to the black night through the small slit of window, or, as now, to the glowering noontide fog enclosing the small, flat yard from which I can see nothing. Only grey mists and ghosts of sheep grazing at their mangers, for there is no green in this mud-brown land. Not in winter. Perhaps there will be in summer. But by Whitsuntide, or sooner, I feel that I shall follow thee in death.

She is ever after me, the old mistress, bidding me drudge through the thousand tedious tasks she lays out for me. I stand at the work in my linen cap and think to myself: This is thy life now, Anne Kyme, and ever more shall be—to spend thy days minding milkmaids and overseeing the carding of the wool and the polishing of pewter, and sewing, and sewing, and sewing. And when it is not she, it is *he*, my so-called husband, who is after me in the night. He will have me regardless of whether I am well or unwell, and most especially when he is angry; and it is for this reason I do try very hard not to make him angry, because he must ever follow his berating of me with his rough mounting, and it is ugly and painful and I abhor it, truly, but seeing as thou hast escaped it by reason of thy death, I think it is nothing that thou ought to have to endure thinking about now.

I do wonder at times, though, if he would not now be so quick to anger if I'd had the wit to hold my laughter on our wedding night and not let it snort and snigger into the room. Even now, when I think of it, I want to laugh. So I must not think of it. I shan't.

No, I *will* think of it. And what's more, I shall tell you, and laugh as long as I like, for I've no one else to tell it to. I should have prepared better. I knew what was to take place in the marriage bed. *A wife must kiss her husband and surrender to all sorts of naughties*—did I not tease you with those very words? Yet I could not, really, have prepared myself for that which caused me such trouble.

His knees.

No, truly. How many wives, I do wonder, may say their fate was laid out for them by their husband's knobby knees? Not many, I'll warrant. This may not be all the truth, but it is surely part, and it began on the very night of our wedding when I came alone to this room, and young Beatrice came to undress me. Do you remember her? The little red-haired serving girl from the kitchen? She is jumpy as a hare, and not well trained, but she is my one gift from Father, besides your dowry chest, which I have brought with me from South Kelsey, and I am grateful for her, despite her clumsy hands and timid face.

'You're trembling, miss,' she said as she unlaced me.

'Am I? It is cold in here.' I knew then my fear had overtaken me, which I had managed to push away, even until the end of the wedding Mass when we two stood liars at the door of the church—yes, liars! For *he* had vowed before God he would love, honour, and comfort me, and I have had none of that from him; and I promised from that day forth to honour, obey, and serve him, and I tell you, my soul roars at the very notion. But, Maddie, I tried. I swore that I would make for him a good and humble wife. But even Beatrice saw how I trembled. 'I shall be warm enough in bed,' I told her. Then, blushing, I added, 'Quick now, bring me my new smock.' She put the smock over my head. It is the fine cambric one you sewed for your wedding night, Maddie. I brought it with me, as I brought all your linens and sheets and embroidered napkins, and your beautiful book, which I keep as I found it, in the bottom of your dowry chest. Beatrice combed out my hair, the two of us quivering like conies in the centre of the room.

Then came a sharp rap at the door, and we both jumped. Beatrice, taking her stub of candle and giving me a long, worried look, went out, and in the next moment *he* came in, wearing a scowl, which he intended, no doubt, should create fear and obedience in his new wife. It failed him poorly. He removed his black gown and laid it in the clothespress, stood before me in doublet and stockings, and I lowered my gaze.

'Turn!' he ordered me. At first I did not know what he wanted me to do, but, glancing up, I saw his arm outstretched and his finger pointing towards the wall, and I understood then he meant me to face away so that he might change his dress. I turned towards the corner. I heard the sounds of unclasped doublet, unbuckled codpiece, all the tug and pull of linen, strange to my ears, until at last I heard him say: 'You may come to bed, wife.' He stood next the bed in his sleeping cap and nightshirt, his face glowing pink. Beneath the hem of his shirt, his legs were pale and thin as hazel twigs. The sight of Kyme's hairless sticks, his two knees like white knobs in the lamp's shadows, well, it made me burst out: 'If thy legs had been any poorer, sir, you'd have need of a barrow to cart yourself about!'

And then, I could not help it, I began to laugh. Oh, you should have seen his fury! Or no, indeed, you should not. His face swelled up red and bloated till I thought his very head would burst, which made me laugh the more, which angered him further, and he stood sputtering at me to be silent! And I, near choking, kept saying, 'Yes. Yes, I will.' But I could not. His fury grew larger. 'Stop!' he yelled. 'Thou insolent, feckless woman, shut thy mouth!' By the time I got hold of myself and quieted my laughter, all hope for his tender care of me, if ever there had been any, was surely lost. And then—

Oh. Never mind. You needn't hear of my pain and embarrassment that night. But I will tell you this: I lied when I said his lips are like a jackdaw's beak. In truth, they are more like a mallard's bill: stiff and hard that way, but somewhat malleable and protruding. His mating, too, is rather like a drake's—excepting, alas, not over with so quick. Though, mercifully, not near so frequent. When at last, snoring loudly, he slept, I lay in the dark, staring up at the tester and burning with shame for what a wife must endure from her husband, until in my mind I would see again his knobby knees and red sputtering face. I would try to hold myself very still upon the bed, so that I might not shake the man awake with my quaking laughter.

He returns on the morrow, or so the old mistress tells me, with a sly lift of her brow and twist to her plump lips, as if this were news I should be glad of. But oh, I dread, Maddie. I dread. I tell myself I shall sit on this ugly stool and watch through the window, and when I see him coming along the road, I shall—what? What shall I do? Push the clothespress in front of the door so that he may not enter? I have thought of that. But even had I strength enough to move that oaken monstrosity, which I haven't: what then? Shall I starve to death in this my marriage chamber? They'll not allow Beatrice to bring me food, and I cannot feed myself on dust motes and thin air, and I cannot escape through this slit of window no wider than my head.

At times, I do think it were well I should starve and die here. Then would Father regret his miserliness which caused my death! He should have forced old Master Kyme to return thy half portion, not offered me to marry his loathsome son in thy place! I vow to sit here forever, but then the old mistress comes and bids me come to supper. I tell her once, twice, thrice that I am too sick to eat. She makes no reply but stands with her arms folded beneath her big bosoms and gazes at me with hard eyes, and waits, and waits. Then I hear my stomach groan aloud with its hunger, and I feel my chin lowering in surrender. How can this be? I who cannot bear to bow my head before anyone! Yet these dank winter evenings I stand meekly and follow that woman to table and make no more protest than a flea but sit in silence while she prattles on about the sly thievery of milkmaids and which of the guildsmen are to provide candles for Sunday's Mass and Cromwell's shameful closing of the monasteries and other such tediums while the bland mutton is served.

So much has changed, Maddie, within me, within all England, in the six months and eleven days since thy death. Yes, I count the days, the hours, nearly. Just as I count my sins, which you must by now be weary of hearing. But what else can I do? I will not make confession to the Vicar Jordan, though the sins soiling my soul would prevent me from joining you even in Purgatory, much less meet you in Paradise, where in my heart I know you must be—I cannot bear to think otherwise. I cannot live!

Yet I fear not to: for if I die this day, I die in mortal sin. Never to see thy sweet face in the Hereafter no more than in this world. There can be no absolution unless I confess what I will not. And, so, I wait. And pray. To you, Maddie, and not the Holy Mother, for you will hear me, and she would not. Did I not cry out to her at your dying bedside? Did I not pray and plead, Mother Mary, have mercy! Have mercy.

He came in the weak dawn hours before the fog thinned, when least I could watch for him or prepare myself. But there was one good thing: it is Sunday. Master Kyme, in his piety, will not take me on Sunday. I felt him standing beside the bed looking down at me as I held my eyes closed, pretending sleep. He bade me rise and wash myself for Mass. 'I am unwell, sir,' I said, but he, still in his riding clothes and with his flattened hair pasted damp upon his forehead, took me by the arm and drew me hard from the bed so that I was forced to scramble to my feet or be dragged over the thresh. He stood me at the wash basin and departed. I did not wait for him to send up Beatrice; I knew he would not. I poured out water from the ewer and began to wash.

They have no chapel in their mean little manor, but we must walk 'most a mile into Friskney every morning, the entire household filing along the mucky road to the parish church whether the sleet falls or the rains come, the old mistress in her gable headdress, and I plodding along in the same. No female will now wear the French hood since Anne the Queen lost her head—not that I believe the old woman ever wore such piquant fashion. I do miss the sauciness of that style, though, our smoothed hair peeking out above our brows. I would welcome even the lightness of coif and veil, but no, I must hie me to Mass in great stiff coverings like the old mistress, my poor little Beatrice trailing behind without even a cloak to keep her warm.

I have been intending to write to Father to send down some lengths of wool to make a cloak for her. I shall need to discover some worthy pretext, however, for they say I mustn't spoil her. Spoil her! Hah! The old mistress smacks her about the ears like a thieving hound if Beatrice so much as lifts her head. For such a skittish one, though, the girl has more stomach than I knew when I begged Father to send her with me. Few enough comforts do I have to be grateful for in these loathsome days, but having Beatrice with me is one.

Kyme and his father were as ever, *he* striding ahead with his hands clasped behind him like an old friar, and his naked-pated old father turning to grin and leer at me from the nick of his eye like a naughty boy. We passed between the clustered gravestones in the churchyard—how they do jut from the earth like God's teeth in the morning mist! Inside the church, Kyme joined his guildsmen, and I stood with the old mistress and the servants. Mother Kyme will ever keep a watchful eye on me to see to my reverence at the kneeling prayers, the sacring, the elevation of the Host—and I do, Maddie, I lift my head and my hands to the Host raised high in the priest's hands beyond the rood screen, but not my gaze, dear sister, for I cannot. Not since the day of thy funeral Mass. No one knows this, not even the old mistress, for all their eyes are on the Body of Christ, and so they do not see my sacrilege. None sees but thee, Maddie, and that Lamb of God whose very Body I did—

No! Hush. Let us not think on these things.

So, yes, this morning I stood with the others for final prayers; we turned to go out, and as we passed from the dimness of the church to grey daylight, the Vicar Jordan stopped me upon the church step. 'Mistress Kyme,' says he, 'if a wife would be obedient to God, she must be obedient to her husband. Is this not so?'

My heart stuttered. All about the churchyard, the parishioners paused, turned their curious gaze towards us. 'Yes, Father,' I said.

'A virtuous woman eats not the bread of idleness,' he said. 'Nor does she steal from her own household! Rather, an obedient wife must do good unto her husband and not evil. Is this not so?'

I stood with my head lowered, my eyes tracing the pocked limestone at my feet. *Steal from her own household.* I knew then Kyme had told him of the stolen sweetmeats, and surely for this purpose: that the vicar would admonish me before the whole world.

'Mistress Kyme! Is this not so!'

'Yes, Father,' I said.

'I pray your transgressions be amended'—his voice was oily with pretence, as if he jested—'lest our parishioners be forced to commit the sins of gossip and idle talk.'

I looked to the villagers gathered in small whispering clutches about the churchyard, saw their pleasure at my disgrace. They have ever spurned me, a stranger from the northern parts, and a gentlewoman, which ought to bring their esteem and has not. 'Wives,' the vicar called out, for their further edification, 'submit yourselves to your husbands, as you must do to the Lord!'

My husband's weighty paw came down upon my shoulder. 'Thank you, Vicar,' he said, and with his fastened hand turned me, and, together with his parents and their servants and my poor little Beatrice trailing after, we departed the churchyard. Kyme moved his fist from my shoulder to grip the back of my neck, kept it there firmly, as a mind for every word of admonishment from the vicar's mouth. I walked with my head high and my neck stiff, pulling as far from him as I dared. I could hear, directly behind me, the great huffing breaths of his mother. I felt her glee at my shaming and thought she would say something to it, but she only asked, 'What news, son, of the wider world?'

'No news, Mother,' he answered, 'but that the executions continue. They say Thomas Moigne will be tried for treason at Lincoln before the week is out.' He gripped my neck tighter. 'Feelings go hard against thy kinsman, wife. From the priests no less than the Crown. Mark my words,' he growled in my ear, 'thy stepsister's husband, Thomas Moigne, will end his days on the gibbet.'

How my stomach dropped to hear him speak this way of our Bridget's Thomas! It is five months since the Rising, and Thomas

Moigne remains in prison, and I do not know why. I pray daily for his pardon—oh, how dared those villeins rise against Henry! And take captive our father and brothers and force them to swear false oaths and hold them at Lincoln a full fortnight so that we knew not whether they lived or died! I wish that Rising had never been! My very undoing came of it! And, yes, it is horrible that rebels' rotting parts hang in churchyards all over Lincolnshire, but I do perceive they brought it on themselves! And I do not believe the Crown will hang Bridget's husband. This is only how Kyme means to put fear in me. Our king is the gentlest, most merciful prince; he will see that Thomas Moigne is no more guilty of treason than Father or Francis, or any of the gentlemen who have been restored to the king's grace. I shall tell this to Bridget. I shall go to her and comfort her, if Kyme will allow me.

First, though, I must see what punishment he will make me for the filched sweetmeats. If I accept my correction with meekness and hold my tongue mild in my mouth and plead sweetly, then perhaps he may be persuaded to allow me to travel to North Willingham to see Bridget. Though it is true I have never yet persuaded him of anything that was not already inside his own will.

– Chapter 2 –

It is a morning like other mornings, Anne coming along the road from the parish church in Friskney, where the people hear high Mass on Sunday and morrow Mass daily before the day's work begins. Walking in front of her, the elder Kymes, her in-laws; they are of the yeoman class, wealthy and pious, devoted to the health of their souls and their church and their stature in the parish in the name of good works. Close beside her, their son, her husband, Thomas Kyme, a grasping man with fair hair, a crushed cap, ruddy face, pale eyes; he, too, is a pious man, jealous of his position in the community, and so, lest any person think he does not have control of his household, he keeps his gloved hand clamped on his wife's neck. Anne feels the weight through the dense layers of wool. Every item she wears is designed to subdue her: heavy kirtle and cloak the colour of dull pewter; bulky headdress, stiff and peaked as a dog's house, with unadorned billets and two rolled layers of black veil. Beneath the gable hood, a linen cap hides her dark hair, though it cannot hide the snap in her eyes, which dart and glare in every direction but towards the man who walks beside her. Following behind are the household servants, among them her young maid, Beatrice, shivering in her thin sleeves, her teeth chattering. The girl steps lightly, carefully, to avoid the worst of the muck, watches the back of her mistress's cloak with sharp eyes.

Anne is not far wrong when she tells her dead sister that her undoing came about because of the Rising—though she leaves out details. Her own part in the trouble, for instance. The Lincolnshire Rising was the opening thrust of the most serious threat against Henry Tudor's reign, and out of it swelled the later, larger rebellion known as the Pilgrimage of Grace, but lately, and most ruthlessly, put down. Across the North Country, the attainders and executions continue. Many plead for mercy, but little mercy is given. Indeed, when word first came of the commotion in Lincolnshire, Henry's fury was of such intensity, some in the Presence Chamber feared the veins in his neck would burst. He began shouting at once in his high, choked voice: 'Send for Norfolk! Summon Suffolk! They are to raise arms and men and ride straight away north to put down this treason! With all extremity are they to destroy, burn, and kill man, woman, and child without mercy, to the terrible example of all others who would rise against their prince!' None who witnessed the king's rage that day would doubt that Henry will have his revenge.

But Anne has not seen the king's fury. She believes yet in his mercy. On this damp, befogged morning, the last week of February 1537, Anne Kyme, nee Ayscough, is fifteen years old, lonely, forlorn, resentful: as furious and full of self-pity as any girl forced to wed against her free will or consent might be. And so, as she walks, she thinks primarily of her own misery.

She recollects with cruel clarity her fear that bright October morning, three days past Michaelmas, her sister but two months dead, when her father's manservant stood panting and stumbling over his words in the great hall at South Kelsey, telling them that Sir William had been taken captive by rebels at Caistor. She remembers, hours later, running to the great hall at the sound of horses' hooves thundering over the drawbridge, finding her brother Francis in the manor door and seeing, beyond him, in the courtyard, scores of snorting horses stepping and turning about with bellowing men astride them, shouting horrible curses, stabbing the air with bills and staves, and on the ground, a teeming horde of commons in stained jerkins and threadbare bonnets, all harnessed and panting and shouting oaths and threats. She remembers Francis bareheaded on the manor steps, his hair like a ragged black pelt on his head, and their little brother, young Thom, prancing on the limestone step beside him. Above all, she remembers her own shock and bewilderment as the mob surrounded her brothers, bound them, lifted them onto horses, while her stepmother, Elizabeth, beside her cried out, 'No! No! Not my child!'

With a dark chill she remembers the tormented days and nights following as they waited for word of her father and brothers: the sense of dread, the cold silence in the manor, the candles lit, the prayers offered, her stepmother's blame-filled gaze. She can feel, even now, the great wash of relief in her spirit a fortnight later when her father and brothers came riding home from Lincoln, weary and filthy and so worn of mien that her heart was wrenched. She remembers that evening, how she'd gone to her father and knelt before him: 'I submit myself, Father. I shall do as you bid me, in this marriage as in all things.' Walking now in the damp fenland mist, she remembers the warmth of her father's hand through her cap when he touched her head, the peace of surrender and goodness she'd felt then, how she'd begun to weep.

What she does not remember—rather, what she shoves away from her memory as she toils along the mucky road with her husband's fist fastened upon her neck—is her own part.

– Chapter 3 –

Oh, the day is glorious, Maddie! The sea winds blow from the east and have parted the skies for once and allowed a weak, pitiful sun to shine through. Cromwell's men have come to close the abbey which stands a mile north of the church on what the people here call Habbey Hill—a bump of land far more like a notion of a hill than a true one, I promise you—and they are even now inventorying and carting away the abbey's silver and gold and precious goods, and for this reason my so-called husband has gone to meet with the vicar and the other men of the village to see what they might do about it—and of course there is nothing they can do against the king's pleasure and Cromwell's orders—but this mission has at the least taken him away and out of my sight. I have allowed to his mother that I am cramped with my courses and bleeding too fiercely to come downstairs for the carding of the wool. Such business is that woman's occupation the livelong day, minding the spinners and carders and milkmaids, and she would have me do the same. And sometimes I will, and sometimes I won't. And today I won't.

Today I shall keep to my room and read thy book in secret and prepare my lessons for Beatrice. I know it is terrible and dangerous and very probably a sin to teach a servant to read, much less to give her lessons from an English Bible whatsoever. But I've sins enough to my soul that I think it of little consequence to add another, and the tedium in this place is so horrible, and the duties I am called to perform so wearisome and unlively to my mind, that I must do *something* to relieve it. Oh, but I take great care when I bring it out, I promise you. I hide it well, tucked far back beneath the linens in your dowry chest; and no one knows I have it, save Beatrice, and she, good girl that she is, would never tell. I open the front board, trace the letters. *The Bible, that is, the holy Scripture of the Olde and New Testament.* How I love the words!

'Come, Beatrice,' I say. 'Let me give you your lessons.'

'Yes, miss,' she says, for she really is a good and dutiful girl, though so annoyingly skittish as to make you want to pull her hair. I sit upon the stool, and Beatrice stands next me twisting her thumbs in her apron as I read.

There are days, I confess, when I take a naughty pleasure in watching her eyes widen and her face bloom crimson when I read to her from the Song of Solomon. '"O prince's daughter!"' I read, and slant my eyes at her. '"The joints of thy thighs are like jewels. Thy navel is like a round goblet, which wanteth not liquor; thy belly is like a heap of wheat set about with lilies . . ."' And Beatrice near faints with mortification. Ha!

Or then, on another day, my temper may be up, and I will hiss at her: 'Hssht! Stand still! Pay attention. Here is this hour's lesson!' And I will read her a tedious hour's worth of begats. Other days I demonstrate for her how to write her English letters, but they seem not able to stand in her mind, or her mind is not able to hold still for them; for whatever I have taught her one day, the next day she forgets—or would have me think so.

This morning I read to her from Genesis: '"And Noah was an husbandman, and he planted a vineyard: And he drank of the wine, and was drunken; and he lay uncovered within his tent." You see this told here?' I pointed the words to her. 'After the Flood, this one righteous man, Noah, got drunk on wine and lay naked within his tent. Now, tell me, Beatrice, is this a sin?'

'I know not, miss,' says she. 'Sounds like one.'

'Indeed, and if sin it is, whose sin is it, then?'

'Noah's, miss?'

'One might think so, but hearken to this: "And Noah's younger son Ham, the father of Canaan, saw the nakedness of his father, and told his two brothers without. And his brothers Shem and Japheth took a garment and laid it upon their shoulders and went backwards and covered the nakedness of their father; and their faces were turned away and they saw not their father's nakedness."'

'Well, I never,' says she.

'Nor me, neither. Now listen: "And Noah awoke from his wine and knew what his younger son had done. And he said, 'Cursed be Canaan! A servant of servants shall he be unto his brethren!'" Therefore, Beatrice, tell me: what is the true lesson in this matter?'

'I know not, miss,' she said. 'It is not good to get drunk and lay about naked, I expect.'

'But then why is Ham's son Canaan the one who receives the curse and not Noah? Nor even poor Ham himself, who could not help that he stumbled upon his old father drunk in his tent: not Ham cursed but his totally innocent *son*! Does this make sense?'

'Not to me, miss.'

'Precisely. That's the lesson, then.'

'Yes, miss,' she said, though her voice sounded extreme uncertain.

'The lesson is, thou saddle-goose: the consequences of sin are unknowable to us, and even the sin itself is oft a mystery, because the mind of God is pure unfathomable.'

'Yes, I can see that, miss,' she said, and stood fidgeting so miserably that I dismissed her to the kitchen.

And now I sit here in the quiet, a slight breeze at the window, thy book open upon my lap, and my eyes free to go where they list, to read front to back, back to front, or I may simply sit and caress the pages thy hands have touched. The breeze and sunlight make me think of South Kelsey in springtime—oh, how I wish we might be there together, riding across the Wolds, as we used to do! I yearn to go home, Maddie! More than anything.

And yet, I am afraid. I dread to see the ice in Mother Elizabeth's eyes declaring all manner of bad things about me. She blames me still, I know. I want to say to her: 'See Thom there! He is well! I did not cost thee thy son!' But I fear it would make no difference.

How was I to know they would take him? Or Francis? They were low men and common, how could anyone dream it? The sound of their coming was like thunder, all those horses galloping over the bridge planks, the knaves astride them all shouting and cursing, it was a fair wretched sea of butchers and farriers and ploughmen, and oh, the stink of man-sweat and lathered horseflesh! And such curses, Maddie! *By the bloody tits of Saint Agnes! By the bleeding feet of Christ!* The villeins were beating their staves against the cobblestones, pounding out threats against Father and Francis, and our brave brother stood on the manor steps in only his doublet and hose—he'd had no time to dress, you see, they came so sudden. He did look so vulnerable, no hat, robe, dagger, yet he strode right down into the midst of them! Oh, you should have seen! He reached up and grasped the nearest wretch on horseback and dragged him from the saddle straight off to the ground—how that act thrilled me! And not me alone but young Thom also, dancing on the stones like a puppet, crying out, 'Francis! Francis!'

Our brother's face was near black with fury, and that wretch's face was black, too, with terror and lack of breath; he bobbed and curtsied and gurgled, his eyes rolling, and Mother Elizabeth stood beside me on the manor step, calling out, 'Francis, no!' Those villeins swarmed Francis, they seized him, Maddie, jerked back his arms, and I cannot tell you—such a fury it unleashed in me! From the manor steps, I shouted at them: 'Pigs! Dogs! Stinking toads! My father will kill you all!'

Mother Elizabeth tried to hush me, she pulled at my arm, trying to withdraw me into the manor, but young Thom took up my cry: 'Toads! Pigs!' he shouted. 'Our father will kill you!'

'Ye are no better than gong farmers!' I cried out in my fury. 'Fit only to muck out gong pits, not fit to come against your betters! Vermin! Pizzlers! Useless voles!'

'Pizzlers!' Thom piped. 'Gong farmers! Voles!'

A farrier in a leather apron rushed upon us, and before I knew anything, he'd picked up Thom and hoisted him onto a carthorse in front of a stout fellow, who at once wrapped his arms around our little brother and held him. Francis was struggling mightily then, but he had no weapon, his arms were bound, and those churls overswarmed him; they hoisted him onto a great horse, and with many shouts and oaths, the mob turned as one creature and roiled across the bridge with their great stink and noise and thunder, our two helpless brothers their captives, and then . . .

Oh. Oh. I do not like to think on this part.

Then, as they passed beyond the manor wall, Mother Elizabeth turned to me, and in a voice as cold as ever I hope to hear in my life, said, 'See what you have done, Anne. Your reckless tongue has cost me my son.' Oh, this is why I dread to go, despite how my heart yearns! Our stepmother was, before that hour, my most stalwart ally. Not ten days earlier I'd gone on my knees to her, pleading for her to intercede with Father that I might be released from this hateful marriage. She stroked my hair as I wept, Maddie. She touched me so tenderly upon my back.

But from the moment of Thom's capture, she became cold and hardened towards me. I'd a thousand times prefer heated words of anger and condemnation! Those, at least, I might defend myself against. But all was frozen silence. Even after they came home safe, Father and Francis and Thom, she did not speak to me, only upon occasion turned her blue eyes upon me—can you remember how blue her eyes are? So beautiful, I always thought them. But not when they are turned cold against thee! Like ice they become! Ah, God. I'll not think of it.

They were none the worse for their ventures when they returned, I promise you, but for a few flea bites and the lice in Thom's hair. We had thought they were held at Louth, for that town was the source of the Rising, but those Louth knaves joined with commons and priests from all over the county—thousands of them, Maddie!—and marched in a great throng to Lincoln. They forced Father and the other gentry to go with them, and for days they roiled and moiled about inside the cathedral, so Francis described to us, and camped all over the city, menacing and thieving and speaking unpardonable treasons.

And then, when but lightly threatened by the king's forces, they must all slink back to their villages and leave Father and Francis and our poor Bridget's Thomas Moigne to deal with the king's anger.

How dared they! *Why* dared they? Henry is king as surely as God is God. How could they possibly think to succeed?

Oh, but hush. Here is the old mistress at my door again. Or rather Mother Kyme, I should say, for this she says I must call her. By the Virgin, I am so tired of her pestering. Will she never under God's Heaven cease?

Oh, Maddie, oh, my heart. I cannot think or pray. I am prostrate with weeping. The sickness in my chest makes me feel I shall vomit or faint. I did not go! I did not go. Even now, this hour, I walk the floor, cast the letter aside, take it up again and read Bridget's words, until I think I cannot bear it. I throw the paper down, and walk and walk, but soon I find her words in my hand once more:

> My dearest Anne, I write thee with as heavy a heart as ever woman did bear within her breast, the sorrow so weighted in me I scarce can lift my pen. I cannot rise from my chair, nor speak, nor walk. O, Nan, he is gone! I know now in what wise our sisterhood is joined, and deeper still, for my grief in this hour is like unto thine at Martha's death, and a thousand times worse. I write thee now with these grievous words: my husband, Thomas Moigne, has this day unjustly and wrongly suffered a traitor's death at Lincoln. I cannot write more now. Come see me, Anne. I beseech thee.

A traitor's death, Maddie! Do you see it? His severed head piked upon the castle wall—our brother-in-law's head! That handsome good man. His eyes dead and plucked by crows as the rotting heads of criminals we have seen there. And our poor Bridget—oh, how can she bear it? How can she *live*? And I did not go to visit her, I did not insist forcefully to my husband—

No. The truth: I did not ask.

How I loathe my selfishness! I have spent these months absorbed in my own sorrow while our sister Bridget suffered. Oh, yes, last night, after the letter came, I did ask—and at once destroyed any hope I may have had in the asking. I stood across the room from him as he changed into his nightclothes, my face turned away, my gaze lowered, as he ever would bid me, and I spoke to him with as soft and beseeching voice as I knew how to force from my throat: 'Sir, I have this day received word from my stepsister. Her husband, Thomas Moigne, has been executed at Lincoln.'

'Well? What of it?' he said.

I turned to stare at him. 'What of it? Why, he's dead, sir! Killed! My sister suffers!'

'I know he's dead, all Lincolnshire knows.'

'You knew?' I blinked at him. 'Why did you not tell me?'

'And what mischief might you have made with such news?'

My meekness fled me at once. 'Bridget is my sister!' I cried.

'*Step*sister!' says he. 'How well I know it. And I suppose you'll be wanting to jaunt right north to Willingham and get your face and my name connected to a traitor's condemnation?'

'Would you prefer I leave your paltry name here, sir? Gladly!'

'You'd best contain that shrewish tongue.'

'I *will* go to her! And from there to South Kelsey for the Easter holy days!' I had not known I would say that, but the words flew from my mouth: 'I have not seen my family these five hellish months,' I said, 'and I intend to see them! You cannot stop me!'

He came close, his voice low, like a cur's warning: 'You'll not go planting yourself in the midst of this trouble. Cromwell's men are yet scouring the country for new heads to set upon pikes. I'll not have my wife traipsing about declaring her kinship to a traitor!'

'He is not a traitor!'

'Tell that to his separate parts quartered and strewn about Lincolnshire!'

'He is no more a traitor than Father or Francis, and they are pardoned!'

'For now.' Kyme glared at me. 'Your father wrote a letter to the king pleading the rebels' cause. He set his name to it.'

'They forced him! Father says they forced him!'

'Your father's name stinks of the Rising, I'll not have the king's spies reminded.'

'Hypocrite! Your very sympathies are with the rebels! I know it. All Friskney knows it—you and the Vicar Jordan!'

'It is not *my* name on a traitor's letter!'

'You should have thought of that before! Oh, how anxious you were to join your name with the lofty name of Sir William Ayscough! You would not withdraw the marriage contract, would not return my father's money, and now must I be here dying in these fetid swamps, wedded to a blood-faced brainless lout!'

His fist came up then, I thought he'd smash me sure, but he jerked away and slapped his open palm against the wooden bedpost and strode out the door in his nightshirt. I stood heaving in a kind of victory, my blood thrilling with the words I'd spat at him. But in the next instant I grew afraid, for I began to think of the trouble I have brought upon me.

He did not return last night and has not returned this morning. Neither has his old mother come to rouse me, which shows what poor standing I am in. Nor has Beatrice come with food to break my fast—not that I could eat a morsel. I am sick to my heart, my stomach, my soul. I lay all the night with my mind roiling. I could not stop seeing our Bridget's Thomas standing upon the scaffold, his light brown hair lifted by a chill sunlit breeze; then I see his bloody guts all disembowelled and burnt before him. I see his head sawed off, his body hacked in four parts, I see it and see it, and I think—oh, I can hardly bear it—I think: *It could have been Father!* It could have been Francis. It could have been the soft blond curls of our sweet brother Thom! But then I think: No, they are pardoned! His Majesty is merciful, he would never allow it! And then I think: But that gentle barrister, that good gentleman, our kinsman Thomas Moigne! And Bridget alone in her suffering! She begs me in her letter to come, but how shall I?

And how shall I go home? Now that I have said the words aloud, I know, truly, there is no single thing else in the living world I desire so much as to go home, to see Father and Francis and young Thom and know they are safe. But I cannot walk fifty miles to South Kelsey, nor even thirty miles to North Willingham to see Bridget. I must have Kyme's permission. I must have a bit of money from his hand and a means to travel, either cart or horse, and a male servant to attend me. But he is furious, I have never seen his anger higher—oh, how I beshrew my reckless tongue! What shall I do now, Maddie, my dearest, my wise sister? How may I change things?

Yes. *Yes.* My heart calms.

I shall be as thee. As meek and lovely. As compliant to his wishes as ever thou wouldst have been. I shall go to him when he returns from the fields for his dinner. I shall curtsy deeply, stand with my head bowed, my gaze upon the floor, and I shall plead for forgiveness. 'I pray you, sir, look with tolerance and pity upon your wife's transgressions.' My throat may choke upon the words, but say them I shall, in a soft and pleasing tone, with a submissive mien and a willing heart, and then may my husband absolve me.

– Chapter 4 –

Francis has come! And what is more—oh, I can scarcely believe it!—I am to return with him to South Kelsey! *Home*, Maddie! Home. Not soon, for he must first travel to Cambridge to see Edward, and from there to London to speak with Christopher in the king's service. But he will return by way of Friskney and ride me with him to South Kelsey for the Easter holy days, and neither my so-called husband nor his distempered mother dare say him no! Oh, I can hardly keep my excitement contained.

But I do contain it. I am become so obedient you would hardly recognize me. 'Yes, husband,' I say. 'No, husband.' 'As you will, husband.' At every moment, I stand with my head bowed and my fingers clasped in tight crosses behind me, and I know *he* believes his great discipline and lordship over me have created a good and obedient wife. Not so. Or I am good and obedient, but not for how he rails at me and uses me to his pleasure—which seems not pleasure, I tell you, but great grunting shudders of pain. But he will keep at it, so I suppose it must cause him pleasure somehow, but for me, none at all. I am docile as a lamb, though, for the pure reason it may bring me that which I wish above all things: to go home.

I want to know why Francis goes to Cambridge and London, but we have had no opportunity to speak privately without Kyme or his doltish father or his old falcon-eyed mother standing near. I fear it is to do with the execution of Bridget's Thomas nine days ago. They say the Crown has not yet had its fill of blood to prove to all England what becomes of those who would rise against their sovereign lord and king—oh, Maddie, there is so much strife and fear in the world, such rumblings of trouble. Our poor Bridget. I shall have Francis stop at North Willingham on our journey so that I may see her. Kyme will never allow me to go there on my own. I have asked lightly, I have pleaded: to no avail. But he'll not keep me from going with our brother, and so I shall have the victory regardless, though

I must be careful never to show it. I shan't show it. I shall be, as the book tells me, wise as a serpent, harmless as a dove.

I am dismayed. I am furious. What do I know of our pig-headed brother? All is not as I thought. This afternoon I looked out the dairy window and saw him striding across the stable yard, and I thought, here is my chance! I stole away from the curd-making, which the old mistress had charged me to watch with careful eye, that the milkmaid not slip a finger into the churn for so much as a lick and a taste—yes, this is her stingy eye, which she would have me create in my own face! But I left the girl to it and ran to follow Francis, making my way through the manure and muck towards the stable. I slipped in the darkened door. At the far end, I saw him standing outside a stall, shifting his boots in irritation as the stable hand groomed the animal within. Francis told the boy to have him readied before first light and see to it he received an extra measure of oats and be watered well, for he would be ridden hard tomorrow.

'Tomorrow!' I cried. 'So soon? We have not talked!'

Francis whirled, frowning mightily when he saw me.

'Have you spoken to Master Kyme?' I said. 'Will he allow me to take one of his horses?'

Francis came and grasped my hand, pulled me quickly away from the stall and the stable boy's listening ears. 'What do you think you're doing?' he whispered.

'Let go, Francis! You're pinching me!' He released me, barked an order at the boy, strode swiftly towards the stable door. I ran to catch up with him. 'Francis!'

But he was already halfway across the yard.

'When are you coming for me?' I cried after him.

Francis turned on his heel and came storming towards me with such a scowl on his face, I shrank back. 'What is the matter with you?' he said, his teeth gritted.

'What do you think is the matter? I am dying here!'

'Hssht! Keep quiet! Can you not see the danger this family is in?'

'I see nothing! Because no one tells me anything! What danger? Francis, include me! Explain it to me!'

'We are beset on all sides!' He tucked his head then, as if half listening over his shoulder, and when he turned back to me his voice was softer. 'Why can you never know your place, Nan? Why must you always be nattering and complaining?'

He studied me a moment, his eyes as grey as the light in this cursed country. I watched his face, saw a decision made. 'Come, walk with me.'

They have not proper walls built of stone here, you know, only a great smudging of the stable yard into the sheep pasture beyond, flimsy cross-wood fences to separate them, a few wobbly stiles. The ground is not frozen firm in winter neither, but all is sog and slop to the horizon, dotted throughout with ugly unshorn sheep in this ugly season. Francis gave his hand to help me over the stile, and at once a flock of ewes came bleating towards us, perhaps forty or sixty of them, some with nursing lambs and some ready to drop this year's bounty, and all of them baaing and begging and bleating at once. 'Here, now! Get away!' Francis flapped his robe at them. 'Hie! Hie!' Still they pressed in on us, their fleece matted and filthy, and the wool all down over their eyes till you would think none of them could see us, but turn and follow us they did, bleating a chorus. They have been used to their rations from human hands all winter, I suppose, and expected it of us, but Francis walked quickly to discourage them, making such rapid and long strides I had to run to keep up. Over his shoulder he said, 'You know about Bridget's Thomas?'

'I know, yes,' I said, panting. 'Oh, I would have gone to her, Francis! I would! But Kyme would not allow me!'

'Yes, and well he did not. What wisdom might that be, to see one's wife visit the wife of a traitor?'

'But Thomas Moigne is not a traitor!'

Francis stopped, and the accusing sheep surrounded us, clamouring. *Maah! Maah!* The look Francis turned on me was grim with censure. 'He was accused for a traitor, Anne, and for that was he condemned. Let no person hear you say otherwise.'

'Why?'

'*Why? Why?* You sound like these bleating sheep. Why must it always be *why* with thee!'

'Because it must! Francis. Tell me.'

He shook his head. 'He was brilliant, Anne. Masterful in defence of himself. In defence of us all! I stood witness at his trial. That alone was as much as I could do for him. He spoke with such eloquence, but his eloquence did not save him. He told the truth, and only the truth—but the truth did not save him! Witnesses were brought forward to swear they had seen him in conversation with the leader of the Yorkshire rebellion, that fool barrister Robert Aske.' Francis turned suddenly and kicked a begging ewe in her side, shouting, 'I have nothing for you!'

The ewe tumbled back, bleating, and Francis's fury rose against them all; he began yelling and shouting and flapping his robe, and the ones nearest began stumbling and scrambling backwards against the flock, till they all turned, a roiling mess of filthy wool and baas and confusion, and fled away from us, running and bleating over the marshes as if scorched by fire; their droppings lay in the stubbly grass like piles of dark steaming pebbles in waves of circles around us. Francis stood motionless, his features hard.

'A traitor's name is allied with the name of this family. The bloodletting is not finished. I've come to caution your incautious husband to cease his public grumblings about the closing of the abbey—he endangers us all! We must not be seen to lean too far to the old religion, nor too far towards reform. Peril lies either direction! Above all, we must be seen to be ardent in our devotion to Henry. And we shall be. When I arrive in London, I will publicly disavow Thomas Moigne and make much of our separation from him. As will Christopher in the king's service, as must Edward at Cambridge. I go there first to instruct him, and it must be done not subtly but loud.'

'But we cannot do that! What of Bridget?'

The look he turned on me then! My heart shrinks to think of it—the coldness there.

'I have seen her husband drawn up by the neck on the scaffold,' he said, his voice not distraught with the telling but dispassionate, empty. 'I have seen him trussed like a pheasant, bound hand and foot, twitching and thrashing as the rope strangled his throat. I have seen his innards drawn out and thrown on the bier, his body hacked into four parts to hang in chains, one part on the green at North Willingham, one within the castle walls at Lincoln. One quarter was sent to Louth to rot with the heads of the instigators—and one part, Anne, this very hour, stinks and rots in an iron cage depended from the oak gibbet erected twelve days ago in the churchyard at Saint Mary's in South Kelsey. Do you understand? The carpenters were sent to set the gibbet four days before Thomas Moigne's trial even began.' Francis drew silent, scowling into the grey distance. 'We will do for Bridget what we can. But that will be very little, and it must be done in secret. Her husband's lands are attainted, they belong to the Crown now. She'll be left homeless, and without support. This is the king's will. And the will of his minister, Thomas Cromwell.'

'But we shall stop at North Willingham and see her, surely?'

He stared at me as if I had offered to jump off the earth and fly. 'Where is your mind, Nan? Have you not heard one word I've just said?'

'My heart breaks for her! When you come for me, surely we can pause one hour—'

'Come for you? I will not *come* for you.'

'But you said! At supper yesterday evening. Speaking to my so-called husband. When all the Ayscoughs are gathered at South Kelsey for the Easter holy days, you said. We shall . . . something, something, I don't remember. When all the Ayscoughs are gathered at South Kelsey . . .'

My voice died away. I understood then how completely I had misunderstood. He did not mean me when he said *all the Ayscoughs*. I, Anne Kyme, was not, would never more be, included by that name.

The look he gave me was more hurtful than either his coldness or his anger, for it was tender, regretful. 'He is not your so-called husband, Anne. He is your husband.'

He turned and walked away. I watched his figure receding into the encroaching mist. Ah, God, I fell into such despair then. I felt as if I would drown in a swell of hopelessness, just as I felt in the dark days after thy death. That grief beyond mercy. That emptiness beyond grief.

But not long, Maddie. Not long.

Before the fog had swallowed Francis entire, I set my mind to planning. Before I heard the iron bell calling the maids to evening milking, I had my plot in place. Before the bell's clangour had ceased echoing across the stubbly, wet pasture, I had already begun to pick my way through the scattered piles of sheep gong towards the stile.

– Chapter 5 –

Francis Ayscough walks quickly towards the Kymes' manor with no thought of his sister's distress. His mind is on the future, as is true of him nearly always. He must keep moving. He must plan. *When all the Ayscoughs are gathered at South Kelsey.* Yes, this is his future intention: to gather with his father and brothers at South Kelsey Hall through the Easter holy days so that they may design and harness a plan. To avoid the worst devastations of the king's vengeance, one must not only take steps to demonstrate one's loyalty, one must be *seen* to take those steps. In this, his elegant brother Christopher's position at court gives them advantage. A gentleman of the privy chamber, one of Cromwell's spies in Spalding at the start of the Rising, Christopher hasn't the king's ear, necessarily, but he has Cromwell's. And that's near as good. In London, Francis will make much of Ayscough loyalty to the Crown, and Christopher will see to it that the right people see.

First, though, he must find Kyme and speak with him a final time. It is not enough to warn or threaten Anne's husband: he must bribe him. Despite the severed heads and rotting limbs hanging in churchyards from here to York, Master Kyme will not practice silence: he must be continually putting his face and mouth in the wrong pot, gathering with the local vicar and merchants and craftsmen to mutter and rail against the new subsidies, the new closures, the new directives for praying the *pater noster* in English. Every word the oaf utters, Francis thinks, puts them all at risk. If threats were enough to shut him, he'd be shut by now. The one thing Kyme understands, however, is money. And so Francis has come with coin in hand to remind Thomas Kyme, if nothing else will, to cease muttering his complaints aloud.

Then to Cambridge to deal with Edward, his studious, passionate, overly religious brother. A mule of a different sort. Edward speaks too zealously of the new learning, too carelessly of English translations and reforms in the church. He must be warned to keep a clamp on his tongue no less than Kyme. Francis must leave before first light to reach Cambridge in good time. Why Thomas Moigne? he thinks, walking fast towards the manor in his wide-legged gait. If his tone was dispassionate when he spoke to his sister of Moigne's execution, Francis's recollection surely is not: he sees his brother-in-law's eyes bulging in pain and terror as the noose strangles him, the brief respite at the rope's release, the greater pain, the greater terror, as his belly is slit open, his intestines drawn out and thrown on the pyre before his living eyes. The beheading was a mercy. Even the quartering, though a bloody horror, is not the worst memory: it is the sound of Moigne's screams. They will be in Francis's ears for eternity, and not the screams only, but how they faded to pitiful whimpers before the man died. In Francis's nostrils, even now, is the sickly-sweet stink of burning organs. He strides quickly across the sodden land to escape it.

As he nears the manor, Francis veers suddenly across the shit-spattered yard towards the stable. He trusts nothing; he will see to his horse's grooming and the extra measure of oats himself. Why Thomas Moigne? This is Francis's great obsession. A hundred commons and priests were given over for execution, but the Lincolnshire gentry have all received pardons—all except Thomas Moigne. Can the king's vengeance be so capricious? What difference between Moigne and Francis himself? Moigne was taken captive by the rebels, as were Francis and Father and dozens of others. Moigne was forced to swear an oath of allegiance to the rebels' cause, as did Francis and Father and all the other gentlemen. These others are not dead, they are pardoned.

But for how long? Francis asks himself. The king is known to pardon a man one day, then turn the next and have him attainted and executed without trial. This, *this*, is what drives Francis Ayscough. For he can see no reason why it should be Thomas Moigne and not himself who suffered the worst of Henry's wrath.

In a driven rush, Francis ducks into the stable, strides towards the rear stall where his horse is being curried, barks a furious oath at the groom.

– Chapter 6 –

The whole of this day's travels, I thought myself quite clever. A maidservant may go about her master's business unchallenged, mayn't she? This is what I told myself. And, indeed, although some stared with ugly leers as I rode past, no man tried to stop me. This hour, however, I do not think so highly of my good wit. I knew our brother would be angry, but I did not quite think how angry. It is fortunate I rode so far behind, not only to keep myself secret but also because the little palfrey I'd chosen could not keep pace. Fortunate, too, that Francis stopped late for his dinner. I thought I had clean lost him, but then I saw his mount tethered outside an alehouse by the side of the road. I waited beneath a great oak until he came from the alehouse and mounted and started again towards Cambridge; and then I rode as fast as I could, whipping the little mare fiercely to catch up with him. He heard me—or rather he heard the mare's hooves ambling at their brisk pace—and he turned in his saddle, squinting to make out this female servant riding astride a fine palfrey, travelling alone. I began to laugh then, and he knew me, and oh, Maddie, how our brother fumed! How he cursed!

I stopped a small distance away, smiling sweetly, until his curses turned to grumbles about what he must do with me now—it was drawing late, you see, and there was no time to return me to Friskney, even if he'd been willing to turn back and lose the whole day. We rode on to Peterborough side by side. He did not speak to me. I knew by his scowls and silence he would return me to my husband next day.

'He will beat me,' I said. 'If you force me to return alone with no protection, he will tear out my hair.'

'That,' Francis said, 'he ought to do.'

'Do you care so little for me?'

'I care that you continually cause such trouble. That your reckless tongue near cost me my life—and not mine alone but young Thom's as well. I care that you have taken your husband's property and left his house without his consent, that you go traipsing about the world dressed like a common milkmaid. That you behave now as you have always done, as if the rules of God's world do not pertain to you. Your wilfulness causes grief to all around you, Anne, and you seem not to care. Why would your husband not beat you?'

And I could say nothing to these charges, for I knew them mostly for true.

'She will beat me,' young Beatrice had said to me not twelve hours before, whispering in desperation in my chamber as she put on me the worn kirtle she'd filched from a sleeping milkmaid's hook.

'Nonsense,' I told her. 'Lace me now, quickly.'

'You know she will.' The girl's eyes were pleading.

'Well, I cannot take you with me, and you cannot find your way back to South Kelsey alone. But when I arrive home next week, I shall have Father send a man down to fetch you.'

'That will be too late, miss.'

And in my more misgiving moments, I fear this may be true. Mother Kyme this hour may be dreadfully misusing her because they found me gone. I swore the girl to secrecy and promised again to send for her and that she should have a reward when she returns to South Kelsey. I told her to lie down on her mat and pretend the deepest sleep, but if no one else discovered my absence, then she must raise the alarm in the morning at the hour when she would ordinarily wake me. 'Pretend all shock and wonder,' I told her. 'Act as if it's the most baffling and miraculous thing. You'll be fine.' Though she did not look fine. She looked terrified. But I shall make it up to her when we are all home again.

I have now more sympathy for her, however, I can tell you, and not Beatrice alone, but any poor servant who must sleep on the floor with the stench of others' odours beneath them and the mice rustling and the fleas. This is Francis's punishment of me. When we arrived at the inn, he allowed the keeper to presume me the lowly servant I appear to be and to point me to the room where female servants sleep. Our brother did not glance my direction but strode straight to the ale room for his supper, and I made no protest but came meekly to the servants' quarters, for what else could I do? I've no proper gown and hood to put on me, even if there were a private place to do so. I was in such a fever to race after him this morning that I brought only a handful of currants and the lone flagon of ale I'd had Beatrice filch for me—all finished hours ago—and so, truthfully, I was grateful for the homely bit of bread and salted fish one of the servants broke off from her portion and shared with me. They asked questions in their flat fenland accents, but I hung open my mouth and pretended stupidity until they left off asking and rolled out their mats and put out the candle and fell to gossiping in the dark. Soon enough I heard their soft snoring, and then I lay on the threshed floor in a pure agony of discomfort, without even a pallet to lie upon, as the other women have, but must I lie on the prickling thresh with the fleas jumping about in the dark and biting.

So I crawled to a corner to sit with my back against the wall and my thin smock wrapped tightly around my legs—not that this keeps the fleas from biting, but at least they haven't the whole stretched-out length of me to feast upon. Here I sit and scratch and squirm and think and talk to you and pray. I repeat over and over these words of our brother: *your reckless tongue near cost me my life.*

II

I See You There, Falling

Cambridge

Lenten Season

1537

– Chapter 7 –

Dearest Maddie, you cannot guess where I am! Oh, but you needn't guess, because you surely know already: I am at Corpus Christi at Cambridge, staying the whole day in secret in Edward's room! And no other person on earth knows that I am here save Edward and Francis. Well, and Edward's tutor, perhaps. Francis made me wait at the stable while he came to warn our brother and pay his tutor to take himself away to an inn or someplace other, but whether he told him about me, I do not know. I expect not. Our brothers seem most anxious that no one should discover me here. They think it will reflect badly upon them to have a sister who rides herself to Cambridge on a stolen pony! Hah!

I know, I know. I should not laugh.

Well, the first hour was not so pleasant. I needn't tell you of the blame Francis heaped upon me, nor how Edward defended me. The first is truer than I care to remember, and the latter is not true at all. Edward did not defend me, you know he would never go against Francis, but neither did he curse and growl at me in condemnation, as Francis did. You would have been proud of how patiently I received the coals of fire he rained down upon me—not loudly, for he dared not make a disturbance that others might hear, but, oh, how he did stride about the room in his cloak and cap, his voice all choked with anger, which he'd borne in silence as we rode together all day. I was mightily relieved this morning when he rode off to London alone to see Christopher and left me here with Edward, who promises to bring me something to eat when he comes from his lectures, and I shall be glad for that—I am famished!

But look how the sun creeps across the floor butter yellow. Outside the window I hear the chitter of songbirds. It is not spring yet, but one can feel the promise. Edward's room is so bare. A rope bed and trundle, a desk, a stool, a trunk, a tiny window. Upon the whitewashed walls, no carpet. Upon the bed, no bolster. No thresh upon the floor, just bare planks, where last night Edward slept, for he insisted Francis have the bed and I the trundle. No fleas, neither. Nor mouse droppings. Our brother's room is as bare and plain as a monk's cell. This pleases me enormously. Would that I had such a quiet, calm room with books.

On the wooden shelf above the desk, I have spied three: two Greek and one Latin. I shan't be able to decipher the Greek, but the Latin is Erasmus's *Adagia*. Do you remember when Thom's tutor challenged me to read from his *Enchiridion Militis Christiani* and translate the words aloud as I read? Hah! He never dreamt I could do it! Thom's tutor, what a tight little man. I made you laugh so when I mocked him, remember? Strutting behind him with my hands clasped in mockery, making his crusty frown, and you would giggle, slap your palm over your mouth, and—oh. Oh. Oh, my heart.

How is it that grief will lie in wait like a highwayman?

How is it that I may walk through the world unsuspecting, my head turned, my thoughts elsewhere, and suddenly grief will leap from its hiding place and flay me open throat to groin?

Oh, Maddie, I would give anything on God's earth—anything! On earth or in heaven! My very soul! If only I could set eyes on you again! I would kneel beside you, lay my head in your lap and beg forgiveness. If I confess, will the grief lessen? Will it go lie in the corner like a scolded dog, beat its hopeful tail against the hearthstones?

I did not weep, you know. I growled and snarled in Mother Elizabeth's arms, and then I grew silent. I remained so as I watched them wash you, dress you, bind your jaw, close your hands on the crucifix, place the coins upon your eyes. Silent through your funeral

Mass and all the stricken days following, my teeth gritted against everything. I wandered about the manor and would not eat and could not sleep. I dreaded to meet your absence as I walked, but I could not sit still. Inside my head, clumps of wet wool crowded my brain, swelled down into my throat. I could not think clearly, nor taste anything, nor read, nor do my sewing, nor dream. And yet there was, at every turned corner, that breath-robbing pain. Each room I entered. *Maddie is dead.* Each hall I walked. *My sister is gone.*

And then, on the day I found your book buried beneath the linens inside your dowry chest, my heart cracked. It grieved me beyond grief, Maddie—it was as if I never knew you! Why would Edward give such a thing to you? Such books are banned by law, they carry a terrible penalty, and you—you were always so *good*. Therefore, I told myself, kneeling on the floor beside your chest, this book must be good. I lifted it out, and my hands trembled. It is not beautifully made, no, but the words are beautiful. I opened the front board. In my mind I see their very shape and structure:

BIBLIA
The Bible, that
is, the holy Scripture of the
Olde and New Testament, faith-
fully and truly translated out
of the Douche and Latyn
in to Englishe

I touched the page, traced the letters. Then, at last, I wept. I sat on the floor a long while, weeping. I grieved every cruel word I'd given you, every gesture of scorn those few short months of your betrothment. I could smell you, Maddie, your sweet scent of lavender wafting from the chest, and I sat in your warmth and benevolence, and I wept and wept. Then I wrapped your book in your wedding linens and carried it in secret to my room. I cannot tell you what a . . . *solace* it became. And is. Your book changed everything. It is what I have of you. Oh, I wish I had it to read now! Instead of this tiresome Erasmus. I should have brought it with me. But it was too bulky to carry, and in any case, I dared not—

No. Let me say the truth.

Let me say the truth to you always, even if I will not say it to the priests. I did not think of it. I was so caught up with my plans to follow Francis, I left your book in its secret place beneath the linens—oh, I pray they do not toss my things about when they discover I am gone! They will blame poor Beatrice. But I shall make it up to her, and when I send for her I shall tell her to bring it, if the Kymes have not found it and destroyed it—though I do not know how I shall get the message to her, since I dare not tell the servant I shall send for her, lest that one betray us, and the girl cannot read, so that is no means to tell her . . . but never mind. Some answer will come. Oh, I hope Edward brings me something substantial for supper. My head aches. I am so very hungry. My stomach has got up such a howl of complaint, you would think one of Francis's scent hounds had followed me here.

– Chapter 8 –

Francis keeps an easy, loping pace towards London, swift but not tiring, his mind filled with anger. Anne. What will they ever do with Anne? He rues all the hours wasted last autumn trying to cajole her to obedience in this marriage. It could not be done. Not with teasing nor browbeating nor banishments, neither: *I shall sit here and starve to a rank skeleton, then see how gladly Thomas Kyme will have me to wife!* And why? Never has Francis understood it. What is so unbearable about the man? A yeoman, yes, but his father has wealth enough, and large landholdings; there is reason to expect Master Kyme will rise in the world. He is not ugly. He does not beat her—although now, with Anne's latest antic, Francis half believes that he should. This marriage has been from its inception as troubling to the family's peace as one high-stomached, ungrateful daughter can make it, and now Anne has turned everything, as is her wont, much worse. Not for the first time does Francis think of how much better all would have been for the Ayscoughs if gentle Martha had lived.

But she did not. And here we are. His horse is ready for a rest and his feedbag. Francis has not stopped the whole day but to water the horse at streams they crossed and allow him to graze on early green grasses, and yet it is still miles to reach London. The light is fading, a damp chill creeping in. By the time he reaches Harlow, a drizzling rain is falling. He is directed to a primitive, foul-smelling inn. The town is, Francis thinks, at once too near London and too far. The streets are teeming with travellers and beggars—the latter, as the innkeeper tells him, made more numerous for the closing of the nearby abbey, all the mendicants and the poor turned out to the streets. Francis sits at a table scowling over his pottage and beer.

He is worried about Edward. His pious younger brother's passion for the new learning is a danger. Francis fears Edward will fail to hold his tongue—especially at Cambridge, where there are so many likeminded scholars, but where there are also, beneath every cobble and prickle bush, conservative spies seeking to sniff out heresies.

Francis sits drinking, thinking. He develops a new plan: he'll seek to have Edward placed in Archbishop Cranmer's household. Yes. It is the very answer. Thomas Cranmer is a man who knows how to believe as he believes in private while convincing others in public he is of their same opinion. He'll have good influence on Edward. And surely his pious brother would delight to serve in the archbishop's household? Francis will bid Christopher at court to assist him; they'll draw on old family connections—the Ayscoughs and Cranmers were near neighbours in Nottinghamshire years ago—and who could have dreamt, Father says, that Tom Cranmer's reticent, scholarly son should become Archbishop of Canterbury? If this can happen, anything may happen in the modern world. Including, Francis thinks, our Edward's rise in the church. He motions the innkeeper to bring him another tankard.

Thinking, cogitating, planning stratagems and protections for his family, Francis takes more drink than is wise in a place where cutpurses may lie in wait around any corner—or in the bed next to you. The innkeeper has said he has no rooms left fit for a gentleman, but Francis may share with two others—'You'll do well enough,' the keeper says, 'if you sleep head to foot.' Francis is drunk and surly by the time he rouses the two snoring men from the bed and pays them a shilling each to take the floor. He lies on his back, smelling the men, listening to their snores, while the room is slowly turning. His purse is knotted tightly around his waist, his saddle secured beneath his head, the hilt of his dagger tight in his fist. He is drifting off, almost dreaming, when a thought comes to him: *Thomas Moigne died because he altered the king's words.*

Francis jerks awake. He lies still, staring up into the darkness. The room turns somewhat faster; the memory roils: the dim chapter house inside the cathedral at Lincoln, priests and commons harnessed with pike and dagger, crowding in against them, and Francis and his father unarmed and helpless in the centre: all the gentry unarmed. A letter had come, penned in Henry's own hand, an answer to the rebels' plea for pardon. Thomas Moigne, as city recorder, was commanded to read it: his calm barrister's voice echoing in the chapter house. A breath's pause, no more than a heart's quiver, but when Moigne began to read again, his voice had changed: it was thick now, slower, more hesitant. A priest, following over his shoulder, cried out, 'Treachery! He lies by not reading all!'

The priest wrenched the parchment from Moigne's hand, sang out Henry's answer: '"How presumptuous then are ye, the rude commons of one shire, and that one of the most brute and beastly of the whole realm, to find fault with your Prince!" Hear it!' the priest cried. 'His Majesty will slaughter us all!' The rebels were furious. They were frightened. They had commanded the gentry to intercede with His Majesty and beg the king's pardon. The pleadings had failed. The king would exact his full vengeance: *your lands shall be attainted, your wives and children put to the sword . . .* In their fear and fury, the rebels turned on the gentlemen. At once there sounded the quick hiss and slide of sword, the snick of daggers unsheathed. They would have slain them to a man.

Even now, Francis remembers his terror, to be standing unarmed in the middle of the round room, surrounded by shouting, cursing rebels. So close to death, Francis thinks. So very close. And Thomas Moigne saved us. 'Spare us!' Moigne cried out. 'We will treat further with the king! We will send another letter!'

With eloquence and calming words, Moigne reassured them: 'His Majesty can yet be persuaded. We shall make our cause clear. Patience, my friends, patience.' For many minutes together, he spoke, using his barrister's logic and gentle ways, until at last, uttering oaths and vile threats, the rebels slunk away. The gentry were safe.

Safe then. Not later. Not Thomas Moigne.

Because the Crown set its vengeance for him.

In the dark, spinning room, Francis clings to this thought: it was Moigne's temerity to censor the king's words that caused them to single him out. How had the king's spies known? Oh, but there were hundreds of witnesses in the chapter house—how might they not have known? *He lies by not reading all!* the priest cried. For the moment, Francis's heart is soothed. Having conjured an act upon which to lay the blame, he believes he might avoid the same fate. I shall never . . . He closes his eyes against the room's turning, rolls to his side. The room ceases its black spinning. It is many hours until daylight, Francis tells himself. I shall ponder further. I may come to a better reckoning. He reaches down to scratch beneath his hose.

In the morning, as he rides towards London with bitten thighs and aching head, he tells himself he should have taken less beer. He should have let the two churls have the bed and slept in the stable. If the bedbugs had not crawled from the straw to feast on him, he'd have slept better. But then, he thinks, rubbing his forehead with one hand, thumb and finger caressing his temples: if he had not drunk so much beer in the tavern, he'd have not slept at all.

– Chapter 9 –

I waited, Maddie. I tried to wait. I sat the whole day quiet as a cabbage, reading Erasmus's Latin till my eyes crossed. But the hours were too long, the insides of my stomach gnawed themselves, the throbbing in my head like a farrier's hammer. No longer did the light slant cheerfully; it seeped into the room like trough water, dirty and diffused. The bells tolled the fourth hour, and still Edward did not come. Men passed outside the door, I could hear their voices, and then the passage grew silent, and I thought, they have gone to supper. I drew the stool to the window and climbed up, but there was nothing to see, only a bricked building across the way, its windows evenly spaced, most of them shuttered, and the ones not shuttered were too dark for me to see inside. Then I spied the bell tower where the bells were ringing. I thought, perhaps Edward is there at vespers? Perhaps I might wait outside the door, and when he comes out, he will take me to an alehouse for supper?

I tore a tiny scrap from the edge of Erasmus and wrote a note for him, in case he should return and I miss him in passing; then I tucked my hair beneath the maid's cap, listened at the door. No voices. No sounds of footsteps. I slipped into the dark gallery and down the stairs.

The lawn was empty, it was purpling dusk already. There were lights in some of the scholars' windows above the square. I ran across the open space feeling vulnerable as a flushed hare, hurried towards the gate through which Francis and I had entered yesterday, but when I stepped into the road in front of the stable, I did not know in which direction to turn. The church bells were pealing everywhere now, up the street, down the street, on the far side of the college behind me. I stood near the stable trying to decide whether to go right or left, and then—oh, Maddie.

I cannot say it.

But I cannot *not* say it. I must tell you, for I can tell no one else.

I felt myself grasped from behind, and in the next instant I was pulled inside the stable. The man uttered no word. I do not know what sort of person it was; I could not see him, only smell him, a fug of ale and onions and sour sweat. He shoved me into an empty stall and tried to push me to the ground, but I clung to the top of the stall wall. All this in silence, Maddie. No words. He was behind me, his slabs of hands atop mine, trying to peel back my fingers, the whole stinking weight of him pressed against my back. I could hear the sound of his grunts, the church bells pealing in the distance. I do not remember my own sounds, but I must have been screaming, because he clapped his hand over my mouth and shoved me against the wood, his nasty hand mashing my lips, and with his other paw he lifted my skirts, pushing against me, he pushed his, oh, Maddie I cannot say it, he pushed his . . . his *member* against me. I wrenched my mouth open and bit down on his filthy palm with all the might God gave me, and oh, he let out such a yell! He mashed the side of my head against the timber till I thought he would crush my brains, and I did hear myself screaming now, or trying to scream, but the sound came a pitiful muffled moaning. I could feel him fumbling at me, grunting; then he took his hand from my cheek to reach down for himself, and in that instant I felt his weight lift from my back, and like an eel from the river I slithered down and sideways, out from between him and the wall, and I ran!

From the stable, into the street, I ran and I ran and I ran, panting, I do not know how long, until ahead of me I saw a lighted vestibule, a low arch, an oaken door, a faint yellow light beyond it: a sanctuary. The door was open.

Within: flickering darkness. The nave was empty, and the chancel. I saw the suffering Christ high upon the wall beyond the veiled rood screen, candles lit near the altar, the scent of incense, wood and stone and must. The saints were dark in their alcoves, looking down. My heart pounded. The blood pulsed in my ears. I heard the little bleats of my own panting. The font stood uncovered near the entry. I dipped my fingers, made the sign of the cross as I eased forwards. But my footsteps seemed to ring against the flagstones, and I stopped.

All was silence. No murmured prayers or confessions, no echo of vespers sung. Only the sound of a cart passing on the street, its wooden wheels rumbling. I turned to look behind, fearful the fiend had followed, but there was nothing. The door stood open, the arched window rising high above it into darkness. I returned to the door and with great effort closed it quietly, stood with my back pressed against it, afraid the man would lurch inside. The feel of that wretch's hands, the stench of him, his terrible reeking weight, his, oh, his ugly hard thing pressing against me—against my very privacies, Maddie! It makes me sick to think it, to speak it. I cannot bear to remember! And yet it is not memory, it is *now,* it is every moment, as if he is still here, rearing and pressing against me, as if he remains continually behind me, atop me, as if—oh, the cur! The slabbering knave!

I stood a long while, trembling. Before me, the nave stretched towards the chancel in warm candlelight. Behind me, the door was cold and solid. I thought, I will stay here until daylight seeps through the windows, then I shall return to my brother's room and receive whatever punishment he will have for me. At once I felt a kind of peace. I edged forwards a few paces.

It was then I saw the friar. He stood in the lady chapel to my right, farther along the nave wall. He was staring at me. The candelabrum in his hand illumed his tonsure, and his pate gleamed. He beckoned me forward. I did not move. He turned and disappeared a moment, the light bouncing and moving with him, and I wanted to run away. But the danger in the street seemed more fearsome than a friar, and so I waited. He appeared again at the far end of the nave and made his way towards me, his brown cassock rustling, his shoes whispering.

When he drew near, he said, 'How may I help you?' I made no answer. 'Shall I come with you? Has your master sent for a priest?' I did not shake my head, but something in my face must have told him that this was not the answer. 'Thy mistress, then.' He waited. 'I have time enough, child,' he said gently. 'Thy mistress, though, perhaps does not have time for thee to locate thy tongue?'

'Not my mistress,' I said. 'I have none.'

'I see,' he said. 'Thy master, then.'

'No.' I saw myself as the friar must see me: a panting servant girl, kirtle and cap all twisted, no cloak about me, and I felt suddenly that he could see what that knave had done to me, what he'd tried to do. My face burned with shame. I would not look at him. The silence stretched long.

At length he said, 'You have broken your Lenten fast.'

I shook my head.

'It is . . . perhaps a worse sin that troubles you?'

I swallowed deep.

'Is this sin a grave matter?'

I nodded.

'Was it committed with intention?'

What could I say? I did not know.

'Did you have rebellion in your heart?'

Ah, rebellion. And what have I been but rebellious, against God, against the Holy Mother, since the very hour of thy passing? 'Yes, your Reverence,' I said.

'And have you repented this sin? Turned from it in true remorse and contrition?' His eyes were kind, brown, the colour of his cassock. They canted slightly away from each other, so that it seemed he looked at me with only one at a time, but such kindness was there.

'I cannot . . .' My gaze strayed to the gilded pyx on the wall within the chancel, obscured by the rood screen, yes, but still I felt it there, as if it burned with an interior heat, as if I could sense the consecrated Host within.

'Cannot do what? Stop sinning? The Lord will help you. He can keep even the weakest among us from temptation.'

'Not that!' I said, for I knew what sort of temptation he meant.

'What, then?'

'I desecrated the Host.'

A great stillness came upon him—the largeness of my sin, I supposed, entering his thoughts. The light from his candelabrum pooled around us—three stubby candles, Maddie, three for the Holy Trinity, but no fourth candle for the intercessor, the Holy Mother, for there is to be no intercession. There never has been! Did I not pray? Did I not beg and plead with her to save you? And she denied me, and I hated her. I whispered, 'I live in mortal sin.'

And then, it was as if saying the words unstopped my tongue, and other words came pouring: 'I have been high-stomached and prideful, full of envy, I have lied and stolen and borne false witness. I have dishonoured my father and my stepmother. I have caused great grief for my brothers, tormented my sister and my poor ninny of a maid, I spilled the Body of Christ on my sister's gown, I have lived in mortal sin, Father: I killed my sister! Oh, I killed my sister! Not with deeds but with the fierce envy of my heart! I hated the Holy Mother, and now I fear, oh, I fear my sister is suffering in Purgatory! And I cannot pray for her! I cannot pay for indulgences, I am not able to help her, no more than I can help myself! And I hate the man who calls me wife, for I am no good wife—I am wretched and wilful and fully wicked in my heart!' I stopped, my pulse pounding. I could not look at him. I could not breathe.

'Yes. I suppose,' he said quietly, 'you are the chiefest sinner in the world. Beyond any hope for salvation.'

I raised my eyes to his face.

'If you think this, then doubtless you are as prideful as you claim.' His mild face was not condemning but kind. 'Paul the Apostle persecuted Christians throughout Judea, you know this? He hunted Christ's disciples, minded the very cloaks of the men who stoned Stephen, yet he became the greatest proclaimer of the gospel the world has ever known. Tell me, child, did Paul go to the priests for his confession? Did he do penance and pay to light candles for prayers?'

I stared at him. I did not know how to answer.

He glanced behind me, to the closed church door. 'I think we ought to retire to the lady chapel. You may sit if you wish, and I shall sit, and you may tell me whereby you killed your sister and all the other particulars of your sins, and also how you came to acquire the accent of a highborn young lady, when your attire says you are not even a lady's maid but only a poor, unwashed girl from the milk house.' He began to make his way towards the chapel, taking his candles with him. I took a step to follow him. Then I turned and fled back outside to the dark street.

I cannot understand my own doings. Why would I leave a lighted place of sanctuary to go back out into danger? I cannot say. Only that I did so. Once outside, I began to run through the darkness, for it was fully night now, retracing my steps at great speed, and when I arrived near the stable, I paused, breathing hard, listening. I was afraid to pass. I pressed myself into the shadows, blacker at the stable's mouth than in the dark street. I heard the restless shifting of a horse in a nearby stall, its softly blown snuffle, but no human sound. I looked beyond the stable's edge, to the wall surrounding Edward's college, and I saw that the great door in the wall was closed. And what if it is bolted? I thought. What shall I do? But the door was not bolted, only latched. It made a creaking groan as I pushed it open and slipped through. I could see the full black square of the lawn before me; there were lights in most all the windows, and my chest swelled in a kind of silent glorifying: I had made my way home!

No. Not home. Most assuredly not home. It is only that I felt it so in that moment; for Edward would be waiting in his tidy monk's cell, there would be warmth, and light, perhaps a bit of supper. I glided like a shadow along the edge of the square to the stairs.

– Chapter 10 –

At her light knock Edward flings open the door, pulls her inside, hissing, 'Oh, thank Christ, here you are! What is the *matter* with you?' He does not stride up and down offering oaths and disparagements, as Francis would do, but stands beside his desk, kneading his unshaven cheek with his knuckles and scowling. 'Father is right, Anne. You've the very dam of the devil in you. What purpose under God's heaven would cause you to go wandering the streets at night? You could have been killed! Or worse.'

Anne knows what *worse* is, and it is for this reason she does not sling words of blame at her brother, though she thinks, why did you not come? I waited! I was near starved to the grave! The stench of the wretch's breath is yet in her nostrils, his weight against her back, his sprung member probing her buttocks, the base of her spine—the memory is not in the past but a continuous *now*: a vile sensory presence that fills her with nausea and guilt and shame.

Later, after she has eaten the pottage Edward saved for her, after her head has ceased to ache and her stomach to churn and the stink of the man is subsumed in the burning fat of tallow candles, she tells him of the friar at the church. 'He was not a lay brother, Edward. The questions he asked—they were as a priest would ask. I'm sure he would have shriven me had I . . .' Her chest tightens. The moment she'd almost followed him flickers in memory. She rises and begins to walk about the room. 'But that seems unusual, does it not? A friar alone in the chapel, the church empty. Who was he? What work would a mendicant do in a parish church?'

'There are always mendicants at Cambridge, Nan. They flock here from everywhere, and scholars commonly join orders after their studies—it means nothing.'

She turns to him. 'Will you? Join orders?'

'Join the corrupt, the misled, and the bestial? No. There are better ways to serve Christ.' Then he seems to think of something. He glances at her curiously. 'What did he say to you?'

'He spoke of Saint Paul, how he became a great preacher of the gospel.'

'Preacher of the gospel. These were his words?'

'Yes. Or proclaimer, actually. "The greatest proclaimer of the gospel the world has ever known."'

'It is true.' Her brother gazes at her a moment, then he goes to his trunk and pulls forth a bound folio—an exact duplicate of the one hidden in her bedchamber at Friskney. 'Here, I'll show you.' He sits beside her, opens the book, turns a few pages, lays it open in Anne's lap. 'So, my too-clever sister,' he says, pointing. 'Read that.' She does not pick it up. She does not look at the pages. Slow, silent tears begin sliding down her cheeks, but her brother does not see. He lifts the book from her lap, begins to read: '"For I am not ashamed of the gospel of Christ: for it is the power of God unto salvation to everyone that believeth . . ."' He continues in a low murmur, but Anne does not listen. Suddenly she bursts out:

'Why did you give it to Maddie?'

Edward pauses. 'Are you crying?'

'Why *her* and not me!'

Her brother's thin face flickers through bafflement and confusion to a slow comprehension. 'She told you? I swore her to secrecy.'

'She didn't tell me, I found it. Buried beneath her marriage linens after she . . . after her death.'

'It was not burned with her belongings?'

'I have it. In my linen chest at Friskney.'

'And what does your husband say to that?'

'Nothing. He knows it not. Nor shall he if I can help it.'

'And how may you help it if you are gadding about the world in a milkmaid's costume while your husband paws through your belongings at will?' Edward stands, and in two steps crosses the room, returns the book to his trunk, replaces the carpet on top of it. 'Why would I not bring this treasure to my most pious and least troublesome sister on the eve of her wedding?'

'Am I not pious?' Her voice is small.

Edward barks a laugh. 'Look at you! Your very cap and kirtle are a lie! You threaten my studies, my reputation, my very *life* here, but, oh, follow Francis on horseback you must! Come to Corpus Christi you must! And now must I keep you hidden if I'm not to suffer the consequences of your indiscretions—and you cannot even be obedient in this but must go traipsing about the city like a girl of the streets! You are not to be trusted, Anne, you never have been—why would I deliver to your incautious hand that which, if discovered, could cause us all such grief?'

'I would not have told anyone! I have not. Only Beatrice.'

Edward sighs, caresses the carpet laid over the trunk. 'It is not so important now. The danger was greater then. Tyndale had been seized at Antwerp, we knew he must burn.'

'So why bring his book to Maddie? Why put *her* in danger?'

He blinks at her. 'This is not Tyndale's Testament. This is the *entire* Scripture in English.'

'I know.'

'Translated by Miles Coverdale.'

'I know.' She had not known. The book does not say so. Miles Coverdale. She has not heard that name.

'It was published on the continent last summer. By grace, three copies came to my hand—the entire Holy Scripture in English, from the Pentateuch to Revelation!'

'I know.'

He gazes at her sadly. 'Yes. You know. I wonder what good it may do you.' He stands, removes his robe and hangs it on a hook on the wall. Anne watches him. The tallest and leanest of her brothers, Edward moves with a kind of stoop-shouldered grace, his scant auburn beard ill-defined in the candlelight. 'You may have the bed tonight,' he says. 'Tomorrow evening we'll exchange.'

In silence she removes her shoes, her cap and apron, lies down and begins her prayers, counting them silently on her fingers. It is only after the candle is snuffed and Edward is stretched out on the trundle that she speaks again. 'I'm sorry,' she whispers. 'I shan't do it again. Run away like that.' He makes no reply. 'You said there were three copies? What did you do with the third?'

'I gave it to Christopher.'

'Not Francis?'

'Of course not Francis. And may he soon come to deliver me from your incessant questions. Go to sleep, Anne.'

She does not sleep but curls on her side, trembling, chewing the inside of her lips, reliving her terror in the stable, her nausea and guilt, for what can that ugly ravishment be but punishment? A chastisement from God for her unconfessed, unrepented sins. Oh, but she has confessed! Her torrent of sins poured out to the friar at St Botolph's! Though it is not a proper confession; she did not kneel at the shriving stool, she has done no penance, received no absolution, her blackest sins yet soil her soul. But I shall go to him again, she thinks, the kind friar in the brown cassock. I shall make a full confession, pray acts of contrition, suffer whatever penance he gives me, that I may be shriven, and so, oh, thanks be to Christ, receive the Sacrament at Easter.

A moment's peace, and then the guilt and terror sweep her again. She cannot rest. Her mind roils now, the wretch in the stable, the friar's canted eyes, memories of her sister Martha sweeping through: Maddie at prayers, Maddie at supper, in the nursery, the solar. A bright autumn afternoon, the road to the village, the light plays and winks through the leaves; her sister throws back her head, laughing, her face to the sky. Anne sees Maddie on her deathbed, her bony finger pointing at the ceiling joint, tracing the imps and devils roaring through the chamber. *Ave Maria, gratia plena Dominus tecum benedicta tu in mulieribus . . .*

Her sister had fallen ill of such a sudden—rushing in from the garden one morning, laughing, her skirt full of asters, and by noontide lying in bed shrieking with the knifing pains inside her head—that the servants were frightened and unhappy to tend her. They crossed themselves and prayed for deliverance, believing that the sweating sickness had ridden north from London. It must be so, they whispered: see the rivers of foul fluid coursing from her face and neck and arm-holes!

But Martha did not die quickly, as one would of the sweat; she remained with them, suffering, for many nights and days. The family tried to keep Anne from the sickroom, but at any unguarded moment she would slip into the chamber and stand staring at her sister's thin chest, willing her to breathe. A chair was brought for Anne to sit and sleep in. She sopped crusts of bread in ale and ground mace and held them to her sister's lips, but Martha's tongue was thick and black, her throat coated with pus; she turned her face away. Anne prayed the Holy Mother to intercede, but no matter how many *ave marias* and *memorarae* she murmured, her sister's torment did not ease.

The last night Martha lived, Anne slept not at all but watched her sister gasping for breath, her eyes roving the ceiling joints, where passels of imps and demons roared through the chamber—or so the servants whispered: Satan sending his minions to snatch the souls of the dying. She watched, frightened, as her sister raised up from the bed, eyes stark, mouth twisted, pointing a thin finger to the darkened crevice where the wall touched the ceiling. Slowly Maddie swept her trembling finger from one side of the room to the other. Anne did not see what Maddie saw, only that her sister perceived with the eyes of the dying, and it was terrible, and terrifying what she saw.

Harder and harder Anne prayed, *Sancta Maria, Mater Dei ora pro nobis pecatoribus nunc et in hora mortis nostrae,* but she could find no comfort in the Latin prayers; she began to plead: 'Mother Mary, save her! Save us! Deliver us from evil, help her! Have mercy upon my poor sister. Mother Mary, have mercy! Have mercy.'

At near daylight, her sister sank down. Anne took her hand. The flesh was warm, the palms dry. She watched her sister's thin chest, the slow, steady rise and fall, her breaths faint and shallow, rhythmic as a heartbeat. Maddie's lips were parted, her face peaceful, her eyes closed. Mother Elizabeth came and stood at the door; she crossed herself and left. A short while later, she returned and opened the shutters, burned sage to sweeten the room, and left once more.

The third time she came, a village boy in altar vestments came with her. The boy spread a white cloth on the small table in the corner and laid there a candle, a crucifix, a silver cup, a clean towel and spoon. Still Anne would not understand, but moments later, when she looked up and saw her father and brothers entering, and behind them the village priest carrying a vial of holy oil and a small silver casket, she understood. 'No!' she cried. 'Do not let him in here! Do not let him! Send him away!'

'Anne.' Her stepmother tried to enclose her in her arms, but Anne turned on her, hissing, 'Get away from me. Traitor! Viper!' Her brother Francis stepped forwards and held her until she grew still. She watched in despair as the priest prepared the sacrament, blessed the Host, poured holy oil into the cup, leaned over the dying girl, exhorting her to confession. 'What hath she to confess?' Anne choked out. 'Can you not see her very goodness?'

Her father said, 'Francis, take her out of here.'

'No,' Mother Elizabeth said. 'Let her stay. Be quiet, Anne.'

Anne drew silent, stood limp and mute in her brother's arms as the priest leaned over the bed with his ear turned; he raised up again, made the sign of the cross, began to murmur the Act of Contrition; then he took up the holy oil, anointed Martha's eyes, ears, nostrils, her gaping, blackened mouth. Her twisted hands. Her curled, fish-white feet. The priest took the Eucharist from its silver casket, blessed it and brake it, began to push a small piece into the dying girl's mouth.

'No! She lives! She lives! Leave her!' Anne tore free from her brother's grasp and leapt forwards, knocking the priest aside, and the Body of Christ fell from her sister's mouth to the sour sheet. The priest at once plucked it up and placed it in his own mouth, making the sign of the cross, as all around the room her family cried out, 'Anne, no!'

Anne, no! Anne, no! Anne, no!

Through the tormented night in her brother's room at Cambridge, Anne tries to push the memory away, as she has done these seven months and more, but this night she cannot stop remembering: the fallen Host, her family's cries, the shock and judgement in the priest's eyes. And the terrible silence that followed. How they all stared at her, stunned at her desecration. How, into that silence, there came a faint sigh, and Maddie's blistered mouth gaped open. Her eyes were partly closed. Her chest did not rise again. Father Sebastian began to pray. *Pater noster qui es in caelis sanctificetur nomen tuum.*

A day and a night and a day, and no word comes from Francis. A rhythm settles: by daylight Anne reads—not Erasmus's Latin but Coverdale's English—and waits for Edward to return, bringing her small portions of ale and pottage or turnips or whatever he is able to procure, for the college keeps Lent very stringently. At the sound of her brother's returning footsteps, she does not scurry to put away the book. The first night, when he saw that she had taken it from his trunk, he did not tell her to put it away; rather, he began to instruct her. He directs her attention from the stories of slaughter and prophets and kings in the front of the book to the Acts of the Apostles in the back. He reads to her of Paul's great conversion on the road to Damascus. She has seen the image in the stained-glass window at St Mary's: Paul struck to his knees, his hand up to protect his eyes, the golden light pouring down.

'Did this happen to you?' she says. 'Did Jesus come to you in a flood of light?'

'Not precisely, no. But I have come to faith through Christ Jesus. I am washed in His precious blood.'

'The blood of the sacrament.'

'The blood of His holy sacrifice.'

'Is this not the same thing?'

'You want learning, Nan. Could you but come with me to the White Horse, you would hear discourse of such learning you'd be clean amazed. Men of the new learning have gathered there for years—you would hardly believe the famous preachers whose awakening came in that tavern. Hugh Latimer, for one. Robert Barnes. Little Bilney.'

'Does it . . . can it ever happen to a woman? Jesus coming in light, I mean.'

Her brother yawns. The hour is late. 'I've never heard so. But I've never heard not. I do not think Paul says much of women, only that they must obey their husbands and keep silent in church.'

'But everyone must keep silent in church.'

'Not the priest.' He is already putting the book away.

'Will the friar at Saint Botolph's know? Whether the light may come to a woman?'

'If he is wise in Scripture through true translation and not through the corrupted teachings that have come down to us, perhaps he will have an opinion.' Edward stretches out on the hard trundle. Four nights now, and Anne still commands the bed. He snuffs the candle. His voice is musing in the darkness. 'I know all the gospel men in Cambridge,' he says. 'I think we should attend Mass at Saint Botolph's on Sunday. You may point out the friar to me, and if I know him and trust him, we can ask.'

They walk in cold March rain to St Botolph's Church in Trumpington Street on Passion Sunday. The season has turned; it is several days past equinox, the minutes of daylight now exceed the dark, but today one would not know it. Today it seems winter will never be done. Anne walks a few steps behind her brother. He ought not to be seen walking with a female whatsoever, he says, and most certainly not with a common milkmaid. She watches the back of his tall figure. The shoulders of his robe are dark with water. His cap is soft, it has no brim. Rain beads his fur collar. Anne tucks her head. Water soaks the veil Edward fashioned for her from a length of linen torn from one of his shirts. Droplets trickle down her neck, slide beneath her smock. Her brother ducks into the church amidst the crowd. She hurries not to lose sight of him.

The inside of the church is dim. The poor light cannot find its way through the stained glass. At the far end, the draped rood screen is covered in its death shroud. The Holy Mother on her dais, the saints and apostles in their alcoves, all seem of a piece with the darkness. Anne stands with the lesser women in the back. She scans the worshippers, looking for a brown cassock, a cowl, but she is not tall enough to see past the shoulders of the men standing between her and the altar. She cannot see Edward's cap now. She cannot see the priest's back within the chancel beyond the rood screen, though she can see the smoke rising from the censer, smell the incense. The stone columns rising to arches seem to close in like marchers with halberds raised. These are the hardest holy days, she thinks. Maundy Thursday. Good Friday. Holy Sabbath, the endless day of despair and darkest sorrow when Jesus lay in the tomb—

An image comes. She wills it away.

But the image washes over her: her sister's body mouldering in the grave, flesh melting from her skull, her beautiful golden hair a rank rag beneath her burial cap, and in the darkness, her eyes hollowed, her teeth bared. Anne has seen what happens to the corrupted body when the life force is gone: the mauled and stinking rats abandoned in the courtyard by the stable cats, the newborn lamb rotting beneath a hawthorn tree. She came across the lamb in the dark time after Maddie's death when she wandered the land around South Kelsey, aimless, without purpose or hope. A sweltering late-summer day. The mowers calling in the fields. The lamb had been abandoned by its mother, dead before it had half lived. She'd been sickened by the smell, the matted wool, the jellied eyes, the undulating life in death as the maggots writhed, and the images swelled over her still, an hour later, as she sat on the ground beside her sister's grave. They arise in her now as she stands swaying at the rear of St Botolph's.

Oh, where is the friar with kind eyes? She looks everywhere, cannot see him. It is all of a piece, she thinks. My sister was betrothed to Thomas Kyme the week of Corpus Christi. *Corpus Christi: Body of*

Christ. The Body of Christ carried in its golden monstrance through the village streets, the people singing, the people praying, Father Sebastian holding aloft the Blessed Sacrament in its golden throne, and here, now, inside St Botolph's, the rector will hold the Host aloft for the people's adoration. *Ecce Agnus Dei. Ecce qui tollit peccata mundi.* Behold the Lamb of God. Behold Him who takes away the sins of the world. It is all part of the same mystery, she thinks, the same convergence, the same impenetrable story.

Anne shivers in her wet clothes, her teeth chattering. She sees Edward now, his soft black cap and furred collar rising above the others, farther along the nave to her right. But the friar is nowhere visible. He is not here, she thinks. She recalls his concerned face, his canted eyes, the stillness that settled on him when she blurted her sin. *I desecrated the Host.* Her mouth is dry. Her eyes ache. She will come again to find him, during vespers or matins or any weekday hour she may slip away. The friar will shrive me, she thinks, that I may receive communion Easter Sunday. I will worship the Blessed Sacrament at the elevation, with my hands and heart and eyes. *Ecce Agnus Dei. Ecce qui tollit peccata mundi.*

But as Anne gets to her feet, her sight darkens, the nave seems to turn black; she puts her hand to a pillar to keep from falling. She stands swaying, sweating, her head pounding the Latin words. When the benediction is sung at last, she turns, her chest shivering, legs trembling, and files out of St Botolph's behind the others into a cold, driving rain.

– Chapter 11 –

I see you there, falling, falling and falling, and yet you reach no place but keep falling as if you will fall forever, your hair is alight. Is it fire? I think it is not fire but light. The light of God. Oh, I burn, my body burns. I hear our brothers' voices, I cannot glean what they are saying, I hear them. I see the friar, his brown kindness like the soil opened for planting, the turned sod. It will be spring soon, is it spring? I had not known I would die in springtime, I had always thought summer, like thee—oh, must I emulate you in everything? Even now when you are falling eternally in eternal darkness? Yet, see there—golden light surrounds you. I think it is light. Is it fire? Oh, do not say it is fire! They do not love me, our brothers, nor even does Father love me, for how may they, when I do not love myself? But I loved you. I loved you, Maddie, it was you who left me! The Feast of Corpus Christi, they came to ensnare you, those Kymes, they came to encase you in wedlock! And you sat at table like a lamb to the slaughter, so meek and smiling, always smiling—why did you? You should have said them no! You should have fled from them, hid your face—oh, Mother Mary protect us! She did not protect us, she did not intercede, and now am I dying, in mortal sin I am dying. I see you across the abyss, the great gulf fixed; you are falling, the flaming bower all about you, your hair lit golden. I cannot come to thee! Maddie, help me! I am so cold. I tremble. My bones shake, my lungs turn to chalk and wax, I am poured out like water—oh, why will they never cease grumbling, our brothers! I cannot abide them! They rumble and grumble, it is like the uttering of thunder in the far distance. No, not thunder—horses! I hear them! They are riding, they come riding, their hooves thundering over the drawbridge, do not let them! Keep them away from us! They will destroy us—they will destroy me! I surrender, Father, I submit myself to thee. But you do not know what you ask! You do not know what he does to your daughter when he comes in the night, he comes creeping, his rough hands, his—I told you! I warned you, Maddie. But you would not be warned! No, you must sit at the window with that secret smile in your mouth, stroll about the manor as if you were the only person ever to marry—and that fool! See him there in the yard, his flaxen hair pasted to his round forehead. He slaps his riding gloves, slaps them! Hard, against his thigh! And you simpering in the bed-curtains, floating about the halls in your new satin sleeves, oh, how I despised you. No! No. That is not true. I loved you! I love you now. Please, do not go. Oh, my sister, do not leave me! You are bone of my bone, flesh of my flesh, our thoughts and minds knit since ever I can remember, every breath that we take—where are you? Maddie, Maddie, why have you forsaken me?

– Chapter 12 –

Francis can scarcely contain his anger. The delay has been burdensome enough, this compelled detour to Cambridge to fetch his sister and bring her home to her husband: two days' miserable ride from London in drenching rain, and now he arrives to find Anne sick with fever and incoherent in bed. Thomas Kyme's ire will not be easily assuaged, further delay will make worse of the matter, and here is Anne again, creating trouble again, for everyone around her, regardless that she is not even awake.

'It is the ague,' Edward says.

'Ague? This time of year? I think not.'

'The doctor says it is. He bled her.'

'You've had a doctor here?'

'How could I not? Look at her, Francis. She is like to die.'

It is true that she looks very ill. She is thin as sticks, her face white as a shroud, the dark hair curling in damp wisps on her forehead. Her skin appears so bloodless you'd think her dead already were it not for the small dry coughs that shudder her chest.

Edward stands beside him. 'Thank God she is quiet now.'

'Quiet.'

'Most hours she tosses and turns, whimpers and moans. Sometimes she cries out, claws at the air or her throat. Since the bleeding, though, I think she is better.'

'How long has she been like this?'

'Three days. We were coming from Mass and—'

'Mass! You had her to Mass?'

Edward meets his gaze placidly. 'Whose reputation is harmed if she is discovered here? Not thine, I think.'

Francis's half-contained rage threatens to spill towards his brother. He turns, covers the room in two strides, walks back again. 'We must leave tomorrow.'

'Look at her, Francis! She cannot ride.'

Francis regards his sister. His mind is calculating.

'I thought you'd changed your mind,' Edward says. 'I thought you had ridden straight home to South Kelsey, and our sister would die here and I should be left to explain things to the dean and my tutor.'

A sharp glance from Francis. 'You know I would not do that.'

'I just could not understand why you did not come,' Edward mutters. He takes his brother's saddlebag from him, sets it on the trunk to dry out. 'How fares our brother Christopher?'

'He progresses. He progresses very well. Cromwell likes him.'

'Cromwell? Not the king?'

'No, yes, of course. His Majesty favours him. But it is Cromwell's good opinion that has helped our brother's progress.' Francis laughs. 'You should see how he struts about in his new doublet, smooth and tawny as a doe's butt it is, his sleeves all slashed and bleeding crimson.' The court suits Christopher—it is a place where, most fortunately for the Ayscough family, their handsome middle brother shines.

'I can well see him,' Edward says as he pours a cup of wine. 'Sit, brother.' He motions towards the stool. Francis throws his cap and riding cloak onto the desk, takes the drink Edward offers. 'We should settle a wife on Christopher soon.' His voice turns musing. 'A Skipwith marriage would not be a bad match. We are thinking of the St Polls for Jane.'

Here is my brother, Edward thinks, herding and nipping: as if arranging marriages for the Ayscough siblings were his purview, not Father's. Of course, he says nothing of a match for Edward: the church will be his bride and dower. So Francis thinks, because he is of the old thinking, and Edward says nothing, neither of his own wishes nor of the priests who are already married, at both Cambridge and Lambeth. 'The St Polls are a good family,' Edward says, handing his brother the filled cup. He thinks in silence: *and of reformist leanings, I hear.*

'I don't think we should settle yet. Jane is a beauty; we might make alliance with a family of greater substance than the St Polls. Perhaps even make do with a lesser dowry.'

The room grows suddenly silent, awkward. Unspoken is the fate of their sister Martha. It had been Sir William's desire to hold the dowry small which caused him to make the misfortunate match with the Kymes of Friskney. Not misfortunate for Martha, as it turned out, but for Anne. And so, Edward thinks, for us all. The silence grows. The brothers sip. They regard their sister. She is so still it appears as if she sleeps the sleep of the dead, except that her brows are frowning. 'When I returned from my lectures the first night,' Edward says, 'I found her gone.'

'What?'

'She returned late, all dishevelled and distressed, and making little sense. She told a garbled story of having gone into a church and met there a friar who interrogated her soundly. I could make no sense of it. Even before she came so ill, she was . . . not like herself. I fear something is wrong.'

'Such as?'

Edward shakes his head. He gazes at his sister. In this profound sleep, motionless as she is, she appears fragile. Like Martha, he thinks. A clot of grief chokes his throat. He'd not been there when Martha died. The family had sent word when she fell ill, but by the time he came from Cambridge, his closest sister was gone. He would transfer that deep affection to Anne, but he and Anne are near opposite in everything: sensibility, rhythms, behaviours, concerns. It is Francis whom Anne most resembles, his bluster and wilfulness, his bold, assured tongue.

'Have you nothing to eat here?' his brother says. 'Oh, never mind. I'll go to an inn and take my supper there. I need to find a buyer for Kyme's mare, anyway. He'll be furious I've sold her, but he'll be more furious if I don't bring his wife soon.' He swirls on his riding cloak. His eyes come to rest on their sister's face. She breathes slowly, evenly, the breaths broken by her sharp little coughs. 'Tomorrow I'll see about hiring a cart. Have you a furred robe here? Or an extra cloak?'

'She won't be well enough to travel tomorrow!'

'She will have to be. We'll take the blanket.'

'Let me call in the surgeon! Let us hear what he says.'

'I've been delayed a week now already, her husband is furious. It will not serve Anne, nor me, nor thee, for that matter, to delay longer. Oh, peace, brother. You know she is not like Martha. She is not fragile and frail but tough as a thistle, and she will prick like one as soon as she comes awake.' Francis picks up his cap, starts towards the door. 'Oh, I almost forgot: as soon as the Easter holy days are past, you are to join Cranmer's household.'

Edward can only stare. He finds his wits before Francis is out the door. '*Archbishop* Cranmer?'

Francis pauses, grins. 'The very one. What did you think I was about in London but preparing your good future? The archbishop is not ready to receive you yet, but he will be come April.'

'What of my studies?' Edward says, but his excitement is clear. For all his asceticism and faith, he is still an Ayscough. His ambition is of a different style than that of his father and brothers, but it is ambition nonetheless: relentless, all-encompassing. To join the household of the Archbishop of Canterbury! There is no prelate but Bishop Latimer so revered among the reformers as a friend of the gospel.

'You're to go just after the Easter holy days.' Francis smooths the rain-roughened velvet of his cap. 'If the Archbishop of Canterbury will have you to serve, what need have you of a sheepskin? Eh?' His sudden heartiness vanishes as he takes one last lingering look at their sister. 'Truly, Edward, it is better to carry her home like this than to wait until she is well. As she is now, her husband will perhaps be moved to pity.'

'But what if she dies?'

Francis does not take his eyes from Anne as he dons the black cap with its drooping white feather. 'Trust me, my brother. She won't.'

III

There Is to Be a Great Feast

Friskney

May

1537

– Chapter 13 –

When I began to rouse from my sickness, my sister's book was the first thought to come into my brain. I was still aching, sweating, the hardness in my lungs like a plug of lead in my chest, but I was not roiling in darkness. I felt myself purged somehow, burned clean. I knew where I was. I knew Beatrice's pointed little face looming over me, her hand holding a spoon of broth. I asked for the book. 'Shh, mistress. I have hidden it.' I felt a wave of peace come over me then, and I sank back into my dreams.

Who can say how many days before we spoke of it again? Quite a number, I think. Time passes so strangely in fever. I know I was able to sit up by then and take a little nourishment. Mother Kyme had been at my bedside with the Vicar Jordan, who leaned over me exhorting me to make confession as if I were dying and this should be my last opportunity, when in fact, I knew that I was coming better. I turned my face to the wall, moaning. When the old mistress and the vicar went out, I sat up and ate the porridge Beatrice had brought for me. 'Come,' I said. 'Tell me a story.'

'Pardon, miss,' she said. 'I think I know none.'

'Of course you know some,' I said. 'I have taught them to you.'

'I forget.'

'What of Noah and his sons? What of Jonah and the great fish?'

She twisted her fingers in her apron. 'I'm but a poor servant girl, miss. I haven't brains for the remembering of stories.'

'But I've read them to you a hundred times!'

'Yes, miss,' she said, and slid her eyes to the door. 'But we oughtn't,' she whispered. 'The vicar says the man that wrote that book is a awful Lutheran and was strangled and burnt.'

'Come closer,' I said. She stepped closer. 'Take the stool and set it here,' I said. She brought the stool from the corner and placed it beside the bed. 'Closer,' I said. She moved closer. I said in whisper, 'My sister's book is not of Tyndale but another man entirely, Master Coverdale, who is a proper Christian and not a heretic and not a Lutheran, so you can stop your gaumless fretting. Now, tell me: what have you done with it?'

'I buried it,' she whispered.

'Where?'

'If I say, miss, you will know, and then we would both be in danger. For if they ask and you tell them, they will know it was me hid it, and then they will make me suffer worse than I suffered when you ran away.'

'Why would they ask? They do not know that I have it.' But the girl remained silent, looking down at her fingers playing with the hem of her apron. *I suffered when you ran away*. I did not like to think of it. I'd seen, when I first came awake, the shadow of an old bruise upon her cheek, laid there, no doubt, by the hand of the old mistress. Beatrice's cheek was smooth now, pale and freckled as an egg. 'Surely you remember our readings,' I said.

'I remember where the book is buried,' she whispered, 'so that you may have it when you want it. But I have forgot what's inside, and I shall stay forgot.'

'Never mind,' I said. 'We'll come to it later.' I was too weak to press further. I laid my head back on the pillow. 'Do you know what they have in Cambridge, Beatrice? A thousand church bells and an alehouse on every corner.'

'Do they, miss?'

'Yes, and the scholars stroll about the streets in their robes and square caps, you'd think it a sea of blue and black angels. Oh, and their manservants, too,' I added, thinking of what might appeal to her, 'following in their wake. Holding their books for them and carrying their dinners. Very handsome they are, too,' I said to tease her. 'A sea of handsome faces. You shall come with me to see them someday.'

'Truly, miss?'

'No,' I said, my eyes closed. 'I am making it all up.'

I heard her snigger, and then the soft thuds and rustlings as she gathered the wooden spoon and broth bowl, the napkins and linens, opened the door quietly, and went out.

That very night my husband came at me with his accusations and his ungentle hands, and I knew then that his mother had been listening at the door as I teased Beatrice: the old gorgon heard my jests about the men at Cambridge, she reported my words to her son, and, oh, the anger in him was so terrible! He snuffed the candle and came at me in darkness. I fought him, I could not help it—it was as if I smelled that knave in the stable. I fought him with my fists, I grappled as never I'd done in all the nights of our marriage, I twisted and rolled, and he forced me over onto my belly, scrabbled my gown above my waist. I writhed and wept while he took me as a stallion takes a mare, as a rutting bull mounts a poor helpless cow, and—oh, it shames me to think of it! I cannot bear it! He said the most terrible words, such filthy words of accusation and blame I hear them yet in my mind; he ground them through gritted teeth against my ear, the back of my head: the worst words that may ever be said of a woman, and he did not cease to say them after he groaned and shuddered and fell off to the side but lay there breathing hard, panting those same terrible words into the dark room.

The next morning Mother Kyme came and told me to get up from the bed: I was to remove myself from my husband's chamber to this incommodious little closet at the rear of the manor, behind her own bedchamber—hers and her husband's. Now must I pass through their chamber at all my comings and goings, and sometimes when I pass, they are already abed, and the curtains not even closed but tied back for the flow of air, and I cannot help but see the old mistress and old master in their nightcaps, snoring away. In this way they contrive to contain me.

But I have hope now. A plan. There is to be a great feast in the village tonight, with the lighting of bonfires and three hogsheads of wine for the people's pleasure, and guns shot off at midnight in honour of the news that came yesterday from London: Queen Jane is quick with child. The feasting and celebrations are to go on all night. Master Kyme has given permission to the male servants to join the feast, though not the females, which seems to me no good justice, but perhaps it is as well: with three hogsheads of wine drunk, there will likely be such disgraceful behaviours as Beatrice or any of the younger maids ought never to see.

But first must we all, the entire village, squire to common, take ourselves to church for Mass, where the *Te Deum* is to be sung. I asked permission to remain here and not walk to church in such heat. I am stronger, but my stomach is still queasy and my head aches at the least weight. But my husband says I must go, and so I must. He tolerates no disobedience, and I make him none since that night, for fear of what he might demand of me. Dingy and close as this room is, I prefer it a thousand times to returning to his chamber. But here is the good thing: Kyme and his old father will go with the others to the village and carouse the night away—abstemious as my husband is, nevertheless, the king's great news must be celebrated—and the old mistress will retire with the roosting hens, as she does, and I shall be free to sneak downstairs and speak with Beatrice.

– Chapter 14 –

Before midnight we stood together in the herb garden outside the kitchen door. I'd skimmed through the old mistress's room like a mouse running along the base of the wall and, downstairs at the servants' room door, beckoned Beatrice. She slid from her mat like quicksilver, and we two in our bare smocks glided outside to the garden. The moon was low in the sky, a narrow white slip of a thing. Beatrice pulled me deeper into the garden, whispering that we dare not wake any of the servants. 'We cannot trust them,' she whispered.

'Not one?' said I, whispering.

'The young girls are too frightened, and the older ones too mean.'

'Hush, then,' I said. 'Show me where you have hidden the book.'

'It is too dark to go out there.'

'Where?'

She hesitated. 'The pigsty,' she whispered.

'The *pig*sty!'

'Oh, it is well covered, miss. I wrapped it in seven layers of cloth and buried it beneath the trough. I dug down deep, too. I think they'll not root it up nor cover it in their dung.'

'But—that is a sacrilege! You must fetch it at once!'

She turned her face to me, her hair springing a dark halo about her head. 'Please, miss,' she whispered. 'I durst not. The pigs will make a great noise and come after me and eat me up!'

'That is as well as you deserve,' I said. 'In any case, I do not know that pigs make such a great noise.'

'You never heard them at the trough, miss, when there's a-many of them and only a little mash. They squeal like they been stuck in the neck at slaughtering season.'

'You could not think of a better place?' She shook her head. The smell of rue and rosemary was suddenly overwhelming, a sickening miasma of sweet and bitter in the summer night air. I was afraid I would be sick again. I looked around for a place to sit.

'Here, mistress.' Beatrice took my hand and led me to a stone bench just outside the garden fence. I did not vomit, but I had to lie a good while with my face pressed to the cool stone, swallowing and swallowing, to keep my supper down. Oh, when shall I ever become well? I thought. I am so weary of being sick.

'Shall I fetch you some ale?'

'God no,' I said. 'It is ale put me here—the bad ale my brother gave me at Cambridge.'

The girl laughed. 'Lord bless you, miss. I shouldn't have thought it was *ale* done it.' She let forth a little giggle. The very idea seemed to delight her.

'Well, it did,' I said. 'Something did.'

Again she giggled.

'Ohhh,' I said, groaning. 'Do not mock me. I am sore sick at my stomach and aching in my bones.'

'I am sorry for your bones, miss. But I should think you'd be happy for your stomach sign.'

A great boom sounded in the distance. 'What was that?' I struggled to sit up.

Another boom at the same distance—the village at Friskney. 'Them's the guns, miss,' she whispered. 'To celebrate the queen's quickening.' In a short while a third boom. 'The Father, the Son, and the Holy Ghost,' she said, crossing herself. There was silence. The crickets again began to chirr. 'Let us go in,' I said, feeling weak. But Beatrice held up her hand. A fourth boom sounded, rolled away. 'There,' she said, with a quick, satisfied nod. 'There's for the Holy Mother.'

It struck me then, what she had been saying. 'What do you mean, stomach sign?'

'Why, the sign of the babe, miss. All the girls know it, though none will say before the quickening, for fear the devil will hear her talk and come snatch it away. You're a mighty good sick, though, and they say that's a promising thing. But *shh*.' She put her finger before her lips. 'I'll not say a word.'

I had not even thought of it, never dreamt it. Yet in the instant I heard Beatrice say it, I knew it was true. I am with child. I stood up from the bench and began to walk towards the barnyard.

'Mistress!' I heard her rasping voice calling behind me, but I did not pause. The sty is well far from the house, but I knew in which direction to walk—even in pure darkness, the stench would have led me. I let myself in. I heard low grunts and snorts on the far side of the pen, but the trough stands near the gate, so I did not need to enter far. I knelt, began to feel along the ground all wet with muck and offal; there was only a small space between the bottom of the trough and the earth. I had nothing to dig with. The girl came into the pen. 'No, mistress,' she whispered, 'not there. Here, at this end!' She got down, began to scrape the muck towards her; it made a sickening sucking sound beneath her palms. 'Shh,' she said, 'we mustn't wake them, they'll think it is feeding time, and with no mash in the trough, they'll think you and me is the feed. Here, now, I've got it. Shh, mistress, let me help you, here's the gate.'

'Let me hold it,' I said.

She put the bulky muck-covered square in my hands.

When we reached the house, we seemed to both see at once what a terrible mess we were in. At the first, we laughed. We stood at the garden gate, and even in the wan moonlight, we could see the stains on our smocks—hers worse than mine, though we were both smeared dark down our fronts. Her bare feet were so covered in mud they appeared as if shod in the moonlight; the soles of my slippers were caked thick with it. We stifled our laughter, looking at one another and pointing. And then she sucked in a gasping breath. 'Oh, God save us, miss, she will kill me! Oh, Mother Mary, help me! How shall I ever get us clean?' She began to weep.

'Hush,' I said. 'Quiet, now. Let me think.' The girl damped down her crying, looking at me as if I held all the wisdom of the saints in my useless head. What I held, in fact, was my sister's book, wrapped in my arms. The mud-stink was horrible, I felt I might wretch and be sick from it, but I would not put it down. 'Sit,' I whispered. 'We shall clean your feet with the tail of your skirt. Then you may slip inside and fetch your clean smock.'

'I haven't one,' she sniffled.

'You haven't a clean smock?'

'I haven't another smock whatsoever.'

'But surely you came from South Kelsey with two smocks? Father would not provide only one change of linen for his servants.'

'I did have,' she said. 'One to fit and one to grow in, but I outgrew the lesser, and the old mistress took it to make swaddling strips for a poor woman's babe in the village, and she told me I should stop growing.'

'But how do you keep clean?'

'We trade out on wash day, me and one of the milkmaids—we take turn about.'

'Oh, that is ridiculous. We shall remedy that, and shortly!' The moon was very low in the sky now. It was dark as dark in the garden. 'Wait here. I shall go up and fetch you one of mine. It will be too large, but you may fasten it with pins.' I slipped out of my shoes. 'Here, hold this.' I shoved the wrapped book into her hands and left her. The old mistress was still snoring when I glided through her chamber, and I was back in the garden with two clean smocks before Beatrice had properly ordered herself. She was sitting cross-legged on the ground wiping her feet. Maddie's book in its mud-cased shroud was a dark square lump beside her. We worked in silence, cleaning our hands, our feet, our faces, putting on the fresh smocks. I picked up the book, began to unwind the wrappings, though the pig stink made me want to vomit; there were layers and layers, as if she'd wrapped it in a winding-sheet. 'Where did you get so much linen, Beatrice? You could have near sewn yourself a new garment with this much cheap stuff!'

She watched in silence as I placed the wadding on top of my filthy smock I'd laid out on the ground. I wiped my hands, paused to look at her. 'That was a falsehood, wasn't it? That Mother Kyme took your old smock for the poor?'

She lowered her head. 'Not completely. She told me to tear it into strips for charity. I only borrowed some.'

'Well,' I said. I took her soiled smock and wrapped it and the filthy wrappings inside my ruined one, held it away from me. The bundle was thick as a swaddled newborn. I looked about for where we might hide it.

'The vicar says—,' she began. Then she released a small, helpless sigh.

'What?'

'The vicar says it is a heresy,' she whispered. 'He says a person will burn in Hell for reading such stuff—and I don't read it, miss! I never! I do not know how! But even to have such a book and hold it, he says a Bible in English is, oh, mistress—he says a person must burn! Not just in the Hereafter, but here! On this earth!'

'Do not concern yourself with the Vicar Jordan,' I said. 'He is a man filled with ignorance and vanity.'

'Oh, please, miss!' She crossed herself quickly. 'You mustn't!'

'I say the truth as I see it, Beatrice. And that is what I see.' I handed her the soiled bundle. 'Put this where you can find it on wash day, but where no one else might.' Beatrice took it, unwilling, curtsied, disappeared into the dark garden. I heard her rustlings, the scent of mint and tansy rising. The nausea roiled in me. I swallowed deep. When she reappeared, a small white slip of a thing coming through the gate like the sliver of moon, I bent to pick up Maddie's book and my shoes, and when I raised up, I had to stand very still a moment, that I might not spew my supper.

'Are you all right, miss?' Her voice was timid, frightened.

'Come,' I said, and we went in.

Through the night I lay in my narrow bed trying to think of how best to tell him. Ought I to inform the old mistress and let her do the telling? She'll be only too glad of it, I thought—truly, this is all she has cared for since the day I married him—but somehow I cannot bear to give her that pleasure. As for Kyme himself, I suppose the news will please him, although one can never know, really, what will please him; for that which would bring another man pleasure only causes this one to grunt, growl, or frown. Oh, saints in heaven, spare me to think of it! I rolled to my side, hung my head over the chamber pot, and heaved; the stink of pig cloyed my nostrils. What on earth was the child thinking? To bury God's Word in a pigsty! I've hidden the book inside the mattress; it is not even a flock bed but loose ticking filled with straw, which I suppose they took from one of the servants. I suppose they deem a straw bed good enough for me. It is lady straw, at the least; perhaps in time it will sweeten the book.

Grey light seeped through the slit of window. I saw the old mistress at the door, her arms filled with clean linens. She turned her eyes from my face to the chamber pot, where my sickness reeked. Then she looked back at me. I saw how the news settled in her, as it had settled in me in the night garden. I met her gaze, the truth of my condition passing between us, and I thought, well, there is no need now to devise how to relay the news to my husband. He'll know within the quarter hour.

But Mother Kyme did not rush off to tell him; she stood at the door glaring, her eyes narrowed. I pushed aside the sheet, sat up, placed my feet on the floor. With both hands I smoothed my smock across my lap, tucked it beneath my legs. My stomach roiled, my mind scurried. Is there a smear of mud on my face? Does she smell the pigsty reek from beneath my pillow? I was in a panic of fear as she came into the room, her expression smug as a peahen. 'So,' she said, standing over me, 'this is precisely why I told him not to meddle with you. I knew all along. Did you think I would be deceived? I who mind the laundering of your linens and know when you bleed? And . . .'—she put a finger to the side of her plump nose—'when you do not.' She hoisted me up by the elbow, pushed me aside, began to pull the sheets from the bed. It ought to be one of the servants here for the bedding, of course, but, no, the old mistress must tend to my sheets herself: all the better to keep watch on me. I feared her discovery of the lump inside the ticking, and I moved to help, but she knocked away my hand.

'Leave it! Oh, we are suddenly quite strong enough to work, are we? Perhaps we shall work hard enough to discharge evidence of our sins?' She tugged hard on the sheets. 'I told him. "Put her away from you, Thomas. Do not visit her at night! Not even when her fever is broken, for if she comes pregnant, then you will know what your wanton wife has been at in the streets of Cambridge!" Here is the sign!' With her foot she nudged the chamber pot, where old bits of vomit mingled with my night-time water. 'Oh, aren't you the very picture of innocence!' she said, because I was shaking my head. I understood then what she was saying, but I could scarcely believe it. I knew, yes, already, how she loathed me, but I have never given her cause to think such things! And yet, what help to deny it? Whatever I say, she will twist my words. The truth must come from her son's mouth. I waited for her to leave so that I might dress and go find him.

But she did not leave. She stood with the soiled sheets in her arms, also waiting. For what? My confession? Prostration? I stepped to the small trunk where they have moved my belongings, withdrew my second-best sleeves, my best damask kirtle, laid them on the bed. Where is Beatrice? I thought. Why does she not come to dress me? I took my rosary from its nail and knelt with hands clasped, began to murmur my prayers aloud to tell her she ought to leave, but still she stood there. I could feel the very distaste and judgement on her face, and I felt myself beginning to sweat. I rushed through the *Gloria Patri,* began the second *Salve Regina,* but I could not finish. The nausea was rising. I made the sign of the cross and started to stand up, but at once the sickness rushed over me, and I sank to the floor again. Now, I thought, while the old mistress stands over me glowering and judging, *now* must I hang my head over the chamber pot, and heave and heave.

Why must we suffer? I do not understand God's mind. Why has He ordered His world so? I feel at times that I shall fly into a thousand pieces, at other times as if I am under a dark veil. And always, at all hours, my stomach betrays me, even when I am careful and nibble as lightly as a mouse on the bread Beatrice brings. This is Eve's curse, the priests say, that women must bring forth children in pain and suffering. But why? Sin, yes, so they tell us—but it is *Eve's* sin, not mine! This makes no more sense than God's curse upon Ham for the drunken nakedness of his father.

At least Kyme and his old mother leave me in peace. They berated me with such shameful language, and then they left me, and now I creep unobtrusively about the manor and complete my little chores and stay out of Mother Kyme's way. I cannot bear how she looks at me. I cannot convince them of my innocence. If I deny it, to their mind this confirms. If I say nothing, the same. I shall never make them believe me. Only Beatrice believes me.

I hope she does.

When the old mother returned that morning—How long can it be now? It seems a lifetime, but I think it is little more than a week—she brought her son, my husband, to accuse me. I sat on the bed unwashed, uncombed, undressed: I had never meant to face him that way! I had intended to go downstairs dressed as the gentlewoman I rightfully am, to speak softly, in well-modulated tones, of this news, and our joy, and thus thwart his mother's ugly suspicions before they could lodge in his brain.

But Beatrice was kept late downstairs—all the girls had extra work that morning, as the men were recovering from their revels—and by the time she came scurrying in to dress me, breathless, profuse with apologies, I had been too sick for too long. I could scarce lift my head. The cheese and ale she brought only made me want to be sick again. I waved it away. 'Come help me,' I said, struggling to sit up, but in that moment they forced their way in—Mother Kyme in her dingy white kercher, her lips pursed in satisfaction, and Kyme with his round forehead red as a cockscomb, frowning and squinting and rubbing his brow, his scowl made all the worse, I am sure, for the wine he'd drunk the night before. The two of them pushed into the tiny, crowded room. Mother Kyme ordered Beatrice out. 'And take that disgusting chamber pot with you!'

Beatrice scooped up the pot and went out. She lingered outside the door, though I did not know it yet, and heard such words spoken of me as I cannot bear to think, and this infuriates me, and makes me ashamed. The old mother's words were as bad as her son's. I've no need to wonder where he learned such curses to grind against my ear when he forced me—ah, God, I shall never forgive him! I shall hate him until the day I die, Christ forgive me, I shall. Because he knew the truth and would not say it! Not to his prideful mother, who in her smugness kept carping, 'Did I not tell you, son? And was it not wise to put her away from you and never touch her from that time till now? For see how our worst suspicions are proved!'

'Worst suspicions?' I spat at her. 'Cherished suspicions, more like.' I turned on Kyme. 'Tell her! Say how you came for your privileges while I yet lay feverish and sick near unto death in our chamber. Like a beast you took me!' Oh, how the anger boiled in his face then! I saw it, and also what I had never thought to see there: his fear. I ground the words at him: 'Tell your mother how you forced me in that manner the priests call bestial. And what will your vicar say when he knows how shamefully you used your wedded wife?'

Mother Kyme slapped me. The sting was nothing like the sting of mortification and outrage in my chest. I would have spat those same words again and again, not caring what violence they might do to me, but Beatrice burst into the room then, panting as if she'd run up the stairs. 'Why, mistress, how have we let it come so late? We must dress you for Mass! All the village is waiting. The *Te Deum* is to be sung at the king's order!'

'Idiot!' the old mistress snapped. '*Te Deum* is not sung twice!'

'Oh, but the kitchen boy said . . .' Beatrice stopped and gaped around the room as if she were stupid. She took the thump on the head the old mistress gave her without blinking. 'Here, now, mistress.' The girl picked up my comb as if nothing had happened. 'Shall I begin with your hair?'

And so, because of Beatrice, the moment was past. It has not come again. They left off their ugly words, left the room, have not spoken of my condition since. Only once, two days ago, when Kyme came to where I sat alone sewing in the small ill-lit corner they call the solar. He came close, leaned over me, and whispered: 'Men know a woman does not get with child unless she has pleasure. I am your lawful husband, yet you fight me like a netted bird, or else you lie upon the sheets cold and still as a dead mackerel. Never once have you had pleasure of me! But it seems you found some at Cambridge.' He pointed at my belly. 'God knows you did not get that of me.' He turned and stalked off. I sat with my tongue cleaved to the roof of my mouth, my heart beating wildly, though whether more in fear or fury, I cannot tell.

– Chapter 15 –

Night. She is sweating. Her stomach cramps. Deep in her gut, the pain clenches. It is as if hot tongs grip her. She wants to walk; she yearns to go striding across the Wolds as she used to do, her breath coming hard, her limbs open. But it is night; the tiny room permits only a hobbling shuffle from bed to washstand. She feels her way to the basin, reaches for the damp cloth. At once the pain clamps down. She bends from the waist, bites her lip to keep from crying out. Breathless, she feels her way to the narrow bed, crawls onto it, curls on her side, praying for morning to come—come quickly! She reaches beneath the pillow, runs her hand over the lump: yes, it is safe. But she cannot read now. She has no fire to light the candle.

Ah, God! The tongs grip! Burning pincers low in her gut. The healing drink the old mistress brings is not helping. Tomorrow, she promises herself, she will be more willing. Tomorrow, she'll take the cup when Mother Kyme brings it, though the drink is so vile, she can never bring herself to finish. Drink it, the old mistress urges. For the sake of the child, that your womb may better hold and keep it. And the woman's voice is, if not tender, at least calm, at least not judging, and Anne thinks, whether she hates me or no, at least she cares for the child. The cramps tighten. A twisting pain low in her belly.

Why did Jesus resurrect Lazarus only to let him die again? Because Lazarus did die again; he is not now in this time walking on the earth, is he? He died, as Maddie died, as all God's creatures must die, and after that the suffering. So the priests say. But why? Sinfulness, yes, disobedience, so they tell us, but what of those who keep perfectly the sacraments, as her sister had done? Maddie had the priest with her, she had the Viaticum, the jewelled cross, the holy water, and yet she died in terror, her poor thin finger, white as bone, pointing to the darkened crevice where the wall touched the ceiling—

In the light of the south window, Maddie turns. *Why, hello, Nan, what are you doing here?* Her sister's eyes gentle in the summer sunlight, the sweet smile on her lips. Wisps of golden hair along her brow, the crown of tawny braid, the scent of lavender, her eyes sad. Anne sees the pain there. The unspeakable grief. *My darling Anne. You do not need to hate me.* Now the memories come roaring through, pulsing with the rhythmic pulse of her womb: her own spiteful self, provoking and criticizing, tormenting, condemning, chiding her sister with icy words of contempt. The last words she spoke to her: *I do not care enough to hate you. Hate you. Hate you. Hate you. A fool such as you.* This is her sin which she can never confess: her own triumphant heart when she saw how perfectly she'd wounded the person she loved best. And it can never be undone. Her sister lay suffering, terrified, dying, and it was too late then, and it is too late now, too late forever, because Maddie is lost to her. Gone. She has nothing left of her, no sweet sense of Maddie's presence, no listening ear, no tender smile, no yearned-for words of forgiveness. She has only her sister's book. Anne sees the words swimming: *The Bible, that is, the holy Scripture of the Olde and New Testament, faithfully and truly translated—*

A spasm takes her, a great rolling contraction deep in her gut. Anne's womb contracts, her womb convulses, the tongs pinch in her lower parts, wave upon wave, it is like the pain of her menses but a thousand times worse, and then the contractions overwhelm her and there is no thought for anything, no past or future, no sin or remorse, only the tyrannical *now* of the pain.

It is near daylight when she feels the warm wetness between her thighs. Beatrice is with her. The old mistress is here. 'Drink this,' the old mistress says. 'It will make it go easier.' She cannot drink. She cannot weep. She did not weep for Maddie. She does not weep for the babe. It is not even a babe but a dark clot of blood passing slick and thick from her onto the bloody sheet, to be scraped into a basin and carried away. 'Stand up now,' the old mistress tells her. 'We have to clean you. We have to clean this bed.' Anne stares at her. She does not move. She is fatigued, emptied, stinking in a pool of blood, but she does not move. She does not blink. The book lies beneath her head; she'll not have it discovered. Her steady gaze feels an accusation to the old mistress, who turns abruptly, barks at Beatrice to clean the bed, and then leaves.

But the straw bed cannot be cleansed of blood; it must be taken behind the stable and unstitched and the straw scattered, the large stain of blood cut from the sacking and buried not far from where the knot of blood has been tossed. New ticking must be bought and sewn in—another mark against her. Another cost for the yeoman farmers. Anne does not care. She knows what they have done to her. What they have done to the unborn babe.

The soul does not enter until the quickening, so the priests say, and that time had not yet come. But the knot of blood would have been a baby—it would have been *his* child, yes, but also her own; and if it had been a daughter, she would have named her Martha, she would have loved her, she would have begun anew, fresh, unblemished, in lovingkindness, in tender care. If only she had not taken the black drink the old mistress gave her! It tasted of fungus and foul herbs and rust—why did she not know what it was? Beatrice gave her such worried looks: 'It smells a fright, miss. Perhaps you ought not drink any more of it? Perhaps it is not so good for the babe as the old mistress says?' But Anne had not listened. She'd held her nose and lifted the cup, and sometimes vomited, and sometimes kept it down. It was enough. She feels no sorrow. She feels rage beyond rage, an impotent anger that now there is to be no Kyme child to prove her faithfulness, and also a secret, unbidden relief. But no sadness. No aching loss. Only the enduring loss at the core of her being, her sister Martha, and even that is changing.

Her strength is returning, and with it a kind of ferocity she had forgotten is hers. With this ferocity comes also rigidity: she is tough and unyielding as ash wood. She informs the old mistress that Beatrice will no longer sleep downstairs with the servants but on the floor in her room like a proper lady's maid, and when Mother Kyme says no, Anne stands with her face directly in the old mistress's face: 'My maidservant will sleep where I say she will sleep. You have done your worst to me, I know this, and God knows it. You'll not do more. Go on, Beatrice. Fetch your pallet.' The old mistress lifts a hand as if to strike the girl, but Anne steps between them, raises her own hand as if to strike the woman back. Mother Kyme takes a flustered step backwards, hurries off in search of her son. 'And much good may that do you,' Anne mutters. She turns to Beatrice. 'What are you waiting for? Bring your things! And quickly.'

The girl has few enough belongings to bring: her rosary; her wooden spoon and comb; the mat she sleeps on, which came with her from South Kelsey; the hand-me-down smock Anne bequeathed her in the garden. She wears her lone linen cap and apron, her woollen dress. She unrolls the mat at the foot of her mistress's bed, comes to stand obediently beside her, pretends to listen as Anne reads. In truth, the girl is praying, her thumb moving silently over the beads hidden in a fold of her skirt. She hopes in this way to stop her ears, hear no heresies, if there be any, and save herself from damnation, if she cannot save her mistress.

Anne reads softly, her voice barely above a whisper, in case the old mistress returns to listen outside the door. She begins with Paul the Apostle. His letter to the Romans. It is Paul whom the friar at St Botolph's spoke of, Paul whom her brother Edward loves to quote. She finds the first verse Edward read to her: *for I am not ashamed of the gospel of Christ*.

'Nor shall I be!' she tells Beatrice. Anne has a new determination. She is going to study her way to God's mind. She is going to read and study and think until she understands God's purpose in slaying every part of His own creation. And where ought she to begin but with His Holy Scripture translated into English from the Latin and Greek? And where therein but with the words of its greatest proclaimer?

She reads quickly through the abundance of sins the apostle has listed, from unclean lusts and idolatry to backbiting and boasting, thankful that at least she suffers none of these. She is slowed somewhat by his discourse on circumcision, whether it be profitable or not, and she glances up from time to time to see if Beatrice is blushing, but the girl stands in silence, a distracted look on her face, and Anne continues. '"There is none that understandeth, there is none that seeketh after God." Oh, but *I* do,' she declares.

Beatrice startles, looks at her.

'"There is none that doeth good, no, not one. Their throat is an open sepulchre. The poison of asps is under their lips."'

The girl frowns uncertainly.

'"For they are all sinners and fall short of God's glory. But without deserving are they made righteous, even by His grace."'

The girl glances towards the door.

'Yes,' Anne whispers. 'You are right, we must be careful. There be some in our own household who say this book is heresy, though it is the very Word of God! Here.' She hands the book to Beatrice to put away inside the trunk. This is the book's new home since Anne crawled from her miscarriage bed, weakened, her thighs sticking together, her smock blood-soaked, and laid it there only moments before the kitchen boy came to lug the stained straw bed downstairs. Anne sleeps now on a thin bed of prickly hay stuffed into cheap sacking, as the old mistress has ordered. The sacking is thin, coarse; little sticks and hard pieces of hay poke up against her. This is intended as punishment, Anne knows, but since she has slept on the bare floor with fleas and servants at that foul inn on the road to Cambridge, she knows herself sturdy enough to withstand such meagre penance. Indeed, she believes herself sturdy enough to withstand almost anything.

IV

As My Heart Desires

Friskney and South Kelsey
August
1537

– Chapter 16 –

Early afternoon, late summer, three months after the clot of blood was tossed in the barnyard. A warm rain is falling; the manor is dank, smells of mould and mildew. The hallo of the stable boy brings Anne to the window. She sees her father's manservant, Will Bard, dismounting in the yard. At once she breathes out *Father!* and runs down the stairs to meet him. But it is not Father. It is a letter sealed with his signet and addressed not to Anne but to her husband. Kyme reads it standing in his lanolin-stained jerkin in the front hall. 'What?' she says, watching his sweaty face. 'Who is it?' Because a letter carried by her father's personal manservant can mean only misfortune—or death. 'Your brother,' Kyme says, and begins to refold the letter.

'Not Francis!'

'The young one.'

'What? Dead? Tell me, Thomas, please.'

She never calls him by name. Perhaps it is this bit of blurted intimacy which causes him to hand her the half-folded letter. Quickly she skims the page. Sir William asks that his daughter Anne be permitted to leave with the bearer as soon as may be practicable: her young brother Thom is very ill. Master Kyme's indulgence in this matter is heartily desired, for the boy, the doctors say, is not like to live. She refolds the page carefully, returns it to her husband without looking up. Her throat is aching, her heart beating hard with fear and anguish. Every nerve, every muscle, urges her to run to her room and begin preparations to travel, but she stands motionless, head lowered, scarcely daring to breathe. The smallest gesture, she thinks, the least action, may cause him to forbid her.

'And how is she to travel?' Kyme asks the servant.

'I am directed to say that Master Kyme's kindness in providing a mount would be most welcome. If this is not possible, I'm to hire a horse in the village, and also a cart to bring Mistress Kyme's trunk.' Will Bard stands erect, eyes forward; his lined face shows no trace of weariness from two days' travel.

'Will you eat?' Kyme says.

'Thank you, sir.'

Kyme sends word to the kitchen. He turns to his wife. 'You may go.' She is not certain if he means she may go home to South Kelsey or if he is dismissing her from the hall. She lowers her head, makes a slow withdrawal, lingering on the stair long enough to hear him tell Will Bard that Mistress Kyme has been very ill herself, for three months now; surely Sir William is aware? She may not be strong enough for the journey. Anne's rage flashes, and also her fear. Surely he would not go against Father! Not with young Thom at death's door? But, yes. Yes, he would. Not in open defiance but in this sneaking manner, *alas, my wife has been ill*—oh, yes, to punish her and demonstrate his dominance. She hurries up the stairs to her cramped little closet.

When Kyme enters a short while later, she is directing Beatrice in hurried whispers which linens to pack in a satchel for the journey, which to lay in the trunk to be brought with Beatrice herself when she comes by cart. Kyme tells the girl to leave. Anne nods to Beatrice: Do as he says. Her eyes say: Stay near. Kyme sits on the narrow bed in his greasy jerkin and blood-spattered hose—he has been castrating the late lambs, stinks of lanolin and wet wool—and indicates with a look that Anne should sit on the joint stool. 'It is a great pity you are too weak to travel,' Kyme says, 'your young brother being so ill.' His expression is falsely tender, his voice smug.

'Oh, but I am well enough!'

'And yet you are so racked by headaches and lingering fevers that you cannot return to your husband's bed.'

She stares at him. So this is it. Punishment for her resistance. Her husband has been after her to move back into his bedchamber for weeks now, not with force but with clumsy, unsubtle persuasions: He has had a new featherbed sewn; it is commodious and comfortable. He thinks it is not helpful to Anne's health to continue to sleep in such close quarters, with so little fresh air; does she not long for greater space and light around her? He will not compel her by force because he knows she will begin to tell things: how he ravished her in violence months ago, hurt her, got her with child in such bestial manner, and then permitted his own mother to give her the black, musty drink that destroyed it. Kyme fears she will say such things in the presence of his old father, the servants, the priest. This is the stance they have held in silence for many weeks. Anne tips back her head, glares at him in challenge. He meets her gaze. His eyes are pale blue, white-lashed, cold. 'If you are well enough to travel fifty miles to South Kelsey,' he says, 'then you are well enough to return to your wifely duties.' He cocks his brow. 'Is this not so?' His ruddy face gloats at her across the dim room. 'Is this not so!'

Her answer comes slowly as she calculates. 'I believe that . . . if I travel to South Kelsey, as requested by my father . . . and after I have spent a goodly visit there, as my heart desires, and seen my young brother before his passing, I believe that . . . yes, when I return, I shall be well enough to . . . resume my wifely duties.'

'And if not?'

'If not, sir, I fear my grief at not seeing my dying brother may create such torment as to cause me to take a backset. I may become very ill once more.' She does not turn her gaze from his. 'It is possible, indeed, that I may never recover. I've heard such things happen. Grief is a great tormentor, as thou knowest. Or perhaps you do not.'

'I've suffered grief enough,' he growls. 'As God has seen fit to saddle me with a disobedient, ill-tempered wife. And so I ask myself: if I were to permit this ill-natured wife to travel such distance alone, accompanied only by a lone manservant, what surety have I, considering all that has gone before, that she will not dishonour her wedding vows?'

'I have never dishonoured my wedding vows. You know that.'

'Oh, have you not? "To be bonny and buxom in bed and at board," as you vowed at the altar—that you have never done!'

'Perhaps if I had a—' She stops herself. *If I had a husband who would touch me gently and not mount me as a bull mounts a poor heifer, not come at me constantly like an insatiable old drake—if I had a husband who might be any man on earth but Thomas Kyme!*

It is only the power of her yearning to go home that keeps her from spilling the words. She lowers her gaze. 'Perhaps if I had the opportunity to visit with my family, I should be restored. Please, Thomas.' She tries to say his name tenderly. 'I will move back with you as soon as I return. I'll do everything you say—you'll never have cause more to rue our marriage. I swear it.' She pauses, does not look up. 'He is my baby brother,' she whispers. 'He's only ten. Can you not grant me this one thing?' No answer. She dares to raise her gaze. He is pulling at his upper lip, staring at the floor. He is wavering, she thinks. Another word may persuade him—in her favour, or against. Better silence or a pleading word? She chooses silence.

At length, Kyme rouses himself, stands. 'Pack what you'll need and carry it with you. We'll not be sending a cart.' He strides to the door.

'But how will Beatrice come?'

'Beatrice will not come. I'll provide a mount and coin for your lodging this night and on your return. Your maidservant remains here, and your wardrobe. Go see your dying brother, stay as long as the clothes on your back may last you. Then you will return home and behave as a humble and proper wife ought. You'll do as your husband and the vicar bid you.'

'The vicar?' The mention of Thomas Jordan baffles her. But her husband has already left the room; she hears his boots clumping through the next chamber. She is sitting perplexed, pondering, when Beatrice puts her head in the door.

'No, mistress. Please! Do not leave me!' The girl's lips are trembling. She is shaking her head. 'You've no idea. Oh, please, miss! Take me with you!'

'But I cannot. You heard him. I dare not go against him, Beatrice. He'll change his mind and forbid me—he'll forbid us both!'

Within the hour, she is mounted on a bay gelding in her woollen cloak to keep the rain off, her fatly stuffed satchel tied to the side-saddle, the lengths of veil caught up on either side of her headdress and pinned. Will Bard takes her horse's rein, leads the gelding out of the yard at a crisp walk—it is almost two o'clock; all haste is necessary if they're to reach Horncastle by good dark. It is the thought of Beatrice that causes Anne to turn and look behind, but she doesn't see the girl at first, only her husband scowling beneath the eave. Then she spies Beatrice in the manor door. The girl's face is puffy and red. The old mistress comes up behind her, and the child flinches. Then she stands motionless, her thin shoulders hunched, hands balled in fists, her tearstained face heartbreakingly still.

They ride north through a fine mist. Water beads her cloak, the gelding's mane. The mud flats reek in the sodden heat. In the fields, the sheep are growing fat in their second wool. Anne swelters in her own woollen covering. When she came down to Friskney for her marriage last November, she shivered and froze in the cart, and Beatrice beside her. Will Bard had accompanied her then as well. Father had sent along his most trusted manservant—for her protection, he said, but also, Anne believed, to ensure that his rebellious middle daughter would fulfil the obligation to which she had agreed: to take her sister's place at the altar. How different that journey from this, Anne thinks. And yet at the end of each, the prospect the same: sorrow, loss, and desolation.

The cart road is muddy, their progress slow. A kind of numbness settles upon her. She cannot think of the past, nor the future, only of how she sweats now beneath the steaming wool, how her neck aches from turning her head to the side to see where they are going. Her feet are propped on the foot brace, her right hand grips the pommel. It is a hundred times easier to ride astride, as she did on her escape to Cambridge. She feels herself tethered to Will Bard by the long leading rein he grips in one hand. She calls to him to release it; she'll guide herself. He turns to look at her. He says nothing, his lined face and grey eyes carefully steady, but she reads his disapproval. Such things are not done. A gentlelady riding side-saddle is always led.

'Let it go,' Anne orders him. 'I'll set the pace. You are too soft with me and the animal.'

He hesitates the briefest instant, dismounts, and walks the leather strap back to her. He could have simply released it and she could have pulled it to her, but Will Bard would no more make such a disrespectful gesture than he'd defy a direct order from the young mistress.

'Your caution is commendable,' Anne says, taking the strap from him, 'but at this pace we'll not reach Horncastle before midnight.' She clicks her tongue at the gelding and passes Bard's horse before he can remount. After this, they make better progress. The track begins to rise gently out of the fens. As the land rises, Anne feels her spirits lifting. Perhaps, she tells herself, Thom is not so ill as they say. He's a sturdy boy, reckless and talkative and so full of mischief. Perhaps they think he is deathly ill only because his usual liveliness is gone. Such thoughts allow her to not dread what lies ahead. The farther from Friskney they travel, the more Anne's natural spiritedness returns. The rain has ceased, though a light fog remains; she thinks of how very soon she will be riding across the Wolds, and they'll not be ash brown and sepia, as when she last saw them, but bright green and yellow with high summer. She tells herself that tomorrow, perhaps, there will be sun, or at least clouds alone, with no rain. The hope flutters.

– Chapter 17 –

It is late, I know not how late, some black hour deep in the night before the sky has begun to lighten even a little. My little brother's cries echo, rising in irregular agonized bursts. Through the window I see a quilt of stars low in the sky, no moon. They have put me in the nursery, where I spent my childhood years, and this makes my heart ache. I want to pray, but I cannot . . . the mysteries, I cannot meditate on them. The prayers feel empty, less than nothing. Edward says I may pray direct to God with my own mouth, but I do not think that I can.

He was the only family member who came downstairs to meet me when I arrived. 'You'll forgive them,' he said. 'They'll not leave Thom's side.' I heard my little brother's cries then, as now: muffled, distant, terrible. Edward took my arm, and we began to climb the stairs slowly, slower still along the passageway towards the west wing. I felt my dread rising, but Edward's presence was a comfort, his great height, his certainty. I am so glad he is here! He came from Lambeth the moment they sent word. It was he who asked Father to send Will Bard to fetch me. He told me this as we walked along the dim gallery. 'Did no one else think of it?' I asked. My brother shrugged. 'Well, I thank you,' I said.

A liveried servant standing outside the door leaned forwards to open it, and my fear swelled so great that if Edward had not had hold of my sleeve, I would have run away. He guided me gently into the room.

Slanting ruddy light from the west window. Father on his knees beside the bed, his black-robed back towards me. Mother Elizabeth stone-faced in a chair opposite. Francis and Jane and young Lisbeth rowed up at the foot. Francis turned, nodded, said nothing. He'd just come in, it seemed, for he wore his riding cloak. Beside him, Lisbeth appeared stiff-necked and uncomfortable in a rose-coloured gown and pearled hood. She is much changed since I last saw her, very grown now, very beautiful. I suppose their marriage will take place soon. My sister Jane gave out a little cry when she saw me, ran to me and kissed me. Mother Elizabeth glanced up then, but the look of blame I had so dreaded did not cross her face. Her gaze slid over me with a glazed emptiness before she turned back to her son.

And there, oh, there on the bed lay my little brother, the poor child, the poor suffering boy: sweating and moaning, uttering his sharp little cries, his sudden hissing intakes of breath. The bedding near his buttocks bore spots of blood. He twisted sideways, whimpered, reached for Mother Elizabeth; she stroked his forehead. Oh. I understand why they do not leave him—you cannot bear to watch, and yet you cannot bear to think of him enduring it alone.

Father got slowly to his feet with many grunts and heaves. He walked towards me, limping slightly, looked in my face a long moment; then he wrapped his arms around me and drew me to him. I felt his shoulders heaving. I began to sob.

Even now, to think of it, my chest tightens. My father has not embraced me since I was a little girl. And I have never, in all my life, seen him weep. He held me so tightly a moment, then he pulled away, wiping his face, clearing his throat. He walked to the far side of the bed, rested his hand on Mother's Elizabeth's shoulder. She showed nothing, her face moving no more than one of the carved saints in the chapel downstairs. Father turned, began pacing the room, limping. He has aged an age since All Saints: his hair gone white, his face worn, and he grimaces constantly with the pains in his feet.

On the bed, day and night, my little brother writhes and squirms; he crawls to the head, where he rocks on his knees, his face in the pillow; he cries out, rolls to his back, clutches his stomach, twists around and turns crossways on the bed, flings himself to the foot, this way and that; they cannot keep him covered. He almost never opens his eyes. They have shorn his long hair, which makes him look older, but his chapped lips are thick and bowlike, like a baby's, and the bone of his skull appears too thin. Mother Elizabeth sits beside him and strokes his head, the back of his neck, and for a short while he will quieten, sleep a little; then he begins to writhe and fling himself about again, crying with pain. He has been suffering this way for many days.

Father sent to Lincoln for the surgeon and the apothecary, Edward says, but they did not know what to do for him. They bled him, gave him wormwood and purgatives, all manner of herbs and potions, but his pain remains. They said there is nothing to be done but let him starve; food only increases his torture. The priest came to perform extreme unction, but my brother cannot die—he remains in the same flinging, crying agony. Mother Elizabeth sits vigil beside him; she prays her beads, gives him sips of ale when he will take them. Father paces up and down, limping and groaning.

It is worse even than Maddie's death because Thom belongs to us all: he is Father's lone child with Dame Elizabeth, and the last she'll ever bear. He is the only one who is blood kin to every one of us; we all cradled him as a swaddled babe, watched him begin to creep, to walk and talk. We have all teased him, ruffled his hair, adored him, and he is dying in agony, and none of us can help him—oh, hear his cries! I do not know how we shall bear it! I don't know that Father can. Or, oh, especially Mother Elizabeth. She buried her first husband of the sweat years ago, and her eldest son, Lisbeth's father, a month after, but Thomas . . . young Thom.

I should go in now to relieve her. She should rest. She should go to her own chamber and sleep a little. I'll take a candle, I tell myself, and go out of the nursery, walk the long, dark gallery to the sickroom where Thomas flails and cries out, and Mother Elizabeth sits with her beads and her frozen face, and her useless cups of thinned ale.

– Chapter 18 –

Anne rises from the narrow bed, takes her candle, but she does not walk towards her brother's room, as she has told herself. Rather, she descends the stairs to the small chapel just off the great hall. Candles are lit beside the altar. The room is stone, and cool, even in summer, cool like a cave, a crypt, a cellar dug deep into the earth. The carved saints seem small to her now, recessed in their stone alcoves, their painted faces flat and plain, dark with soot, but familiar, like the small beds and panelled walls of the nursery. They make her heart hurt the same way.

Kneeling, she makes the sign of the cross and begins to pray, *in nómine patris, et filii, et spíritus sancti.* The words come unbidden now, as they would not do before; it is the feel of the cold pockmarked floor beneath her knees, she thinks, the smell of incense and stone and must. *Pater noster, qui es in caelis:* the words murmur through her lips, effortless, familiar; she does not have to think. Christ Jesus taught his disciples to pray not in Latin, Edward says, but in their own common tongue. Not *pater noster* but *Our Father*. She begins the prayer in English: Our Father who lives in Heaven, holy is Thy name . . . deliver us from evil, forgive us our . . . forgive us—

In her chest, a great clamp squeezes, tight, so tight she cannot breathe. She hears young Thom's cries overhead, faint and plaintive through the stone, muted, as from the very grave itself. Oh, my sweet brother! He is suffering. Help him. Edward says he will go to be with Christ in Heaven the very instant his soul flies from his body, as we must all fly—but how does Edward know? It is not what the priests say. They say all must suffer in Purgatory for expiation, to be made pure enough for God's Presence, and her prayers can do nothing for Thom, neither here nor in the Hereafter, for she is wholly wicked in her heart, and she can no longer feel her sister in the darkness; she cannot hear her anywhere, cannot pray her little brother to life no more than she could reach Maddie falling, falling and falling, her golden hair aflame, and now their baby brother is suffering, he is dying. *God. Heavenly Father. If You must take him, take him now. Do not let him suffer more. It is unbearable how he suffers.*

Silence. All is silence but for the sound of her breathing, the rhythm of her blood, her pulse in her own ears. She feels nothing, but that her heart hurts. Her knees hurt. She is alone, terrified, drowning in emptiness.

God, she prays. *I am lost! I am frightened. I do not know what to do. Help me, God! Help me.*

A warmth settles upon her like a mantle, a sense of calmness, peace. Her clenched heart slowly opens; her breathing slows, deepens, becomes even. She feels herself bathed in warmth and love and an ineffable, permeating sorrow so tinged with tenderness and mercy she feels it does not, cannot, arise from within her but has eased inside her from without.

Yet there is no source, no Presence, only this calm suffusion of peace washing through her, a balm to her spirit. The peace assures her that all will be well, all is love, all is forgiveness, the fires of Hell will not touch her, will not touch her little brother, her sister. Anne remains so, kneeling, not seeing, not praying, not thinking, only breathing.

By the time she comes to herself, the candle she carried downstairs has guttered. She unclasps her hands, gathers the loose folds of her shift, rises stiffly. Her knees are frozen bone, her lips tremble, the tyranny of the body returns, and she discovers she is famished, her neck aches, she is shivering with cold. But she is not frightened. It is true what Edward says: there is nothing to fear. She twists a candle free from the candelabrum to light her way back upstairs. She glides swiftly along the gallery towards Thom's room, ghostly in her white shift, her dark hair loosed from its cap, her palm cupped in front of the flame.

Outside the door, the watchman is asleep, slumped against the wall, his halberd laid on its side. She slips past him, in through the creaking door. Mother Elizabeth sleeps in her pillowed chair, her coif tugged sideways, her hand on Thom's arm. The boy lies on his back, his other arm flung above his head. Anne is relieved to see his young face so peaceful, his eyelids soft, his brow smooth; he is not frowning, not moaning or crying out, he is not—oh, God; oh, no; oh, Jesus Lord, is he gone? Have her prayers to end her brother's suffering ended this way? Her heart quivers, a caught bird; she eases quietly to the bed.

Standing near, she sees her brother's narrow chest rise in a long, slow inhalation, pause, then sink in an equally long, torturously slow exhale. Anne watches Thom's chest. After many seconds he breathes in again. Still she watches. Any moment, she thinks, any breath could be the last one. But Thomas breathes. Slowly, rhythmically, peacefully, he breathes. She touches his forehead: it is not clammy with sweat, not marble cold or burning hot, but warm with life, warm as a child's face should be warm, smooth and dry and delicate. *Oh, my little brother; oh, Thom.* She is not weeping—she is too wrought-up to weep—but her relief is as large as if a great stone has been lifted from her chest. She tips out a bit of wax onto the near table, sets the candle, draws the stool to her brother's side. The tenderness she feels towards him, the vast and aching love—it is like what she felt in the chapel. Her little brother will live! Yes, and not that only: he will thrive! His hair will grow out again, she thinks, touching gently his scabby scalp. He'll be handsome and darling as ever. Our darling Thom.

She must tell Edward! She must find him and tell him. And ask him. What was it, then? The peace and confidence that swept her in the chapel, where did that come from? It was not God, she thinks. God is holy might and fear. God condemns sinners to Hell, condemns even the penitent to Purgatory. God demands blood sacrifice and fire and death: for expiation of our sins must we suffer; God sent even his own Son to suffer. The peace she felt, it could not have come from God. Her mind is roving now, her restless, questing mind; she has no fear, she is only hungry, in her mind and in her body. Her stomach growls. She has a thousand questions. A soft snore comes from the far side of the bed. Anne studies her stepmother.

Dame Elizabeth's face is not frozen now in lines of distress; she rests peacefully, as Thom rests. She has seen the change, Anne thinks. She was here when the fever broke and the pain ended, she witnessed the miracle—what can it be but a miracle? For through the whole of the night Thom's cries pierced the manor, and now the sky is greying, and he is at peace. The release came when they had lost all hope—

No. When Anne herself had lost hope.

When she prayed for his release, and the warmth entered, that blessed peace. In the bed, her brother whimpers, turns on his side towards his mother, and at once Elizabeth awakens. Her eyes go first to her son, then lift calmly, without surprise, to Anne's face. 'You should go to bed, Anne,' she says quietly. Her voice tells nothing of the rift between them.

'It is you who needs rest,' Anne says. 'I'll stay with him. He'll sleep a while now. I shall be here when he wakes.'

But Dame Elizabeth sits holding her sleeping son's hand as the light lifts outside the window and the morning opens, birdsong and cockcrow, the creak of harness, the snuffle of horses, the reapers' voices in the yard as they prepare to go to the fields. Anne watches her stepmother, who has been aged by Thom's illness, as her father has aged—only differently. Anne's father has become stouter, more florid; he suffers more with his gout and swollen knees; he grumbles and grunts continuously. Mother Elizabeth has grown wan and thin, her hair greying faintly, as sand-coloured hair greys: a fading, a bleeding away of colour. Anne sees it at her temples and above her brow where her coif has been pulled aside. The lines on her forehead are etched deep, but those at the corners of her eyes and mouth are delicate, faint. She is still beautiful. She has always been beautiful to Anne's eyes. I shall name my daughter after her, Anne thinks. Martha Elizabeth, as Maddie said she would do. In her last months, as she prepared for her wedding, Maddie often—

Anne stops her mind. She stands. 'Shall I send for something to eat?' She doesn't wait for a response but goes quickly to the door. In the hallway she nudges the servant awake, shushes his stumbling excuses, asks for bread and ale and something nourishing to break Dame Elizabeth's fast. 'And warm broth for my brother. For myself, the same as is brought for my mother.' She turns quickly from the servant's confused face.

Thom is still sleeping; the covers have been pulled up over his shoulders, only his round knob of head peeking out. Her stepmother is at the window, looking out at the new day. Anne goes to stand beside her. There is deep silence between them, an awkwardness, a knowledge. But it is not the cold silence of last October. It is not thick with anger and blame.

'The day will be fine, I think,' Mother Elizabeth says at last.

'Yes. Very fine.' To the west the land is flat and wooded. Never put to the plough. Her father's hunting grounds. 'Lisbeth is coming quite grown,' Anne says.

'Yes.'

'And beautiful.'

'Yes,' Mother Elizabeth says. 'Her manners are impeccable, her gracefulness most pleasing. Her skills at sewing and singing and dance are well learned.' The bitterness in her voice baffles Anne. 'Your brother wishes the marriage to take place before Michaelmas. And so it shall.'

'You would prefer the marriage be postponed?'

'I would prefer, had I a preference, that it not take place at all. But I have no authority in the matter. As you, above everyone, must know.'

'But they've been betrothed forever,' Anne says. 'It is not the same as me.'

'No,' Mother Elizabeth says. 'It is not the same.'

'Has something happened?'

Her stepmother sits in the high-backed chair. She is silent. Her hands are spread open on the coverlet. Anne sees the blue veins like minute rivers, her rings large and ornate, bloodstone and topaz and opal, and the one lapis on her right hand. When Anne was very small, that blue stone was loose in its setting; it would tick lightly against the gold when she patted the children to sleep. Mother Elizabeth would do that, stay with the little girls in the nursery sometimes, patting their backs, singing soft lullabies. Anne goes to her, lowers herself to the floor beside the chair. She touches her brother's thin leg. 'I prayed for him. I prayed so hard. And he is better. But I prayed even harder for Maddie. And she died. Why?'

A long silence. 'It is not for us to understand the will of God, Anne, but to accept and obey.'

Anne rests her elbows on the coverlet; her fingers are laced, her hands make a single tight fist beneath her chin. She looks at the hunt tapestry on the wall, the crucifix beside it. 'I am trying to be obedient,' she says. 'Acceptance, though. That is much harder.'

A soft snort beside her. When she looks over, she sees her stepmother gently smiling. 'Indeed,' Elizabeth says. The long weeks of Anne's rebellion tumble into the space between them: long days when she would be banished to her chamber because of her stubborn refusal to submit to her father's will. A small sigh escapes her. A similar sigh comes from her stepmother's breast. Anne begins to laugh, a low, quiet sound, and Mother Elizabeth laughs, too, not loudly, a low shared murmuration, quickly erupting, just as quickly subdued. They draw serious and silent again.

Anne whispers, 'I am truly sorry, Mother—' The word upticks on the end, as if she would continue with her stepmother's Christian name, but then she doesn't. She leaves it simply as *Mother*. 'For everything,' she says. 'All my disobediences. My frowardness and rebellions. But especially for causing those churls to take Thom. I did not know they would do that.'

'But they did,' Dame Elizabeth says. 'At the loosening of someone's reckless tongue, they did.'

'I know.' Anne wants to say *I know, but,* and then enumerate her many self-justifications. She leaves off *but,* says only, simply, 'I'm sorry.' She feels the warmth of her stepmother's hand on her head.

Then the hand lifts. Her stepmother reaches to smooth the coverlet over her son's legs. 'God returned him to us safe then. And today

He returns him to us again. This is not the false healing the dying sometimes make.' Her voice is calm, stoic. 'My first husband did so. He roused from his fever, called for his robe and his boots, got out of bed, ate a little supper. A few hours later, in the night, when I no longer watched over him, he died. But Thom is returned to us, and I shall believe it, and thank God for it, until evidence should force me to know otherwise.'

'But his fever is broken, Mother. Look. His pains are gone. He is coming well, really and truly. I know it.'

'Do you?'

Anne answers with the firm confidence that was hers an hour before in the chapel: 'I do.'

For two days more, she rests in that confidence. Two days more, as her little brother continues to improve, as he sits up and takes a thin gruel and later porridge and does not cry out; as her father ceases his pacing and sits at dinner in his riding clothes and later returns from Lincoln with the doctor, who pronounces the sickness past, the boy mending; as the priest comes at daylight to say Mass and Mother Elizabeth retires from the chapel directly to her chamber and sleeps the day and night around; as her burbling sister Jane and the silent, stiff Lisbeth sit with her in the solar, sewing, with nothing of any real interest to say, and she leans towards them, smiling, with quiet benevolence. Above all, Anne's certainty is unshaken as she walks the summer road with her brother Edward, talking and listening and talking. 'What was it?' she says. 'That peace I felt in the chapel. Where did it come from?'

'The Comforter,' he says. 'Christ Jesus promised to send us a Comforter to abide with us and teach us.'

'Why have I never heard of this?' she says.

'Oh, but you have, you've been saying it all your life: *in spiritus sanctus*. It is the Holy Ghost, Nan. In the Gospel of John, Christ Jesus says, "That comforter, even the holy ghost, who my father shall send in my name, shall teach you all things." And listen, Anne, to what He says after: "Let not your heart be troubled, neither let it be afraid."'

'But I am not afraid, Edward. Not anymore.' She looks up at the sky. How blue it is. How open. To her left, her father's sheep meadow rolls lush and green towards the village, the dirty pale dots of her father's flock spread out across its bosom. On her right, the rye fields glint gold in the late summer sunlight. And directly ahead, shimmering on the horizon, the softly undulating green slopes of the Wolds. She feels she could nearly burst with happiness.

Just so, for two days more, her heart remains untroubled. Two days more, she is peaceful, joyous, contented—until the last evening, when Francis comes to find her in the nursery after supper and tells her to be ready at first light for the journey home to Friskney.

'No!' she cries. 'Francis, not yet!'

'Thom is better now, Nan. There is no reason for you to linger. Your husband is anxious for your return. Will Bard will accompany you home.'

'But I *am* home!'

Francis does not answer. He turns and departs the nursery as if her protests were no more significant than a child's.

Book Two

Lincolnshire

1541

I

He Paces and Grieves in the Night

Friskney

August

1541

– Chapter 19 –

He paces and grieves in the night. I hear him outside our chamber, my husband, walking up and down, sobbing in great ragged breaths. I try to open my heart to pity, but it comes not so easily to me—not for him, though I know what grief is, to have lost Father at Easter, and young Thom four years ago, and Martha, dear sweet Martha, scarcely a year before that. My own sorrow ought to bring me to compassion. I pray that it might. But my husband's misuse of me, and of our son William, is worse since his old father died, and it makes hard my heart. I pitied the old master, at least. I treated him as kindly as I might, though it was difficult when he would be flinging his arms about, knocking at one's face or whatever part came near.

Oh, I cannot think which is worse: to have your mind yet keen, like Father's, imprisoned inside a body that is decayed and helpless and must be hoisted about and turned in bed, or to be like old Master Kyme, completely brainless inside a knotted, sturdy body that ever must walk and wave its arms and rove aimlessly, so that your son must bind you to your bed with fast cords. I think this is much of where my husband's vociferous grief comes from. Yet had he not tied him, the old man would have wandered off through the marshes and drowned. I might remind my husband of this, and also of the mercy that his mother did not live to see his father's end. God is merciful, I might say, can you not be thankful? But any talk of God from me is not welcomed by Master Kyme, and so I say nothing. I try not to draw his wrath when I can help it. Nor do I pity him enough, truthfully, to want to relieve his suffering—even so much as to remind him of God's grace in this as in all things.

Sometimes, as yesterday, I do look to draw his anger towards me, but that is only to deflect it from our son. We were in the boy's room, Beatrice and I, sorting his clothes for the journey and telling him, no, you may not take that; yes, you may have your spinning top and your ball, but your sword and scabbard remain here. His uncle Edward serves now as one of the King's Spears, and the term has taken the child's fancy. He was excited, yes, and rowdy, jumping about on the bed and making noises and slashing at the air with his play sword. We are all excited, even Thomas, though he will not admit it. But just think: Henry and Queen Catherine in Lincoln! And my brothers to take part in the ceremonies, and also Bridget's new husband, Sir Vincent, as lord mayor; and the king is travelling in such vast progress, they say, as has never been seen in all England: how may we not be excited?

Thomas came into our son's room and saw him prancing and immediately barked out, 'Master Kyme! Get down!' I turned at once. It is always a danger when Thomas addresses the boy as 'Master Kyme.' Alas, William did not respond quickly enough, and Thomas stepped to the bed and jerked him to the floor by his arm. Young Will landed with a great thump and a howl, and I rushed to stand between them. It helps nothing to defend the boy, and in fact only brings down more of his father's wrath. 'Thomas, there you are!' I said. 'I've been waiting the whole morning! How do you expect me to make all these decisions? I know not which of your gowns to pack nor where to send anyone to fetch you to ask!'

'You know well enough where to fetch me,' says he.

'Do I? You may be at your accounts or you may be off in the fields or the stables or the sheep meadow. How am I to know? I cannot be taking my time to chase you about!'

'*Your* time. Your precious time, which you spend half on your knees and the other half indulging your ill-mannered son.'

'Or I suppose I might send to find you at the vicarage, where you plot away hour upon hour in secret with your papist priest!' This was guaranteed to rouse him, and soon we were arguing as we stormed out of the room and into our own chamber, and Beatrice was then able to lift my sobbing son from the floor and soothe him, as I heard through our heated words, my ear cocked towards the little room.

Now he threatens to make me stay at home while he and the household travel to Lincoln. But I know he will not do this. Francis has written specially to have me there. Have *us* there, myself and young William. It will be the first time we are all together since Father's burial, where we hadn't the opportunity nor any good place to truly talk. Jane and her husband will come from Snarford, and Edward and Christopher are already travelling on progress with the king, and we shall all be together in Lincoln—we are to stay at Bridget's home at St Catherine's a mile south of the city gate, I with my little family, and Jane with hers, and so may we all visit to our heart's content. I tell Kyme how fortunate we are that I have such well-placed relations—and living so near the city centre! There'll be no lodgings to let for miles around. My husband only frowns. Which makes my heart laugh. It is a small, bitter laugh, true, but filled with delight: the two powers under Heaven most precious to me are God and my family. Well, Master Kyme has ever been after God in his papist, self-righteous way, and half his life he schemed with his old father to marry into the Ayscoughs. Now, when I mention either, all I get from him is that pinched little frown. Thus are we reminded of that age-old lesson: take care what you pray for, lest God, in His infinite wisdom and humour, decide to give it thee! Ha.

We leave at dawn. I would plead with Thomas to allow William to ride with me or sit with Beatrice in the cart, but it would serve no purpose but to make him harsher with the boy. No son of *his* will ride with women. He'll hold William before him astride his great horse, the poor child clinging to the pommel and straining to look behind to see me, until Thomas cuffs him and tells him to straighten and turn front. This is how we made our way to Stallingborough in shivering March weather for Father's burial, and thus shall we ride to Lincoln in summer's languid heat.

Oh, I pray it stays fair. The king's progress was delayed for weeks by heavy rains, which has caused me no small amount of concern. I had thought to be well settled at Bridget's by this time. Each day my pregnancy shows a little more. Thomas does not yet know. I would not have him know—he'll not forbid me to go for arguing, I think, but he might forbid me for the sake of the child. Only Beatrice knows. She whispers in secret: 'Oh, do you dare travel now, mistress? And on horseback?' I whisper in return: 'The slow sway of an old nag? And I riding as a gentlelady with my knees propped and my skirts wrapped? It would be far worse to bump and thump about in the luggage wagon, believe me. Hush now,' I tell her. 'There'll be no danger.'

And I hope, truly, that there will not be. I would not endanger my unborn babe for anything, but I would not stay here, neither. Nor do I wish for Will to go alone with his father, who descends into such cold rages when the boy flinches from him or freezes and turns silent the moment he draws near. It is strange. Young William, with his round head and flaxen hair, is the very image of his father, but Thomas cannot abide him. There is that in the boy's temperament which rubs his nose the wrong way, though I cannot understand what it is. Perhaps William is too much like me. Perhaps the child I carry will be a son more pleasing to my husband, and then may he dote upon that one to his heart's content.

Although, in truth, I hope not for another son but for a daughter. My little Martha Elizabeth. I pray daily for the Father's will in this, as in all things, but I cannot help my hope. In any case, it will be no matter. William is eldest and heir, and Thomas Kyme can do nothing to abort that.

II

The King's Retinue Draws Near

Lincoln

August

1541

– Chapter 20 –

9 August 1541. Lincoln. The king's retinue draws near. His Majesty is on his Great Northern Progress, travelling in all pomp and splendour, to receive the submission of his subjects. The small capital city is overwhelmed. For weeks now, the highborn of Lincolnshire have poured into the city. In their most sumptuous trappings, they parade up and down the cobbled roads from the River Witham to the glorious cathedral atop the steep hill, trailed by their servants in new livery, their exquisitely clad children, their elegantly coifed and sleeved wives. They've brought with them their finest mounts and sleekest dogs. Mingling amongst them are priests and priors, tradesmen and merchants, tanners, glaziers, glovers, labourers from towns and villages across Lincolnshire, all come to make grovelling submission to His Majesty, that the besmirched name of their county be severed from that unconscionable Rising four years past.

The sun is bright. The weather warm. The important men of the shire array themselves along the road as they await their sovereign, gentlemen astride horses on one side, burgesses and commoners on foot along the other. Among the lords and gentry, it is hoped His Majesty will offer not only forgiveness but perhaps also new grants and licences at (it is hoped) not too dear a cost. Francis Ayscough, on horseback, is here. He is squire and landowner of his own means, inheritor of his father's estates at Stallingborough, Nottinghamshire, and Yorkshire, as well as the vast Hansard lands at South Kelsey, which came under his purview at his marriage to young Lisbeth and have been enlarged at his good tending. He has a new town house in Lincoln, and a new son. Across the road he spies his stepbrother-in-law, Sir Vincent Grantham, lord mayor of Lincoln, squinting in the bright sunlight, perspiring, his chain of office glinting upon his shoulders.

Ah, here. A great satisfaction. His kinsman Sir Vincent will have a great part in the ceremony: it will be he, as lord mayor of Lincoln, who surrenders the sword and mace. This marriage has been one of Francis's most successful endeavours: his widowed stepsister Bridget wed to Sir Vincent. She who dwelt in poverty and shame after Thomas Moigne's attainder lives now in wealth and comfort at the suppressed priory of St Catherine's, with her husband, Sir Vincent, and two young daughters.

Bridget is not in attendance at today's ceremonies. Indeed, there are no women here at all, save, far back at the rear of the encampment, the camp followers who service the king's guards. One might gaze across the land as far as the eye will carry and discover only the faces of men: highborn, lowborn, yeoman, craftsman, merchant, priest. They have come to confess their treasonous rebellion, and to offer their abject, grovelling submission: five years following the Rising, this final act remains. There is a prescribed ritual. All know their parts. On the horizon now, a faint line of dust. Soon the heralds and trumpeters are making a great noise: the king's Majesty approaches!

Emerging from the choking haze, a phalanx of five hundred marching archers, longbows drawn. Henry rides towards them upon his enormous black charger, huge and imposing in a velvet cloak of Lincoln green. Behind him, his young queen, Catherine Howard, lovely in crimson velvet, is seated upon a pale palfrey, followed by her ladies and the rest of the mile-long train. It is a stunning display. Henry and the queen's Grace turn off to the side and are escorted to their royal tents, where they dismount and enter to rest and change their apparel before the grand entry into Lincoln. They do not come out again for a long while.

Not for a very long while.

The afternoon lengthens. The burgesses and commons shift their weary legs. The gentlemen try to hold their mounts steady, but their horses shake their reins, step side to side, restless, uncertain. No man dare say a word. The hours drag on. The heat and dust oppress. Thirst chokes every throat. All eyes rest on His Majesty's tent, the closed door, the lack of stirring. With trepidation the important men of Lincoln await their king. What if, Francis thinks, the king's willingness to accept their submission has changed? That would be very bad for Lincolnshire. Very bad for the hopes of Squire Francis Ayscough.

What Francis does not know—what none but the privy grooms in fearful attendance know—is how profusely, and with what agony, the king's leg ulcers suppurate. He lies upon the royal bed groaning and raging as his dressings are changed. Inside the queen's sweltering tent, his young bride, sheathed in cloth of silver, sits bored and restless with her ladies, awaiting word. The king curses. He roars. He bats hands away. Without, in their ragged rows on the yellow plain, the good men of Lincolnshire pray. Charles Brandon, the Duke of Suffolk, strides between tents, a massive, bearded bull, grumbling at the delay. As premier peer of the north, Suffolk has planned the Great Northern Progress. One of the grandest moments is to be when His Majesty emerges from Lincoln Cathedral as the lowering sun lights the spires with flaming sunset light—golden orange! Magnificent!—that all may be struck by the king's glory! If the ceremonies are delayed, Henry will emerge into a shadowy close at dusk. The portent will be less portentous. The glory less glorious. Suffolk looks around for a messenger to send word to the bishop to shorten the Mass. Ah! Near the tents, he sees a stirring! The heralds of arms don their coats. The gentlemen pensioners take their places. Now, at last, the king's Majesty and the queen's Grace emerge.

Henry strides forwards, a grandiloquent mountain apparelled in cloth of gold, his diminutive queen like a slender silver tassel at his side. His broad, florid face shows nothing of his pain. They mount their beautifully trapped horses. The train falls in line, begins to move slowly along the hard-packed road, where the gentry have dismounted and await their sovereign on their knees. The mayor and burgesses are on their knees. All the important men of Lincolnshire are on their knees. They cry out in loud voices: 'Jesu save your Grace! Jesu save your Grace!'

Francis Ayscough, kneeling amongst them, cants his eyes upward, scanning the procession for his brothers. He spies Christopher, handsome in tawny velvet with slashed sleeves of claret silk, mounted on a fine-looking sorrel within the king's train. Christopher meets his eye, makes a warning frown, a lowering gesture with his forehead as if to say: do not be caught, brother, peeking about when you ought to be grovelling before your king. Francis, reading his brother's face, at once bows his head more abjectly, turns his gaze to the ground.

At the appointed place, His Majesty lifts a languid hand. The train halts. The city recorder rises and takes a step. At once he goes to his knees. He rises again, takes another step, unrolls an enormous scroll, and reads aloud the people's submission, with all its fawning humiliations, abasements, its listing of vast monetary gifts and fine victuals. The quaking man kisses the parchment and hands it to a page, who walks it to the king, who takes it and gives it to the Duke of Norfolk. Now it is Lord Mayor Sir Vincent Grantham who humbly comes forward to present the sword and mace of the city. Surrendered, the heavy silver mace is returned to Sir Vincent to carry in the procession. His horse is brought 'round, and he is placed in line behind the two dukes, Norfolk and Suffolk, with the burgesses behind him. The gentlemen of the county mount and take their places, two by two, behind the mayor and his brethren. On the crowded dusty plain, the trumpets blare. The drums sound. The royal retinue begins very slowly to move.

Nearby church bells begin ringing; the peals echo, meet themselves. Soon bells farther distant begin to sound, one igniting the next in every direction, as the king's train, near a mile in length, moves slowly across the bridge over the River Witham, enters the city, and begins to climb. Francis Ayscough rides anonymously with the gentry, up and up and up, winding towards the magnificent cathedral at the crest. Women and children and the lesser men of the county throng the streets, hang from the upper windows, crowd themselves a dozen deep along the walls at the Lincoln Edge to peer down upon the king's magnificence. They wave their kerchiefs and cheer *Jesu save your Majesty! Long live the king!* Their voices are like the piping of little frogs in the great cacophony of church bells and trumpets and drums.

In the cobbled square at the crest of the hill, within the press of people mingling near the cathedral, Anne waits with her family. The pealing bells obliterate every thought and sensation but the resonant thrum in the chest, the ears, the back of the throat. The crowd swells. Anne raises herself to her toes, shouts in her husband's ear: 'Put William on your shoulders!' It takes many repeated shouts and gestures before Kyme hoists the boy to his shoulders, just as a cry goes up—*he's here, he's here, His Majesty approaches!* The people push back to make room, compressing the space. Anne is crushed against the stone building; she loses sight of her husband and son, can see nothing but the hulking backs of the huzzaing men in front of her. Desperately she looks about. Where is William? Ah, there. She breathes. She sees the boy's cap above the others; he sits on his father's shoulders, his plump legs gripped in his father's hands. She sees her son lift his two small fists in the air and cheer. All around her the people cheer: His Majesty is passing! Oh, the grief, to be so near and yet not to see him! Never mind. It is enough that her son should see him.

But it is not the massive gold-encrusted mountain her son cheers, but his own uncles, Edward and Christopher, whom the boy sees passing within the king's train, and far behind them his uncle Francis, astride his great stallion, forcing his way into the crowded square. The lord mayor and burgesses are turned off to the side by yeoman guardsmen, but Francis Ayscough dismounts, drops his reins, and shoves himself through the throng of people to make certain he is among the highborn who follow His Majesty through Exchequer Gate.

Beyond the gate, in the minster yard, the crowd opens and spreads, a contained river pouring into an open estuary. In the centre, a Turkey carpet lies upon the ground beneath the canopy of estate, and upon the carpet: a small embroidered stool beside a great kneeling-cushion covered in cloth of gold. Upon the cushion, a jewelled crucifix. The king and queen alight slowly, grandly. Henry's face is flushed, his teeth gritted, as he strides to the canopy. Here is his magnificence, the excellence of his pretence, his great masking: Henry walks in excruciating pain, but he limps not. He lowers his tremendous bulk to kneel upon the gold-covered cushion, but he grimaces not. The queen is escorted to her stool by her ladies, and Henry takes his bride's hand. From the great carved wooden doors of the cathedral, the Bishop of Lincoln issues forth, resplendent in gold-trimmed vestments and white mitre. At once the bells of the cathedral go silent—a silence that makes its ponderous way from the minster yard to the castle square and beyond, across the city, where, one by one, the church bells cease.

Within the minster yard, Francis casts about for his brothers. Ah, there, beyond the carpet where the bishop stands extending the great crucifix for the king to kiss. Christopher Ayscough, in silk and velvet, is kneeling, but Edward, as one of the King's Spears, stands at attention in his red coat with gold braid as the bishop murmurs the Latin blessings, swings the gilded censer, and the ever-pious Henry lifts his face, eyes closed, towards Heaven. Francis catches Edward's eye. A communication passes: Come to my town house this evening if you are able to get away. Edward nods, an almost imperceptible gesture. An arched brow from Francis. Bring Christopher. A shrug. If I can, I will.

At length, His Majesty rises—it requires two strong men at each elbow to help him—and turns, takes the queen's hand. The massive gold mountain and his lissome silver tassel proceed into the great Roman cathedral to hear Mass. The sun lowers. Above the minster wall, the great western face of the cathedral begins to glow amber, deepening quickly to a gleaming, impossible orange. A hush settles upon the yard, seeps out into the cobblestoned square, the nearby streets of the city. The crowd edges forwards, listening, as within the Cathedral Church of the Blessed Virgin Mary of Lincoln, the glorious choir is singing: *Te Deum laudamus*:

Thee, O God, we praise!

– Chapter 21 –

Anne sits with her sisters Bridget and Jane by candlelight in one of the smaller chambers at St Catherine's priory, Bridget's home. The children are abed, the men gone. 'What did you think of her?' Bridget asks. 'The new queen. Is she as beautiful as they say?'

'I didn't see her,' Anne murmurs. 'Nor did I see the king, even. The press was too great.'

'Nor did I,' says Jane. 'Why did you not come with us, Bridget? You could have failed to see them for yourself.' Jane means to be humorous, but Bridget merely looks at her. 'Well?' Jane says. 'You did not ask *if* we'd seen them.'

And this is true. For two hours the women sat silent at supper listening to their husbands' discourse on the day's events, their approbations, criticisms, and boasts. After the meal, when their husbands left to join Francis at his home near St Swithins, the women gathered in this close chamber to talk. Jane eyes her stepsister carefully. 'You seem well enough now.'

'I'm fine,' Bridget says.

'Then why did you not join us?' Anne asks. That morning Bridget had professed to feel too ill to undertake the long walk into Lincoln, the arduous climb to the cathedral, though she'd seemed then, appears now, in the peak of health.

'Are you with child?' Jane asks bluntly.

'That is not the reason.'

'What, then?' Anne says.

Bridget rises, goes to a near wall to smooth the arras. 'How does one make a home from stone cells created for perfect discomfort?' she says, without turning to face them. 'It is a puzzle.'

'You've worked miracles, Bridget,' Anne says. 'One would hardly know it for a priory.'

'If you discount the frescoes,' Jane says. 'And the tortured saints splayed about in the great hall. And the leering imps. And the gold inlay in the tiles. And the great painted ceiling arching overhead the moment one enters.' Jane smiles above the cup in her hands.

'Really, Jane,' Anne chides, 'you're terrible.' But Anne, too, is smiling. Jane makes a dry jest of everything. She seems never to be dispirited, never discontented or unsure of herself. It is her happy marriage to George St Poll, Anne believes. To Jane and her husband, as with other reformist believers, the artwork at the priory is as idolatrous as plaster saints and rood screens in churches, and she'll not hesitate to say so. Still, Anne thinks, her smile fading, you needn't insult poor Bridget. Anne watches her stepsister's back as she strokes the tapestry, a scene of snarling dogs and rearing horses, the bloody breast of a wild-eyed hart pawing the air. 'Why did you not come with us?' she says. 'It is a formidable honour, your husband riding at the front of the king's procession, directly behind the peers.'

'Oh, yes,' Bridget says. 'The glorious *peers*. Suffolk and Norfolk. Seventy-six men hanged in one day at Carlisle on Norfolk's order—such is the glory and benevolence of the *peers*.'

'Had my husband had such a grand role in the proceedings, you could not have torn me away.'

'Well. So may it be with you, Anne. Your life is not mine. Nor mine yours.'

Anne and Jane exchange a look.

'Just speak,' Jane says. 'Tell us.'

Bridget gestures around the tiny room. 'What do you see?' The sisters turn their gazes. Two small tables, a candelabrum, the three oaken chairs. Clean rushes on the floor. No fireplace or windows. The stone walls above the tapestries glisten with sweat. The doorway closes with only a heavy damask curtain, open now to admit the gallery's dank air. The room smells of age and must, ineffectively masked by beeswax candles and a bowl of crushed rose petals on the wine table. 'A monk's cell?' Bridget suggests. 'A close, cramped room where men arose in the dark for matins and lauds? Where they wore hair shirts and buggered one another and flogged their own backs?'

Jane shivers. 'Ugh. Don't tell us. Doubtless such brutalities and worse were committed here—and all the more reason for the closings!'

But Anne, who has spent hours of her life cloistered inside a dark room against her will, says, 'This is a nun's room.'

'The prioress, actually,' Bridget says. 'The cells of the nuns are much smaller.'

'There were nuns here?' Jane says.

'Saint Catherine's was a double house.' Bridget cuts Jane a look. 'I'd have thought you knew that.' Bridget gazes out the open door into the dark passageway. 'The door between had seventeen locks, and in the centre, a little slot the length of a man's finger, no wider than his thumb, where the nuns made confession. It was reinforced with iron.'

Jane laughs. 'The better to keep some canon from poking his member through, no doubt.'

Bridget continues in her dreamlike voice. 'They were all turned out, of course, at the closing. Nuns and canons alike. The canons received pensions. The nuns did not.'

'Where did they go?' Anne asks. 'With no pension for their keep?'

Bridget shrugs. 'Home to their families? The back streets and dark alleys of London? No one knows.'

'Your concern escapes me,' Jane says. 'For canons and priors? For the women religious? Are you saying it was wrong to suppress these corrupt houses?'

Bridget looks at her. 'You do not know their lives, Jane.'

'No more do you.'

'I live where they lived. I see much, and sense more, in the very bones of this place. In the walls, the vastness and constrictions. The cold, cramped cells.'

'Oh, fie,' Jane says. 'And I suppose you've smelled blood where they flogged themselves? Which is, as you well know, clean contrary to Scripture. Where does it say in the Great Bible that Jesus Christ flogged himself?'

'You heed the royal commissioners' foul rumours, I see. Sleep well tonight, Jane. Perhaps you'll dream of holy canons buggering one another in that chamber where you sleep.'

'The commissioners speak true, Bridget,' Anne says. 'You know the king would not have allowed the closings if—'

'The king would not have! The *king* would *not* have!' Bridget turns blazing eyes against her. 'The king would not have what? Disembowelled my agonized husband and burnt his bloody entrails before his living eyes? Ordered the butcherly deaths of thousands on the whims of his own fancy? Oh, the king, the king, the king! Why should I care to look upon the king!'

'Hush!' Jane has hurried to the archway and drawn the curtain closed, though damask will surely not hold secret such treasonous words. Anne is standing now, stroking Bridget's arm. 'Yes, dearest,' she says soothingly. 'We know.'

'You do *not* know.' Bridget glares up at her. 'None of you know,' she says through gritted teeth. 'Neither you nor your lordly brothers who go sucking around in the king's wake! And my husband, Sir Vincent, the same.' She turns on Jane. 'And yours! The only one who does not crawl bellywise to the tyrant is Thomas Kyme, and that only because he is not permitted to draw near!'

A rigid stillness descends on them. A lengthy silence. The women stare into emptiness. At supper, Thomas Kyme sat glowering while Bridget's and Jane's husbands recounted the day's glories, their own parts in the proceedings. Anne's husband had not been asked to participate—not even so much as to kneel in the dirt with the commons at the king's passing. Tension threaded the air then, hangs in the room now. Jane rearranges her sleeves. '*Tyrant* is a dangerous word, Bridget. You'd best take care who hears your fulminations.'

'I did not intend to *fulminate,* as you call it. Did I not seek to withdraw quietly from the day's pomp? But no—my sisters must be at me all the evening asking why did I not go!' Bridget's face is defiant, yet she too lowers her voice. 'I fear him, yes, as we all must, but I despise him more fiercely than that. I'll not be a part of this grovelling! So there. It is out. Betray me to the king's men if you like, and I shall go in that same cold hatred to my death, where, God willing, I shall meet my beloved Thomas—though they'll not quarter me, as they did my husband, but burn me, as they did Lady Bulmer. The king himself ordered her condemnation, it is said—and for what? Her loyalty to her husband? Disloyalty to the Crown? I say it is because she and Lord Bulmer were not properly married—for you know how our thrice-married monarch is such a moral stickler for the sanctity of marriage!'

'Hush!' Jane whispers. 'You'll have us all at the stake, and our husbands with us.'

'No,' Bridget says. 'Our husbands will not join us. Nor our brothers. They are too sycophantic and grovelling for that.'

'My husband is no sycophant!' Jane's voice rises. 'He is a good and worthy man, and a loyal servant to my lord Suffolk. And as to our brothers: what else might you expect them to do? And how, pray tell, would *you* have survived without Francis's help? How might you have all this?' She gestures around the room. 'Proper food and warmth and lovely little gowns for your daughters? Think, Bridget. Remember how it was.'

'Rest assured, Jane. I remember.'

'As do I.' Anne kneels beside Bridget. 'I understand your grief, my sister. I don't *know* it, but I understand it. And I understand why it turns to anger. But . . .' Anne cannot think how to say all she feels. She wants to defend Henry; she knows him for a faithful prince—did he not commission the Great Bible to be translated into the common tongue and placed in every church throughout England? It is because of Henry that she, Anne, may read the Bible openly and her husband dare not say anything against it, for it is at the king's order. And yet . . . the butchery. It is as Bridget says. Only last summer, three devout men of the gospel were burnt at Smithfield while three papist priests were being hanged, drawn, and quartered, and all this but two days after Cromwell's execution, which is the most shocking death to Anne. How could Henry execute the minister most responsible for bringing God's Word in English to his subjects? Why slay papists and gospel preachers in the same hour? She has no means to comprehend it, and so she shuts her mind to the notion. She strokes Bridget's shoulder, but the muscles are rigid beneath her hands. Anne gives one final gentle pat. 'We must pray,' she says, bracing her belly with her palm as she stands. 'God save us from anger—not His wrath only, but our own.'

'You had more charm,' Jane says dryly, 'before your piety took such hold.'

'I am not being *pious,* Jane. I'm only saying the truth. Look at her.'

'She looks fine to me. Pink and plump as a goose. Are you not fine, Bridget?'

'I'm irritated, that is what I am.'

'At *us*?' Jane quips, as if shocked.

'At everything. At how you two glorify Henry no less than, than, than—everyone! Every lord and lowborn in the kingdom. Shall I tell you other fetes of your glorious sovereign? Before he left London to come north on this oh-so-magnificent progress, this most merciful prince of yours ordered the Tower cleared of prisoners—not by pardon, Anne, not by mercy, but by execution. The old Countess of Salisbury, you know she'd been held for two years? That venerable old lady was sent to the block to be slaughtered by an inexperienced young lout who chopped at her neck for a quarter hour till she finally came dead.' Bridget snorts at their doubtful expressions. 'Oh, yes. It is one of the perquisites of being married to a man of such civic authority as Sir Vincent: I hear all the news from London as quickly as it rides north.' She settles her gaze on Jane. 'I hope your husband's closeness to Suffolk will protect you, but I would not stake my life on it. Nor should you. Not in these changing times. Not with the changing laws, the changing . . . oh, look at us! Look at our husbands arguing at dinner! They stand in such strained relation to the Church and the Crown and the new laws that indeed they do not *know* where they stand. Whose loyalty lies with whom? Who believes what, and why?'

'*We* know what we believe,' Jane says. 'And where our loyalty lies.'

'And where is that?'

'Why, with God! With His Holy Word. What is the matter with you, Bridget? Has living with nuns' ghosts addled your brains?'

'I should not, if I were you, be so quick to proclaim the gospel, Jane. You know the papists are in the ascendancy now.'

'I'll not deny my faith!' Jane says, but her voice is at a whisper. 'Not at your table, nor anywhere else.' Indeed, Jane and her husband have expressed their opinions openly; they've felt protected in doing so by their close connection to Suffolk and his wife, Katherine Willoughby—at least until Cromwell's fall, this was so. Now, though, no one in Henry's England is completely sure of his position. Jane whispers: 'Salvation is not by the Mass and paid indulgences but by grace through faith, as Paul says: Not of works, lest any man should boast.'

'Ah, thank Christ none of us has a boasting husband,' Bridget says.

Jane blinks at her a moment, then laughs. Bridget begins laughing. Anne is silent. She brings her wine to her lips, but the smell nauseates her, and she sets the cup down. Jane and Bridget might well laugh at their husbands' boasting as if they are only braggarty boys. They'll not be forced to pay this night for their men's inadequacies. Anne had noted her husband's glowering silence as Sir Vincent and Sir George revelled in their places of honour, the grandness of the king's progress, describing for their wives the sea of fluttering pennants, the gloriously trapped horses, the dust, the colour, the sound—and as they spoke, Anne read her husband's every impatient gesture, his silences, his frowns. That he'd not been allowed to take part in the ceremonies galled him. That he'd been forced to stand with the women and children in castle square, only to be shoved back, pushed aside, trampled at the king's approach—this had eaten the whole day at Thomas Kyme. Now, to sit at table listening to these fine gentlemen of the county, with nothing of his own to say of the day's glories: it was beyond endurance.

And so he'd jumped in with a foolish boast: that he'd watched Henry stride through the crowd a full cubit taller than any man on earth. Sir George had turned to him: 'When did you see the king walking? His Majesty did not dismount until he was inside the minster yard.' Kyme's voice had hovered between defiance and jest when he answered: 'And how do you know, brother, that I did not follow and slip inside the gate?' At the sudden scrutiny of the others turning to him, he said jovially, tipping back his ale, 'Marry, brothers, have we not all heard how the Great Harry stands nineteen hands tall? But I did see him ride his great courser through Exchequer Gate, and that was something.'

Anne did not raise her gaze. Such a foolish boast. So easily disproved. She'd neither smirked nor defended him silently; she had thought only: This will not serve me well this night. Thomas had tried to retrieve his dignity by turning the conversation to religion, fervently defending private masses for souls in Purgatory, and there came at once a haggling argument, of which Jane took part, though Anne did not. She watched her husband. Faced with in-laws citing Scripture to support their positions—men higher born than he, more keenly educated, better dressed, better read, more importantly placed in the county—Thomas Kyme had argued his points ineffectively, by repetition and stubbornness, his neck hunched into his shoulders: a dull bulldog, unpersuaded, building moment by moment deeper feelings of ignominy and rage.

She will be the one who pays for his ignominy. Tonight, in bed, she will pay. Her hand goes to her belly. She had hoped to wait until they were home again in Friskney, perhaps even until the quickening, but she must tell him tonight. It will do no good to pretend sleep. When he is angry and full of wine, as he will be this night, he is not deterred by her sleeping. He'll come in berating her brothers, their adherence to the new evangelicalism, its austerity, its emptiness. This will be how he rouses himself. In his cups, and in their absence, he'll call them reprobates and time servers, no men of true faith but joiners for political reasons—and there'll be some truth to it. Certainly for Francis, alliance with the new religion had been an act of political expediency: the strongest repudiation of the papist rebels who'd risen up against the king five years ago. Before Cromwell's execution, it had seemed the most prudent path. Now the path is less certain. For Christopher, it is and has always been a matter of the royal supremacy: he has ever acknowledged Henry as Supreme Head of the Church in England. But for Edward, Anne knows, it is a matter of devout faith. As it is for her. As it had been for young Thom, while he lived.

The thought of her tender young brother catches at Anne's chest. Four years, she thinks. It hardly seems possible. The last time she saw him, he was sitting up in bed, chatting happily with Mother Elizabeth, his scalp pink on his shorn head, his ivory chessmen scattered about the covers, the oaken chessboard on his lap tipped askew. He'd died hardly a week later of the lingering ravishes of his fever, not upon his bowels, the surgeon said, but upon his weakened heart. Thom died in late summer when the Wolds were, as now, bathed in yellow sunlight. If it is a boy, she thinks, caressing her belly, we'll name him Thomas. My husband will profess the child is named for him, but I shall know in secret that he bears the name of my sweet baby brother. And I shall call him Thom, not Thomas. Will and Thom. Or Martha Elizabeth, pray God. Will and Martha. Not Maddie. I shan't call her that. Just the simple, pure sound: Martha. Sister of Mary. Sister of Lazarus. Sister of Anne.

'Oho, I see now.'

She looks up. Jane's brows are raised in that ironical hitch. 'My lovely fecund sister.' She tips her cup at Anne's belly. 'Not Bridget with child, I see, but you. Now, there's a pleasant subject we may turn our thoughts to.'

– Chapter 22 –

Ah, the uncertainties of the age. What do they muse on, then, these five gentlemen and their sullen yeoman brother-in-law sitting before the fire in Francis Ayscough's fine town house near St Swithins after the servants and wives are abed? It is August, it is sweltering, the men sweat in their summer doublets, but Francis has bid the spit boy build a fire—for what purpose? To demonstrate the new fireplace and chimney he has had installed in this ancient building that never had one before. To give light and a centred place to fasten their gaze as they drink. They are not, as Anne conjectured, arguing religion. They are not recounting the day's glories and their own triumphs, nor anticipating the aftermath of the king's Great Northern Progress, how conditions in their county and, more significantly, their own positions might henceforth change.

No, in this moment, well into their fourth flagon of wine and second tapped firkin of strong beer, the men are gossiping about the king's bed. Specifically: how the king keeps to it alone these nights on progress, does not visit his young bride excepting briefly before he retires, to kiss her cheek and bid her good sleep.

'This is fully opposite to last summer,' Christopher says. 'Last summer we slept in attendance outside her door every night. Now it is rare beyond rare. He grows more celibate as he grows stouter, have you noticed, Edward?'

Edward shrugs. 'You would know better than I.'

'We have all noticed. The dressers say it is the odour of his leg, that he'll not subject her to it, that he is too embarrassed and in too much pain to bed her. The gentlemen of the bedchamber say it is more likely that he cannot perform his duties and that it is this mortification which prevents him, more than the stink.'

They do not say his name. They do not call him by any of his royal titles. They do not say 'the queen.' They use only pronouns, *he, she, his, her,* as if this could protect them should some untrustworthy person be lurking near the open door to hear. But there is no one. Francis has sent his servants to bed, even the boy who serves the wine. His wife, Lisbeth, has been asleep for hours, tossing restlessly in her damp summer linens, the new leaded glass windows opened to the night air. It is only these six men, drinking in fellowship, linked in kinship, entertaining one another with men's gossip, and none will betray the other, Francis thinks. No word spoken here will go out of this room—for to harm one would be to harm all. He lifts his cup, takes a long draught. 'Stoutness has naught to do with virility,' he says as he plunks the cup down. The others laugh.

'Has it not?' Sir Vincent says. 'Your girth bears witness to that, I suppose.'

'And my son!' Francis's newborn son is two months old, a plump, healthy boy named for Sir William—the fifth William Ayscough in the family's long line. And it is true: Francis has grown stout on the blessings of prosperity—not fat, but solid and square-built, a hulking shag-haired bear, very like his father. He has made excellent use of the Hansard estates, has added to the already large holdings with two new land grants from closed monasteries and a small priory near Caistor—and now this fine old large home in Lincoln, which he is presently gutting and making entirely modern to please his wife, with newly built fireplaces and chimneys, an enlarged kitchen, an indoor privy being built at the rear. Soon he hopes his young family will spend more time here than in South Kelsey, for it is in Lincoln that Francis cuts a public figure. He can, he believes, anticipate knighthood in the not distant future, given a reasonable skirmish or some small war whereby he may prove himself as his father did at Touraine thirty years ago. Francis yearns to be known as Sir Francis, not merely Squire Ayscough. In good time, he tells himself. All in good time.

He drinks, gazes about the room; his shoulders rise and fall in a slow yawn of satisfaction. His brothers are elegant and polished as any gentleman in the king's service: Christopher sleek in silk and velvet, leaning back in his chair, his handsome features limned gold in firelight, blue eyes, dark hair. Beside him, Edward leans forward, elbows on knees; he is not so handsome as their middle brother, but he is refined-looking in the king's livery, with his close-cropped auburn hair, his long ascetic face. Opposite are the husbands of his sister and stepsister, Sir George St Poll and Sir Vincent Grantham, two of the most prosperous and prestigiously placed gentlemen of the county. How might Squire Francis Ayscough not be confident of his own and his family's promising future?

His glance falls on Thomas Kyme scowling at the fire as he sips wine and wipes his forehead with his open palm, tugging with stubby fingers at the wisps of pale hair plastered there. Francis's mood falters. The one flaw in his placid musings. Anne's husband. There are men of the yeoman class, certainly, who climb through profitable marriages and increasing wealth to the rank of landed gentry. Master Kyme is not one of these. He's proven himself adept enough at gaining lands and profit, but he has not, alas, proven adept at advancement. Thomas Kyme remains an uncultured sheep farmer, a churl, a bumpkin—and a secret papist, Edward allows. But Edward sees papists everywhere. Francis shrugs, takes a long drink. Kyme may yet make good progress, he tells himself. What Francis ought to do is take the fellow more firmly in hand, instruct him by example in the proper ways of gentlemen. Not tonight, however. Not during this time of His Majesty's presence in Lincoln, when Francis may prosper himself under the auspices of his brothers' placement—two Ayscoughs in the king's service now.

'Edward!' Francis calls out. His lean and lanky brother is standing near the fire, one arm resting upon the mantel. 'How like you your new placement as one of the King's Spears?'

'It hardly seems new, brother, at a year and a half. I stand it well enough.'

'Though you preferred service with the archbishop,' Christopher says.

'I did.'

Christopher turns his handsome smile to the room. 'Other pensioners sneak away to see their wives when they have a bit of time, but not my devout brother. Where you'll find Edward on his day off is in a skiff being rowed to Lambeth.'

'Were we permitted to travel farther than twelve miles from His Majesty's person,' Edward says, 'you'd find me on the road to Cambridge. As it is,' he shrugs, 'I enjoy the archbishop's erudite company. And his excellent wines.'

'But how shall we ever find you a wife in the archbishop's palace?' Christopher says. 'Though it did not prove impossible for the archbishop.'

'You might keep a closer tongue,' Edward says, his voice low. He cants his eyes at his brother, a warning, which Christopher instantly heeds: smiling, he claps his hands, leans forward.

'Oh, but our brother looks fine in his gallant red coat with all that fancy gold braid, does he not?' he says. 'The ladies at court trail around after him, dropping their handkerchiefs in his path and making dog eyes.'

Sir George gestures with his gilded cup at Edward's knees. 'Careful you don't singe those pretty hose.'

'Oh, he'll not singe himself,' Thomas Kyme growls. It is the first he's spoken in an hour. 'This side of Purgatory, at least.'

The men all turn to look at him. Oh, let us not, please, Francis thinks.

'You'd warn me of the fires of Purgatory?' Edward says, smiling.

'I'd warn any man to look to his sins and his manner of living, and to keep the sacraments most healthfully, that he die a good death and shorten his torment.'

'Here, Thomas,' Francis leans over, 'let me fill your cup.'

But Kyme will not retreat. He narrows his already half-masted eyes at Edward: 'You would leave your own father to suffer the fires of Purgatory for a thousand years.'

'If I believed in papist superstitions, I would not. But my faith follows the Word of God, not the false constructions of the Bishop of Rome.'

'And what do the king's bishops say of the sacraments in their book? And of Purgatory?'

'What does Saint Paul say? Or James? Or John or Peter? What, indeed, does our Lord and Saviour Christ Jesus say?'

'Brothers!' Francis says. 'Let us leave this topic and speak of subjects more profitable!' He turns to his stepbrother-in-law Sir Vincent. 'Let us hear, sir, how goes your case in Chancery on the new enclosures?'

'Ah, the enclosures!' Sir Vincent takes his cue. 'These villeins are a nuisance, but I doubt not that the courts will hold me in good stead. Do you find, Master Kyme, that your locals are stubborn and contumacious against the new laws?'

'I have good relations with my locals,' Kyme says. 'I pay them fair for their losses.'

'Do you? And how do you make good profit, then?'

'I profit well enough.'

'Ah. I'm keen to hear your methods. My commons would hold me up like highwaymen. Ah, yes. Well, then. It is late.' He gets to his feet, looks about vaguely. 'I suppose we'll have to see to our horses ourselves?' He frowns at Francis. 'I can't think why you sent the servants to bed.'

'I cannot think why, either,' Francis says. 'Here, one more glass, and then I'll rouse the stableman.'

'Well. Perhaps one.' Sir Vincent sits. Another round of malmsey. Their faces shine red in the firelight. They are all quite drunk. 'I cannot think why you lighted that blasted fire, neither.'

'Nor I.' Francis shakes his head.

'My best velvet doublet,' Christopher says with mock sadness. 'Stained with sweat.'

'Why do you wear velvet in August?' Sir George says.

'You're wearing velvet.'

Sir George looks down at himself. 'So I am,' he says with mild surprise. 'But I do not complain of sweat stains. See? There's your rub.'

'What rub?'

Sir George shakes his head. The thought is too difficult to follow. 'It was quite a day, was it not?' A genial chorus of agreement. They have done themselves proud.

'How long will he remain in Lincoln?' Francis asks, a question for his brothers in the royal service, but it is Sir George who answers: 'He tours the castle after dinner tomorrow. Our lord mayor is called to be in attendance.' A nod to Sir Vincent, who, seated in the great chair, nevertheless bows from the waist. 'After that,' Sir George says, 'God knows. He remained at Grimsthorpe three days beyond what Suffolk expected. The duke had to scour all the villages miles around for provisions. Pray God the bishop has laid in sufficient stores. If His Majesty likes his accommodations in the palace well enough, he may decide to stay the week.'

Francis looks to his brothers: Is this true? Christopher nods. Edward is not looking at him; he is still gazing pensively, and not kindly, at their brother-in-law Kyme, who glares at the fire as if he'd like to throttle it to ashes. It is time, Francis thinks, to take this situation in hand. 'I shall go to castle square tomorrow,' he announces, 'to see His Majesty pass. A more intimate setting than today's tumult, I trow. Will you join me, Thomas? We might have dinner at the White Hart before.'

The red-rimmed gaze Kyme turns on him is at once suspicious, filled with resentment, and unwillingly flattered. 'Oh, *now* I'm to be invited, am I? Master Thomas, will you go with me to castle square? Master Thomas, will you join me for dinner? Master Thomas, never mind you were left like a dog to be over-swarmed by villeins so that even His Majesty's head could not be seen. Let us skulk about the edges of the king's retinue tomorrow, when all the significances of the most important day have bled away. Let us go like beggars in the low aftermath, when even a kicked dog may look upon the king.'

'If you'd rather not,' Francis says, his measured tone a warning, 'you are free to decline. I shall be pleased to dine on the White Hart's fine pheasant alone.'

Kyme, realizing that the invitation is about to be withdrawn, lifts his cup towards Francis, dips his head, a slow blink of the eyes. 'I shall be honoured, sir,' he says, his words mildly slurred. The angel of silence descends. They all stare at the dying fire.

'Tell me,' Edward says, breaking the quiet. 'How fares my sister?' All three in-laws look up, but it is, of course, Thomas Kyme he addresses. 'And our nephew, young Will? How is he?'

'My son was a naughty snipe today,' Kyme says. 'I had to discipline him a dozen times. His excitement at seeing the king caused him to forget his manners. But he is coming along admirably, and he is healthy, thanks be.'

'And Anne?'

'She is well enough.'

'Well enough? What does that mean?'

Kyme shrugs, takes a long drink. 'She is well.'

'Another round, sirs?' Francis pours. 'So!' He claps his hands, pulling them back to a topic upon which they can offer unconflicted opinion: 'He ne'er visits her at all? That seems strange to my mind. But they sleep at the Bishop's Palace tonight. Now, *that* is a fair place. Fairer even than Grimsthorpe, wouldn't you say, George? He'll go to her tonight, don't you think? I suspect we'll be hearing gossip of a different sort tomorrow.'

'Let us hope,' Christopher says. 'And so we all pray.'

'And so we all pray.' Francis, well soused in stout beer, thinks to himself, yes, so we all pray, and it will not hurt our advancement should Henry find himself, shall we say, hungry, this night, in the Bishop's Palace in Lincoln. And should he get a son on Queen Catherine there, so much the better. A second son, the all-important second heir should the delicate Edward, God preserve him, fail to thrive. The king will think well on Lincoln should this night prove fruitful, and what serves Lincoln serves Lincolnshire, and what serves Lincolnshire serves the Ayscough family. Yes, yes, Francis thinks, draining his cup, all is well this night for Sir Francis Ayscough and his kin. Not yet openly 'Sir Francis,' of course: but soon, he tells himself, twisting around in his chair to refill his vessel. Soon enough.

– Chapter 23 –

Late morning, Edward's messenger arrives with a request for Anne to join him for dinner in castle square. Her husband would have forbidden her, of course, but Kyme left early this morning, with bloodshot eyes and flushed snout, to go Anne knows not where. She dresses for the walk quickly. Beatrice kneels to brush the road dust from her hem, glancing up hopefully from time to time. She had pleaded to go with them yesterday: 'May I please, sir! I can carry Master William for you!' But Kyme had said no—out of the plain spite of his heart, Anne thinks. It would have been Beatrice's first time ever in Lincoln; what could it have hurt? 'You shall come with me,' she says. The girl's face brightens. 'Run tell Nurse we'll not need William till evening. Quickly, now! It is a good hour's walk to reach the square.'

In fact, the walk takes much longer, for once they pass Saltergate, Anne must keep stopping to tell Beatrice to come along, come along! The girl walks slowly, turning her head side to side, staring at all the citizens in their finery, a lady here fingering the wares on a clothier's table, a gentleman there in a fine new cap, a carter beating his mule's rump as it brays and balks. 'Is there always so many folks about, miss?' Beatrice whispers.

'There were more yesterday. Thrice as many, I should say. Can you not walk a little faster?' Anne says, though she is making slow enough progress herself, for they have started up the steep hill now, the buildings crowding in on either side, ancient mortar and stone. 'On yesterday's climb,' Anne says, huffing, 'I had to walk. With my hands on my skirts. And my eyes on the backs in front of me. Hold a moment.' She stops, leans against a wall to catch her breath. 'The people were packed so closely. Like sheep in a chute tumbling and scrambling. I was afraid to falter, for fear they would climb over me and mash me into the stones.'

'That sounds terrible, miss.'

'It was not so terrible,' Anne says between panting breaths, 'when I believed I would see the king. It seems terrible in retrospect. All that sweat and work for nothing. Master Kyme had to carry William the whole way, you know. Which made him not the least happy.'

The two look at each other, blink an instant, then laugh. They begin the climb again. The road grows steeper. They trudge without speaking; they are hot, thirsty. Anne's stomach begins to quease. She needs something to drink, bread to calm her stomach. Lining the road are food and ale shops, but she does not pause to look inside the windows. What purpose? She has no money. Yesterday the people moved all one direction—towards the crest. Today men and women stroll both up and down the hill. Two common women stand gossiping in front of a butcher shop. Anne steps into the lane to go around them. Beatrice follows her. A priest comes walking fast down the hill towards them, and they move to the other side to let him pass. The climb begins to ease at last, and then the lane flattens, opens into the cobbled square.

'Oh, my,' Beatrice breathes, her head tilted back as she gazes up at the cathedral's spires. They are too near to get the full effect—the beautiful façade is hidden behind the minster wall—but still the girl turns to her mistress with wonder. 'I seen it from far off my whole life. I just never thought it would be . . . so . . .' She bites her lip, turns to gaze up at the cathedral again. 'Please, miss,' she says softly, 'after you have your dinner, may we go in to pray?' Anne eyes the helmeted men with raised halberds guarding the gate. 'I think not today,' she says. Beatrice's countenance drops. 'Well,' Anne says to cheer her, 'perhaps after His Majesty leaves.'

She steps briskly into the square, looking around for the inn. The King's Arms, Edward's note said. People are strolling everywhere, burghers and their wives, men in soiled caps and leather jerkins, ladies in sumptuous kirtles, street jugglers, sweets sellers, beggars sitting on the stones in front of the gate. Beatrice stares at the women's fashions—so many colours and qualities of fabric, such varied sleeve styles, satin kirtles, jaunty caps. 'Help me look,' Anne says. The girl turns an uncomprehending face to her. 'The inn, Beatrice! The King's Arms!' Beatrice points behind Anne, above her head. Anne turns to see the brightly painted sign above the door, the golden lions and fleurs-de-lis, the great crimson crown. One could not miss it, and yet she had walked right past—no doubt, Anne tells herself, because the crumbling old building looks not at all a decent inn, but more a shabby old tavern. 'Come!' Anne hurries to the door, steps from the bright sunlit square, alive with colour and activity and bejewelled women in bright dresses, into the dim, ale-smelling tavern.

She glances around. Only men's bearded faces—merchants and tradesmen, gentlemen wearing the king's badge, others in liveries she doesn't recognize. 'Anne!' Edward is coming towards her—what a relief to see his warm, familiar face. He embraces her, then holds her away to examine her. 'Look at you! Plump as a partridge! I believe marriage to that scowling papist actually suits you. Where's the boy?'

'We didn't bring him. The walk would be too much for him two days in a row.'

'Yes, I suppose. I'm pleased to see it is not too much for my sturdy sister.' He takes note then of Beatrice standing behind her. 'Oh,' Edward says, frowning; he glances towards the rear of the tavern, where, through a half-open door, laughter and curses pour forth in coarse accents: the servants' tables. 'I've seen no other lady's maids here, Anne.' He looks at Anne, then at Beatrice, then back at Anne, as if to say, what shall we do?

'Thank you, miss,' Beatrice says. 'I'll wait outside.' She hurries out the door as if she cannot escape fast enough. Frowning, Anne watches her leave.

Edward takes her arm. 'I've a table for us near the window. I'm sorry I could not do better than this rude tavern.' He steers her towards a small table in a wooden alcove, slightly elevated, dark wood, carved chairs, no padding. 'With Lincoln crowded as it is, I'm afraid this is the best I could manage.'

Through the wavy partitioned glass, Anne sees Beatrice lower herself to the cobblestones, wrap her skirts tightly about her legs, look up towards the cathedral spires. Anne turns to Edward. 'How are you?' she says.

'I'm well.' There is something tense, guarded, about him.

'No, really, Edward. How are you?'

'Good!' It is almost a chirp. 'I'm fine. It is merely discomfiting to find oneself at once so pampered and simultaneously a prisoner, that is all.'

'A prisoner?'

'Poor choice of words.' His slight let-us-not-speak-of-unpleasantries shrug. 'All right, then. What shall we have to eat?'

She searches his lean face. 'You do not like your life at court?'

'Of course.'

'Of course what? You like it or do not like it?'

He studies her in silence. She feels he is weighing her, measuring—what? Her trustworthiness? Her circumspection? 'I did not choose this life, Nan,' he says. 'Someone put my name forward, I know not who, nor why. I know only that a letter came to the archbishop saying that a "certain lord" had recommended me for one of the new positions. Cranmer was compelled to write a letter of reference for me, and I was compelled to leave his service, which had suited me right well, to become one of the King's Spears, which suits me not at all. But one does not refuse such a recommendation.'

'Surely, though, Edward, to be at court? To be so well positioned—'

'You sound like Francis. I'm no privy counsellor, Anne. What do you suppose we do all the tiresome hours, we gentleman pensioners? At Greenwich or Windsor or Whitehall? We attend the king's masques. We dine. We dance. We carp and argue or stand about whispering behind our hands. Some play kiss-the-lady behind the curtains. Others fawn over the latest fashions or look to create new ones. It is tedious beyond bearing.'

'It cannot be more tedious than shearing season in Friskney, believe me.'

Her brother laughs. For a moment, his tension eases. He waves the innkeeper over, orders pies and bread and ale, sends the man away with an injunction to hurry, his sister is famished. 'Coarse fare, I'm afraid,' he tells Anne. 'I'm sorry.'

'I'm hungry enough, I'll not sneer at it. Anyway, it's as good as you brought me at Cambridge. Turnips, turnips, and turnips again. I was grateful any night you showed up with a mess of pottage.' Edward laughs again. She would never have thought to see him laugh at her recklessness back then, all those years ago when she stayed a fortnight in his room. 'Oh!' she says, suddenly remembering Beatrice. 'May we not send something out to my maid? She'll be half starved by now, and I know she's thirsty.'

Edward goes to the back to order food and drink to be sent out. Anne looks through the wavy glass. Beatrice's image is fractured into parcels by the lead partitions. She's no longer gazing up at the cathedral but squinting the opposite direction, towards the castle, her attention rapt. Trying to make out the gruesome knobs on the ramparts, Anne thinks. A shudder passes through her. All these years. Is Thomas Moigne's skull yet spiked on the ramparts amidst the others? Must Bridget turn her gaze away each time she comes to the city centre? Her stepsister's sorrowing face swims before her, her bitter voice in the tiny candlelit room. *You must know, Anne. You above anyone.* Almost the same words Mother Elizabeth said to her years ago, in Thomas's sickroom: *A woman has no choice in these matters, Anne. As you above all others must know.* What is it I must know?

'The king,' Edward says, taking his seat again, 'has an astonishing capacity for particulars. He knows at all points who is to be in attendance upon him, who is released, and for how long, and where that gentleman may be found should he fail to return at the proper hour. When I first came to court I thought it was Cromwell who kept such strict accounts, but Cromwell is dead a year now, and yet we are kept rigorously ordered—not by a minister, you see, but by His Majesty himself. My life is entirely circumscribed by my master's whims, his loose or firm stools, his mood and appetite.'

'Sounds like *my* life,' Anne says.

Edward cocks a brow. 'I'd not have thought Thomas Kyme a man of any especial capacity for particulars. Anyway, this is not what I wished to talk about.' He reaches across the table, takes both her hands. 'I need to warn you to take close care.'

'Take care how?'

'When you go to the church in Friskney, do not stand at the Great Bible and read.'

'What? But that is my prerogative!'

'It soon may not be.'

'What makes you say that?'

'It is no accident that the Six Articles were passed before Cromwell's fall. Very easily may the same forces that destroyed him come to destroy us all. Already they agitate to have the Word in English taken from the people.'

'Who does?'

'Stephen Gardiner, Norfolk, the conservatives on the council.'

'But surely the king does not listen!'

'Oh, he listens.' Edward releases her hands, leans back. 'Henry is far more malleable than he knows. We all in our ways must lie low. Since Cromwell's beheading, our eyes in the privy chamber are dimmed. Ralph Sadler will have naught to do with us openly. Our friend John Lascelles no longer serves as the king's sewer but lives in exile in Nottinghamshire.'

'What of Christopher? He's there.'

'Christopher is not one of us.' At her sharp look he says, 'You know that, Anne. Or you ought to know it.'

And, yes, she supposes she does know. Christopher is, above all, a courtier: he is consummately the king's man. Whichever way the religious winds blow, Christopher bends with them—provided they blow not against Henry.

'We must pray and read and believe as we rightfully believe,' Edward says, 'but circumspectly. In secret. We've done it before, we can do it again. We shall lie low, you and I,' he says, 'until the time is right. I shall pretend to be grateful to be one of the King's Spears.

And you, my brave sister, shall pretend to be pious and humble. The piety suits you right well, and the humility not at all, but here we are.' He smiles as if to coax Anne to smile, but she is baffled, furious, dismayed. To read the Great Bible in All Saints is her most rare and satisfying pleasure! She takes Beatrice with her and walks to the village; they slip through the church door and stand with their heads together at the lectern where the Great Bible is chained. Anne turns the rustling pages, murmurs the words to Beatrice. The book is so beautiful. Ten times more beautiful than her old Coverdale, it is an object worthy to be called Holy Scripture, the frontispiece designed with such intricate grandeur: Henry on his throne handing down the Bible in English to all his people.

'But Henry *brought* us the Word!' she bursts out. Edward motions her to quietness.

'He authorized it, yes,' he says, his voice low. 'He did not *enjoin* it. He had different voices in his ear then—Cromwell's for one, and Cranmer's, and even Hugh Latimer's. Now he heeds the whispers of that snake Stephen Gardiner, and Norfolk, even Thomas Wriothesley, I'm told. They murmur in the king's ear that it is this reading of the Word in English which causes disquiet in the kingdom.' Edward reaches again for her hands. 'I ask you only to take care, Anne. You have your Coverdale. Read it in the privacy of your room.'

'Privacy! I have no privacy.' She jerks her hands away, glances through the leaded pane at Beatrice. The girl is standing now, looking east towards the cathedral. People are milling about. 'I am not afraid, Edward,' Anne says. 'I try to submit myself in good faith, as Saint Paul directs me, but I'll not forbear to read Christ's Holy Word! Not at my husband's admonition, and certainly not at yours! My king says not only that I *may* read it but that I *must!* I know the passage well, I have quoted it often enough: "One book of the Bible of the largest volume in English, and the same set up in some convenient place—"'

'Those are Cromwell's words! Not Henry's. And Cromwell is dead, Nan, his words are dead, and the conservatives move swiftly.

They look to deny the Scripture in English to any man below the rank of gentry, and then it is to be allowed only to men. To men, Anne. Not wives.'

She feels the blood rising in her face, her anger so lightly contained she does not know what she might do, but Edward scatters it by snapping her attention to the window. 'Look!' The square is thick with people; they begin to press together, as yesterday, squeezing back against the walls. Their faces are all turned to the east. Inside the tavern a murmured excitement is rising, and many of the merchants and burghers begin to move towards the door. 'What is it?' Anne stands to see over the heads of the people on the street. She cannot see Beatrice now. Low voices sweep through the dark room: *The king. The king. The king. His Majesty approaches!*

'Edward!' she cries out. 'It is the king!' She starts towards the door, but Edward stops her.

'Stay here with me. It's safer.'

'But—the king is coming!' Anne had not dreamt she would have another opportunity to see him. 'I must go out there!'

Edward has hold of her arm. 'I paid a hardy penny for these seats, Nan. You'll see better from here.'

She looks through the glass. It is true they are above street level, but the glass is thick, smoke-coated, wavy, partitioned into crude diamond shapes that allow no unbroken perspective, and the crowd outside is growing larger, and the men pressing back against the tavern walls are now blocking her view. 'He'll be astride his great horse,' Edward says. 'Half a man taller than anyone. You needn't worry. You'll see him.' He convinces her, and she sits. 'His Majesty comes to tour the castle,' Edward explains. 'There'll be no heralds today, but there will be noise enough announcing his approach.' Anne hears the voices outside rising at a low, steady hum; it is not so large a crowd as yesterday, nor so finely dressed, but at an equal pitch of excitement, and so dense she cannot now see the far side of the square. And then she thinks of her maid. She stands up again. 'What?' Edward says.

'I must retrieve Beatrice.'

'You'll never find her in the crush. Anyway, you're always telling me how resourceful she is. I expect she'll find a tree to climb somewhere, like Zacchaeus.' He is smiling. 'She'll be at the tavern door the moment the excitement passes. It is better to wait for her here than to be trampled in that mob.'

Anne remembers the sweat and closeness and helplessness she'd felt in the pack of men yesterday, her panic at not being able to see her son, the stink of man-sweat and horse droppings. She puts her hand to her womb, sits down. Together they watch as the mass of people sways with anticipation towards the east, washes back once more against the walls; it is like the ocean's tide sucked and pulled by the moon, though it is not the moon's force that draws them, but more like the sun's. And then the roar erupts into a great cacophony, and the people push forwards to see, and at the same time back away to make room, pressing against the window till Anne fears it will be smashed in. But the leaded partitions hold, and the huzzahs grow louder, and within a heartbeat, Anne understands that the king is passing; all the people are cheering, turning their heads slowly, following the passage, but there is no king astride a great courser rising above them—just a great ripple of movement in the centre of the square. Anne is on her feet, and still she can see nothing but the gold-fringed top of a scarlet litter gliding smoothly towards the castle. She gathers her skirts and climbs onto the chair.

'Nan!' Edward is half shocked, half laughing.

'Where is he? I see nothing!'

Edward climbs onto his own wobbly chair. He says something to Anne, but she cannot hear him for the noise outside the window; but as the tumult wanes, the people turning towards the west now, and those bowing in the centre with doffed caps now rising, the tide beginning to move and roll after the procession, Anne looks at her brother. She can hear him now: 'Really, Nan, I'm so sorry. I wanted you to see him. I did not think of this. I knew the queen would be carried in her litter, but that the king should be carried also—this never occurred to me.'

'A litter! Old sick men ride in litters! Not the King of England!' Anne glares at him. 'Why did you not let me go? I might have gotten close enough to see him!' Her brother ducks his head, a small shrug. The merchants and burghers are beginning to return now, the tavern door opening and slamming, the room filling with laughter and oaths. Edward leaps agilely from his perch, reaches up a hand to steady her as she climbs down. Anne straightens her skirts, adjusts her veil. Her hands are trembling. Her disappointment is more piercing than yesterday. Oh, why did Edward bring her here, only to create a worse disappointment? 'Will you come with me to find my maid? Never mind. I'm quite capable of strolling amongst the rabble myself.' She turns.

'Anne, wait!'

She ignores him, wades through the tide of men. At the door she is forced to step back to make way for two gentlemen trailed by their manservants; then she pushes through to the outside steps.

At once, a thousand terrors rain down. There, in the thinning square, not six rods from the tavern door, Beatrice crouches on the stones, her back bowed, her face in her hands. Above her stands Thomas Kyme, raving and roaring, and behind him is Francis, yelling at him to stop. 'Speak, you damned harlot!' Kyme shouts. 'Where is she? I'll have you flogged within an inch of your life!' He strikes Beatrice on the side of the head, and she pitches sideways to the cobblestones, silent as a sack of barley.

'Leave her!' Anne cries. She runs straight at him. 'Leave her alone!' Her husband's closed hand is raised to strike the maid again, but as Anne rushes up to him, he wheels and strikes her the prepared blow.

A sharp red blackness, a burst of light, an after-explosion of pain. Anne is sprawled on the ground before she knows she is falling; an instant later she understands that Kyme has struck her in the face with his fist. She hears her brothers shouting, the voices of other men, other women, the excited chittering of strangers, and then her brother Edward is kneeling beside her, repeating her name like a question: 'Anne? Anne? Anne?'

As soon as she is able to move, Anne rolls to her side. She pushes down her skirts to preserve modesty, but she keeps her eyes closed, in part because the throbbing in her face will not allow her to open them, but also because she does not wish to see strangers' eyes staring at her. Francis and her husband are shouting at each other, cursing, and she thinks, oh, Francis, do not argue with him, it will only bring me harder trouble. She groans, not from pain, but from dread. She feels a light touch on her back, a faint little patting, as one might pat a baby to sleep. To that sweet touch, Anne surrenders. The world closes around her.

She awakens alone. What hour it is, she does not know. There is no window. The room is very small, lit with rushlights, the bed hard and narrow. The crucifix scar on the wall, the stone niche beside it, bared of saint or Virgin, tell her this is a nun's chamber. So, she is returned to the priory. But this is not the room where she slept before with her husband. Where is William? And Beatrice? Oh, now the memory sweeps her: the blow from her husband's fist, men's voices cursing and yelling above her, the girl sprawled on the cobblestones. Anne tries to rise, but the pain knocks her back. She lies still. Her jaw aches, her neck, the back of her head. Even the winking light makes her wince.

Oh, why did she not think? When the crowd swelled to follow Henry, how did she not know Thomas Kyme would be amongst them? He'd left early, and where might he have gone but to Lincoln? She knew Beatrice was alone in the square, vulnerable as a newborn kit—she knew, but she did not put these parts together. She sees the girl pitching sideways, oh, and now she feels the blow to her own face, feels herself sprawling, the pain blossoming like a black rose across her cheek. The shame swells in her, the mortification. But then the memory: the soft, delicate, comforting touch on her back. She thinks, *It was Maddie*. She believes it was her lost sister, kneeling behind her to comfort her.

In the small room, the burning rushes cast dancing shadows, but the shadows do not make her afraid. *Though I walk in the valley of the shadow of death, I fear no evil. Thou art with me. Thy staff and thy sheephook comfort me.* They comfort me. They were comforting to me, she thinks, those soft, motherly pats. She is thirsty. She wishes Beatrice would come.

When she awakens again, her husband is leaning over her, the spite in his face bitter, puckered, small. 'You'll not see that strumpet again,' he says. 'I warned you, didn't I? She's out on the streets now, where she belongs.' Anne opens her mouth to answer, but the shooting pain makes her cry out. Her hand flies to her jaw, the tears spring sudden and hot; she glares up at him, the pain radiating. Beneath her hand, her face is swollen, taut, burning. He rears back, leering, leaves her there.

For many days she remains in the sweltering chamber, her jaw bound closed with linen as the jaws of the dead are bound, unable to talk nor chew. She finds comfort in her enforced silence, however, for she sees how it angers her husband. Her stepsister Bridget comes in the evening, gently unbinds her, holds the chalice to her lips. Anne drinks the thinned ale in tiny sips, allows the watery gruel to enter her mouth and sit clumped on her tongue until she can force herself to swallow. Even this she would not do were it not for the child: her stomach roils more fiercely when she does not eat, and so she allows her stepsister to feed her, offers silent thanks to Bridget with her eyes each day as the gossamer crack in her jawbone slowly mends.

III
She Holds Her Silence
Friskney
Autumn
1541

– Chapter 24 –

By the Feast of the Nativity of the Blessed Virgin, she is able to chew, can open her mouth to yawn a little, and yet she remains silent—not as a devotion, the way a nun might, but simply to goad Thomas Kyme. The strength of her closed mouth, the constancy of it, infuriates him. She holds her silence, in the nun's cell at St Catherine's, through the long, jarring journey to Friskney. Each step of the horse's hoof is an agony, but she does not cry out. In silence she follows him as he carries their sleeping son to his room, waits as he lays the boy down, and then she crawls onto the narrow bed beside the child and falls into a dead sleep.

It is late in the night, she is deep in her exhausted slumber, when he comes for her. He pulls her from the mattress, across the floor, over the threshold, into their chamber. She does not resist but goes entirely limp, allowing all strength and tension to drain from her body so that when he tries to hoist her onto their bed, she is boneless, formless: an unwieldy and immovable weight. His arms are strapped around her chest, but he cannot lift her onto the high mattress. He drops her to the floor. 'Lie there, then!'

She gazes up at him. He stomps to the other side of the bed, snuffs the candle, climbs onto the bedclothes, and closes the curtains, even though the room is sweltering warm. Soon she hears him snoring. She gets up and goes to the little room and lies down on the small rope bed beside William. The following night the same happens. And the next night. And the next. Each dawn the bruises beneath her arms and across her swollen breasts are darker. The fourth night, as her husband drags her, she says, through gritted teeth, 'Do not drop me again, Thomas. You are like to hurt the child.'

He does drop her, though, there and then, loosening his grip in sheer surprise, and she sinks to the floor. She lies still, looking up at him, one hand spread protectively across her womb. Her husband curses. He pulls back his bared foot as if to kick her, but he does not kick. She sees the slow recognition wash over him. 'You'll not beat this child out of me,' she says. The words come thick and garbled through her closed teeth. 'Your mother purged the first, with your help and blessing, but you'll not have this one. You'll not.' She rolls to her hands and knees, stands, returns to her son's room. Kyme does not stop her; nor does he drag her across the floor again. But from this hour, his rigid control over her grows worse.

She is forbidden to leave the house except to walk with him to the village to hear Mass. No longer is she able to slip away to stand quietly in the nave at All Saints and read. She is watched continuously, if not by Kyme himself, then by his fearful servants. The loss of Beatrice is hardest to bear, but even that punishment will not crush her. If this is Kyme's purpose, to crush me, she thinks, he has failed himself miserably. She keeps to her son's room, where she reads her Bible openly, spends hours on her knees in prayer. It might be worse, she tells herself. It surely could have been worse for Beatrice. Anne knows what Kyme does not know: that her brothers would not see the girl turned out to the streets but hid her away for a time, and then sent her home to South Kelsey. Jane came to the priory when they were all yet at Lincoln and whispered in Anne's ear that secret news.

A brisk autumn morning. Anne sits on the three-legged stool next to her son's bed, her sister's tattered Coverdale open on her lap, her stub of candle drawn near—there is little natural light here—while the boy plays on the floor near her feet. The child chatters endlessly, as if to compensate for his mother's silence, but he seems not to mind that they are always together, most often alone and most often in this small room, which is always close, a bit foul, for there is no fresh air here, and the linens want washing. The boy will be hungry soon, Anne thinks. He'll begin to ask for food, and she'll need to carry him downstairs to beg morsels from Cook, who doles to Anne and the boy precisely what Kyme says they must have, though sometimes he'll add the tiniest ort more if he thinks it can be spared without discovery. Anne is pondering how to persuade from him, with pleading gestures and hungry eyes, a bite of leftover mutton to go with their bread, when her husband enters the tiny room. The boy flinches when he sees his father. Kyme hoists the child by the arm and carries him, howling, two long strides to the door, where he sets him on the floor on the other side, shuts the door against his wails. Anne maintains her empty, flat expression, though the boy's cries pull at her—and what new condemnation is this? What punishment? Hers, or young Will's? Hers, no doubt.

It is because I did not go with him to Mass yesterday, she thinks. For weeks her bound jaw allowed her to remain at home when Thomas walked with his son and the servants to All Saints. But her jaw is healed now, the binding discarded. Nevertheless, yesterday, in thin morning light, when he commanded her to rise and dress for Mass, Anne sat on the bed in her linen smock, undressed, unwashed, refusing in her cold, stubborn silence to go with him. Kyme had been furious as he slammed out of the room.

But she sees now, as her husband turns from the locked door, his face cold, determined, that this is not why. He steps towards her. Against her will, Anne flinches and shrinks back; her hands close around the book, but he wrests it from her. Methodically, without apparent anger but with appalling strength, he begins to rend it; he balances the spine with one hand against his chest, and with the other he tears out pages. 'The vicar says wives should not,' Kyme grinds out between gritted teeth. 'Therefore, thou shalt not.' The worn folio comes apart with a sound like ripped membrane; it tears at her teeth, her chest. Anne watches without speaking, though her soul cries out in protest. She has been so careful! Each morning she turns the pages gently, as if they are delicate as blown glass; each night she wraps the book in linen when she puts it away. Her sister's Coverdale was ever poorly made, of cheapest paper and ink, thinly glued, but for all that, and for all the book has suffered these five years, the words of God had been legible. In grief she watches the book disintegrate slowly beneath her husband's hands. The torn pages in large, ragged shreds rain down upon her. Outside the door, her son howls.

Now, for a time, Anne is truly bereft. Without her Bible to read, without Beatrice to hear, without sunlight or air or the chattering presence of her son—for Kyme has removed the child to their old chamber and hired a village woman to care for him—Anne feels her strength waver. She realizes she knows only bits and scraps of Scripture, words that have stayed in her mind as she read, some held there intentionally, others unbidden: *In the beginning was the Word and the Word was with God . . . for God so loved the world that He gave his only begotten Son . . . wives, submit yourselves to your husbands as you do to the Lord, Jesus wept, Jesus wept.*

Jesus wept.

One bright frostbitten morning, Anne rises from her knees beside the bed, teeth chattering, jaw aching, her breath a white mist in the frigid air. She dresses herself in her mothy wool—two smocks beneath, two kirtles, one set of sleeves, a simple coif and veil, slightly soiled—and strides briskly into her husband's room. He is not there. Brilliant sunlight slashes across the floor through the side window. She goes down the stairs, crosses the frosted yard towards the road. The October sun makes her squint. Without haste, looking neither right nor left, she walks the cold mile to the church. She leaves the door agape behind her when she enters, goes directly to the wooden lectern near the chancel where the Great Bible is chained. With trembling fingers—more from cold than from fear—she lays open the great board. Her eyes graze the frontispiece, which she has traced many times: Henry on his throne handing down the Word of God, Cranmer and Cromwell on either side, the people below crying out *Vivat Rex! Vivat Rex!* and in the clouds above, Jesu Christo, small, benignant, mild, His arms open in blessing as He gazes down upon His servant, the disseminator of His Word, King Henry VIII. She turns the pages until she arrives at the centre, begins to read aloud, starting low and quiet, but soon she is reading as audibly as any priest might intone his Latin. Her back is towards the door. Her voice is calm, distinct, slightly raised. She has not spoken a word aloud in fifty-three days, yet she does not croak or whisper. For half an hour she reads undisturbed, until a passing hod carrier, hearing a woman's voice inside the church, pauses, looks in, then hurries off to find the vicar.

Thomas Jordan, when he arrives, does as the hod carrier had done: stands outside the door and listens. He recognizes the voice—or he presumes it; for what other woman in all the parish would do as Mistress Kyme does? What others have even the knowledge of reading? The words are, he thinks, from the Book of Psalms: *In the Lord put I my trust: how will ye then say to my soul that she should fly as a bird upon your hill?* A pause. A rustling whisper as a page is turned. The vicar steps through the door. 'Ah, Mistress Kyme!' he says, as if surprised to discover her. 'I'd no expectation to find you here. May I ask what you are doing?'

'"For lo, the ungodly have bent their bow and made ready their arrows in the quiver,"' Anne answers, without looking at him, '"that they may privately shoot at them which are true of heart."'

'Have you your husband's permission to be here?'

'"For the foundations will be cast down,"' Anne reads, '"and what have the righteous done?"'

All pretence gone, he swoops towards her, robes flapping: a black crow with wolf eyes. 'Cease, woman! Wanton! Abominably trained!'

She places her finger on the page to trace the words: '"His eyes consider the poor: and his eyelids try the children of men."'

The vicar's hand clamps down upon hers, his signet ring like a branding iron searing ice and not fire into her skin as he scrapes her hand from the Book. 'I know well that your husband has not given you permission to be here! He comes to me daily with his complaints: she is at all hours at the Bible and on her knees, she neglects her wifely duties, closets herself away from her husband to read that heretical translation. I told him: Remove it! Take it from her! Show your wife her proper place!'

'My place is here.' Her eyes are steady upon him: the same mild gaze with which she so infuriates her husband. 'Do you not know the law, Father? Shall I quote it for you? "One book of the Bible of the largest volume in English, and the same set up in some convenient place within the said church that ye have care of, whereas your parishioners may most commodiously resort to the same and read it." Am I not your parishioner, sir? According to the king's decree, then, I am following the law, for I have most commodiously resorted here to read it.'

'The law does not say that you are to make a spectacle of yourself,' he hisses, 'and swank about the chancel and simper.'

'Simper?'

'You are too bold, Mistress Kyme! Get thee home and return not to this place until your husband returns with thee!'

Anne laughs. In fury the vicar turns and storms out of the church—scurrying off, as Anne will soon learn, in search of Thomas Kyme. She reaches forth her hand, gently smooths the vellum. Softly, aloud, she reads: '"Upon the ungodly he shall rain snares, fire and brimstone, storm and tempest: this shall be their portion to drink."' She repeats the words aloud as she commits them to memory. She goes on to the next verse, softly, her voice calm, her heart full.

At the door are gathered some village women. She senses them first, then turns to look. There are three, in dingy linen caps and soiled aprons, their eyes huge, their faces aghast. I have given them something strong to gossip about this night, Anne thinks. At their skirts are four children, foremost among them a little girl of perhaps eight or nine years, with tatty brown hair and a dirty face, her fist clutching a toddler boy's hand. Anne smiles at her. She turns back to the tome and leafs through the pages. When she comes to the Book of Saint Matthew, she finds her place, the xix chapter. '"Jesus said unto them, suffer the children, and forbid them not to come to me, for unto such belongeth the kingdom of heaven."' She turns to look. The children are solemn. Their mothers the same. Anne reads on.

By the time she reaches the end of the chapter, the women are well inside the door, and the little girl, still clutching her brother's hand, stands halfway along the nave. By the time the vicar returns with Thomas Kyme, Anne has reached the xxiii chapter, and the women are standing in a half circle at her back, listening. '"Woe unto you, scribes and Pharisees, hypocrites! for ye devour widows' houses—"' When the men enter, the women scatter, bobbing and begging pardon, clutching their children's hands. The little girl is the last to disappear, dragged along by her mother, turning to cast one last lingering look towards Anne as she is pulled away.

Anne's husband charges towards her.

'Hello, Thomas,' she says. 'Must you break my jaw again? Here in the house of the Lord and before the very eyes of the village?' Thomas halts, turns to look. Townsmen have followed them and now stand four deep at the door, elbowing one another for a better view. Anne places her hand on her swelling belly, the ancient gesture, says clearly and distinctly: 'Will you slay this child, too, as you did our first?' A small gasp from the crowd. 'Will you chain me, bind me, gag me to keep me from coming here to read God's Word? "Husbands, love your wives." Does not Paul say this? Oh, but you would not know, for you have never read it. Therefore I will tell you: Yes. Yes, Saint Paul says: "Husbands, love your wives, even as Christ loved the church"!'

The vicar stands at Kyme's elbow, whispering, 'Forbid her! Discipline her!' But Thomas Kyme has heard no utterance from his wife's lips for two months—that she speaks at all stuns him. That she speaks with such cold clarity confounds him. He falters, looks from his wife to the priest to the villagers at the door. Anne pages through the Bible to Saint Paul's letter to the Ephesians: '"So ought men to love their wives as their own bodies,"' she reads. '"He that loveth his wife loveth himself." Do you not love yourself, Thomas? I think perhaps you do not; for I know well that you do not love me.'

With both hands she lifts the heavy pages from the left, the weighted cover, folds it over to close the Great Bible. She dips a shallow curtsy to the vicar, walks through the silent nave, her shoes making a quiet rhythm on the stone floor; she parts the crowd at the church entrance, descends the limestone steps, and begins the walk towards the manor, where her son is.

From this hour, Anne is changed. The forces that have moulded her have been cumulative: from her conversion in the manor chapel as her young brother lay suffering to the pain-filled nights at the priory as her jaw healed; from her despair at the loss of Beatrice through long weeks of fasting and reading and prayer, to the final hammer blow: the destruction of her English Bible. Maddie's book. God's Holy Word. The last precious piece of her sister on this earth. A determination has settled in Anne, a strength and a kind of fearless serenity. Through the chilly autumn into the dark of winter, as her belly swells, she returns to the church when she chooses, reads the Word as she wishes, commits long passages to memory. Sometimes the village women see her walking and slip away from their tasks to follow, stand at the door, and listen. Anne makes no set pattern; she may come once in a week, or thrice, then not again for a fortnight. Neither her husband nor the vicar nor the village women know when she will 'most commodiously resort to the same and read' (how she loves the phrase!), but she believes she has the force of law behind her, despite Edward's vague warnings in Lincoln; more importantly, she has the will of God. She goes when her husband is occupied with work and cannot set for her an argument. He does not raise his hand to her again, whether from shame or instruction of the vicar, or perhaps even the force of her own strength, she does not know. Only once, early on, as she wraps herself in her woollen cloak for the walk, does Kyme enter their chamber. 'Where do you think you're going? No! You shall not! I forbid it!' But Anne lifts her head. The unabashed gaze. She smiles at him. 'You should not have destroyed it, Thomas. Then might I remain at home to read.' She pulls the woollen cowl over her headdress, goes on her way.

Book Three

Lincolnshire

1543–1544

I

My Reputation Flies before Me

Friskney

Spring

1543

– Chapter 25 –

Francis writes that I must comport myself 'in a more conformable manner.' Conformable to what? I might ask. Or to whom? But I know his intention: the will of my husband, he means, and the Vicar Jordan and that unholy murther of priests at Wrangle and Wainfleet, and also, no doubt, such men at Westminster as attempt to change God's laws to suit their schemes. I have word of that already from Edward: they have passed their statute forbidding the free reading of Holy Scripture in English, just as he warned me almost two years ago they would do. My ears were deaf then, that hard day in Lincoln, but I see now how true Edward told me.

But God is not mocked, and His laws cannot be changed by lords and commons at Westminster, no more than by these dreary fenland priests, nor by the prelates at Lincoln, who, Francis's letter assures me, condemn me for 'a certain contumacious woman in Friskney, high-stomached and prideful, who would argue with priests.' My reputation flies before me, Francis says, and my family grumbles that their good name is linked to a woman of poor repute. My family? It is Francis himself who grumbles, I think. 'Henceforth,' he writes, 'thou must keep to thy home and thy wifely duties.'

Or else what? I think.

My home and my wifely duties. Indeed. And what of my duty to my Lord and Saviour? What has Christ Jesus charged me to do?

And what would Edward say to Francis's admonition? Two letters from my two brothers, both set about with warnings, both in the same week. Edward's letter I have hidden. Two days later, Francis's own messenger stood at awkward attention while I read the letter twice again. 'Wait here,' I told him, and went quickly to the desk where Thomas keeps his records, picked up the quill, uncapped the inkpot, and turned my brother's letter over to the unblemished backside to write:

> Brother, I commend me very heartily unto you, trusting in the living Lord that you be in health, and daily praying that you continue in the same. As to your concerns: if my reputation must suffer for how I serve my Lord, then why should I protest? For what else doth Christ teach us? As it is written in the ix chapter of the Gospel of Saint Luke: 'For whosoever shall be ashamed of me and of my words, of him shall the Son of man be ashamed.' I am not ashamed, Francis, and must do as Christ bids me. And how is my maid Beatrice? Please to give her my kind regards and tell her I remember her often, and also commend me to thy lady wife Lisbeth, and to our stepmother Elizabeth. Oh, how I should love to see her face! Tell her that Father's namesake here, my William, grows tall and sturdy, and waxes strong. As I trust your son William does also. And now in haste, for the hour runneth quickly, I close. By the hand of your loving sister, Anne Kyme.

I rushed the messenger to his horse with a flagon of ale, his pannier stuffed with victuals, that he might be well gone by the time my husband should return home. Then I went to the boys' chamber to read to them until my husband's return—at least as much as young Thom would allow me. He is such a fussy child, our Thomas, and demands more of me than ever did Will at this age. He is forever climbing out of his cradle and creeping fast across the floor, dirtying his gown and getting into everything. He can toddle when he wishes, but such slow ambulation is not swift enough for him: he drops to all fours and creeps fast as a whippet, or he cries and wails, 'Hold you! Hold you!' demanding to be picked up. He cannot be contented then until I lift him to my shoulder and stride about the chamber, though he is chuffy as a little shoat and much wearies my arms. William, meanwhile, contents himself at our feet. They are as unalike as two brothers may be, Will and Thom, and here's the wonder of it: their father dotes on the younger, his namesake, as he thinks, who is fretful and demanding and in appearance a dead-out Ayscough, and is hardest on the elder, his heir, who is his very image for likeness and the kindest child in the world.

I sang to Thomas until he slept, and then I took William on my knee to show him the drawings in my prayer book and read to him until he, too, fell asleep. I laid him on the bed beside his brother, the hangings open to catch the breeze. Only then did I have time to fully ponder the meaning of Francis's letter. There was a sternness in the language that is not like him. His gruffness I am familiar with, but not this stern and staid manner. *Keep to thy home and thy wifely duties.* This does not sound like Francis. Worrier that he is, and burdened as he always believes himself to be with the fortunes of this family, he nevertheless exhorts us through charm and cajoling, and there is not a whiff of cajoling in that letter; and as for charm, a winter badger has more. As I thought on it and prayed, asking the Lord's guidance, I came to see the letter's true meaning: Thomas Kyme set him to write it. Of course. But when? Did my husband travel to South Kelsey sometime to persuade Francis? Perhaps he contrived to meet him at Lincoln. Oh, it hardly matters. I know the source of the injunction, the *why* if not the *how*: Thomas Kyme sees he will never control me. He harangues and forbids me, threatens to beat me; he has had the priest to lecture me and give me false penance, and still he cannot keep me from the Lord's work. Last winter he discharged the nurse who minded the children so that there would be no one to care for them when I walk to the church. I am not dissuaded. I take the boys with me. Now Kyme hopes to persuade me through family obligation, but this will have no better effect than the others.

I looked to the window. The sun was lowering. The yearning was strong in me then to walk to All Saints. It is not the edifice that draws me, not the glass windows with their images of saints and disciples and the widow's mite, but the blessed Word of God chained like a prisoner at the lectern—but for how long? Edward's words in his letter repeated themselves before me: *The forces of wickedness are in the ascendancy.* I went to William's room, pulled the small cedar chest from the wall. It is my dead sister's carved dowry chest, where I first laid my hand upon God's Word. Now it holds, in secret, beneath William's little linen gowns and tunics, Edward's letter, which reached me surreptitiously two days ago, and which I'd read in haste then, being mindful that Kyme would be calling for his supper, and also, I confess, misliking its news. Now mine eyes traced again Edward's words:

> Mind yourself, Anne. Mind all that I have told you. The forces of wickedness are in the ascendancy—Norfolk, Gardiner, their enterprising minions. They'll not stop till all of England is returned to papist superstition and idolatry!

He named then the law: An Act for the Advancement of True Religion and for the Abolishment of the Contrary.

> Hear me, dear one, and take heed. This is the very language of the law: 'No woman or artificers, prentices, journeymen, servingmen of the degree of yeomen or under, husbandmen nor labourers, shall read the New Testament in English.'

I traced, and traced again, the words: *No woman.*

> It is better that you read in the privacy of your home, your quiet little room alone, than to have no recourse at all. Put on the armour of God. I shall tell you more when I see you, God grant it, though I know not when that will be.

But Edward knows that I have no Bible to read in the privacy of my home. I have written him about it. *Put on the armour of God.* It is in

Paul's letter to the Ephesians. Put on the armour of God, something, something . . .

I stood and walked about the tiny room, reciting. '"For we wrestle not against flesh and blood, but against rule, against power, namely against the rulers of the darkness of this world."'

Yes. And after? What comes after?

'"Stand therefore . . ."'

Through the open window I heard my husband's voice hallo the house. He'll see to his horse, I thought, and the day's count of new lambs before he comes in. And then he'll be ravenous, demanding his supper. I should go down and see that Cook has all to the ready. I continued pacing.

And if the Bible may not be read by any but prelates, lords, and gentlemen, I thought, glancing down at Edward's words, does this mean the king's men will come and remove the Great Bible from All Saints? Will they remove English Bibles from all the churches in England, carry them to London, and pile them in a great heap in front of Paul's Cross and burn them, as was done with Tyndale's Testaments? My heart tightened. I refolded and replaced Edward's letter. In our chamber I paused to lay the bolster beside the baby so that he might not roll off. I knew I must hurry. I wanted to be gone before Kyme finished in the stables.

Put on the whole armour of God, I said to myself.

Stand therefore, and your loins gird about with truth.

Yes. And then what is it? What does it say?

Take the helmet of salvation and the sword of the spirit,
which is the word of God.

– Chapter 26 –

The glass shows her eyes black, her throat swollen, striated with perfect violet marks the shape of his thumbs and fingers. She reaches up, feels the naked, plucked place on the top of her head from where he dragged her up the stairs by her hair. She'd not been afraid for herself then but for her sons wailing and shrieking on the bed. Here now, upon the same bed, in gloomy daylight, Anne lowers the glass to the coverlet, lies very still. The house is silent. She remembers pleading with him to carry her to the other room so that their sons would not see. Or trying to plead. But Kyme's fingers were too tight about her throat. 'I'll kill you.' A low one-note growl in his throat. 'I'll kill you, I'll kill you, I'll kill you.' And she'd believed that he would. The ceiling tilted then, the room swam dark, and she swooned.

When she came awake—how much later? she cannot tell—she lay sprawled on the floor, and Thomas Kyme was sitting beside her, weeping. On the bed, the boys were huddled against the headboard. William held his baby brother between his legs, both arms around him. The children were quiet then, or in any case she could not hear them over the groans and sobs of her husband; she could see young Will's shoulders heaving, his chin trembling. *Oh, my poor child,* her heart cried. She'd smiled at him to tell him all was well. But his eyes did not believe her.

Kyme had ridden her down on the road to Friskney—he was beside her before she'd registered the sound of hoofbeats and could run. He'd snatched her up by one arm and heaved her over the horse's withers, the pommel gouging her stomach, and cantered back to the manor yard. Her old trick to fall limp and unresisting served no purpose but that he'd dragged her over the threshold on her back by her arms. Then her coif was torn off and the top of her head was burning fire as he pulled her up the stairs by her hair, the back of her head thumping against the wood, thumping and thumping. And then she heard her sons' screams.

The silence in the manor now is painful, deep and cold, like a tomb. Kyme has taken their sons to his cousin Margaret in Wrangle. He will not say when he'll allow them to return. Last night he brought the vicar to look at her, to show the priest how he had disciplined his wife. This, Anne knows, is the cause for his great fury, for he said as much as he sat weeping and groaning on the floor beside her: that he is seen by the priest and the people of the village as a man who cannot control his wife. A weak man, a nowter. A powerless and impotent fellow with an unquiet marriage, who has never been, and shall never be, as high and mighty as his high and mighty wife. She remembers the vicar's cold eyes as he stood gazing down at her. 'I shall pray for you, Mistress Kyme,' he said. 'And do you the same, in true contrition, that you may be forgiven; for our Lord is merciful. I trust that henceforth we'll not see you standing in the chancel mouthing heresies or gadding up and down the country corrupting our servants and children. Keep to thy home, woman, and to thy wifely duties, that thy husband and his household be found pleasing in God's sight.'

Keep to thy home and thy wifely duties.

So Anne knew then who had directed Francis what to say. If my reputation spreads, she thinks now, struggling to swallow, it is the cruel vicar who spreads it. She closes her eyes, listening to the silence. She throbs all over, it hurts to turn her head. She hears the heavy clomp of Kyme's boots on the stairs. Her breath quickens. Her chest tightens. The tang of lanolin and sheep dung. She turns her head, and the pain shoots. He stands at the door, cap in hand. His brow is broad and red, glistening with sweat. He wears his shamed dog look. 'Cook wants to know will you be having your dinner?' he says. 'You've not eaten in two days. You'll not get your strength back this way.'

'I am strong enough.' Her voice creaks like a jaybird's.

'It is time you were up and about and tending to your household. I cannot be minding my own tasks and my wife's both.' His words are harsh, but his tone is surprisingly gentle. What? she thinks. Does he believe I'll find him gentle now?

'When I am up and about, Master Kyme,' she says, 'I doubt you'll like the tasks I shall be attending.'

He blinks and stares. Suddenly the pretend gentleness is gone. He comes to stand over her. '"Oh, it is the king's *decree*."' His voice trills, his eyes roll: mocking her. '"We parishioners must repair to our churches and—" How does it go? Say it!'

'"Whereas your parishioners may most commodiously resort to the same and read it."'

He shows his teeth. 'But I have news for you, wife. Parliament has made a new law! Shall I tell it to you? The Bible is not to be read by any woman in England!' His face gleams with triumph, but Anne merely looks at him. It is no news to her. Edward's letter said the same. Her calmness infuriates him. 'With mine own ears I heard it declared! At Wainfleet! In the town square!'

'The town crier cried the law?'

'Not the crier, the vicar of Saint Mary's. He read it out loud, that all the priests gathered from across the diocese might hear. So you see, wife, you have no justification.' His grimace grows wider, his gloating face more sinister, and she knows now why the beating was so vicious: he'd thought to return home and confound her with this news, and instead found her walking to All Saints—his great triumph diminished into scrabbling on the road after his wife. His dignity was damaged. Always it is about his dignity. 'You have no recourse in the law *now*,' he says. 'To go gadding about reading and spouting nonsense like a madwoman. Here is the law for your obedience: a wife must be in submission to her husband!'

'Not if he would murder her, Thomas. The law does not say that.'

'You're not dead, are you?'

Anne pulls aside her gown, turns her neck to show him. She watches his eyes. 'I ought to go to Francis and let him see how you've used me.'

'I have corrected you, that is all—as a husband must do when his wife comports herself unseemly and neglects her duties.' He leans over her, teeth gritted, speaking low: 'Or when she spouts heresies in her own home which, if he were to denounce her to the authorities, would kill her far quicker than he.' He steps away again, his look at once victorious and sly. 'Your brother agrees with me. As he has told you from his own hand.'

'And how would you know that? No, let me guess. From the Vicar Jordan? That papist priest with whom you conspire daily.'

'He is not a papist! It is against the law to be a papist.'

'Is it?' Anne rolls to her side, every movement a stab wound, and climbs out of bed.

'You think me ignorant, don't you?' Kyme growls. 'You think I do not know things, but I know things. I know the law confirms the sacraments, and that your heretical teachings do not.'

She pulls herself upright, turns to face him. 'It cannot be heresy to follow the true Word of God.'

'Who says it is the true word? Vicar says it is based on Tyndale's translations, and he was strangled for a heretic.'

'Ah, strangling is the proper end for a heretic?' Anne touches her bruised throat. 'And here I thought the law said a heretic must burn.'

'Will you never shut your smart mouth! I ought to send you back to your family as Vicar advises!'

'Send me, then! I should be only too happy to return to South Kelsey!'

'You think your brother will welcome you with open arms? I promise you, he will not. He loathes the rumours about you! I've spoken at length with him.'

'When?'

'It is not your business when. Your business is to tend to your sons and your wifely duties!' Kyme leans towards her. 'You know, as I know, that above all else, the mighty Francis Ayscough cares about his own advancement. He'll not cherish a sister who impedes that in any way.'

She continues to glare at him, but her heart sinks. For she knows it is true. 'My brother loves me,' she says. 'He esteems his family above all things.'

'I have the authority of Parliament behind me to make you cease your reading and prating, and your brother will enforce it no less than I.'

'My brother believes in the gospel.'

'Hah! Your pompous brother Edward at court, perhaps. Not Francis. Francis believes in Francis. The world is not as it was, wife. We return to the true religion daily, hourly, so Vicar says, and now we have the law to prove him.'

'"True religion,"' she says flatly. It is a slip of his tongue. *True religion* is what papists call the old ways; it is how they cloak their desire to return to the authority of Rome. 'Do you quote the vicar now,' Anne says, 'or only your own papist yearnings?'

'I have not said that!'

'Haven't you? I see we have a mighty union here, Master Kyme. A most even-handed marriage. How shall it end, I wonder. Perhaps you'll denounce me to the authorities and see me burnt for a heretic? Or I could denounce you for the secret papist you are and see you hanged, drawn, and quartered, like those Carthusian traitors.'

'I'll slap that froward tongue right out of your mouth!'

'Ah. Then I should have to write a note to Francis when I arrive tongueless, to explain what you have done to me.' She turns and makes her way across the floor to the clothespress. Suddenly her husband is behind her, gripping her by the shoulders, digging his fingers. Anne stands very still. 'It is not only the vicar who knows what you did to me,' she says quietly. 'It is all the household. The servant boy sees my blackened eyes when he comes for the chamber pot. He sees your cruel lacerations at my throat. Whose work most damages your fine reputation?'

In fury he shoves her into the clothespress. The pain bolts through her, face to groin, and it is only seconds later, as an echo, that she realizes how hard he slammed the door as he left. Vicious enough to break it off its hinge.

II

Have I No Allies Here?

South Kelsey

Summer

1543

– Chapter 27 –

They stood in the manor yard, staring at me. I could tell nothing from their faces, neither Francis nor his lady wife, Lisbeth, nor our step-mother nor any of the servants gathered to witness my ignominious arrival. I thought, blessed Jesu, have I no allies here? I saw Beatrice then, standing back behind Lisbeth; she did not meet my gaze. I could scarcely recognize her, she has grown so tall. 'So, Anne.' Francis cleared his throat. 'Must I say you welcome? Shall I . . .' He gestured vaguely. He wore his velvet robe and feathered cap, though the day was warm already; he must have been preparing to travel somewhere. Or preparing for visitors? Not this visitor: not his disgraced sister, cast out violently by her husband and sent to him on a dray mare accompanied only by a turnspit. I dismounted, stood waiting. They stared at my face in silence. I've not seen a glass, but I know what I look like. My fourth beating in three months. Not the worst, no, but I pray God it is the last. Mother Elizabeth came from behind Francis and kissed me. I could have wept with relief. But I held my expression still.

'You'll sleep in Thom's room,' she said. 'They're razing the east wing, there is no habitable place to sleep there.' She turned and made her way up the steps. Lisbeth, following her grandmother's example, came to me and kissed me. 'When you're settled, you must come to the solar. We are sewing a dozen new smocks for the poor women in Lincoln. I'll send up food if you're hungry. Ought we . . . to send for the surgeon?' She glanced uncertainly from me to Francis.

'There's no need,' I said. 'I've no bones broken, no bleeding wounds. Bruises will heal.' I glanced again at Beatrice, or rather at the place where Beatrice had been standing, but she'd vanished, along with the rest of the household servants. Did Francis give an order I hadn't heard?

'Come,' Lisbeth said, and motioned me to follow. I had no trunk or satchel to have sent up. I wore the clothes he'd cast me out of the house in and brought nothing more. I heard Francis directing the turnspit to the stables as I followed my sister-in-law into the great hall. Kyme had sent the boy with me, not for my protection, but to be certain to get his mare back. He always makes good on his threats, does Master Thomas Kyme. I might wish he had not taken so long to make good on this last one, to cast me out of my house, were it not for my children. He thinks by shaming me, he will bend me to his will. He thinks by withholding my sons from me, he can cause me to be other than I am. But how can I? It is neither my nature nor God's purpose.

'You'll be comfortable here,' Lisbeth said, opening the door to young Thom's room. 'Francis had the furnishings changed, all the hangings and bedding. Grandmother would have kept it all, but . . .' A shrug. *You know Francis*. 'Edward and Christopher stay here when they're visiting from London.' She crossed the room to push open the shutter; light and air poured in, the scent of meadowsweet and yarrow. 'We do keep it closed when they're not here.' She turned to smile at me. The smile drained away slowly; there remained an expression of quiet horror.

'Do I look so ghastly?' I said.

She came to me, lifted a hand as if to touch my cheek, dropped it back down. A worried frown knit her brow; her eyes roved my face as if marking the number of bruises. 'Francis is devastated,' she said.

'Francis is.'

'He is furious.'

'With me?'

'No! Of course not! Well, perhaps a little.' She shrugged. 'Only that the conflict remains so raw between you and Master Kyme. But his fury is greater that his sister should be so used.' I suppose my scepticism must have shown, for she said as if I'd argued: 'You are his sister, Anne. How would he not be furious? He loathes how your husband treats you. I've often heard him say it.'

'I wish he'd had such concern when our father compelled me to marry him.'

She looked at me. 'Francis could not help that.'

I saw then what I had not really considered: Lisbeth loves my brother. Or in any case she will defend him. She wants him to be right.

'No. I suppose not.' I turned to the room, a sorrow welling beyond my ability to contain it, and also an incredible fatigue. 'I think I should like to rest now. May I rest? I'll come sew with you later.'

'Of course!' She took my hand, held it between hers. 'You'll be fine,' she whispered. 'Francis will take care of everything.' She squeezed my palm and went out. I wish I had the confidence in my brother his lady wife seems to have. I thought back on the letter, not two months past, written in my brother's own hand. *Conform thyself. Keep to thy wifely duties.* I felt an old aching bruise in my chest. I walked to the window, returned and circled the bed, paced to the door, again to the window. I saw then the turnspit coming from the stable on the little pack pony he'd ridden, leading the larger mare. He'll sleep in straw on a stable floor tonight, I thought, remembering how Kyme had thrown a few coins into the dirt, enough for only one night's lodging. The turnspit climbed down from the pony and scrambled to collect them. I would have left them there.

A timid knock at the door. I opened it quickly, hoping it was Beatrice, but it was a boy from the kitchen carrying a tray with a napkin-covered trencher, a goblet of wine. The child stared open-mouthed at my face. I scowled at him, made a dark grimace, and out he scuttled.

The next knock, perhaps a half hour later, was not timid but firm, three sound raps of clean authority, and so I knew better than to hope for Beatrice. I went to the door, assuming and dreading it to be Francis—I did not feel prepared to speak with him—but it was

Dame Elizabeth. She cradled a basin of water, a white cloth folded on the basin's lip, clean linens beneath her arm.

'Come in,' I said, breathless. 'Come in, Mother. Here, let me take these.'

She shrugged me off, carried her burdens to the washstand. There was a long moment before she turned to look at me. 'Sit,' she said. I lowered myself to the joint stool. She removed my coif and veil. The water stung with herbs, but I did not flinch. I closed my eyes. She pressed the warm cloth against them. The soothing scent of comfrey and rue. 'Who is caring for your children?' she asked.

It was a while before I could speak. 'I don't know. The last time, he sent them to his cousin Margaret.'

'The last time.' An acknowledgement, not a question.

I nodded. She lifted away the cloth, but still I kept my eyes closed. I thought I would shatter if I looked at her. My throat worked, I could not swallow the sobs. I heard the little trickle of water as she wrung the cloth into the basin. Now the rustle of her skirts as she moved to sit, a little grunt and a sigh as she hoisted herself onto the bed. I opened my eyes but trained my gaze on her pale slippers peeking out from beneath her hem.

'I take it we're to understand,' she said, 'that your husband has put you away from him?' This, too, was more comment than question, though her voice lifted at the end. I glanced up to see her face. She is as beautiful as ever, even now, though more lined and faded. Like Francis and Lisbeth, she has put on flesh. The Ayscough household eats well at South Kelsey Hall, clearly. 'Of course, Francis will go and talk to him,' she said, 'but I do not know what good it will do. He's talked to him before, he's censured him, threatened him, even, I believe.' She gazed at my face, her expression resigned and sad. 'I cannot see the solution, Anne.'

I said nothing. I have seen a solution, but I thought it best not to say.

'It is unfortunate you don't believe in the saints,' she said lightly. 'You might pray to Saint Uncumber for deliverance.'

'I believe in some saints. I believe in Saint Matthew. I believe in Saints Mark, Luke, and John. I believe in Saint Peter, Saint Stephen, the Apostle Saint Paul.'

'But not she who delivers wives from their abusive husbands?'

'I believe in those whose names appear in Holy Scripture.'

She sighed. 'That again.' My stepmother is not a friend to the gospel. She is not opposed, necessarily, but nor does she seek it. She remains very traditional in her religious practice and her prayers.

'I've never known a wooden saint to deliver a poor wife from her husband,' I said. 'Have you?'

'I don't know. So the stories say.'

'The stories say the saints may grow new limbs and open sealed wombs, they say all sorts of things. I could make a thousand pilgrimages to any shrine you like, and it would make no difference in my situation. Saints cannot intercede to God for us. And indeed, we need no intercession, for we have the very Lamb of God seated at His right hand to serve as our Intercessor. Saint Paul says in his epistle to the Romans—'

'You have grown marvellously tedious, Anne.'

I met her eyes in silence for a time, then turned away.

'I'm sorry,' she said. 'I don't mean to be unkind. But, as I understand, it is this perpetual spouting of Scripture that causes such dissension in your household.'

'It is not that. I promise you.'

'Francis will do what he can. I just think you might try to be more cooperative at home.'

'I should conform myself, should I? Deny my faith?'

'I didn't say that.'

'You seem to have changed your views of my brother. Before their marriage, in this very room, you told me you'd as soon his marriage to Lisbeth not go forward. Now you parrot his words.'

'Francis is good to my granddaughter. He progresses in the world and carries us with him. I'll not speak against him.'

'Will you tell him I'm not yet well enough to come down? I shall be with them at dinner tomorrow, and afterwards I'll join Lisbeth and her women at their sewing.'

Her expression was blank, unrevealing, as she gazed across at me. 'I'll tell him,' she said. With a few pushes of her arms and a few small grunts, she stood up from the bed, stepped to the table to collect the basin and washing cloth. 'Here are clean linens for you. They're Lisbeth's, but I think they'll fit. Perhaps a bit large.'

'Thank you, Mother.' She turned to look at me. I wanted to kneel in front of her, kiss her hands. 'I have missed you,' I said. 'I truly have.'

'And we have missed you, Anne.'

'Really? Your froward stepdaughter with her reckless tongue?'

'Even she.' She smiled. 'Change into these and rest. I'll send someone with your supper.'

'May I . . . do you think I might have Beatrice? For my maidservant again?'

'Beatrice serves Lisbeth now.' My disappointment must have shown, for she added, 'Ask Francis. If Lisbeth agrees, he'll allow it, I suppose, for the time you are here.'

'And how long will that be?'

'You must ask your brother that as well.'

'Until he is able to threaten and charm and cajole Thomas Kyme into being a different man than he is? I'll be here till the end of glory, in that case.'

'Many women make bad marriages, Anne.' She smiled sadly, started towards the door.

'I am not going back.'

Mother Elizabeth halted.

'I'm not sure where I'll go,' I said, 'but I shall not return to Thomas Kyme.'

'But you shall.'

'I shall not.'

'You cannot abandon your children, Anne.'

'I've not abandoned them! I've been torn away! Cast out!'

'And you shall return to them, and love them, and cherish them, and train them up in the way they should go.'

'And pray to Saint Uncumber to deliver me from the hopeless torment of my marriage?'

She looked at me a moment, her lips clamped. A wash of sorrow swept her face. Without speaking again, she turned and went out.

It is just as well, I thought. What good to argue? No purpose to argue, to tell her again what she is unwilling to hear: that I cannot be shaken from what I have already determined. I will not live in the same house with him. I'll gain my children somehow, and I will not return; for there is one threat Thomas Kyme has yet to fulfil, which he vowed again yesterday, with his hands at my throat: that he will kill me.

I pray for strength, I pray for discernment, and a good plan, but I have no doubt as to the rightness of my course and the righteousness of my matter. Kyme would fulfil this threat, as he has fulfilled all the others, if I were to return to him. And I do not believe that my Christ, my Lord and Saviour, wishes me to go willingly to such an unpurposeful death.

– Chapter 28 –

Dust from pulverized stone hangs in the air, though the workmen have not slung hammer since yesterday dusk. It is Sunday, they are at their church and their dinners, but still the grey dust sifts through the hall, coats every surface, puts grit beneath the teeth, chokes the throat. Francis stands at the end of the second-floor gallery holding aside the heavy carpet hung there as barrier, gazing into sunlit air. His men are removing the walls, stone by stone, a task near as formidable as the raising of them must have been four hundred years ago. It is no easy thing to tear down a twelfth-century castle, but Francis Ayscough is determined that the ancient hall shall come down, and a newly built manor house of brick and fine timber rise to take its place. He has pored over the plans: the approach through the arched gate flanked by octagonal turrets, the enormous brick manor house, the garden, the orchard, the enlarged courtyard. The old hall will not be fully demolished for months yet; the new manor will require many months more to build. It is slow work, and tedious, and tremendously expensive. Francis has petitioned for materials from one of the suppressed priories to help ameliorate his costs. If necessary, he'll sell some of the Ayscough holdings in Yorkshire, and, of course, he feels certain that one of his lucrative lawsuits will soon be successful. Francis Ayscough will always be successful. Of this, he has no doubt.

Except . . .

A cloud passes over the sun. A troubled thought passes over his spirit.

Except, there is this misfortunate matter of his sister and her churl of a husband and the trouble they continue to put Francis to—put his whole family to. Anne has not come out of her room for three days. Dame Elizabeth has been in to see her, and his wife has; they say she is ill. And well she might be, or too ashamed to show her face. He frowns with the recollection of Anne dismounting in the courtyard: her torn veil, bruised eyes, damaged mouth—oh, the damnable whoreson knave! Francis ought to ride straight to Friskney this hour and drag the fool out and beat him to quivering jelly! Anne can be exasperating at times, yes, they all know it, she has ever been a bit of a thorn, but, God's blood, man, control your wife—don't half kill her! Francis turns to face the dark hall.

All is quiet. The others are at St Mary's, his entire household, except for Anne. Well. He supposes he must go now and speak with her. He has avoided, delayed, kept himself occupied with his many necessary occupations since she came. Even now he cannot admit how much he dreads to look at her, how he fears he'll find no better words than the helpless sputter he offered on the day she arrived. But what is there to say except go home, sister, contain yourself, do not behave in ways that cause your husband to beat you? With a sigh, he begins the long walk towards Anne's room. His heels echo loudly in the empty gallery. At the chamber door, he stands a moment, frowning, knocks once, and enters.

His sister sits beside the window, a piece of stretched linen on a hoop in her lap. She gazes steadily from her bruised eyes, calmly, without curiosity or question. Her lips are less swollen now, but the gash there is crusted and ugly. On her cheekbone blooms a dark violet rose. Her head is uncovered. The sight of her hair loose on her shoulders discomfits him—it is too intimate, too immodest. And yet it causes him to see her in his mind's eye as a little girl, her long hair loose and flying, her screams of laughter as he galloped around the courtyard with her on his back, snorting and pawing like a stallion: he himself so young then, and sturdy, the child on his back light and leggy as a fawn. The memory makes his chest ache.

'Welcome, brother.' She flicks a quick gaze to the corner, where he sees now his wife's maidservant bent over her sewing. So it is arranged, he thinks. Dame Elizabeth came to him two days ago asking if the girl might attend Anne during her stay. 'What does my wife say to it?' he'd asked. 'She's amenable.' Dame Elizabeth's affect had been flat and seamless as a board. He was unable to tell her opinion in the matter. 'If Lisbeth thinks it good,' he'd shrugged. Here the girl sits, so she must have thought it good—but the maid ought to be at Sunday Mass now, he realizes, as all servants must be.

'Why have you not gone with the others to hear Mass?' he demands, but the girl does not look up, and it is Anne who answers.

'Look at my face, Francis. Will you have the whole village to gossip?' Then she adds, as an afterthought: 'I've told Beatrice to stay with me.' She touches her hand to the side of her head. 'The pain is better now, Beatrice. You may bring me my veil.' The girl stands, bobs a quick curtsy to Francis, retrieves a linen coif and veil from the counterpane, and takes it to Anne. She moves as if to place the cap, but Anne takes it from her. Another quick curtsy, and back to the joint stool with her sewing in her lap; she never looks up. Francis stares at the top of his sister's head, the pale, ragged oval spiked with short black hairs. 'Do not concern yourself,' Anne says. 'It is months old. The hair grows back.' She touches the side of her head. 'It is only the pain that still visits.'

'I'll thrash him to a puddle when I see him,' Francis mutters.

'Will you?' Anne gathers the length of her hair in a loose bunch, stuffs it beneath the linen coif. 'And much good may that do you. But it'll not benefit me. Nor your nephews, my sons.'

Francis turns and strides the room. It is as he feared: he has no words, neither of comfort nor of resolution. All that occurs to him is to chide her, and he cannot bring himself to it—though surely if she would only hold her tongue, if she'd not argue with him, increase his anger . . .

'She'll come with us to Lincoln,' Anne says. She is arranging her veil at her neck. 'It will be a satisfaction to her, though she cannot bring charges herself.'

'What? What are you talking about?'

'When we go to Lincoln to pray the peace against my husband, Beatrice shall come with us. She'll swear to his treatment of me, if they'll allow her. Do they allow servants to testify?'

Francis tries to sort out what she's saying. 'It is not a crime to beat one's wife, Anne.'

'It is a crime to kill her. Or do you prefer to wait until after he's murdered me and then wreak vengeance upon him?'

Francis turns away from her bruised, placid face. Common law allows that a wife may plead for peace from her husband if his beatings are like to kill her. It is not a subtle action, nor a private one. 'Evidence is required,' he says. 'A woman's life must be in danger.'

'You'll give evidence. Beatrice will.'

Francis glances at the girl, who appears not to be listening, though of course she is—a servant always is listening.

'My face will give evidence,' Anne says.

He looks at her again; the swelling about her eyes is no better, the discolouration worse. And that great blackish gash at her lip—oh, damn the brute! Damn him. 'Very well. But one doesn't pray the peace before the sheriff, Anne, but with the justice of the peace. And it would not be in Lincoln but in Boston, your own district.'

'Boston is not good,' Anne says. 'He conducts business there; the guildsmen all know him, the merchants and priests.'

'Nevertheless, this is how it is done. Look. I haven't the time to go now. Next week, perhaps.'

'Our evidence will be poorer next week.' She touches the scab on her lip.

'Yes, all right. Soon, then. Before your . . . before the evidence heals.' He throws another glance at the maid, who still does not lift her head. In his mind he sees the girl crumpled on the street in Lincoln, her dazed and broken look, the shouts of the onlookers. 'I think it will not be necessary to bring Beatrice. My wife may not be able to spare her.'

'But I want her to come,' Anne says. 'I'll speak with Lisbeth.'

'*I* shall speak with her!' Francis grips himself. 'If she's to be spoken with. You presume too much, Anne. Why cannot you be more circumspect?'

'You mean why can I not comport myself in a more conformable manner?' Her tone makes quotations of her words; they flutter at the edge of his memory, familiar somehow, though he cannot recall from where.

'All I mean,' he says more gently, 'is that my wife is mistress of her household; she determines where her servants serve.' He moves to stand over his sister, awkwardly lays a hand on her shoulder. 'I'll speak with Lisbeth when she comes from Mass. Are you well enough to travel? Ah, of course you are. You rode a carthorse from Friskney.' He gives her a brisk little pat, starts out, pauses and turns, frowning. 'You might . . . for the journey, you might put on again your torn veil.'

When the door closes behind him, Beatrice looks up. For an instant the two women stare across the quiet space; then, quickly, Beatrice lowers her head. Anne says, 'Certainly you'll come.'

'Yes, madam.' Beatrice picks up the linen she is sewing. Her needle pricks in and out rapidly.

'I hadn't mentioned it before only because I had not thought we would go so soon—but, of course, I see that we must. Bruises are more eloquent than words. I should have ridden straight to the constable three months ago, instead of waiting in my room for my sons to return.' She looks for a response. None comes. The girl has been with her two days now and has hardly uttered two words. 'I understand well the punishment of silence, Beatrice,' Anne says. 'I do not understand what I'm being punished for.'

Beatrice looks up in alarm. 'Goodness, no, madam! I would never presume!'

'Then why the long face? Why do you say nothing but *Yes, madam, no, madam, as you wish, madam*? You might at least call me Mistress Anne.'

'I . . . I am not certain what I should call you.'

'I just told you. Mistress Anne.'

'Yes, mad—mistress. My mistress wishes me to say *madam*, so I thought perhaps you too prefer it.'

'Well, I do not. Beatrice, lift your head. Look at me. What's wrong? You act as though we're strangers.' The girl holds her eyes on Anne's face a moment before she skims them away, to the bed, the tapestry on the wall, the open window. She appears trapped. 'What?' Anne says. 'You do not wish to go to Boston?'

'If my mistress bids me, yes, of course I shall be glad to go.'

My mistress. The words cut Anne like a scythe. This is the trouble—or it is Anne's trouble, though it seems not to be Beatrice's. All this time Anne has been remembering the girl as she last knew her: young, guileless, gape-mouthed, clever but ignorant, spirited but obedient. Anne has missed her as one misses a helpful digit, a thumb or forefinger, suddenly cut off, or at other times she longs for her as listener, student, confidant. Surely, Anne thinks, Beatrice has missed her the same way. That the girl has a new mistress, new allegiances, a new way of speaking, curtsying, sewing, dressing hair—these are discoveries Anne finds intolerable, and so, since she cannot tolerate them, she disallows them; she chooses instead to believe that Beatrice's stony silence is grounded in resentment. 'I would have sent for you if I could,' she says. 'Master Kyme would not allow it.'

A nod of the kerchiefed head. The swiftly darting needle.

'I was so relieved to hear you'd come safe to South Kelsey. I didn't learn that for weeks, you know. Until Jane told me. I often ask about you. Do they tell you I ask for you?'

The girl shrugs.

'I'm grateful to my brother for that, at least. That he brought you here. Do you know, young William cried for you for ages.'

The girl looks up. 'How is he? The young master.'

'Oh. He's coming so grown, Beatrice, you'd hardly know him. And Thomas, too—well, but you've never seen Thom, have you?

My baby. He's . . . he's a chuffy handful.' She must take care now. She must hold herself very firm as she speaks of her sons. 'Master Kyme hired a woman from the village to mind them for a time, but William was nothing so attached to her as he was to you.'

'Really, miss?' the girl says, pleased, and then her face reddens that the old familiar word has slipped out.

Anne laughs. 'I always did prefer *miss* to *mistress*,' she says. 'And either to *madam*. Though what I shall be called now, I cannot think.' She laughs again, and then, in an instant, she is crying, her face in her hands. Wrenching sobs shake her shoulders.

Beatrice looks to the door, all around the room, back to her former mistress. No one has told her anything but that she must report to this chamber to attend to Mistress Kyme. Dutifully she has done so, but the ruin of Anne's face is so disturbing that she's not been able to look at her. The swollen bruises, the crusting scabs set her heart to race; she thinks of the old mistress at Friskney, how she would twist and pull Beatrice's ears, smack her mercilessly about the head, leave blue-black marks on her arms from the pinch of her fingers. 'Madam?' Beatrice whispers. 'Mistress Anne? May I . . . ? Should I call for Master Francis?'

Anne shakes her head. She raises one hand, palm out, keeps the other over her eyes. Her shoulders heave. Beatrice remembers her sprawled on the ground in castle square, her tumbled skirts, her curled and heaving back. Beatrice had reached over and laid a hand on her back, patted lightly, but then she herself was wrenched from the ground, and in the next moments she saw her mistress lifted onto a pallet and carried into the nearby inn. Never to be seen again—at least not by Beatrice. Not until a few days ago, when she'd watched her dismount in the courtyard, her clothing mauled, her eyes staring out of black swollen circles. Anne's sobs begin to lessen. When she uncovers her face, it is red and glistening, and more swollen than ever, but she has regained control of herself. 'Forgive me,' she says. 'It is hard to speak of my children.

Oh, Beatrice, he thrashed me in front of them! The first time, he did so and afterwards sent them away. Now he sends them away first, and then the beating.'

Beatrice stares. Anne continues in a low murmur, as if she fears someone outside the door might be listening. 'I knew it the moment I came in. The house was so quiet, the servants vanished, and he alone there in the hall to meet me. I listened. Turned my ear to the nursery. No sound.' She speaks in a monotone, like an old recitation. 'He will not say where he has sent them. The first time, he sent them to his cousin in Wrangle, but I think now he does not, for she would judge him harshly, with her clamped mouth so like his mother's, for all the trouble he puts her to. They were with her almost a month then.' She swallows a sob. 'Now I do not know where they are.'

This last causes Beatrice to look up. Something powerful from the past rises in her, a kind of protectiveness she used to feel. 'Master Kyme would see they're well cared for, surely. And when you return, they'll be—'

A terrible thought occurs. She remembers young William's terrified stillness whenever his father came near.

'Madam,' she whispers, 'does he harm William?'

'Not with blows,' Anne says. 'Oh, Beatrice, you know him. You know how he bullies Will—he expects so much of him! He demands that he act as a grown man when he's only a little boy! I do not mean he should be coddled, of course not, but neither should he be shouted at and berated and treated with such contempt. Why is Kyme like that? How does a man not love his own son?'

'I couldn't say, miss,' Beatrice murmurs. She picks up her sewing. 'Perhaps Master Francis can find out for you where they are. Then you'll be at peace until you go home.'

'That place is not home, Beatrice. I do not intend to go back there. Not ever. Only once, to get my children, and then never again.'

The girl stares at her. 'How is that possible, miss?'

Anne stands, lays her embroidery hoop aside. Beatrice scrambles quickly to her feet, watches as Anne begins to walk about the chamber. This is as she used to do—how many times has the girl seen her pacing the four walls of a room? Countless times. An uncountable number. 'I pray without ceasing,' Anne says. 'I ask for guidance, that the Father's will be done. But now we see through a glass darkly, Paul says, and so it is. I am able to see only as far as the next task. I pray to be carried through, and to have the next step revealed when the time comes for me to take it.' She pauses, turns to Beatrice, her face lit with fervour. 'And it will be, you see. It always is!' She begins again her restless walking, wall to wall to wall.

'May I ask, mad—mistress, what that is, your next task?'

'Why, I've told you. We go to Boston to pray the peace against Master Kyme, then to Friskney to fetch my sons. After that, I cannot say.'

'But how will you fetch them,' the girl says timidly, 'if you do not know where they are?'

Anne stops. She stands very still. 'He must bring them home sometime. They are too young to live in another household. Perhaps they are in Friskney already. God will return them to me. Did not Jesus say "Suffer the little children to come unto Me"?' She goes to Beatrice, takes both her hands. The maid is half a head taller than the mistress. The intimacy of the gesture discomfits the girl; she ducks her head, frowns. 'He has returned *you* to me,' Anne says. 'How will He not also return me my sons?' She turns, begins to walk again. After a few moments, Beatrice realizes she is murmuring beneath her breath. At first she thinks the mistress is praying, but the sound does not have the rhythm of prayers. Has the mistress lost her mind?

Anne catches her questioning look, and laughs. 'This is my method,' she says, without a break in her steps. 'I commit Scripture to memory walking. And, walking again, I retrieve the verses, word for word. Oh, but of course. You couldn't know.' She pauses, turns to look at her. 'Thomas destroyed the Bible you so carefully preserved.

He tore it apart with his hands, shredded the pages, burned what was left.'

Within Beatrice now, the memories tumble: her mistress sick nearly unto death in the bed, the bloody sheets, the buried book, the secret lessons.

'I had to find other methods,' Anne says. 'I went to the church to read, despite his vile threats, and the threats of the Vicar Jordan. Oh, don't look so distressed, Beatrice. This turn is my salvation! Listen. Master Kyme has violently driven me from his home. Therefore, I am not under subjugation to him. The Apostle Paul says so: "Bear not a strange yoke with the unbeliever."' She holds the girl's gaze a moment, and smiles. 'In Scripture is every answer, Beatrice. *Sola scriptura*. Don't worry. When we return from Boston, I'll teach you.' She begins to walk again, murmuring verses.

– Chapter 29 –

Alas, I must make a new plan. The journey to Boston was less than worthless. Francis found reasons to delay—the work on the east wing, the mowing, a visit he must make to Nuthall to oversee his tenants. In the end we rode down a fortnight later. Beatrice did not come with us, and I did not insist. My eyes were only faintly rimmed yellow-green by then, my mouth healed. There was no evidence of Kyme's misuse of me—only my testimony, which I was not allowed, even in my brother's presence, to speak. Francis's esteemed influence reaches not so far south in the county, unfortunately. The justice listened only a short while. 'I'm familiar with Thomas Kyme,' he interrupted. 'He is the largest landowner in his area, a good shearman and landlord, and renowned for his piety. I see no justification for bringing this insubstantial case to the quarter session. When you return to your husband, Mistress Kyme, you must mind yourself, that such corrections are not necessary.' Mind yourself. I'm always being told to mind myself.

'See here, sir,' Francis said, 'we are telling you he is like to kill her.'

'Evidence, sir. Where is your evidence?'

'Look there!' Francis said, waving his hand at my face. 'See it!'

'All I see is an unchastened wife whose reputation for disobedience scuttles about the district. She must go home and fall to her knees in proper humility; then perhaps her good husband will forgive her.'

'He is a vile man and not at all a good husband!' I cried out. But Francis bundled me out of the room.

So now I wait. I pray for guidance, but no clear light has yet come to me, and I cannot search Holy Scripture for answers, as I have none, and I cannot walk to the parish church to read, because Father Sebastian, at word of the new act forbidding it to be read by any but clerics, nobles, and gentlemen, and fearing some subtle infraction, unchained the Great Bible from the nave and hid it away. I've written to Edward to send me a small Testament, if he can get one. I look every day for his messenger from London, and in the meantime, I recite to Beatrice all the verses I can remember and ask her to recite after me, but she only mumbles or pretends not to hear.

My life is so tedious. I sleep in the guest room wearing borrowed linens. In the afternoons I sew in the solar with Lisbeth and her servants, though my handwork is clumsy and unlovely as ever. Lisbeth says I needn't feel badly, it is only lying-in smocks for the poor, but I know how useless and unhelpful are my contributions. I cannot go forwards, and I cannot go backwards. I cannot see the next movement. And, oh, how I miss my children! Yet I cannot return to Kyme's household. I cannot. I will not!

At least I have Beatrice with me, for a mercy. Daily she becomes less wooden. Our old comfortableness has not yet returned, but her stiff formality has, at the least, eased. Though I cannot shake her of her superstitions. I have tried. Yesterday she wanted to go to the chapel to say prayers for her dead father, it being his death anniversary, and I told her, 'You need not pray him from Purgatory, Beatrice, for there is no such place. In Holy Scripture we find only two places for the soul to fly after it departs its earthly shell: to be with Christ in Heaven, or else to that eternal separation and suffering in the Lake of Fire known as Hell.'

She said, 'Yes, miss,' and crossed herself. 'May I go now to pray?' I waved her away.

When I have my Bible again, I shall show her. As Hugh Latimer showed me. Indeed, as he showed all who were gathered at St Wulfram's to hear him that day.

This is one of our secrets, Edward's and mine—that he carried me to Grantham to hear the sermon of God's great good preacher Hugh Latimer, not to South Kelsey to see Father, as he'd told Master Kyme he would. This was in the bitter Advent season after Thom died. Bishop Latimer stood in the pulpit and thundered: 'Show me where the word *purgatory* is writ even one time in this book!' His white hair and beard and cassock were all lit with light, his great Bible raised Heavenward in two hands. 'I submit to you, people, that ye cannot, for it *is* not! Oh, ye brain-sick fools, ye hoddy-peaks, ye doddy-polls, why will ye pay more heed to some priest's nattering than to God's Holy Word!'

Ye hoddy-peaks. Ye doddy-polls. Well. I shan't call Beatrice that. But I shall open the Holy Book, when I get me one, and show her: Heaven or Hell, one place or the other. And my sweet Maddie is in Heaven, and Thom, too. I know this, and it comforts me. By faith shall I join them there at the appointed hour, with Christ Jesus our Lord. *This day shalt thou be with Me in Paradise*. In the meantime, I pray for wisdom and insight and, may it please my Lord and Saviour, a sign.

Jesu Lord, help me. This is not the sign I asked for, this letter to my brother Francis from Master Thomas Kyme. *Send to me, sir, at your earliest convenience, and by what conveyance may prove most commodious, my disobedient, lawful, and, by now, let us pray, well-chastened wife.* He mentions nothing of his abuse of me, how he cast me aside like worthless chaff, says not one word about my sons, only demands that Francis send me back.

'I suppose you'll be all right there now,' Francis said vaguely. 'I suppose he has learned his lesson.'

'You do not suppose that,' I said. It was the two of us alone—I'd sent Beatrice out the moment Francis appeared with the letter in his hand and his false sorrowing expression.

He went to the window, reached out to touch the sill, ran a finger through the dust.

'Will you send me straight away, then? I'd hoped I might spend Christmas.'

'Not so long as Christmas, but . . . perhaps we might delay a little. Master Kyme speaks of my convenience. I shall send word that I find it not presently convenient.'

'*You* find it.'

'There is nothing to be done, Anne. You are his lawful wife. It is an unbreakable union.'

'How is it that the king receives his divorcements at will?'

'First, the obvious: he is king. Secondly, his were not divorcements but annulments. A divorce does not allow for remarriage.'

'How does one seek an annulment, then? An everyday person, I mean.'

'It isn't done.'

'But if it *were* done? Must it be through the archbishop?'

'I believe a person would take his case to the bishop's court in Lincoln.'

I felt my heart rising. 'And there do what?'

'It must be proved there was no valid marriage.'

'But mine is not valid! Saint Paul says if a faithful woman has an unbelieving husband who will not tarry with her, she may leave him. Kyme will not tarry with me. He cast me out, you know that!'

'And now demands to have you sent back.'

'He is an unbeliever, Francis. A papist!'

'You must not say such things. We do not know from hour to hour how the screw will turn.'

'*I* know,' I told him. 'I know what the Apostle Paul says.'

'An annulment declares that one was never truly married.'

'Nor am I! Not properly. Not in the eyes of God.'

'If you receive an annulment—unlikely, but let us say it could happen—what would that do to your sons?'

Everything dropped. My heart. My stomach. If Kyme and I are not truly married, then my two sons are bastards. 'Which would be worse for my children? To be bastardized by the law or to find themselves orphans whose father killed their mother and was hanged for it?'

'You make dramatic claims.'

'If I go to him, Francis, I go to my death. Oh, perhaps he'll not intend to kill me straight away, only to fear me a little, bend me to his will. But the beating will begin, his hands will close around my throat, and he'll not be able to stop himself. He'll squeeze and squeeze until I swoon, and so it will happen that one day my sons will not be in the room screaming, one day the servants will have all been sent away, one day there'll be nothing between Kyme and the devil that drives him, and in a few short moments, which will feel to me like an eternity, I shall be dead.'

Francis was looking at me. There was sorrow in his eyes—not conjured now but real—and also a kind of helpless fear.

'You must promise to bring William and Thomas here,' I told him. 'Raise them as Ayscoughs. Do not let them bear the burden of their father's name. He'll be hanged for a murderer by then.' I wiped my face. My heart hurt terribly. 'I know you do not wish to send me to my death, brother. But you do.'

A flickering passed over him, a muscle twitched along his jaw, his shoulders slumped. I've seldom seen Francis appear defeated, but he did so then. Within the instant, he roused, shook his head, dusted the grit from his fingers. 'Our cousin Brittayne comes from London next month!'

'Here?' I said. I did not know why this should cheer him. The name echoed faintly, a distant cousin from our mother's side. I hardly remembered him.

'No, of course not,' Francis said. 'To visit his mother at Lincoln. Brittayne is well regarded at Middle Temple, much admired for his acumen. He'll have sound advice in the law. Perhaps he knows a way I do not see.' His old bluster and confidence returned, Francis came and took my hands. 'Cheer up, Nims. He comes at Michaelmas, that is not so long now. I'll go to Lincoln and meet him. You shall come too, if you wish.' He chucked me beneath the chin with his finger, as he used to do when I was a child, and went out.

III

It Is No True Marriage

Lincoln

Autumn

1543

– Chapter 30 –

Anne sits in the alehouse near Saltergate watching her cousin and brother converse. They speak of fellows they knew together at Cambridge, court news, London news. Francis asks after Brittayne's mother. Anne would not have thought this sombre behatted crow to be her kinsman had Francis not jumped up to embrace him. He is a tall man, with a long face, large hands, and a barrister's pallor that is not helped, she thinks, by the unrelieved blackness of his robe and over-large hat. He bowed to her formally as he sat down, has not glanced at her since. His mother was cousin to their mother and came often to visit them in Stallingborough, or so Francis says, always bringing her young son with her. This was before their mother died and Father remarried and moved the family to South Kelsey. But Anne was very young then. She has no memory of the man sitting before her.

Francis, however, knows Brittayne well; they were at Cambridge together and have kept correspondence since. Francis follows his cousin's progress, as he would any kinsman who seems likely to rise in the world. And their cousin Christopher Brittayne does rise, Francis tells her: his influence at the Inns of Court is very strong. He is admirably skilled in civil and common law; he will surely have wise advice to give. In this moment, however, he seems more intent on hearing news of their former fellows at Cambridge. Fidgeting, impatient, Anne waits for the conversation to turn to her own matter. Food is brought, two tankards of beer consumed by her brother, and a stoup of ale and a small glass by her cousin and herself, before their talk turns at last to her marriage. Rather, her un-marriage, as

Anne thinks. Francis begins, but Anne soon takes over, laying out her case plainly and simply, and when she is done, Brittayne stares at her for one whole long minute, then turns to Francis: 'My cousin your sister seems to have little understanding of the law.'

'I understand the law, sir,' Anne says.

'She seems to be under the impression,' Brittayne goes on, speaking only to Francis, 'that an indissoluble contract can be dissolved.'

'It is not a valid contract!' Anne bursts out. 'Therefore, not a valid marriage! No more than the king's marriages were valid!'

'Anne.' Francis issues his low one-note warning.

'Perhaps my cousin your sister does not know to what trouble the king was put for his annulments?'

'If the Archbishop of Canterbury can provide annulments for the King of England,' Anne says, 'surely the Bishop of Lincoln may grant one to a poor Lincolnshire gentlewoman like me.'

'On what grounds?' Brittayne says to Francis.

'I have told you,' Anne says. 'It is not a valid marriage.'

Brittayne pulls at his lower lip. 'Was my cousin your sister joined to her husband in holy matrimony by a priest?'

Francis nods.

'A contract was sealed?' Brittayne says. 'The banns declared, opportunity given for any man to step forward and declare just cause by which they might not be legally married?'

'This all was done,' Francis says sadly.

'For Maddie!' Anne cries. 'The contract was made for my sister!'

Brittayne looks questioningly at Francis.

'Our sister Martha,' Francis says. 'She died of fever, God rest her, before the marriage could take place.'

'Perhaps,' Brittayne says, 'there might be a case based on affinity. That the man Kyme was previously married to her sister.'

'They spent no night together,' Francis says. 'Indeed, they hardly met.'

Brittayne pauses a good while, pulling at his nose. 'My cousin your sister has lived with her husband for a number of years?'

'Seven,' Francis says.

'And she has borne him children?'

'Two sons,' Francis says.

Brittayne shakes his head. 'I do not see how to make of such a public union an invalid marriage—and even if one could, this would bastardize the children. Kyme would be free to marry again, and any issue from the new marriage would be his rightful heirs.'

'I have explained this to her.'

'Please stop speaking of me as if I'm not here,' Anne says. 'I'm here, and I tell you I have my authority in Scripture!'

'Unless this Kyme chooses to claim them as his bastards,' Brittayne goes on speaking to Francis, 'they'll be cut adrift. How will they be supported? Do you intend to accept them into your home, cousin, and raise them with your own licit offspring?'

'Yes,' Anne says.

'No,' Francis says.

'Francis, you promised!'

'I believe, as the conversation ran, you informed me that I *must* promise, not that I in any particular manner *did* promise. And then, if you'll remember, it was to bring them to South Kelsey in the event your husband murders you. In which case, of course, you would yet be married, and they would be legitimate heirs.'

'You are against me! This is a ruse! A false little play to make me think you support me, when all you want is to send me back to Thomas Kyme to my death!'

'I look to keep you from making a mistake, Anne—one that will devolve not only upon you but upon your sons. And me. Upon our whole family.'

'He is violent, then?' Brittayne says. 'This Kyme?'

Anne snorts. 'You may say so. Tell him, Francis.'

'He carries his domestic discipline too far. It is of great concern.'

'I am so relieved at your *concern*, brother.'

'She should pray the peace against him,' Brittayne says. 'The authorities will enjoin him from excessive violence.'

'We have tried that,' Francis says.

'That is not the cause! Kyme is an unbeliever, Master Brittayne, and I may not remain yoked to him.'

'An unbeliever?' For the first time Brittayne appears surprised.

'A believer in false doctrine! In papist superstition! The Apostle Paul tells us that if the unbelieving one departs, let him depart, for a brother or sister is not under bondage in such cases. Such is my case, sir! Tell him, Francis. The man cast me out of his house, and I am not under bondage to him; so says the Word of God, and this is the case I shall bring to the bishop!'

Brittayne remains silent a long while, staring down at his large hands spread open on the table. After a moment, he says: 'Her husband is quite violent against her?'

'Alas, yes. It seems so.'

'This is my advice, then.' He looks up at Francis. 'Which I offer not in my capacity as lawyer but as a devoted kinsman and friend. Suggest to your sister my cousin that she seek not an annulment but a divorce from bed and board. This will not dissolve the marriage, but she'll be allowed to live apart in honour, and in this way, she might at least protect her sons.'

'But I want the marriage dissolved!' Anne bursts out. 'It is no true marriage! "Be ye not unevenly yoked with unbelievers," so says Paul to the Corinthians! An annulment is just, sir, it is right, it is the very commandment of God through His apostle Saint Paul, and if you've no better advice to give, then plainly you must say so!' She is panting in fury. Brittayne looks at her fully now, and indeed all the men and the few women in the alehouse are looking at her, as is also her brother, who is scowling. 'Sit down, Anne,' Francis says. She retakes her seat, folds her hands in her lap, though her bodice is heaving.

Brittayne pulls at his earlobe. 'Will you ask your sister to quote these scriptures again?' Anne does so, reciting the Great Bible verbatim, and citing the chapters. As she quotes the apostle's words, she sees something indecipherable pass over Brittayne's face, a kind of placidity, a calmness. 'Here is my new advice, then,' he says. 'Let my cousin your sister plead to the bishop's court as a chaste and faithful woman seeking annulment based upon said scriptures. Offer them in Latin. Most definitely do not say them in English. Bring a cleric. At least one. More if you can find them. Might your village priest attend with you? Any evidence of canonical support would help. Also, you must hire an ecclesiastical advocate; he will present your case to the bishop's court.' He suddenly stands. 'And now, cousins, I bid you good day. I leave for London tomorrow and have much business to settle before I depart.' He does not bow in Anne's direction but gives a quick nod to Francis and is out the door before Anne quite realizes he is leaving.

'Well,' she says, disgusted, watching his black hat disappear beneath the stone arch of the gate, 'that was no help.'

'He was as helpful as he knows how to be.'

'And as rude. He might have glanced at me once, if he'd not speak directly to me.'

'You'll have to get used to such behaviour. No Englishman is going to condone a wife leaving her husband.'

'I did not leave Kyme,' she reminds him. 'And he is not my true husband.'

'He is, Anne. You bear his name.'

'Then I'll not bear it!' But she sees the distemper growing in her brother's face and so changes the subject: 'Why do you call him by his surname?'

'Brittayne? Oh, that became our custom at Cambridge.'

'Why does he not call you Ayscough?'

'There are several Ayscoughs and only one Brittayne. He has no brothers, his father and uncles are dead. He's the last of his line, unmarried, and likely to remain so.'

'Why?'

'Oh, for the love of Christ, how should I know? Drink your ale, Anne, and spare me your questions.' Francis waves at the innkeeper to bring him more beer.

* * *

After All Souls, the household removes to Lincoln for Advent, and Anne with them: the entire family squeezed tightly into Francis's town house near St Swithins, and now is the ecclesiastical advocate for Anne's case procured. He appears at the door on a grey day of sleet and bitter wind: a round man with a round face and many papers in his satchel, a light, constant cough, a deep frown, and a wine-reddened nose. Francis welcomes him, sits him, and Anne begins at once to quote Saint Paul's letters to the Corinthians. It is hardly a moment before the advocate says no, that is no good justification.

'But it is, sir,' Anne says.

'It is not. I'll not use it. Do you hope for the well-being and future security of your children?'

'I do.'

'Then you must plead not for an annulment but for an authorized separation—a divorce from bed and board.'

Anne glares at her brother. He nods, frowning his sincere frown. This, she thinks, is at his persuasion: Francis does not wish to see his nephews bastardized with no right of inheritance; nor does he wish to have care of two disposed bastards for the rest of their natural lives.

'This solution would, of course,' the advocate says, 'preclude remarriage. For either you or your husband.'

'Remarriage is of no importance to me. This would allow me to have care of my sons?'

'Perhaps.'

'Only *perhaps*?' she says.

'It is your sole hope, madam. Certainly, it is the only hope by which they'll remain your husband's heirs. So. Yes?' Reluctantly she nods. He takes out quill and paper. 'Now. There is only one cause by which a woman may plead for divorce from bed and board, madam: adultery and cruelty.'

'That is two causes,' Anne says.

'Ah, but a woman must demonstrate both,' the advocate answers, licking his lips, dipping his pen. 'Thus it is considered to be one plea.

And seldom granted, you do understand? So. Your husband often beats you to the point of death, though you are a chaste, pure, and faithful wife. Your lewd husband . . . ,' he says, writing, not looking up, 'has often committed . . . adultery against you.'

'That pious prig?' Anne says. 'I could only wish.'

At the advocate's suddenly lifted head and her brother's shocked look, she mutters, 'It is a jest, Francis.' Then to the lawyer: 'No, of course not.'

'But we must declare that he has.'

'I'll not swear to what I do not know to be true.'

'You needn't swear it, then. We shall merely allege.' The man writes a few notes. 'It will be for the venerable court to decide yea or nay.'

Anne thinks of Kyme's mortifying use of her, how he would come at her so brutally sometimes, from the rear, as a stallion mounts a mare—what is this but an abomination of God's law? Her face burns with shame. Very lightly she nods. The advocate writes her assent. Quickly he completes the plea in his inelegant Latin, has her sign it, sands and seals it to be sent on its way through the many hands, inspectors, processes through which it must travel. Not before Candlemas, he tells her, is her plea likely to come up in the bishop's court.

'Oh, please, not so long as that, surely?'

'Patience, Mistress Kyme. The law turns slowly, and canon law more slowly still.'

IV

The Winter Has Been Harsh

Lincoln
Winter
1543–1544

– Chapter 31 –

The winter has been harsh, the roads so wretched that we were not able to bring Christopher home to Lincolnshire to bury him. Edward writes that our brother is laid in the churchyard at St Mary's, Hampton. He was thrown from a horse. This seems near impossible to believe, our Christopher was such an able horseman, but Edward says it was a misfortunate and unaccountable accident. He was riding up from Westminster on the darkest day of the year, late afternoon, winter solstice. The mud had thawed and refrozen a dozen times, Edward said, into jagged, hard ruts, and the road was crowded with carts and wagons, suppliers, all making their way towards Hampton Court Palace, and our brother amongst them, threading his way through the purveyors and overladen wagons. He passed a carter's mule, which startled, kicked, and brayed at that moment, and Christopher's horse shied, stumbled, and went down, bucking as he fell—or just beforehand, Edward said, because Christopher landed yards away. He did not die with his beautiful face buried in the road's mire, thanks be, but facing towards Heaven, perfect and handsome in his furred riding cloak, with his neck broken.

I wonder that I do not feel Christopher's death as I have felt the others. Perhaps it is that I've only read of it in Edward's letters, and so my heart does not quite believe. Or perhaps—yes, I think it is this—it is because my faith is increased. At Maddie's death I had none, at Thom's only a little, at Father's a little more. Now I doubt not that I shall see Christopher in Paradise, as our Saviour has promised; for, though he was ever a worldly man, our courtly brother did profess a long time ago, Edward says, his perfect faith.

We all remain at Lincoln, but I have moved from Francis's house to stay with Bridget at St Catherine's. It is not as comfortable here, but the tensions between my brother and myself are too constant—no matter how I try to hold my tongue, it seems my opinions must somehow slip from me—and I do not wish to prick his irritation to the point he'll not go with me when I take my case to the bishop's court. The day after our New Year's gifts were passed, we had a dour fight. Argument, I should say. Disagreement. I told him I would go to the cathedral to read from the Great Bible chained there. He said I must not, that the priests would be furious, that I ought not flaunt myself in public until we have brought forward our case.

'*Flaunt* myself? To stand quietly in the minster and read God's precious Word?'

'It is against the law, Anne.'

'They have amended the act! You know that. We are no longer forbidden! A gentlewoman may read the Word to herself alone—oh, Francis, I must go! It is a terrible thirst, a craving in me—I need to refresh my spirit!'

'No,' he said. 'You'll not do it.'

'I shall.'

'This is the very disobedience of which your husband complains!'

'Ought I to obey that papist farmer and the craven words of my brother, or ought I to obey the Holy Word of God? "Until I come, devote yourself to the public reading of Scripture, to exhortation, to teaching," Paul says in First Timothy. All Scripture is breathed out by God, Francis, and profitable for instruction in righteousness. You cannot stop me.' I turned to go.

'Where is the bishop's court?'

'What?' I halted in the doorway.

'Where in all the great warren of buildings within the minster walls lies the bishop's court? By what means will you contact your advocate? Where will you find him, and how shall you pay him?'

Francis's voice was cold but calm. I met his gaze. This was not his false sad look, nor his dark flashing anger, but a look of weariness, as if it would require very little for him to give up on my case entirely. I saw no profit in defiance. Not then. Not with Francis. Stiffly I curtsied and left him. That evening, I told Beatrice to pack my trunk, and we removed here to St Catherine's next morning. Beatrice does not like to be here. No more, in fact, do I: the stone walls are cold, the fire in our room smokes and spits and throws sparks on the rushes, which we are forever having to stamp dead, and yet the fire does little to warm or cheer us. But, as I tell Beatrice, it is only a little while. Just until my case comes to court. 'And then what, miss?' she says. 'Shall we return home to South Kelsey?'

'I don't know. My brother is so . . . never mind. There is no need for worry. Has not every step unfolded in its proper time and place and sequence? Be not anxious for your life, our Lord said, but seek ye first the Kingdom of God and His righteousness, and all these things shall be added unto you. I feel the hand of God on me, Beatrice. I'm not anxious for my life. Nor should you be. We shall be led in the path of righteousness for His name's sake, as the psalm tells us.'

'Yes, miss,' she says.

In the meantime, I prepare myself. The advocate assures Francis that my case will be heard in the new year. He has come twice more, to advise and question me. He says I must address the court as 'this venerable court' and the bishop as 'worshipful sir.' He asks for more details of the conditions of my marriage. I answer him always the same: my husband beats me, I have no certainty of his infidelity, but nor do I have certainty of his faithfulness, so I will not testify one way or the other. I let the advocate write down what he will. In any case, I have determined in my own mind what I shall say to the bishop, and it will be no lies or prevarications but only God's holy truth.

– Chapter 32 –

The day is cold, damp, and grey, a bitter north wind to slice through the bones: it is late February, the beginning of Lenten season. Her brother walks before her on the steep climb to the cathedral; her maidservant trails behind. This morning, as they waited at Francis's home for the advocate to join them, a messenger arrived, saying the advocate is ill with fever and cannot attend her at consistory court this day. Francis wavered then, worried, saying they should postpone, but Anne could not abide the delay. 'It must be today, Francis! You'll represent me. You know the law.' 'Not canon law,' he muttered. But he'd allowed himself to be persuaded—he, too, for his own reasons, wishes no further delay. And so, singly, as rowed ducks, they approach the minster yard.

They enter through the western gate. Francis guides her towards the great arched doors of the cathedral. Anne looks up in surprise. She'd thought the bishop's court would be somewhere in the many ecclesiastical buildings inside the minster yard, but they enter the cathedral directly, and Francis turns her immediately to the right. A small, narrow door. A granite-walled room. Within, from the southern window, cold light slants. A skull-faced man stands at the door, bony and wizened as a cadaver; this is the court summoner, or apparitor, as he is known. He crosses his great ceremonial mace in front of Francis, turns him away. Nor is the maid allowed to enter. Gesturing roughly with his mace, the apparitor motions Anne to her position: a narrow wood-panelled stall in the centre of the room. Before her, enthroned, sits the bishop's chancellor. She stands alone, shivering with cold. She looks around for Bishop Longland.

'Who represents you, madam?' the chancellor says.

'My advocate is ill, worshipful sir.'

'And your witnesses?'

'They've been turned away, worshipful sir. They wait without. My maidservant and my brother.'

The chancellor raises his magnifying spectacles to his nose, peers at the document before him. He tilts his head back to peer down at Anne. His eyes, made huge and grotesque by the thick circles of glass, return to the paper. He lowers the page and spectacles at the same time, shakes his head contemptuously. 'You are not half killed, Mistress Kyme. I see by the looks of you that you are a healthy young woman who ought to be at home with her children.'

'I may not go home, sir. Master Kyme—'

'Be silent. You are not to speak unless this venerable court asks of you a question. Now.' He shakes out the scrolled paper. 'We have searched out your case, madam, and we see no justification for the many falsehoods alleged here.' Anne becomes aware of a rustling murmur behind her. She turns to see a score of priests crowding into the tiny room. 'We have sent our representative to your home parish in Friskney. We have spoken with your vicar, Thomas Jordan, and indeed with the defendant of these scurrilous accusations himself. We find no blemish in Master Kyme's character or reputation. No evidence that he beats you or behaves with any moral turpitude. We *do* hear many shameful accusations pertaining to his wife. That she gads about the country gossiping and gospelling where she ought not. That she abandons her children to the care of strangers and her husband to a cold bed. That she reads Holy Scripture to common men and women in open defiance of the law.' The chancellor waits, gazing at her in expectant silence. Behind her, the rustling murmurs. 'Well?' the chancellor booms.

'There is a question, worshipful sir?'

'Yes! Yes! What have you to say for yourself?'

'Only that I have not offended the law. I read Scripture to myself alone, as the law permits me. Also this: it is God's law, not man's law, which gives justification for my plea. In Paul's letter to the Corinthians, he says—'

'You'll not teach us what Saint Paul says! It is an abomination for a woman to speak so, and I think, as I look at you and hear you, that your husband is well justified in his complaints! Your suit is dismissed, madam. Master Goodrick, see her out.' The apparitor steps forward.

'I would speak with Bishop Longland, sir. I should like to appeal—'

'Peace, woman! Will you risk the stocks as well? Be glad you've no worse judgement than this. Go home to your husband, Mistress Kyme, and behave as an obedient Christian wife ought!'

In the grey light of the courtroom, she alone in the panelled stall with the black robes lining the wall, the men rustling and murmuring behind her, the apparitor like a death's head at her elbow, Anne lifts her chin, looks directly into the cold eyes of the chancellor. 'He is not my husband, sir,' she says. 'And my name is not Kyme.'

On the frigid walk back down the hill towards St Swithins, Anne does not speak. Francis tells her she must do as the chancellor has ordered; he is sorry, he has tried, he'd hoped, truly, for a better outcome, but he fears he has little choice now. 'Damn it all!' He stops, rubs his forehead. 'I paid good money for the advocate. Why did I not wait for him to represent you!' He walks on. Anne walks with him in silence. Beatrice follows. 'Yes, all right,' Francis grumbles. 'You may remain here through Holy Week. But then we all return to South Kelsey, and I shall see to your repatriation, Anne. I really believe that I must.' Anne does not argue. She bids her brother goodbye at Saltergate and walks with her maid to Bridget's home at St Catherine's.

She'd held out hope, yes, but not expectation. It is not to be. Very well. She accepts this. She'll seek redress at the king's court in London. She has been thinking on this for some time. King Henry is the great disseminator of God's Word in English, he has had his own false marriage relieved through an annulment grounded in Scripture; therefore, who better to acknowledge that she is unevenly yoked in a false marriage than His Majesty himself? Or his courts, anyway. She is not sure how this is done, nor how she'll travel to London, nor how she'll maintain herself once she arrives, but she is confident that God will provide. More compelling to Anne just now, more troubling to her spirit in these hungry days as the Christian world moves towards Christ's Passion, is the fact she still has no Bible to read.

Late one morning, a chilly day of promising sun halfway through Lent, Anne takes Beatrice with her and climbs the long hill to the cathedral. They enter at midday. The noontide sun makes cheerful patterns on the flagstones. Masses are being held in several of the small chapels within the nave. Anne breathes in the dusky odour of incense, the low murmur of Latin. She does not pause at the beautiful carved font on its pedestal near the door but walks directly towards the reading table in the south aisle, where the Great Bible is chained. Beatrice quickly dips her finger in the font, crosses herself, hurries after her mistress. The minster is very busy, priests and prelates strolling everywhere, many people come to hear Mass or pray in the chapels. Anne opens to the Gospel of Saint Matthew. She is careful not to look at Beatrice nor to move her lips as she reads.

In time, however, she feels herself watched. From the tail of her eye, she catches the hard stare of a priest in a violet chasuble. Soon he is joined by another, and then a third. Anne continues to read in silence. Other priests and deacons come and stand nearby, glaring, sometimes muttering together, but they do not speak to her. She feels her maid's restlessness: the girl stands near the stone wall, shuffling, clearing her throat, trying not to draw attention to herself. It is only as a mercy to Beatrice that Anne ceases reading at last. She closes the Great Bible, centres it carefully on the table, arranges the heavy chain neatly along its base, and without a word or a look at anyone, turns and departs the minster. Beatrice follows quickly, her relief palpable as they emerge into the bright minster yard. Anne tells herself that the next time she walks to the cathedral, she'll leave the girl at home. In the evening Francis comes storming into the great hall at St Catherine's: 'Mother of God, Anne, what is the matter with you?' he roars. '*Why* will you court such trouble and condemnation? You'll not go there again!'

'Who told you?'

'I forbid it! The law forbids it!'

'I know the law, Francis, and its amendment: "Provided always that every noblewoman and gentlewoman may read to themselves alone and not to others any texts of the Bible or New Testament."'

'To themselves *alone!* In private! Not in the most public place in all of Lincolnshire!'

'Does it say that? I take the words to mean to herself *only* and not to others. Do they accuse me of reading to others? I promise you, I did not. Did I, Beatrice?'

'No, madam,' the girl says formally. She manages to make the word sound at once like *no* and *yes.*

Anne frowns. 'Go see to my supper, please. I'll take it in my chamber.'

'Yes, madam.' The girl curtsies and leaves. Anne endures another half hour of her brother's haranguing, until his anger and impatience are spent—although not his fear. She sees it in his great agitation, his restless pacing.

'What are you afraid of, Francis?' she says.

Her brother stops, gazes at her a long moment. 'I am afraid you do not know what you are unleashing. I am afraid you'll bring coals of fire down upon us all. That you'll persist with your wilfulness in such degree that we must all suffer—my wife and her tender heart not the least. We have lost Thom and Christopher and Martha. I would not lose you, too.'

'The priests will not kill me. They are too cowardly even to speak to me. They only come near and stare with cold eyes—as if stares and glares might harm me. I've not offended the law, Francis. And I shall not. I'll take care.'

'You do *not* take care! You parade yourself in public, flaunt your wit, your learning, your unwifely demeanours for all the world to see! All right. All right. It is near time for us to return to South Kelsey anyway. I'd hoped to wait until after Easter, but never mind. We'll go next week. Have your girl pack your trunk; I'll send someone 'round for it on Friday.'

'And then what?' Anne says.

'Then what *what?* We return to South Kelsey.'

'And do what?'

'Damn it all, and *live*. Just live.' He snatches his cap off the mantel. 'I do not exaggerate, Nan. The priests will put you to great trouble, so they have promised. Do not go back to the cathedral.'

'I'm not afraid of priests, Francis. No more here in Lincoln than in Friskney. What can they do to me? I do not offend God's law nor Parliament's nor the king's.'

'You offend the laws of common decency! Mind me, Anne! I mean it!' He jams his cap on his head and goes out.

Always before it has been *Mind yourself, Anne*. Now it is *Mind me*. At the least, she thinks, he does not speak of returning me to Friskney.

Next morning before daylight Anne walks to the cathedral alone. She has determined she'll not endanger Beatrice with her necessities, nor anyone else in her family. The streets are empty, quiet, cold. Mist shrouds the valley in greyness. She wraps her cloak more tightly, holds her rushlight high enough to see her feet as she climbs the hill. In the minster yard, priests and acolytes glide ghostlike in their white surplices towards the cathedral; their candles glow in the mist like bobbing cats' eyes as the bells peal the call to matins. Anne follows them; when the last enters the cathedral, she extinguishes her rush, slips in behind. Candlelight flickers near the font. In the distance the last priest's skirt disappears into the choir. She hears their voices, rising, falling, rising, as they sing the morning prayers. Quietly she goes to the table and opens the Bible to read. It is not long before two priests discover her: they stand at a distance, frowning. Anne senses how they want to rebuke her, but they say nothing. After a while, their duties of office calling them to other tasks, they drift away. In their place, others come. And so it is throughout the day: priests, prelates, and priors come to look at her. None speak to her, although they often whisper together. An hour before vespers Anne closes the Book, walks down the hill to St Catherine's, repeating in her mind the words she has read till she has them by heart. The following morning, she arises early to go to the cathedral again.

For six days she reads in the minster. Every one of these days the priests come and stare at her. By two and by two they come, by five and by six. Anne meets no man's gaze but reads as deeply in silence as if she were alone in her chamber. She makes no sign of recognition to show that she knows they are there. Throughout the cathedral, the rituals and masses and prayers and offerings continue, the murmur of Latin, the clink of coin, the shuffle of soft soles on stone, but around the Great Bible, in the south aisle of the nave: a circle of silence. Only once, at the last, does one of the priests speak to her, an ancient fellow with white whiskers and stained stole. 'You display yourself a learned woman capable of reading God's Word,' he smirks. 'I enjoin you to look to Saint Paul on the proper conduct for a woman in our holy mother church!' Anne does not raise her eyes from the page, though she is not able entirely to keep hidden her smile. What does Paul say of women in church but that they must keep silent? And have I not kept purely silent all these six days?

The old priest leans near, the must of age and unwashed skin wafting from his collar, his breath, the soiled crepe of his throat. 'Why do you smile, woman? Look you to the thirty-first chapter of Proverbs and mark God's Word there! See how you defy every conduct of a virtuous woman! Thou art none but a wanton and a wayward whore!' He pulls away, taking his stink with him. Anne quietly turns the sacred pages—not to the passage in the Book of Proverbs he mentions, for she knows it well: *Who can find a virtuous woman? For her price is far above rubies.* Anne need not study that passage to commit it to memory. Rather, she leafs forwards, to Solomon's beautiful Song of Songs, and continues to read. *For behold the winter is now past. The rain is away and gone.*

– Chapter 33 –

When I returned to St Catherine's that last evening, I halted, my chest tightening, the moment I entered the gate. Francis's stallion stood saddled in the courtyard. I stepped back, thinking to slip away and return only after he'd gone. I was filled with the spirit, the pleasures of my recitations on the long walk from the cathedral, and had no desire to listen to my brother's harangues. But then I saw that on the other side of the stallion stood tethered a small saddled mare. What? I thought. Has Lisbeth come with him? That would be most unusual; she seldom stirs from the town house except to cross the street to St Swithins for Mass. A hard nip of fear gripped me. Is there trouble? Perhaps Mother Elizabeth has taken ill? Or one of the children—or, oh, no, it could be one of my own sons! I hurried to the door.

In the great hall Francis sat in quiet conversation with Bridget's husband, Sir Vincent. I did not see my stepsister, nor Beatrice. Francis rose from his stool, came gently towards me with his head tipped forwards: his sincere, concerned look.

'What?' I said. 'Is someone ill? Please, not my sons!'

'No, no, it's nothing like that. Or . . .' He hesitated. 'Not exactly. But you must come with me.'

'Where?'

'Hurry, now, here's your cloak. I'll explain as we ride.' He draped my riding cloak over my shoulders and swept me out the door so swiftly I did not have time to think. He set me on the small horse, mounted his own, and rode quickly ahead of me through the gate. When we came to Saltergate, he turned east, and I thought we would go to his house by St Swithins, but Francis cantered on towards Lindum Road, continued up the incline till we passed along the back side of the cathedral by Pottersgate. We rode hard, north and east, on the rutted road towards Nettleton, so I knew then we were on our way to South Kelsey, and this caused me even more to fear. The sun was near setting; we would not reach even Market Rasen before dark took us—what terrible difficulty drove this terrible haste? I called out to Francis more than once, but he only kept to his swift, controlled canter and did not turn to look at me.

Night caught us before the market town, of course. I would have ridden on in the dark, but Francis insisted we stop at the inn near Faldingworth, and it was there, in the common room over supper, that my brother Francis and I had our last fight. I pray it was our last one. He leaves for France soon. He said he must deliver himself to the Duke of Suffolk within a fortnight, bringing threescore fighting men of his own hire and good harness to join the duke's forces. 'The king prepares for war, Nan, and all of England with him.'

'This is your urgency? Not my sons? You've frightened me half to death!'

'I'm sorry. It was necessary. I had to get you away from Lincoln before the priests do to you as they boast that they will.'

'Which is what?'

'Give you great trouble, Anne. Imprison you. Put you to the quest.'

'They've had plenty opportunity already and have not.'

'Ergo, you have come away in time.'

'Ergo, they have naught to imprison me for. So you thought it best to deceive me with this unnamed urgency? To trick me here to this louse-ridden inn with no maid to serve me, no change of linen, not even a comb?'

'You're more easily deceived than persuaded.'

'Not for long,' I said. 'And now you'll return me to Thomas Kyme to be killed.'

'No,' he said.

'I do not trust you.'

'Nor I you.'

'Do not trust me how?' I said. 'To be other than the honest, faithful woman I am?'

'I cannot trust you not to return to Lincoln and make of your life and our family's lives a butcher's shambles!'

'It is your reputation you care for more than my life.'

'I care for both! God's blood but you'd make any sane man mad!'

Then we argued back and forth over the poor pottage and poorer ale for perhaps half an hour, he grumbling, I disputing, until at last in a temper he thumped his fist on the table: 'I've told you I'll not send you to Friskney, now believe it! But I promise you this: you'll stay at the manor until I return from France. You'll not parade yourself to the parish church, you'll not stand about flaunting yourself in public, you'll remain in your rooms and do your, I don't know, your blasted *sewing,* and comport yourself as a gentlewoman. And when I return, we'll see to your marriage!'

'And my sons.'

'And your sons!'

'And if you do not return?'

He sat glaring. He had no answer.

'And what shall I do if Kyme comes for me while you're gone? I have no protection but you, Francis. I'll have none till you return.'

'Ah, you admit I'll return, then?'

'I pray you will. Brother, please. Do not leave me to the mercy of Thomas Kyme. You know he will come for me. And you know he is not a merciful man.'

'What would you have me do!' he cried, smacking the table again. He did not intend it as a question, but I answered him anyway:

'Send me to London,' I said.

He sat blinking as if the words were so strange, he could not comprehend them. 'Send you to London,' he repeated. I told him then of my plan to seek an annulment in the Court of Chancery at Westminster—or perhaps Star Chamber, I said. I did not know which was proper, though I presumed our cousin Brittayne would know. At first Francis shook his head in disbelief. Then he laughed. Then he asked just where did I think I might live in London, and I said, 'With Edward,' and he said, 'At court? Hardly. Not without His Majesty's express invitation. In any case Henry will soon lead the invasion at Picardy, and Edward will go with him.'

'I'll not sit and wait pliantly for Kyme to come kill me.'

'He'll not!' My brother's vehemence was meant more to convince himself than me. He sat in silence, thinking, turning his spoon over and over on the pocked table.

'What will you do,' I said, 'lock me in chains? You cannot keep me, Francis. You know the moment you leave to join the duke's forces, I shall leave, too.'

And he did know. I saw in the slackening of his shoulders, the cold rigidity of his features, that he knew: he would have to clap me in a dungeon to prevent me from following my conscience, and God's plan.

Book Four

London

1544

I

By God's Hand

London

Summer

1544

– Chapter 34 –

London! Oh, London. I scarce can believe I am here! And our rooms so close to the Temple, the very Inns of Court—it is as if I live and walk and breathe in a waking dream. Beatrice can scarce believe it either, though she is not near so well pleased at the prospect as me. I understand her unhappiness. She has lived her whole life with wide-swept spaces around her, the scent of growing barley and wet wool and sheep gong, not cramped narrow alleys banked in shadow and the stink of chamber pots and cooking water sloshed in the streets. 'But look!' I say, and point to the spire of St Paul's. 'See how close we are to the very steps of that holy cathedral!'

Beatrice shrugs. 'The spire of the cathedral at Lincoln is taller,' she says, and bends to pull the chamber pot from beneath the bed. She walks to the window carrying it like a sacred chalice, opens the shutter, flings the contents into the street.

For myself, though, I like very much to be here. I carry great hope. Francis arranged with Brittayne to find these lodgings for me with the Widow Hobbes, and though they be dim and cramped, yet they serve perfectly, for from here it is but a short walk to Chancery, where, God willing, my case will be heard next Hilary Term. So says my cousin Brittayne. He has barely to step out his door at Middle Temple to come speak with me, carrying his messages from my brothers, bits of news, my allowance, his own stiff advisements. He is one of us, Edward says, a true believer in the gospel—although, if this is so, our cousin's faith brings him little joy, I must say. I never knew so uncomfortable a man. But he is helpful, if awkward, and with Francis mustered for the war and Edward preparing to go to France with the king's forces, Brittayne is my closest male kinsman here, and the one I may best turn to for help.

And really, why do I doubt him? At my first inquiry he brought me a Testament: it is Tyndale's banished translation, tattered and worn, and small enough to hide inside one's sleeve. I'd hardly known there were any left in the world, so many have been gathered up and burned, although one wonders why. I find few differences in the translation from my own dear lost Coverdale, excepting in the glosses. Edward says it was for his so-called heretical glosses that William Tyndale was strangled in Germany and afterwards his body burnt. Some call that a mercy, that he was choked to death before burning, but I have been strangled at the hands of Master Kyme and I do not think it much a mercy. Every evening, however, as I read aloud from Tyndale to Beatrice, I am grateful for the risks my cousin took to bring it to me, and so my original antipathy towards him has changed.

Brittayne is also the person who, at Edward's bidding, introduced me to Master Lascelles—they're old friends from Henry's court, my brother Edward and John Lascelles—and for this, too, I am grateful. We met at an alehouse in Poultry Street. Lascelles and I talked of Scripture for nearly two hours, while my cousin looked on in his staid and stiff manner. Master Lascelles has promised to call for me soon and accompany me to a close gathering in Bread Street, where, he says, I shall find a group of like-minded believers such as I've never seen. God's gospellers, he calls them. Believers in the evangelical truth. There I shall hear the true and holy gospel read, he says, despite the wrong-headed laws set by Parliament.

And so I see that by God's hand I have come to this place where I may find men and women who are my kinsmen in faith and in spirit, if not by blood—though Brittayne is both, it seems—and therefore, how may I not be glad?

Francis, of course, would argue. He would say it is not by God's hand but by Francis's own that I have come here. And certainly it was my brother's hand which laid coins in mine for our journey; he who supplied our mounts and the two manservants who travelled with us; he who arranged for my allowance, charged Edward to see that Brittayne attends to my welfare. Then he took himself off to France with the Duke of Suffolk as comfortably as if he'd come to the notion on his own. But I remember his face that night at the inn at Faldingworth. I see again the fear and pride there, and his anger, and so I say God may use my brother's failings as easily as He may use any other means to bring me to the place I must be.

'If you please, madam, how long before Master Brittayne comes again?' It is Beatrice, with her long face and her 'madam.' This is her little resistance. It is 'miss' and 'mistress' when she is not unhappy, and 'madam' when she is stiff with misery.

'Day after tomorrow, I think. Are we poor again?'

'We've two farthings left.' She stands awaiting instructions.

'Yes, all right,' I say. 'But not that dark bread, Beatrice, it hurts my—'

. . . jaw to chew, I meant to say, but she is out the door towards Cheapside before I can spit out the words. Poor child. She receives meagre fare, I think, in the kitchen with the servants. She seems always to be hungry. Mistress Hobbes owns the house in receipt of her dead husband, a famous barrister of Inner Temple, as she often tells me, although it seems the great man did not leave her a very great income, for the widow is extremely spare in her portions, and parsimonious with her salt and spicing besides.

Oh, look there! How the westering sun gleams on the curved dome of the Temple! Not glowing orange, as at Lincoln in summer, but this cool, mild cream colour. So peaceful and inviting. I shall ask Brittayne if one who is not a member of the Inns of Court may worship there. Or, indeed, whether a woman may enter the Temple Church at all. Or perhaps Master Lascelles will know. He studied law at Furnival's Inn, Edward says, and is wise in so much Scripture. I shall ask him when he calls to take me to the gospel meeting, which will not be long now, I pray.

– Chapter 35 –

Master Lascelles escorts Anne through the crowded streets at great speed, his young servant and hers struggling to keep pace. He is not a tall man, hasn't a lengthy stride, but he is possessed of a type of fiery urgency that corresponds to Anne's own. The two hurry along, heads together, talking of religious texts, certain words in translation, Cranmer's new English liturgy, which the king has approved but not yet implemented. 'Soon, though, Mistress Kyme,' Lascelles says, waving her into Bread Street. 'Very soon.'

'Please, sir,' Anne says, 'I should like better to be called by my Christian name.'

Master Lascelles bows graciously. 'Mistress Anne.' He steers her into a narrow alleyway, down a short set of stairs, and into a large room crowded with great wooden beer butts, hogsheads, barrels: it is the backroom of a brewery that faces onto the next street. The room is filled with men and women of every age, class, complexion: a mishmash gathering, which seems no surprise to Anne but is a wonder to her maid. The girl stands against the back wall with Lascelles' servant boy, Jack, and stares. She's never seen such a confusing conglomeration: prentices rowed up beside gentlemen, merchants cheek by jowl with brewers, fine ladies seated next to washerwomen, fishwives by tanners, tailors beside priests. Her mistress takes a seat near the front, plucks the small Testament from her sleeve, and opens it as familiarly as if she were in her own rooms.

Beatrice pulls away from the sharp scent of Lascelles' boy, who is leaning too near, and watches an elegantly dressed woman stand and open her own small book and begin to read: not in silence, as did Mistress Anne in the cathedral, but aloud before God and all this hotchpotch assembly. Beatrice knows it is against the law for women to read God's Word aloud, but no one here appears troubled or surprised to hear a woman reading. The woman is perhaps a merchant's wife, Beatrice thinks, eyeing her fine rose-coloured skirt and clever hat, but she is clearly well educated, for she does not stumble once over the words. She pauses to turn a page, and at once Master Lascelles jumps up to offer his explication.

Or perhaps that's what it is. Beatrice cannot, in fact, quite tell what he intends. He seems to be arguing, for his round chest puffs up and his voice deepens, but his words are not said with anger, though he waves one fist about emphatically. In his other hand, a large Bible is splayed open. 'Submit yourselves to God!' Master Lascelles declares. 'Resist the devil, and he will fly from you! So says James the brother of Jesus! And hear this: he who spites his brother spites the law! What art thou that judgest another man?'

But is not everyone in this place disobeying the law? Beatrice knows that common men are not to do this, only clerics may do this: read Scripture in English in public, aloud. She looks to Mistress Anne to see her reaction, but she can tell nothing from the back of her mistress's head. A chapped-looking woman in a white linen cap gets to her feet.

'Oh, watch this!' the servant boy Jack whispers, elbowing Beatrice. 'She's a Lollard, that one! She'll go to blaspheming here in a minute.'

'Thou sayest well, Brother Lascelles,' the woman says. 'But let me put to you this.' She brandishes her Testament. 'James says we are to confess our sins to one other, don't he? "Knowledge your faults one to another." We do not need to make confessions to priests! Therefore, I ask you . . .' She glares pointedly around the room, where several priests in black cassocks are scattered throughout the crowd. 'Who are these men among us? They are like to be spies!'

A grumble runs through the room, some *ayes*, some *nays*, some general disgruntlement. Lascelles raises his voice: 'Should we not seek to reform the church, Sister Joan, rather than, in a frenzy of destruction, tear it down?' As the low rumble continues, Mistress Anne rises and steps forward. Master Lascelles waves the people to silence. Anne's voice is clear in the quiet room:

'In the sixteenth chapter of Matthew we read "Upon this rock I will build my congregation, and the gates of Hell shall not prevail against it."' She looks kindly at the raw woman in the linen cap. 'If

Christ Jesus Himself says the gates of Hell shall not prevail against it, how then shall we? We cannot. We dare not. What disobedience that would be. But I find my mind troubled in this manner . . .' She gazes out over the room, her brows drawn in a faintly puzzled frown, which Beatrice recognizes as prelude not to a question, but to one of her mistress's firm opinions. 'What is meant by this word *congregation*?' Anne glances meaningfully at Master Lascelles. 'Some say the word ought to be translated not as "congregation" but as "church."'

An even more discontented murmur ripples through the crowd. This is an old argument.

'I am told,' Anne continues, 'that this Greek word, *ekklesia,* being translated literally, means "they who are called." But are not we here this evening they who are called to carry the gospel of salvation? Then *we* are the church, the congregation, the *ekklesia* of which Christ our Lord speaks. I think it matters not, therefore, that some of us be of the cloth and others common, some learned and others ignorant. For the Apostle Paul tells us in Galatians there is neither bond nor free in Christ Jesus, neither man nor woman, but we are all one thing in Him. *We* are that holy apostolic universal catholic church, which Christ our Lord founded upon the rock of faith. "Therefore, be ye courteous one to another," Paul says in Ephesians, "merciful, forgiving one another, even as God for Christ's sake hath forgiven you."' She smiles at the chapped woman. Then, as quietly as she rose, she sits back down.

'By the blood,' the servant boy breathes.

John Lascelles stands blinking, one hand half lifted in the air.

When Anne returns to her lodgings that night, very late, almost midnight, she is flushed with excitement, a wildly beating heart; she thinks she'll never sleep. Beatrice lights a candle, undresses her, and Anne, holding tight to her Testament, kneels beside the narrow bed to give thanks that God has led her into fellowship with His people, these true gospel believers, to whom she entirely belongs.

In his own lodgings not far distant, her new friend John Lascelles revels in his own sense of belonging. He has been struck by Anne's grasp of Scripture and its meanings, her ability to interpret and remember and quote. For the first time since Cromwell's death four years past, John Lascelles feels he has found a spiritual peer. He and this young woman from Lincolnshire, this sister of his friend Edward Askew, share a religious fervour that is coequal, passionate, grounded in Scripture, and has nothing at all to do, Master Lascelles assures himself, with her feminine appeal.

He begins to call for Anne every evening, escorting her to evangelical gatherings in disparate corners of the city, from Blackfriars to Bishopsgate, St Bartholomew's to Fletchers Hall. He likes best to walk with her on Sunday mornings to St Mary Aldermary in Watling Street to hear the fiery sermons of Dr Edward Crome. John Lascelles is a Reformist of the corrupted church, as he often says, not a radical believer in blasphemous new ideas. Nevertheless, upon occasion he takes Anne to hear the words of Zwinglians and Lutherans, and even Anabaptists, and after each meeting they explore together what they've heard, holding each new thought or idea up to Scripture. *Sola scriptura.* They are in complete and unified agreement on this singular fact: the answer to every dispute under God's heaven is to be found, can *only* be found, in God's Holy Word.

But as Anne's belief increases that in London she has at last found a home, her unhappy maid Beatrice longs every moment to *go* home. The girl does not like the city; she does not like the air, the crowds, the smells, her daily monotony of tasks. She has more than once found herself lost and been forced to ask strangers to direct her. Always she feels that they are laughing at her stupidity, her ignorance, her northern accent, her dress. She is miserable, homesick, perpetually hungry. Her mistress takes midday dinner with their scrimping landlady in the dim hall off the withdrawing room, but Beatrice must eat scraps with the cook and serving boy in the dark kitchen below stairs. She eats her cold supper with Anne in their rooms in the evenings, and it is only here that the girl feels she has enough to eat.

And so when Master Brittayne brings her mistress's allowance, Beatrice is out the door to the stalls on Cheap as quickly as she can get away. She purchases bread and ale most days, dried fish on meatless days, gooseberries or black currants if she can get them, other victuals that might be bought not too dear and eaten without cooking, for they have no means to cook in Mistress Anne's rooms. Thus, Beatrice returns to the stalls almost daily, until the money is ended, and then they are forced to wait one or two days for the cousin's return, tempers short, stomachs growling, and only their meagre late-morning dinners to sustain them.

It is on just such a day, then, that the girl stands outside the widow's door, hungry and irritable, waiting for her mistress's benefactor to arrive. The air is sweltering, the sky overcast, the sun a dull coin past its zenith in the whitish haze. Beatrice stands well back beneath the jetty, watching towards the west, the direction from which Master Brittayne always comes. He is very late today. She'll have to walk fast to reach the stalls before the day-old bread and bruised fruits have all been pawed through and the best pickings plucked away.

Her eye is caught by something to the south in the distance: within the sea of men moiling the street in their black law robes and soft, shapeless caps, she spies the tall figure of Master Brittayne striding towards her—not from Middle Temple, as ordinarily, but from the direction of the river quays. Trotting along beside him, pumping his short legs, is Master Lascelles. She watches them, curious. Her mistress's cousin is tall, pale, loose-limbed, lean as a pillar, beaked as a crow, a man who speaks little and reveals less; he always seems a bit sour on the world, but he is, she believes, wise in his reserve. Master Lascelles, on the other hand, is short, ruddy, thick-limbed, loquacious: he talks more than any person of quality she has ever known. She thinks him incautious, puffed up, but also exuberant. Her mistress admires him greatly. He is, at the least, not a tedious person. Beatrice steps back as they approach swiftly, Master Brittayne's black robe flapping about his knees, and Master Lascelles puffing and red-faced, his legs churning double time. They do not see her: their eyes are on the widow's closed door. Master Lascelles darts forwards and raises his plump fist to knock just as Master Brittayne reaches over his head and raps twice, very hard. He elbows the shorter man aside, saying, 'You'll not do it!'

'I shall,' Master Lascelles says.

'I tell you, it is unwise.'

'They are friends of the gospel, sir! They have powers of persuasion with the queen, and I *will* bring her to meet them!'

'You'll not expose my cousin to such danger! Not while she is under my care!'

'But do you not see? It is part of the Master's plan! They come tomorrow to Saint James Palace! I have it all arranged!'

'Her brothers would have my hide.'

'Your hide or your head, sir? Which will you lose for the love of Christ?'

'Do not impugn my faith, sir!'

'Nor you mine!'

The two men stand inches apart, glaring, and Beatrice cannot tell, should it come to blows, which might prevail: Master Brittayne has the advantage for height and disdain, Master Lascelles for weight and pugnacity. But the door opens, and here stands the Widow Hobbes, frowning, fluttering her swollen fingers at her chest. 'Gentlemen! Your voices! Will you have the commissioners down upon me?' She hurries them through the door and closes it with a firm thump. Beatrice stands in the greyness beneath the jetty, blinking in wonder. That the two know each other well she understands now: their sniping had the intimacy of an ancient argument between old friends. This observation is soon swept aside, however, as she considers Master Lascelles' words: *They come tomorrow to Saint James Palace. I have it all arranged.* What Master Lascelles wants, what he intends, as Beatrice sees now, is to take her mistress to see the queen.

She hurries to the closed door, slips lightly into the house, where the Widow Hobbes is piping uselessly at the two gentlemen arguing in the front hall. Mistress Anne comes down the stairs. The widow stays only a few moments, pacing back and forth, fluttering her hands, before withdrawing to her private quarters. Beatrice remains quietly beside the door while the men talk over each other, and her mistress listens, seeming to side with neither gentleman, until her eyes open a little wider, spark a little brighter, when Master Lascelles explains that he has arranged for her to meet with the queen's ladies.

'The war is near finished,' Master Brittayne interrupts. 'Your brothers will soon come from France.'

'I do not hear that the war is near finished,' Master Lascelles says. 'I hear the siege at Boulogne goes on most tediously!'

'My advisement,' Master Brittayne says, 'is that you take no rash action until your brothers return.'

Anne glances over then and sees Beatrice. She turns to her cousin. 'May I have my allowance now, sir? My maid is near faint from hunger. See her there?'

The small purse is thrust into Beatrice's hand. She does not wish to leave—she wants to know what they are saying: will her mistress really be taken to see the queen? But at Anne's look, she goes out, hurries to Cheapside to gather their supper, rushes back to the Temple district as quickly as she is able, but by the time she returns, the visitors are gone. She and Anne take their supper in their rooms. The bread is stale, the cheese mouldy, the ale off, but her mistress says nothing to it. The girl dares finally to ask: 'Will you go to see the queen, then, miss?'

But Anne does not answer. In a moment she stands, brushes the crumbs from her bodice, withdraws to the cramped bedchamber; and soon Beatrice hears her praying. It is the same as always, Mistress Anne reading her Testament aloud and murmuring prayers, except it is not dark yet. This evening Anne has gone to her bed while the sun is still slanting light into the room.

* * *

That night, from her pallet, Beatrice hears her mistress crying: choked sobs, swallowed gulps, as if she is struggling to hold in the sound. The girl lies very still, filtering in her mind the afternoon's conversations, trying to retrieve what might cause her mistress to weep. She can think of nothing. But then, she did not hear everything the gentlemen said. She rolls from her mat.

From the doorway she sees Anne on her back on the narrow bed. The shutter is open. Moonlight streams in, turning ghostly her white smock and bedsheet. Her dark hair pools on the pillow; she is not wearing her cap. The back of her hand is laid across her mouth, fingers open, palm facing the ceiling, but her little shudders and sobs escape around it. She has grown so thin, Beatrice thinks. Her smock looks flat as a pressing board.

'Madam?' Beatrice whispers. 'Mistress Anne?'

Anne swallows. Clears her throat. Using her elbows, she pushes herself up, scoots back until she is sitting with her shoulders against the wall. 'Yes?'

'Are you . . . can I get you anything?'

'My children.'

'Beg pardon?'

'If you could get me anything under God's Heaven to ease my pain, it would be to bring my sons.'

The girl does not know what to say. Her mistress never speaks of her children; a person would think she has pushed them so far from her heart that their welfare impinges not the least on her consciousness. Beatrice has secretly thought this more than once, and if she has judged her mistress for it, well, God forgive her, but a servant sees what she sees. She would never, of course, say such words aloud. Beatrice considers now that her judgement may have been wrong.

'Please sit down.' Anne takes in a ragged breath; it gets caught in her diaphragm with a shudder, like a sobbing child. She clears her throat again. 'I am, I believe, a righteous woman. So I strive to be. So I pray.' In the moonlight, her face is drawn and pale, her eyes dark and swimming. 'I pray for Will and Thom,' she whispers, 'that they be returned to me. I pray for their well-being, their salvation, their health. I pray for their father: that his eyes will be opened, that his sins be forgiven. That his anger will be tempered, and he'll not raise his hands against our sons.' She pauses. Her throat works. 'But I am not there to protect them, you see.'

'Has something happened, miss?'

Anne gathers herself, answers quietly. 'My cousin Brittayne tells me that my case at Chancery will go against me because I am a woman who has abandoned her children. This is not what he came here to say, I think, but this is nevertheless what he said. He became angry because I said I would accept Master Lascelles' invitation to meet with the queen's ladies. He thinks it foolish, a reckless exposure to rumours and gossip and the spies of the commissioners. I think his anger is more at my resistance to his guidance than to any true danger. And he was truly angry. He did not shout, as Francis would, but the crimped whiteness around his mouth, his tight lips, told me how angry he was. And his words. He said I ought to return to Lincolnshire and take care of my children. He said there is little hope for my case unless I do, for there is no viler creature on earth than a mother who abandons her children.'

A harsh sob barks into the room. Anne sits a moment, holding herself. Then she wipes her face with her sleeve. 'I said to him: "Where in Lincolnshire must I go, sir? I've no better hope in South Kelsey than if I remain in London, for Kyme will not allow them to come to me. If I return to Friskney, Thomas Kyme will kill me." My cousin said, "You do not know that." "Oh, but I do," I said. "Why do you think my brother has sent me to London?" Then Master Lascelles said, "Mistress Anne, follow your conscience! Follow the Father's will!"

'And this I must do, Beatrice. I know it. I pray and I pray. But I cannot tell what the Father's will is.'

– Chapter 36 –

'Her Highness remains at Hampton Court,' Lascelles says breathlessly, hurrying Anne along a dim gallery, 'since the king departed for France. Although she comes to Westminster at times. In her capacity as regent. But the court comes not with her. It is only God's wonder.' He breaks off, puffing. 'That they come here now. The queen's ladies, I mean. Here we are.' He waves Anne to precede him as the gallery opens into a vast hall. The opulence stuns her: tapestried walls, painted ceiling, gold leaf accents on the king's arms repeated endlessly along the cornices. On the far side: a carved door flanked by two guardsmen in red and gold livery. Nearby a young page stands at attention next to a tall, thin groom with pinched nostrils. Lascelles raises his voice: 'Master John Lascelles, former sewer of the Outer Chamber, and Mistress Anne Kyme, visitor, to see my lady Herbert and the Duchess of Suffolk!' At the groom's arched brow, he adds, 'We are expected.'

'Ayscough,' Anne says. 'Anne Ayscough.'

'*Ass*-coo,' the groom says, looking Anne up and down: she has donned her best gown, but it is showing wear, the grey velvet faded, worn slick in places. Her bodice is plain, her sleeves too slender and spare for the day's fashion. On her head she wears a simple coif and veil, suitable for London's streets or her visits to gospel gatherings, but not elegant enough for St James Palace. Anne feels herself blush. She tilts back her head, meets the groom's gaze.

'Ah-*skew*,' Lascelles corrects him, elevating the pronunciation. 'Mistress Anne Askew, sister to Master Edward Askew, gentleman pensioner and royal cupbearer, who is this hour by the king's side at Boulogne, and who'll not be pleased to have his sister maligned by the likes of you!'

The groom blinks, nods to the page; they bow and withdraw. Anne looks about the room. She has had a letter from her sister Jane which convinced her to accept Master Lascelles' invitation: Jane says Katherine Willoughby, the Duke of Suffolk's wife, is a true friend of the gospel and looks forward to meeting her. The letter came next day after Lascelles' and Brittayne's visit; she'd taken it for a sign. Now, though, she is less sure. She feels acutely her uncertainty in this place, and also, if she is to be honest, her poverty, which she never feels in the breweries and basements where they meet with their Bible friends. The page returns and ushers them into the next chamber, through which they pass into the next, and the next: four antechambers in all, until they reach one where the pinch-nosed groom stands waiting. This room is smaller, somewhat less ornate; here are chairs and cushioned benches for sitting, a slant of sunlight through glazed windows.

Within moments there is a rustling at the far door. The page enters, followed by two richly dressed ladies in royal blue and bright yellow satin. The yellow lady carries in her arms a liver-and-white spaniel, which she sets on the floor before she approaches quickly and takes both of Anne's hands. 'And here, as promised, is young Anne Askew all grown up! But then, we are all of us grown since our halcyon days in Lincolnshire!' The lady laughs. Anne inclines her head, smiling. This is, of course, Katherine Willoughby, Duchess of Suffolk, of whom she hears so many lively tales from Jane. 'And who should have thought we'd see each other in London?' the duchess asks, as if they are old friends—though of course they cannot be, as they've only just met. 'Come, Gardiner!' She scoops the pup back into her arms, turns to the lady in blue. 'My dearest Anne, may I present my distant neighbour Anne, who is sister to our steward's right faithful wife, Jane St Poll. Anne, here also is Anne, my lady Herbert, sister to Her Highness the Queen. And now we have too many Annes! Anne my lady Hertford, Anne my lady Sussex, Anne my lady Russell, and—no, Gardiner! Naughty boy! Don't nip!' She sets the pup on the floor, where it skitters after her skirts as she sweeps to one of the carved chairs below the window. 'You may go.'

Her dismissal is to the groom and page, but also, it seems, to Master Lascelles, who nevertheless remains standing. Anne takes the chair between the two ladies, which the duchess indicates. The servants have withdrawn. The ladies stare at Lascelles. Anne smiles: 'Thank you, John. I appreciate your good escort. I shall . . . we shall . . .'—she looks to Katherine Willoughby for confirmation—'send for you when our conversation is finished.' The duchess nods. Lascelles appears confused, affronted, and helpless all at once. This is clearly not the turn he'd expected. With a frown and a cursory bow, he retreats. The ladies burst into laughter.

'What?' Anne says. 'Don't laugh. He is my dear friend. He sees at all points to my introductions and well-being!'

'Yes,' Lady Herbert says. 'And brags of you as if he'd fashioned you out of whole cloth!'

'Or sprang you from Jupiter's forehead!'

'Or plucked you from Adam's chest!'

'What are you talking about?'

The ladies laugh again. 'You've no idea how the fellow boasts of you,' Katherine Willoughby says. 'Or how he inserts himself into the boasting: *he* is the one in all London who has discovered your brilliance.'

'Truly, you must be the most brilliant scholar to ever take up a Latin primer!'

'Female scholar, that is.'

'Female scholar indeed,' Lady Herbert says. 'Not that we've ever heard of such a thing.' She smooths the taffeta lining of her sleeve. 'Your skill with Latin, Mistress Anne, if it proves true, is an attribute which recommends you to my sister the queen.'

'And her knowledge of Scripture.'

'And your knowledge of Scripture.'

Anne glances from one to the other. Their jewelled biliments, brocade bodices, startling colours in the sun make her want to squint. Really, she does not know what this is about. Lascelles said they were to join the queen's ladies for private devotional study. He told her not to bring her Testament, the queen's ladies would provide. She had expected a larger gathering. She had not expected this cryptic mirth, or that Lascelles himself would not remain with them. She sees that the two women are studying her, their eyes narrowed in judgement, yet the smiles keep playing about their mouths.

'Really, my dear,' the duchess says, 'you'll have to see that your Pygmalion does not fall in love with you.' They burst into laughter again, then draw serious at last.

'All right. Now, my young friend,' Katherine Willoughby continues, though in fact she and Anne are near the same age, 'your sister Jane has charged me to see how you fare. You look terribly thin. Do you eat well? Jane fears you suffer in London with no close kinsman to see to your welfare.'

'Our cousin Brittayne sees to me well enough.'

'And, of course, you have your mentor, instructor, and great discoverer, Master Lascelles,' Lady Herbert says. They laugh again, mildly.

'I don't see what's so amusing,' Anne says. 'He breaks no bounds of propriety.'

'No, of course not,' the duchess says. 'It's just that he has written four letters of introduction and visited Hampton Court twice and hangs about after privy council meetings seeking an audience with the queen. If he weren't in such good graces with the archbishop, he should have been tossed on his ear long ago. But he does hold good standing with Archbishop Cranmer, who admires the stalwartness of his beliefs, if not the rashness of his proclamations. The archbishop holds also enduring fondness for your brother Edward, as does Her Highness the Queen. She is willing you should join us for study at some point and show off your great learning.'

'But not today,' Lady Herbert says.

'Not today,' the duchess echoes.

'I see,' Anne says. 'Then why am I here?'

'You are here that we may look at you,' the duchess says.

'And examine you.'

'Determine if all the lauds Master Lascelles offers are borne out in your character.'

'And also, if you please,' Lady Herbert says, 'we should like to hear your explication of this.' From her capacious sleeve, the queen's sister withdraws a small bound leather volume. The title page is hand-painted, the Latin script elegant as a medieval scribe's: *Psalmi seu Precationes ex variis Scripturae locis collectae. Anno Domini M.D. XLIIII.* 'May we hear your translation, please?'

'Psalms or prayers collected from various passages of Scripture,' Anne reads. 'In the year of our Lord one thousand five hundred and forty-four.'

Katherine Willoughby produces a bound volume of her own: this one edged in gilt, with a jewelled clasp. She opens to the title page, hand-painted in gold leaf, royal blue, richest crimson. *Psalmes or Prayers taken out of Holy Scripture*. 'Please continue.' She follows along in her exquisite book as Anne turns pages in the Latin volume.

'The first psalm,' Anne translates as she reads, 'for obtaining the remission of sins.' Her words flow smoothly, a low, melodious stream: 'O Lord of Lords, God Almighty, great and dreadful, who by your word have made heaven, earth, the sea, and all things contained—'

'Thank you.' Lady Herbert plucks the book from her hand, turns pages, returns the volume to Anne opened near the back: *Precatio pro Rege*. 'And here, as well, if you please.'

'A prayer for the king,' Anne murmurs. The duchess follows along in her own volume. 'O Lord Jesus Christ, most high, most mighty, king of kings, lord of lords . . .'

In a very short while, the ladies are satisfied. 'Thank you,' Katherine Willoughby says, and returns her book to her silk purse. Anne's eyes follow the small volume as it disappears into the yellow maw. She has never seen a book of such exquisite quality: it must have cost a duke's fortune. 'You'll do nicely.' The duchess bends to lift her whining pup to her lap.

'My lady sister mislikes to read Latin.' Lady Herbert shuts her leather volume, returns it to her sleeve. 'Oh, she is quite capable, I assure you. But she finds the labour tedious, the language staid and arcane, and she has many urgent concerns to occupy her as regent. In this, you shall help her.'

Anne looks up, surprised. 'I? Help the queen?'

'Her Highness has a great project in mind,' the duchess says.

'A very great project indeed.' Lady Herbert leans towards Anne conspiratorially. 'Erasmus's paraphrases of the gospels are to be translated into English and published and distributed for the edification of Christian minds throughout the king's realm.'

'Shh,' Katherine Willoughby says, cupping her hands over her pup's ears. 'Master Gardiner mustn't know.' Her eyes are bright with mischief. The queen's sister puts a finger to her own lips, nods solemnly. Then they both laugh. Anne smiles vaguely. She has no idea what they are talking about. 'You'll be sent for when the time comes.' The duchess stands, Lady Herbert joins her, and Anne scrambles to her feet as the guardsmen seem to appear from nowhere. Within moments, the ladies have taken their little leather books and spaniel pup and gorgeous gowns off to other quarters, and Anne is left alone in the opulent chamber wondering what has just happened.

Master Lascelles arrives to collect her, ushered into the chamber by the disdainful groom. Her friend says nothing during the long walk back to the Temple district, though Anne tries several times to engage him. Lascelles takes his leave at her doorstep with a curt bow and few words: 'Clearly you know your way now, madam, your introductions are achieved; you'll make your own arrangements to meet the queen's ladies forthwith, I assume.' And off he marches towards his lodgings near Newgate Market. Anne stands staring after him, thinking that this is the most baffling day she has ever lived.

– Chapter 37 –

A fortnight later comes a bold knocking downstairs. Anne hurries to the door, hoping to find her cousin Brittayne with word at last of her brothers in France, and also, pray God, her allowance, for her purse and stomach are coming mighty thin. Instead, she finds a royal messenger with a sealed letter summoning her to wait upon the queen's ladies at Hampton Court Palace on Monday morning at ten. She is to bring with her 'all pertinent texts,' although Anne does not know what is meant by this. She owns no texts except her Tyndale. But yes, she'll bring that. Good. Very well. And then? Or rather, what she means is: and how?

How is she to travel a dozen miles upriver to Hampton Court? It is too far to walk, even if she knew which roads to take, which she does not. A hired boatman could carry her there, but Anne has no money. She has not seen her cousin Brittayne since he walked off in a cold stride the day she said she would go with Master Lascelles to meet the queen's ladies. Twice he has sent his servant with money, but it was little enough, and her allowance is whittled to nothing. She has had no communication with her friend John Lascelles since he quitted her at the doorstep two weeks ago, and although she has missed their evening forays to the gospel meetings about town, she has not sent to ask for him.

But it is to Master Lascelles she now turns, penning a hasty note and sending it with Beatrice to his lodgings by Newgate: *My dearly beloved friend in Christ, I greet you well . . .* She beseeches him to call for her on Monday next, at the earliest possible hour, to accompany her to the nearest river quay, where, if he is so able and willing, he might hire a boatman to row them both together to Hampton Court Palace, where she is asked to be in attendance on the queen's ladies. *When my brothers return from France, we shall happily repay you. By me, your devoted friend in Christ, Anne Askew.*

'What did he say?' Anne asks when Beatrice returns looking sweaty and harried.

'Nothing, miss.'

'But did he read it?'

'Yes, straight away. I told him I was to wait for an answer.'

'And he made none?' The girl shakes her head. 'But what did he *say*? Surely he indicated yea or nay?'

'He grunted.'

'Grunted?'

'At the end. When he'd finished. He grunted like an old dog lying down for its rest, folded the page back together, and retied the string. Then he said, "Thank you, Beatrice," and shut the door in my face.'

Anne is alarmed by this news. She sets out for Newgate Street immediately, Beatrice trailing unhappily behind. At the door the young servant Jack scratches his arm, the back of his head. 'Master John is at his prayers. You want I should interrupt him?'

'No, please, do not trouble him,' Anne says, sweeping past. 'I'll wait.'

The room is dark, dingy, spare, and smells of boiled cabbage. Anne seats herself on the wooden bench. Beatrice stands with her back to the cold hearth. Jack has apparently disregarded her words not to trouble his master, for within moments Lascelles appears. His face is tight, reserved. He bows formally. 'How may I be of service, Mistress Kyme?'

Anne studies him, trying to grasp this change. 'John. What's wrong?'

Lascelles lifts his chin, pulls himself to his full meagre height. His words and manner are exceedingly formal. 'I'll be pleased to render you good service, madam, if you care to explain how it is that I, your lowly, ignominious servant, may assist you. Of course, there are certain services I may not render, as there are certain books and tracts I may not read. Certain privy chambers where I may not enter.'

'Privy chambers?'

With the barest flick of his eyes, he indicates the two servants.

'Beatrice,' Anne says, 'will you wait outside, please?' Slowly, with several suspicious backwards glances, the girl goes out. Lascelles nods at Jack, and the boy vanishes into the back room. When they are alone, Lascelles seems to deflate like a bladder, the puff and air going out of him, and Anne sees that he is not only angry but deeply hurt. She goes to him, places a hand on his arm, but he jerks away, strides to the window, stands looking out. 'I see I've offended you,' she says. 'I am so sorry. If I've overstepped the bounds of courtesy in some way, please forgive me.' His back remains closed and hard as a fist. 'Talk to me, John. What have I done?'

'I know not, madam. What *have* you done?' He turns. 'What texts did you study in secret with the queen's ladies? I suppose they gave good lessons in mockery and derision? I suppose they teach you how to titter on cue?'

'What in heaven's name are you talking about?'

'You didn't hear, I suppose, what mine ears can never forget. Although how that is possible I cannot imagine, since you stood hardly an arm's length from the duchess as she sniggered. They swept you to their pale bosoms, while the guardsmen swept me out the door like last night's refuse.'

'That's not true! When did they?' But it is true, of course: he'd been dismissed like a serving boy before he'd hardly entered. She also remembers—*now* she remembers, although for many days past, she has pushed it away—her friend's face when he returned to the audience chamber: downcast, sullen. She had been unwilling to see his hurt then. She sees it now and knows that he stood outside the door and listened as they laughed at him, while she, Anne, his dear friend in Christ, said nothing to stop them. She'd been so full of her own excitement at the ladies' attentions, at being in the royal palace, that she allowed them to mock her friend with hardly a word of protest. A cold silence fills the room now. Anne searches for something to say. The silence deepens. Lascelles' head is bowed. Is he praying? His lips do not move. His eyes are not closed. He stares at the plank floor. His forehead is shining with perspiration. 'I'm sorry, John,' she says, and gathers herself to leave. The room is so quiet she hears the whisper of her own linen, the soft sigh of velvet, as she moves towards the door.

'You shall have the money.' Lascelles lifts his head, looks at her with baleful eyes. 'I'll not go with you. I'll not subject myself willingly to such mockery again. But I'll meet you at the dock on Monday and pay the boatman.'

But on Monday morning, at the appointed hour just after daylight, Master Lascelles arrives at Temple pier wearing a new doublet and a dark coat of finest wool. He pays the waterman and, without explanation, climbs into the small boat himself, holds out his hand to Anne. It is a two-passenger wherry. There is no room for her maid. Anne looks back to see Beatrice on the pier, her white cap smudged pink in the rosy dawn light, staring after them, frowning.

The day is calm, the river mild. The wherryman faces them with his long-practiced blank expression, as if he is both blind and deaf. The stink of the river causes Anne to hold her sleeve before her nose, but the light slants ruddy from the east, bathing the towers of Westminster in a ruby glow as they pass. The soft, rhythmic thunk and creak of oars, the faint plash as they rise and re-enter the water, lulls her until she feels she might fall asleep. This silence between her and Lascelles is not like the silence in his room two days ago, stiff with anger, but rather comfortable, mild, somehow expectant. Who will speak first? Anne drowses. Not I, she thinks. They are several miles upriver, moving well with the tide, when Master Lascelles begins to talk.

'Orphaned at nine, I was. My brother George, my sister Mary, and myself. Our neighbours, the Hercys, became our benefactors; they saw to our upbringing. But it was my brother George who insisted I be sent up to London to study law.'

Anne looks up at him. Always their conversation is of religious matters, of interpretation and faith. Lascelles never speaks of his personal life.

'I was at Furnival's Inn close on to three years.' His profile is blunt, self-conscious. 'Then George sent me to Master Cromwell with letters of introduction. Master Secretary, he was then. Lord Privy Seal. Vicar General. He had so many titles in those days. Henry made him Earl of Essex, too, you know. That last spring. Then he cut off his head.' Lascelles spits in the water, glances front at the boatman, who does not even blink. 'He was a hard master,' he murmurs, 'was Master Thomas Cromwell. But a good one. Devoted to the gospel in spirit, not merely in words. People don't think it, but I know it is so.'

Anne watches his face, listening.

By the time they reach the landing stage—which seems, actually, in her estimation, not so very far: the river journey has passed very quickly—she knows many things about her friend. A great deal that he has told her. Much more that she perceives. She knows that his bitterness over the execution of Cromwell endures. That his brother George in Nottinghamshire is very wealthy, while he himself is not. That he is not a widower, as she'd presumed, but rather that rarity, a well-positioned gentleman—of the minor gentry, to be sure, but a lawyer of good prospect—who is past thirty and has never taken a wife. She knows that it is by choice he lives simply, in rented rooms of little comfort, so that he may devote the fullness of his life to the sharing of the gospel, but that he also secretly yearns to return to court. He was employed as the king's sewer during Cromwell's reign, has not been employed there since. That he rests much hope in the reformist leanings of the new queen, Katheryn Parr. That he purchased his new doublet and coat to impress the haughty yeomen of the guard at the palace. That he carries, unknown to himself, the hard, hot nugget of perpetual resentment smouldering in his chest.

The clunk of wood upon wood startles her when the boat smacks the pier. The wherryman steadies the vessel. Master Lascelles scrambles out inelegantly, quickly reaches for her hand. Through the trees, on the rise above the river, Anne sees twinned red brick turrets. Lascelles takes her arm, and together they climb the stairs to the gate. Anne suddenly feels as if she's forgotten something. She stops, turns to look back. She sees only the wherryman pulling his cap down over his eyes as he settles in for a nap.

The palace grows larger, redder, more imposing as they draw near. 'This is Base Court,' Lascelles murmurs as they enter through the gatehouse. On three sides, windows look down upon the great courtyard, across which Lascelles strides, chin high, towards the guardsmen at the far entry. He lightly dips his head this way and that. 'My lord Hertford resides in those rooms with his wife, Anne Stanhope. When he is at court. But he is in France now, of course. As is my lord Essex, the queen's brother. His accommodations are just there. Yonder are the quarters of Thomas Wriothesley. Likely *he's* about.' Lascelles' voice is bitter. 'He nearly always is. He played Judas to my master Cromwell, you know, and is now left at court to skulk about the queen and utter his treacherous mutterings.'

At the far passage, they are halted by the guardsmen. Lascelles argues; he speaks in elevated diction, flicks invisible dust from his own fine woollen shoulders, asks Anne to produce her summons, which the guards scan with suspicion. Eventually they are waved through. They move through a chain of rooms, and at every passage another pair of guardsmen bars them. They are questioned, looked up and down. Anne shows them her summons; the guards run their fingers over the broken seal, testing whether it is genuine. She understands now why Master Lascelles has spent money to purchase his fine new clothing: the guards do not examine him nearly so high-handedly as they do her. Their eyes pass contemptuously over her brown riding cloak as if it were stained with offal. Could they see how worn is the velvet of her kirtle, she thinks, they'd cast her right down the landing stairs to the Thames. 'I'm glad you came with me,' she whispers as they pass through another rude screening. 'I doubt I'd have made it past the first interrogation.'

Lascelles smiles. 'I once talked my way into His Majesty's withdrawing room and remained there three hours, watching the king and his gentlemen gamble most marvellously at cards.' She sees the little puffed-up pride in his swagger, which, in her gratitude, she is happy to forgive. At last they reach the Great Hall. 'Now,' Lascelles says quietly, 'we must be subtle.' Anne looks around. The long, bright hall is crowded with richly dressed men strolling about in the slashing sunlight or talking together in twos and threes. 'Petitioners,' Lascelles whispers. 'Lawyers mostly, aspiring courtiers. Burgesses, of course. Stay here.' He strolls away. A few of the gentlemen nod to him. They do not look at her. It is as if she, in her faded clothes and feminine aspect, cannot be seen. The guardsmen cross their halberds at Lascelles' approach. Their weapons glint silver, their scarlet uniforms bell over their leggings: they are wonderfully stern and forbidding, but Lascelles speaks familiarly with one of them, a congenial smile on his face. The guardsman laughs. Within moments Lascelles returns. 'We're in luck. It is my old card partner. He is one of us, Anne.'

As unobtrusively as possible, they make their way across the crowded hall, but Anne senses now the curious gaze of the petitioners, the crimped lips of courtiers. When she and Lascelles reach the far end, they are admitted at once, escorted by Master Lascelles' friend through more chambers, each room more ostentatiously appointed than the last, until they reach the queen's audience chamber, and halt to wait outside the door as they are announced. They enter, and Anne has the barest instant to see the queen seated upon her dais before she bows and steps back on one foot, bends her knees to make the deepest obeisance possible, her eyes to the floor. She feels Lascelles bowing beside her. A woman's mild voice says, 'You may rise.'

The tableau is stunning, like a painting, as if each figure has been artfully arranged for the viewer's pleasure: seated at varying heights around the dais are six ladies—the queen's sister and the duchess among them—resplendent in jewelled colours, bright blue, yellow, ruby, green, violet, rose. None matches the quiet brilliance of the queen at their centre. Her gown is crimson velvet, the sleeves embroidered in gold thread and folded back to display ermine lining, the satin under-sleeves caught with jewelled clasps. A diamond and ruby brooch gleams from her bodice. At her throat, a close-fitting pearl and ruby necklace. In her lap, a small velvet-bound prayer book, tethered to her waist by a long, gleaming strand of pearls. When Anne dares to look at the queen's face, she is eased by the placid, curious expression she sees there: the queen's brow is broad and pale, her auburn hair smoothly parted in the centre, adorned with a pearl-encrusted hood. Her lips are thin, her nose piquant, her chin narrow and receding. And her eyes, close together, smallish, light hazel in colour, are bright with intelligence and good humour. She is altogether appealing, if not beautiful, and the kindness in her face makes Anne want to weep. Katherine Willoughby rises and comes to her, takes her hand, draws her forwards.

'Your Grace, may I present our young Latin scholar, Mistress Anne Askew, whom we have told you about.' The duchess's tone is humorous, ironical. Anne cannot tell if she is being laughed at. 'She is sister to His Majesty's cupbearer Edward Askew, as your Grace knows, and also sister to the wife of my lord husband's steward, Sir George St Poll. She is come of a worshipful stock, your Highness, and with such fulsome recommendations'—a quick glance at Master Lascelles, but no snigger—'as your Grace's ladies have seldom heard.'

'So,' the queen says. 'You've come to aid us with our translations.'

'Yes, your Highness,' Anne breathes. 'If it please your Grace.' Her heart is beating so fast.

'We have some degree of urgency, you should know. You've heard of His Majesty's great siege at Boulogne? And for God's most glorious victory we humbly pray—'

A low-throated *amen* reminds Anne of her friend's presence.

'Master Lascelles,' the queen says.

'Your Highness.' He makes another deep bow.

'Here you are.' The queen's voice is neutral, her gaze flat. 'I trust you are well.'

'Very well, your Highness,' Lascelles says. 'Thanks be to Christ.'

'Thanks be.' The queen eyes him toe to head. Her expression reveals nothing. Perhaps, Anne thinks, her friend has committed a *faux pas* by accompanying her? His name was not on the summons. 'Your protégé proves your endorsement, Master Lascelles. We are not unimpressed.' She returns her gaze to Anne. 'My ladies mentioned our project on the translation of Erasmus, yes? But we have, as well, a second project in mind.' The queen unclips the small book in her lap from its jewelled chain and hands it to one of her ladies, who brings it to Katherine Willoughby, who in turn places it in Anne's palm. 'Our work, which we undertake as a New Year's gift for our entirely beloved husband, must needs be . . .'—the queen pauses, smiles—'discreet.'

There is a light rustle and stir among the ladies, followed by a slow, preening settling. How is it, Anne wonders, that the ladies all have identical colour of hair? The visible wisps and peeking curls are all the same precise reddish blond as Her Highness the queen's. Is it possible that the ladies are selected for their colouring?

'As we should like to be finished before we depart on progress at month's end,' the queen continues, 'we think it prudent you remain at court rather than travel daily from London. That will be too many hours lost, you see. My lady Denny will escort you to your chamber.'

The lady who rises is plump, a bit older than the others but with the same bright tint of hair, and beautifully dressed in violet taffeta. Anne understands that she is dismissed. She turns to leave, and at once feels Lascelles' grip on her elbow. He gently pulls her to join him in facing the dais; he bows deeply, then, stepping backwards, begins to withdraw. Anne takes his example, curtsying fully, withdrawing slowly, facing the queen. The little prayer book is clutched tightly. She glances down. On the crimson cover, in elegant gold letters: *De Imitatione Christi.* The violet-clad lady has come behind. 'Follow me.' She walks towards a set of stairs leading down. 'That will be all, Master Lascelles,' Lady Denny says, without looking back.

'I thank you, my lady!' he calls. 'My kind regards to your husband!' With both hands he waves Anne to follow her. 'Go,' he mouths. 'God bless you. I shall come again soon.'

That night, kneeling in her linen smock on cold stones in a small, bare room that is not nearly so well appointed as those she passed through on her way here, Anne remembers the tug at her thoughts as she left the landing stage by the river: that uncertain feeling that she'd forgotten something. She'd felt bare then, as if some familiar article of clothing had been left off. It is, of course, not some*thing* she'd forgotten, but some*one*: her maid. In the rush of leave-taking, Anne did not think to ask Lascelles to carry a message to tell Beatrice she'll not be returning this night—nor, apparently, for some nights to come. Anne prays with one part of her mind, and with another she contemplates how to send Beatrice word. She'll inquire about this tomorrow. Indeed, she'll ask whether she might have her maidservant join her. She should like to bring Beatrice here, to this cold little room in Hampton Court Palace, to tend to the needs of her perplexed, elated, altogether physically uncomfortable mistress.

II

A Woman Is

Hampton Court Palace
August
1544

– Chapter 38 –

They have given me a borrowed lady's maid, who comes early to bring me fresh linens and dress me, returns at night with candle and bread and ale to put me to bed. Her name is Lucretia; she is brusque and heavy and speaks with a West Country accent, and she is not young. She seems always to want to be finished with me so she can return to her duties—she serves the queen's cousin, Lady Lane—and at times displays a shortness that borders on discourtesy, but I do not say anything. I am not a person elevated enough to share a room with one of the queen's gentlewomen, nor low enough to be lodged with servants, and so they have given me this small, dim closet, which suits me well, in fact, for its closeness is familiar, and I am able to pray and read here in solitude. But it gives me no discernible status, and so the maid does not know what level of deference to pay me. How she makes me wish for my Beatrice!

Master Lascelles has not come again, and so I do not know if Beatrice knows where I am. I've sent her two letters in care of the Widow Hobbes, but I do not know if she has received them or was able to learn their contents if she did. In the first letter I told her to ask Mistress Hobbes to help her—the good widow is a devotee of the gospel and reads rather well—but whether Beatrice can trace out my words well enough to read my instructions, I could not swear. Though heaven knows I've tried to teach her. She can write the Our Father in English and her full name, Beatrice Beckwith, and is able to puzzle out some words in Scripture, if I insist, but she does not take to it naturally, that I will say. I printed out MISTRESS HOBBES very large and plain on the first missive, thinking Beatrice can surely puzzle out that much and calculate the rest, but I've received no answer, and so I remain in this prickle bush of uncertainty.

Before first light, Lucretia comes. She lays out a fresh smock borrowed from some gentlewoman twice my size, which is always well laundered but never properly pressed, and roughly bathes my face, my arms and feet. She holds the smock above my head with the neck hole open to receive me, then cinches the waist tight with a long length of ribbon folded twice. She puts on me my kirtle and bodice, pins my sleeves, and no longer *tsks* at the worn nap and faded colour, though her face holds the very expression of *tsk*. She plaits my hair roughly—much harsher than ever would Beatrice—and, as she winds it up to pin it, asks me for the eleventh, twelfth, thirteenth time if I would like her to apply the powder that will turn my hair 'a proper colour,' as she says. This solves the mystery of why the queen's ladies all have her same tint: the first morning Lucretia came, she withdrew from her bag a jar of yellow ochre powder and went to comb it into my scalp. I batted her hand away. I didn't know what she was doing. 'But you must, madam!' she insisted. 'All the ladies wear it!'

'It is a vanity,' I told her, which is true but was perhaps not wise to say. I think it set up her antipathy for me straight away. She does not now attempt to apply it, but she never fails to ask. I demur, and she turns without a will-that-be-all, beg-your-pardon, by-your-leave nor nothing, and out she goes.

So then I am dressed. If she has brought me bread and ale, I consume them. I say my prayers, read my Testament, write, wait to be summoned. Sometimes the groom comes as early as eight of the clock, sometimes well after dinner. We are all at the beck and call of the queen's duties as regent in the king's absence at the war in France. Sometimes I am bidden to their Christian studies, other times to set down by hand my translations. I like best the hours of study with Queen Katheryn and her ladies, though I was sore surprised when the groom first brought me to join them.

He led me, that first morning, into the queen's privy apartments, which are stunning beyond measure, with exquisite arrases and gold-threaded cushions. There, in an inner sitting room, were her ladies all arranged in subdued colours. Beautifully dressed, to be sure, but in muted browns and rusts and dove greys, their heads bent over their needlework.

'Come, Mistress Anne!' the Duchess of Suffolk, Katherine Willoughby, waved me in. 'Come join our little confabulation!'

The groom accompanying me bowed himself out. The ladies all lifted their heads. A beat of silence, and then, from beneath embroidery hoops and nestled lapdogs and stretched linens, there emerged in the ladies' hands rustling pamphlets—eight and ten folded pages, I could see, though I could not read what they were. The duchess laughed at my expression. 'What did you think, my dear? That we only tittle-tattle and stitch linens?'

'I do not know what I thought,' I said.

Again the duchess laughed. I had with me the small velvet-clad book, Thomas à Kempis's *De Imitatione Christi,* supposing this was what I'd been summoned to translate, as the queen's Grace had intimated the day before. I sat on the low stool the duchess indicated, and opened it, ready to do whatever might be bidden. There came then a rustle and a sigh, a whispered *Hush!*, and the ladies all stood, and I stood, and we all made our reverences as Queen Katheryn entered. She wore crimson, as before, but without brocade or jewels this morning, and walking with her a cleric in black cassock and cap, who stood to one side as the queen seated herself on a cushioned chair near the window. The ladies all sat again, gathering their pups and pamphlets and sewing hoops. 'Whom shall we read this day, ladies?' the queen said. 'For our minds' edification?'

Her sister, Lady Herbert, said, 'We have at hand, your Grace, the writings of Marguerite de Navarre, of whom your Grace is most fond, as we know. Also a printed sermon by Bishop Latimer and a pamphlet containing an exegesis on the paraphrases of Erasmus. We await your Highness's pleasure.'

'And what have you there, then?' It took a moment for me to realize she was addressing me: her gaze was on the small crimson volume I held.

'It is *The Imitation of Christ*, your Highness,' I answered, puzzled, for she herself had seen it delivered to my hand only yesterday.

'Oughtn't we all to imitate the life and habits of our Lord and Saviour?'

'Yes, your Highness,' I said.

'Then perhaps this *Imitation of Christ* ought to be our reading today?'

'Yes, your Highness.' At her slight frown, I continued, 'Shall I read it aloud, then?' She nodded. 'In Latin or English? I can do the translations as I go, but it will be slower and more tedious.'

She glanced at her ladies. 'In English, I think.'

I stood to read. The wren-and-dove-coloured ladies held their pups and their needlework, desultorily punching needles through linen or stroking silky ears as I read, and so we went along for a while, until the priest stepped forwards and whispered in the queen's ear. She inclined her head, smiling slightly. I had paused at their whispers, having reached only the third page.

'The archbishop wishes to know,' the queen said, 'how fares your brother, his former clerk Edward Askew?'

'The archbishop?' I glanced at the cleric, who stood smiling kindly beside her, then blushed at my ignorance. But surely the Archbishop of Canterbury would dress more splendiferously? 'I do not know, sir.'

'*Your Grace*,' the duchess whispered.

'Your Grace,' I corrected. 'I've had no word as to my brother's welfare, but I hope to hear soon. I pray good health for him. For both my living brothers, who are both at Boulogne. My brother Francis serves with my lady of Suffolk's husband, the duke.'

'Then they'll both be present at a great victory soon, we pray.' The archbishop smiled, his eyes warm and sad. 'If I know Edward, he is making himself quite safe and comfortable, even as he serves His Majesty admirably.'

'Yes, your Grace.'

'Where have you learned such good Latin?'

'From my brothers' tutors. Not gladly on the tutors' part, I should say, but with my father's blessing. Or, to be wholly truthful, not his blessing so much as his indulgence.'

'Indulgence,' the archbishop said. 'I see. And what do you think of these words of encouragement and exhortation from Thomas à Kempis you share with us today?'

I thumbed the pages. 'I think, sir—begging your pardon. I think, your Grace, there is nothing here to speak against God's Word.' He nodded. 'Except that it is not God's Word.'

He watched me in silence a moment. 'Go on,' he said.

'See here. In the fifth chapter (for I had read deep into the book the night before): "Truth ought to be what we seek in reading Scripture, not eloquence."' I translated roughly. 'This I do not disagree with. But here: *Curiositas nostra sæpe nos impedit in lectione Scripturarum:* "Our curiosity often impedes our reading of Scripture when we seek to understand and discuss what we ought simply to read and pass by." But if we read and pass by without investigation, without applying our minds to uncover the whole of God's truth, how can we be said to truly read God's Word?'

A look passed between the queen and the archbishop, a kind of unvoiced familiarity, as if they knew each what the other was thinking. 'It is our habit,' the queen said, 'to study texts that serve as guides for Christian living.'

'Yes, your Highness,' I said. 'I wonder, though, if it is better to study an interpretation of the life of Christ when we might study the very words of Christ Himself, in His gospels.'

'The problem, of course,' the archbishop said, and cleared his throat, 'is that this violates the law.'

'Not for gentlewomen and ladies.' I looked around the room. 'As we all are. Saving your presence, your Grace.'

'And if it should happen,' Katherine Willoughby interjected lightly, 'that a gentlewoman or lady is unable to read these gospels in total silence but must murmur along as she reads?'

I turned to look at her. She was smiling, her eyes wicked with humour. I began to comprehend. 'I have seen such things happen,' I said.

'And if there are other ladies or gentlewomen nearby'—she stroked her dozing spaniel—'who cannot stop their ears as she reads, what then?'

'That is not the fault of the reader,' I said.

'And if God's Word,' Lady Herbert put in, 'being seeped unconsciously, and without intention, into the room, should happen to cause some nearby lady or gentlewoman to ponder aloud its meaning?'

'Why, that, too, is not the reader's concern,' I said, smiling broadly, for I understood all now. A gentlewoman in russet velvet stood up then, turned, and lifted the cushion from her chair. This was Maud Lane, the queen's cousin and Lucretia's mistress, and soon to become my favourite of the queen's ladies, though of course I could not yet know this. From beneath the cushion she withdrew a large Bible. 'I feel moved to read of Scripture to myself alone this morning,' she announced. 'If you cannot stop your ears, ladies, this will of course be your concern and none of my own.'

'Naturally,' Katherine Willoughby said. 'And if your throat tires, my dear, you may feel free to pass your book to me. I never tire of reading aloud to myself alone.'

The queen inclined her head, a subtle gesture. The archbishop, bowing slightly, withdrew as the ladies laid aside their pamphlets and sewing and, amidst rustlings and whispers of linen and silk and paper, brought forth from various bench compartments and purses and cleverly sewn cushions a veritable wealth of Bibles, of so many shapes and sizes and of such beautiful quality, you'd think you had stepped into God's library. The queen's own was covered in soft dyed leather the colour of a dove's breast.

'Ephesians,' Queen Katheryn said. 'Shall we begin with Paul's letter to the saints at Ephesus?'

And so my introduction to the queen's Bible studies began. I was being tested, of course, to try my circumspection and prudence, my quickness, even, I suppose. Had I failed, I would not have been brought again to their studies, I'm certain, but would remain here at this desk in this cramped room with inkhorn and penknife, translating the Latin text of *De Imitatione Christi*. And, indeed, I do spend most of my days here with Thomas à Kempis: I am bidden to distil essence from essence, that the queen's Grace may reform my clumsy words into her own graceful phrasings, to make a book which shall be printed in secret by the king's printer, I'm told, for a New Year's gift for His Majesty. And so I read and cogitate and scratch down my translations. I do find much of excellent devotion in the work—although I find also passages that offend. Father Kempis writes of man and Christ only, for instance, and I want to say: Is it men alone who yearn for Christ and desire to grow close to Him? Doth our living Christ draw unto Himself only the hearts of men? That is clean contrary to Scripture! To wit: the woman at the well, Mary Magdalene, the woman with the issue of blood, *et aliae*.

Nevertheless, I am bidden to translate for Queen Katheryn, and so I do. Though I find silent ways to amend. Where the writer says *Quod homo non sit curiosus scrutator sacramenti*, for example, 'A man is not a curious searcher into the holy mysteries,' I might, for the greater truth and the queen's reading pleasure, rephrase the words as if they say *Quod femina sit curiosus scrutator sacramenti*: 'A woman is a curious searcher into the holy mysteries.'

Because is it not so? A woman is.

– Chapter 39 –

Anne is pleased to have made a new friend of the queen's cousin Maud, Lady Lane. Or perhaps it would be more accurate to say that the cousin has made a friend of her. Lady Lane pays close attention to Anne's words at their Scriptural studies. If by chance Anne is still below stairs when the ladies gather, Lady Lane will send Lucretia to fetch her. She invites Anne to supper or to walk with her in the palace's formal gardens, where she imparts court gossip, news, bits of information about the queen's history. It is from Maud Lane that Anne learns that the queen knows the great preacher Hugh Latimer—and not Latimer only, but also Myles Coverdale: the very Coverdale whose translation of Holy Scripture Anne unearthed from her sister's dowry chest years ago. 'He is alive, then?' Anne asks in wonder.

'I've not heard that he isn't.' Maud bends to sniff a flower. It is evening. Anne's third week at court. They are on a footpath between the great plats of lawn stretching down to the river. 'He remains in exile at Antwerp, of course.'

'I should so like to meet him! Do you think an introduction would be possible?'

'Oh, he'll not return to England now. No Bible man will. Certainly not while Wily Winchester holds sway—though he, too, is on the continent, at Boulogne, supplying the king's troops with beer and victuals, though I'm told he manages so poorly the men curse him behind his back and call him Stephen Stockfish.'

'Who?'

'Stephen Gardiner. The Bishop of Winchester. And a more ruthless, cunning papist you'll never find, though of course he pretends not to be. Don't you know him?'

'I know the name. Gardiner. Is that not also the name of my lady of Suffolk's dog?'

'It is!' Maud laughs. 'Katherine Willoughby has such a naughty sense of humour!' She takes Anne's arm, and together they stroll.

'For a purported man of God, Stephen Gardiner is as vile as any man living. Except, perhaps, for Thomas Wriothesley. But then Wriothesley does not pretend to be a man of the church.'

'My friend John Lascelles spoke of Master Wriothesley.'

'Indeed?' Maud turns, interested. 'What did he say?'

'That he is not with the king in France but here at court.'

'Alas, yes.' Maud makes a wry face. 'He presides over the queen's council, more's the pity. But you mustn't call him Master Wriothesley, my dear—he is lord chancellor now. Well, more's the pity for that, too, in my opinion.' Maud makes a wry face. 'He and Stephen Gardiner are a ruthless, conniving pair. At the least, they are on separate continents now, we may praise God and King Henry for that. His Majesty took Gardiner to France with him and left Wriothesley here to serve Kate in her capacity as regent—though my lord chancellor will truly serve no woman. He has nothing but contempt for the queen.'

'Contempt! How is that possible?'

'Oh, with Wriothesley, it is possible. Believe me. His letters, when he must be away, are filled with flattery and obsequious assurances, but when he sits at council, his lip curls with the most exquisite disdain. You should see Kate imitate him!' She lifts her lip in delicate distaste. 'The ladies in the privy chamber laugh and laugh!'

'Will the queen come again to our Bible readings?'

'Why, certainly! I think when we return from progress, she'll be at leisure to join us once more. If the war is going well. Or is finished. Unfortunately, you'll be gone then.' Maud cuts her a glance. 'We shall be sorry to lose you. We've never had someone like you among us—a person with so much Scripture by heart.'

Anne blushes, the warmth of pleasure rising. She does not know what to say.

'We leave on Sunday next.' Maud pauses, then adds: 'You'll return then to London, I suppose.' She often does this, offers a statement that is actually an inquiry: When you leave court, where will you go? Maud strolls placidly, waiting, then speaks as if there'd been no silent query. 'One day, we pray, the queen will have sufficient influence that we shall no longer need to study the Bible in secret—oh, surely it is God's will that all of the king's subjects know the gospel!' She smiles at Anne. 'Though perhaps we needn't all of us have every word by heart.'

'I do not have every word,' Anne murmurs.

'Really? Before you joined us, we ruffled through so many pages, had to begin at the beginning and read through till we found what we wished to know. Now we simply say *faith,* or *forgiveness,* or *circumcision,* you point us at once to the precise chapter.'

'You've never asked about circumcision!' But then she sees the way her friend is smiling. Anne laughs. They stroll in companionable silence a while.

'Tell me, then,' Maud says, 'how *do* you know so much Scripture?' It is not an implied question but a direct one, and whether it is for this reason, or because of the warmth of the moment, or the flattery, Anne doesn't know, but she finds herself describing how she used to walk to the parish church in Friskney to read the Great Bible because she no longer had her sister's Coverdale, and then she finds that she must back up and tell how she came to have her sister's Bible—and how, later, she came to not have it. She does not say Kyme ripped out the pages, set fire to the mangled remains, only that her so-called husband took it from her.

'So-called?' Maud says, her eyebrows raised.

'It is a long story.' Anne looks away. The sun is setting. The muddy Thames gleams a dull silver. The words her cousin Brittayne spoke a month ago are like molten lead in her ears: *there is no viler creature on earth than a mother who abandons her children.* Anne clears her throat. 'It became my habit,' she says lightly, 'to commit God's Word to memory. Even now, at day's end, I take out my Tyndale and put to mind whatever chapters we've studied that day.'

'That is quite marvellous,' Maud says. 'And equally marvellous that you keep a copy of Tyndale's translation. You know, of course, should the wrong person discover it, you could be brought up on charges.'

'I know.'

'Stephen Gardiner has a nose for Tyndale like a scent hound.'

'Then I am glad Bishop Gardiner is in France now.'

'We are all glad for that, my dear.' Maud stands looking out over the bronzing horizon. 'They think themselves so clever. How they twist the king's language. "The Act for the Ad*vance*ment of *True* Religion."' Her voice drips sarcasm. 'What would they advance but their own positions? Gardiner and Wriothesley, their snake-in-the-grass minion Richard Rich.' She turns to Anne, frowning. 'Wriothesley appeared to favour the gospel in Cromwell's time. But his faith has gone to Rome now. Or, more accurately, to the tutelage of Stephen Gardiner. Though, truly, who knows what Thomas Wriothesley believes? Whatever will serve his own interests, if you ask me. And his wife is the same, though she is one of the queen's ladies—or was, before grief at her son's death seemed to addle her wits.'

'The loss of a child,' Anne says quietly, 'might well bring one to maddened grief.'

'Yes,' Maud murmurs. 'This is so.' They stand in silence. The season has not yet turned, but there is a hint of change in the air. On the river the boatmen hallo one another. In the garden, the chirr of insects rising and falling. 'Have you lost a child, then?' Maud asks.

'Not through death.' Anne begins slowly; it is a tiny window. She says only that she has two sons but was forced to leave them behind when she came to London. 'Oh, but I came for a good reason!' she says, as if her friend might think otherwise. 'I came to seek an annulment!' Now she wishes she could call the words back. But she has begun, and so she continues. 'He is a papist. We must not be yoked with unbelievers, so the Apostle Paul says in Corinthians.'

'My lord husband adhered to the old religion. I could not turn his mind. Even so, he was a man of great faith.'

'Did he beat you?' Anne asks.

Maud glances at her sharply. 'He was a good man. An honourable husband.'

'I envy you, then.'

Lady Lane studies her a moment. Then she turns back to the view. 'Who is caring for your sons?'

Anne takes in a deep, ragged breath. 'I do not know. I fear what their father tells them about me. Worse, I fear that when I have them again, they'll not remember me. Do you think that they will?'

'A mother's touch is a powerful memory, I find. Shall we sit?' Lady Lane makes her way to a stone bench and seats herself, pats the empty space beside her. 'How will you proceed with this . . . undertaking?'

'My cousin the lawyer says I must go to the Court of Chancery.'

'Ah, well. That is misfortunate. The lord chancellor, Thomas Wriothesley . . . well, I have told you what he is.'

'He will preside over my case?'

'All cases in Chancery are under his supervision. And those at Star Chamber as well.'

'Does he disdain all women, then? Or only the queen?'

Maud snorts. '*Disdain* is a mild word for it. In any case, no. He does not disdain his wife, I think.' She plucks a broad leaf from a nearby plant, begins to fan her face and neck. 'I am not much fond of Jane Wriothesley,' she says, 'but I understand her grief. As my cousin perhaps does not, for Kate has never borne children. She wrote a letter of condolence to Lady Wriothesley, and her words were true enough to Scripture, but they were not very sympathetic. She told her she oughtn't to lament her son's death with such inordinate sorrow, lest God take it that she questions His will. The queen's advice, as you may imagine, was not happily received. Soon afterwards, my lady Wriothesley left court. Now there is even greater antipathy between the lord chancellor and Katheryn, and there was enmity enough already.' Maud grows silent, gazes out over the river. The leaf lies unattended in her lap. 'I have lost two,' Maud says quietly. 'My son shortly after his birth. My daughter a few months later. I do not doubt that they are in a more perfect place. I do not question the Father's will in this, as in all things. But I grieve them. With all my heart. Every day.'

Anne reaches over, touches the back of her friend's clenched fist. They sit in perfect silence as the companionableness between them settles into something deeper.

The sun is below the horizon now. The garden is bluing. After a long while, Anne says, 'I wonder that God's love does not save us from grief. And yet it does not. Even our Blessed Saviour suffered. At the death of his friend Lazarus, Jesus wept. I've not lost a living child, but I have lost loved ones whom I loved so deeply I thought I should die from sorrow. Sometimes I am very afraid that I have already lost my sons. And I . . . I lost a child before it drew breath. Some might think that a small matter. But it was not a small matter.' She sits holding back a moment, and then, as if a dam has broken, her words pour forth: she tells of her husband's jealousies, his vile accusations, the black drink her mother-in-law gave her, the clot of blood taken out to the barnyard and tossed away. 'It was not even a child,' she says carefully. 'Only the promise of one. But for its loss I am very sorry.' Soon she is describing how Kyme dragged her up the stairs by her hair, beat her mercilessly in front of her children, sat on the floor afterwards, weeping. She tells how he ripped pages from her Coverdale Bible, broke its spine, torched it in the flames. Her words are terrible, but she speaks them calmly, in a low, breathless voice. 'I miss my sons,' she says. 'I pray God every day they'll be returned to me. Am I wrong to be here, do you think? My cousin Brittayne says I am. He says I am the vilest creature on earth.'

'No!' Maud grips her hand. 'Don't think it! Never think it, Anne. Listen. Why would God give you such gifts if not to use them? Any day you come among us, do we not learn of the gospel? You must trust God that your sons are not lost to you. And when the queen returns from progress, you must come to us again and teach us.' She pats Anne's hand affectionately, practically—not at all as if Anne had just poured out her soul. 'Ah, look there. The watch lights are being lit. We must go in.' Lady Lane rises, begins to climb slowly towards the palace. Anne follows. Her heart is warm, her feet light.

* * *

Later, in the cramped dimness of her little room, she takes out her Testament to read, but her mind will not settle. The court leaves on progress soon, and Anne will return to the dull routine of her dull dinners with the dull-as-dust Widow Hobbes, her daily rote lessons to Beatrice, and, yes, of course, her evening gospel meetings with John Lascelles, but . . . oh, how is it that her former life seems now so tedious, when it had seemed so wondrously exciting before? She knows now why her brothers changed after their time at court, why they never came home again to live in Lincolnshire, nor wanted to—not even Edward. Anne feels the same. Even if she might be no more than an inky transcriber sitting at a scarred desk in a dingy corner, she would still prefer to be here. How she shall miss her conversations with Lady Lane, their companionable warmth, their fevered discussions of Holy Scripture!

But already there is a flurry of preparations, barked orders, careful packing of bedding and wardrobe and plate. They'll travel first to Woking, Maud tells her, and then perhaps later to one of the royal palaces farther south; for Her Highness must keep the king's children well away from London, where there is just now a hard outbreak of plague—oh! my poor Beatrice. Anne is swept with guilt. Yes. There is plague in London, and she knows this, and she has not even considered Beatrice's welfare, nor hardly thought of her. Nor has she considered her friend John Lascelles, how he fares, why he has not returned to see her as he promised. *Oh, I am selfish and absorbed with foolish pride! Jesu Lord, forgive me!*

Anne rises from her stool; her forefinger marks her place in her Testament, but she cannot read. She paces the floor, not to commit verses to memory but to try to tame her thoughts, which dart and swoop like swallows; she cannot contain them. She thinks of her children, her sisters, the summer Wolds in Lincolnshire; she thinks of her maidservant alone and penniless in London, her brothers Edward and Francis at the siege of Boulogne—and what if they should be killed there? Englishmen die every day in Picardy. The stories roll across the channel with horrific details: hunger, dysentery, skirmishes, stabbings; there is an outbreak of plague also in Calais. Anne pauses in the centre of the tiny room, eyes closed. She feels her infant son in her arms, her sweet baby William, pressed against her chest as he nurses, his silky crown, the milky half-sweet-half-sour scent of him, his tiny hand kneading her upper arm. She feels young Thomas tugging her skirts, his little child's voice pleading, Hold you! Hold you!

There is no viler creature on earth.

She kneels on the stone floor to pray.

When Lucretia comes early next morning with her breakfast, Anne tells her to please inform Lady Lane that she must depart for London as soon as possible to collect her belongings and her maid, and from there travel home to Lincolnshire. She has completed her translations and will deliver them to the groom this morning, with a written request to Her Highness for permission to leave court. But she will require a conveyance of some sort, and she has no money. Would Lady Lane, as her friend, please see to her passage?

In just over an hour the burly maidservant returns. 'Compliments of my mistress,' she says, and presents a linen-wrapped parcel. Anne waits until the servant withdraws. She knows what it is before she unwraps it—or perhaps it is just that the moment is so life-changing, she simply tells herself later that she knew. The cover is brown calfskin, the volume a folio, much finer than Maddie's. She opens the front board, traces her fingers along the words:

BIBLIA
The Bible, that
is, the holy Scripture of the
Olde and New Testament, faith-
fully and truly translated out
of the Douche and Latyn
in to Englishe

Anne sits holding it, caressing it; she recalls the blush of warmth in her breast yesterday, her pleasure at Lady Lane's words: *We've never had someone like you among us—a person with so much Scripture by heart.* After a long while, Anne rises. She replaces her Tyndale beneath the bolster, holds the Coverdale in her arms, and goes to join the queen's ladies.

III

Sanctus, Sanctus, Sanctus

London

August into Autumn

1544

– Chapter 40 –

Beatrice has not responded to Anne's letters for the simple reason that it has not occurred to her to do so. She has never written anything except the alphabet and the few short verses her mistress would write out and bid her copy, certainly nothing so complicated as a letter. She would not even know how to begin. In any case, communication is from the mistress to the servant, not the other way 'round, and so Beatrice merely puts the two missives atop the cupboard and from time to time unfolds them, frowning as she studies the words. She does know Anne's whereabouts, however, and has since the afternoon of the day she left, because Master Lascelles came rushing from the pier directly to the Widow Hobbes' front door, exclaiming with great excitement where Mistress Anne is and what she is doing and that she may not return until the queen dismisses her. This mightily impressed Mistress Hobbes, who fluttered and tutted about the hall and suddenly became, if not kind to Beatrice, at least less curt. Master Lascelles gave Beatrice money for her keep and told her she must continue to attend their gospel meetings while her mistress is at court, and Beatrice, not knowing any words to say to a superior but *yes, sir,* finds she has agreed.

Thus, in her mistress's absence, Beatrice walks each evening with Master Lascelles and his boy Jack to evangelical gatherings around London, and also, on Sundays, to Mass at St Mary Aldermary, where the rector, Dr Crome, most marvellously repeats in his sermons the same words she has heard in basements and backrooms all week. This is very strange to Beatrice, and strange, too, is the new manner in which she sees Master Lascelles: he is not the puffed-up, proud man she had thought, but a kind man who calls her by name and inquires if she's had enough to eat. The Widow Hobbes, however, is less solicitous. 'You've too much time on your hands,' she says, lips pursed, arms folded, her own fluttery hands caught in the clefts of her armpits. 'Idle hands are the devil's playthings! I'll find work for you to do.'

Beatrice bobs her head, retreats to Mistress Anne's rooms, where she waits quietly until all is silence downstairs because the widow is napping; then Beatrice slips out to Cheapside for her supper, or she walks to the quays to stare across the river at the brothels and pestilential houses. She has never lived in a place where the plague was so raging. The very notion fills her with fear. The gatherings in their gospel meetings have grown smaller as the rumours darting about the city grow wilder: A hundred dead in Southwark! They lie stacked like cordwood at the gates of Lambeth Palace! The bearers cannot keep up with the scores of bodies that must be carried to the burying fields! Master Lascelles tells her not to listen to such tales; Christ the Lord will protect them. Still, as they return in the evenings, when they pass a house with a padlocked door and a large red cross nailed to it and English words written upon the wood asking God's mercy upon the misfortunate inhabitants boarded up inside with their misfortunate sick, Beatrice shudders and holds her hand over her nose to prevent the effluvium from entering as she hurries past. She notices that both Master Lascelles and Jack do the same.

It is true, though, what the widow says: Beatrice does have too much undedicated time on her hands. During the empty days she feels restless, useless, without direction. She is nearly twenty years old and has spent her entire life in service; she has always been told where to be, what to do, how to serve, how to speak. She cannot imagine any other purpose. She ponders the notion of returning to South Kelsey, perhaps to serve Mistress Lisbeth again, but she hasn't any money to travel, and in any case, Master Lascelles tells her that Mistress Anne will soon return. But it cannot be soon, for it is long already, and the Widow Hobbes would have Beatrice's idle hands scrubbing floors in the kitchen under the serving boy and cook, for she has said as much, and that would be an unbearable reduction and mortification, and Beatrice will not do it if she can help it. So she hides herself in her mistress's rooms and scans her mistress's letters and says her Latin prayers, and waits.

In the third week she begins, during the widow's nap time, to walk to St Paul's to hear Mass. She lights candles for her dead father, stands before the Blessed Virgin, feels the comfort of the holy prayers murmuring through her, *Ave Maria, gratia plena, dominus tecum, benedicta tu in mulieribus*. Her spirit is bathed in calmness to hear the beautiful kyrie eleison sung, the Eucharistic prayers murmured, *sanctus, sanctus, sanctus*, her heart lifting in worship and wonder when the priest elevates the Host, *per ipsum, et cum ipso, et in ipso*; she is soothed, sanctified, as she gazes up at the sacred Body of Christ.

Early evening. The days have shortened. Mists from the river ghost the streets. They are walking north towards a meeting in Holborn when young Jack stops still. 'Look, master!' He crosses himself, stands staring. In the mud, not five rods distant, a man's half-naked body lies staring sightless at Heaven. The nose and lips are black, the clawed fingers black also, and at the neck and below the armpits, angry black welts ooze blood and pus. He cannot have been dead long. The stench is unbearable. Master Lascelles grips Beatrice's elbow and pulls her backwards, his kerchief covering his nose. Together they retrace their steps, hurrying back to the Temple district. Before they reach the widow's door, Master Lascelles stops on a corner, panting with exertion. He lowers his kerchief. 'I think we need not mention this to Mistress Hobbes,' he tells Beatrice. 'I think, too, perhaps we'll not attend meeting tomorrow. Nor, perhaps, indeed, again until plague season is past.'

This is fine with Beatrice. She has become increasingly uncomfortable at the meetings, though she cannot say why, and at the same time she has felt compelled to hide from Master Lascelles her daily visits to St Paul's. She does not understand this, but the feeling is strong in her, and it makes her uneasy. And now, oh, now: the sight of the dead plague victim fills her with such horror, she'll gladly go to Mistress Anne's rooms and stay there till the pestilence is past. She starts to leave, turns back. 'Tell me again, sir, if you will: when may I expect my mistress?'

'Soon.'

'Yes, sir, but when is soon, sir?'

'I don't know! How can I know? No person from the city is allowed at court, for fear of contagion! But it cannot be long now. Pray for her, Beatrice. Pray for us all.' Master Lascelles covers his nose again, jerks his head at Jack, and the two hurry away.

And Beatrice does pray. Several times a day she kneels beside her pallet with her beads, the small wooden crucifix clenched tight; she touches fingers to forehead, breastbone, shoulders, *In nómine Patris, et Fílii, et Spíritus Sancti*, prays the rosary around, counting with her fingers, pausing long on the final prayers. *Salve Regina. Mater misericordiae. Ad te clamamus exsules filii Hevae.*

Holy Queen.

Mother of mercy.

To thee do we cry,

we poor banished children of Eve.

At first she thinks it is a phantasm. Then a dream. But when she realizes it is truly her mistress standing in the doorway in the grey light of morning, the wash of relief and happiness that surges through Beatrice is beyond any joy she has ever known.

'Oh, mistress!' The girl scrambles to her feet, slipping her rosary into her pocket. 'Here, let me help you!' she cries, though her mistress carries no heavy bag, only a wrapped parcel clutched to her chest. Mistress Anne remains standing in the doorway, blinking, staring, as if she's been spirited here in a dream and, awakening, cannot fully grasp her surroundings. Behind her, in the dim hallway, the Widow Hobbes, still in her nightcap, flutters and frowns.

'We have tried to keep good order,' the widow tuts, 'but your maidservant, madam, well, I could not help it, if all is not in order, you'll not blame me. How fares the queen? And His Majesty's children, they are well? And what news of the king's Grace? He is hale and hearty, I suppose?' She is still talking when Anne steps inside the room and shuts the door. The widow calls through the closed door: 'I'll have my dinner at eleven! Please join me! I should like to hear all the court news!'

The room now is even dimmer. The poor light from the window in the next room barely seeps into this one. They stand in silence a moment. Then Beatrice goes to her mistress, reaches up to unclasp her cloak, and with that simple gesture, all falls into place. All is as it should be. The world, for Beatrice, is properly ordered once more.

But something, she gradually perceives, has changed in her mistress. Anne prays no less often, reads her Bibles no less assiduously—she has two now, a large one and her small one: the contents of the wrapped parcel—and begins within the week to instruct Beatrice in her letters. But her instructions come gently, her voice is patient and kind; she sits in silent contemplation, sometimes for hours, and she is altogether quieter, calmer, stiller. Beatrice finds herself walking carefully, speaking only what is necessary—Will you have your breakfast now, miss? Shall I dress your hair?—as if Anne were a leavened loaf in the oven, rising, and any jarring slam of a door, any bang of a dropped kettle, might cause her to deflate in an instant.

Master Brittayne comes. What passes between the cousins, Beatrice does not know; she waits inside the room while they speak in the outer hall. She can hear their low murmurs, her mistress's new gentle voice, Master Brittayne's hesitant rumble, but the words are not plain enough for her to hear. When Mistress Anne steps back inside, she is smiling benignly. She hands Beatrice coins to purchase their supper. Peace, it seems, has been made.

Days later, Master Lascelles arrives. Beatrice follows her mistress down the stairs. Master Lascelles' hair is sleek, his cap new. 'Boulogne has fallen!' he cries. 'We are victorious!' Mistress Anne nods.

She knows. Indeed, all London knows. The bells have been ringing for hours. 'You look well!' Lascelles says, gazing at her with shining face. 'Doesn't she?' the Widow Hobbes offers. 'The queen's court agrees with her, does it not?'

'And you, my friend?' Anne says. 'You are well?'

'Look at me!' Master Lascelles thumps his chest. 'Thick as a mule and twice as hearty!'

'And what of our friends at Holburn? And Ludgate and Whitechapel? One hears such terrible stories.'

'All are well!' Lascelles booms. 'So far as I know. The plague has passed. Or is passing. Or will soon pass, I think.' He cuts a glance at the widow, but when he turns back to Anne, his face is still radiant. 'When will you join us again? We have missed you!'

'This evening,' Anne says.

'Oh, ah, yes. I see. Let me . . .' Master Lascelles flaps his hand vaguely. Beatrice suspects he had not intended to return to their meetings just yet. 'I shall need to make inquiries. Tomorrow, perhaps? Yes, tomorrow evening, I think. Or perhaps the day after.'

As they eat their cold supper in their rooms that evening, Beatrice ventures to ask her mistress what she has been longing to know since the bells began pealing the news that the war in France is ended: 'When shall we go home, miss?'

Anne smiles. 'Not soon, Beatrice. My case cannot come before Chancery till next term.' She draws quiet a moment, then adds softly, 'I must go as I am led, Beatrice. Or stay as I am told. For now, I deem my work to be here. In London. Among the believers. Perhaps later I shall be sent forth to share the gospel, as others were sent.'

Two nights later they begin their evening visits to the various gospel meetings about the city: Master Lascelles and Anne striding rapidly in front, heads together in fervent conversation, Beatrice and Jack coming behind, as if there'd been no interlude from the first time to this.

It is here, in these secret prayer rooms and brewery basements and merchants' halls, that Beatrice sees how deep is the well of change within her mistress. Anne has always been quick to offer her opinions, quoting snippets of Scripture to support her convictions. In the earlier time, others would rise to argue or recite their own verses.

But now Mistress Anne stands before them and reads from her splayed Bible in such bold, crisp, melodic tones, and then explicates what she has read in such simple language, with such confidence and clarity, that it seems no one will rise to dispute with her. It is almost, Beatrice thinks, as if her mistress were preaching—except that she is a woman, of course, and stands in no pulpit, and does not raise her voice shouting like Dr Crome. The girl sees how the others regard her mistress with respect and honour, and a kind of affectionate awe, and the same so for Master Lascelles, who gazes at Anne with rapt attention when she is reading or speaking.

Beatrice, though, in her secret heart, thinks Mistress Anne leaves many mysteries unanswered. If it is not the real body and blood of Christ in the Blessed Sacrament, Beatrice thinks, why do the priests say that it is? Would not God have struck them dead ages ago for such a lie, if it were a lie indeed? If the miracle of the Mass is not a miracle, if the consecrated Host is mere bread, as evangelicals say, then why does Beatrice feel such wonder and adoration when she gazes upon it at the elevation? Why does her spirit feel so pure and right and sanctified when she prays at Easter with God's body melting on her tongue? And why is she filled with such uneasiness and longing these dreary autumn days when she can no longer slip away from their rooms to hear Mass at St Paul's? Beatrice does not question her mistress. She would never argue or dispute with her, and she knows herself too ignorant to do so anyway. She is a good girl, obedient, deeply grateful that Anne has returned; she studies her letters, follows her mistress and Master Lascelles to their meetings, listens to the gospel read aloud in English again and again, but Beatrice remains unpersuaded. She knows what she knows.

Book Five

London and Lincolnshire

1546

I

What Sin Had She Committed

London
March
1546

– Chapter 41 –

Ash Wednesday, and Anne emerges from Dr Crome's sermon at St Mary Aldermary, her heart lifted, her spirits keen. Beside her walks her friend John Lascelles. Behind her, coming slowly, her servant Beatrice. It is a year and a half since Anne made acquaintance with the queen's ladies. She still visits them from time to time when the court is at Whitehall or St James; they meet in the queen's privy rooms, in secret, to study Scripture, but she no longer writes translations for Queen Katheryn—such services are no longer needed. Where Anne serves, whether privately among the queen's ladies or openly among evangelicals in London, is in delivering the gospel. She offers it especially to those who cannot read it for themselves, freely quoting Paul and John and Luke and Matthew. Her knowledge of Scripture is prodigious, celebrated, renowned. The fair gospeller, they call her.

Gliding from the church shadow into grey morning light, Anne pauses. Before her, crowding up and down the steps and into the street, are dozens of brothers and sisters in Christ waiting to speak with her, greet her, offer the sign of peace. These are my people, she thinks tenderly. Her dearest kin in the Lord, whose faces, thoughts, temperaments she knows as well as her own. Anne descends the steps, takes the outstretched hand of a flushed laundress who waits for her. Faces turn to her; an old memory flickers: a cold late-winter day years ago in Friskney; she'd walked out of the church into muddy light, as today, and there, on the pocked limestone steps, the Vicar Jordan stood waiting. Behind him, all through the church yard and into the muddy lane, the villagers of Friskney turned to look at her. The vicar had admonished her in front of them, berating her loudly for . . . what? She cannot recall. What sin had she committed to earn such public shaming? Beatrice will know. Anne glances back, smiling, to ask her.

Beatrice stands on the top step, staring into the street. Anne, still smiling, turns to follow her gaze. Two men in livery are shouldering their way through the crowd, grim-faced, purposeful. In an instant they surround her, and then she is in their custody, being marched between them north along the street. It is a moment before she grasps what has happened. Behind her she hears cries, shouts of anger and outrage; she recognizes Lascelles' voice, and Beatrice's: 'Mistress Anne? Mistress Anne!' The girl is panting, running behind them. 'Go back!' Anne calls over her shoulder. 'Find Brittayne! Tell him I'm taken up!'

'You're not to speak to anyone!' The man to her right tightens his grip. And from her left: 'On strictest orders!'

'Whose orders?'

But the men squeeze her arms tighter, walk faster, propelling her as if she were a puppet, a toy pony on wheels; she hears Beatrice's panting breaths receding as the men hurry her north across Cheap, turn her west and then north again, to Gutter Lane, where the severe face of Saddlers' Hall stands glowering: one of the finer livery halls in London, though hardly the finest—and certainly the cramped room to which the two men escort her is not fine. Whose men the guards are, she cannot tell. She does not recognize their badges.

'Stand here, madam.'

And here she stands. The scene is familiar. Nine frowning men rowed up behind desks, and she to stand in the centre, facing them. She tilts back her head. But these are not justices, and this is nothing like the Court of Chancery at Westminster, where last autumn she'd stood facing the lord chancellor and his judges scarcely ten minutes before her plea for divorcement was dismissed. Nor is it much like the proceedings last summer, when she'd been arrested with two others for violation of the Six Articles and brought before a jury at Guildhall. No witnesses had come forward to accuse them, and they'd all been released—to the open rejoicing of their supporters who filled the great hall. But times then, for evangelicals, were not so perilous as these. The warnings are whispered in every gospel meeting throughout the city: the Bishop of London seeks heretics beneath every bush! Beware Lord Chancellor Thomas Wriothesley! Stephen Gardiner has returned from France with hissing malevolence, the conservatives are in the ascendant now, arrests are made daily for offences against the Act of Six Articles—be aware, brothers and sisters!

But why is Anne taken up alone?

'Mistress Kyme,' says the merchant-looking fellow in the middle. He is neither old nor young, neither kind nor gruff, handsome nor ugly, gentleman nor common. He is of a type she sees every day on the streets of London: shopkeepers, mercers, tradesmen, the fellows whose wealth and civic engagement engine the city. 'You've come before us today to answer to certain accusations.'

'And who may you be, sir?'

An old fellow in a green bonnet says, 'We're to ask the questions, madam. You're to answer.'

'Master Christopher Dare,' the first man says. 'Member of the Common Council and chairman of today's inquiry.'

'Not a member of the commission, then?'

'Silence!'

Anne turns her eyes along the row: to the left of Master Dare are four men of equivalent age and station, with fine caps, dour looks, and dark coats; to his right three more the same, and at the end, the old man in the green bonnet glaring. It is he, the old man, who ordered her to silence, she thinks. The room has an air of familiarity, and uncertainty. This is—what? A citizens' quest?

'Tell us, Mistress Kyme.' Master Dare glances down at the scrawled page on the desk before him. 'What say you to the Sacrament?' he reads. 'Is the bread hanging over the altar the very body of Christ, really?'

'Am I charged with a crime, sir?'

'You must answer the questions!'

Master Dare continues reading: 'If it should fall from the pyx and a mouse eat it, doth that mouse ingest the very body of God?'

This is an old poser designed to trick one into offending the Six Articles. Anne is not so easily gulled. 'Can you tell me, Master Dare, for what cause Saint Stephen was stoned to death?'

The man glances at his fellow inquisitors. They are all frowning. This is not in their script. 'I cannot,' he answers finally.

'Then, sir, I'll not resolve your vain questions.' Her voice is pleasant, but her mouth is tight, her eyes sharp. She refrains from remedying the man's ignorance: Saint Stephen was stoned because he went among the people sharing the gospel of Christ. The Sanhedrin brought false witnesses against him. Master Dare squints down at his page—the hand it is written in is not familiar to him, she thinks. He finds it hard to decipher.

'It is reported, Mistress Kyme, that you have said that you would rather read five lines in the Bible than hear five Masses in church. Is this true?'

'I wish you would not call me Mistress Kyme. My name is Anne Askew.'

'Is it true!'

'I confess I have said no less. For the one edifies me greatly, and the other nothing at all.' She has dropped her pretence of gracious cooperation. 'As Saint Paul says in his first epistle to the Corinthians: if the trumpet gives an uncertain sound, who will prepare himself to the battle?'

The men glance at one another. They have no idea what she is talking about. Christopher Dare reads on: 'It is reported also that you have said that if an evil priest ministers the sacrament, it is of the devil and not of God.'

'No, sir. What I have said is that it matters not what manner of man ministers unto me. His evil condition cannot hurt my faith, for in faith and in spirit do I receive the body and blood of Christ.'

A whisper as of a soughing wind runs along the row of men: *in spirit, in spirit, in spirit*: is this not a violation? Sectaries hold that the Blessed Sacrament is not the real flesh, blood, and bone of Christ but His symbol in spirit.

'I suppose you think that you have the spirit of God in you?'

'If I have not, sir, I am but a reprobate and cast away into damnation.'

There is a murmured ruffling. Surely this is blasphemy, for a woman to speak so? Christopher Dare motions to the back of the room. Anne turns to see the two liveried men guarding the door. One comes forward. Master Dare speaks to him quietly. The man leans down to answer in Dare's ear, and at Dare's curt nod, he straightens and goes out.

'I have sent for a priest, madam. He is near at hand and will soon join us. Would you care to sit while we wait?'

'I've no need of a priest, sir.'

'He is here to examine you, madam, not shrive you.'

'I see. No, I'll stand. Thank you.' And she remains motionless, arms folded over her satchel, looking calmly at the row of men, who murmur with heads together, avoiding her gaze. The priest comes. He is plump and pale, wears a white surplice and stole as if he has just come from Mass. She does not know him. He takes the seat next to Dare, and the others are forced to shift over. 'Good morning, madam. How do you?'

'I'm well, Father. And you?'

'I am sad today, for I hear unhappy reports of your unseemly doings.'

'Doings, Father?'

'Your reputation is greatly noised about. We hear that you speak against the Sacrament of the Altar—a violation which, as you must know, condemns the offender to the fire.' The priest leans towards her, his voice firm: 'What say you to the Real Presence, then, Mistress Kyme?'

'On that point, Father, I've said to Master Dare all I have to say.'

A hurried scratching of pens as the men scribble their notes. Anne watches them, her chest tight. This, then, is how they mean to manipulate her, for offence against the First Article: *that after the consecration there remaineth no substance of bread and wine, nor any other substance but the substance of Christ.* The penalty for denying the Real Presence is death by burning. She does not speak again, but at every repeated question, she smiles. The interrogation continues, the same questions over and over. Anne begins to sway slightly. They have not relieved her of her cloak, have offered nothing to drink; the room is airless, close. She grips herself, stands straighter. Tensions rise. The men are hungry by now, thirsty, in need of a piss. At last Master Dare explodes: 'Send her to my lord mayor! I can get nothing from her, and I don't suppose I shall if we sit here till the cocks crow! Take her out! Take her to Master Bowes!'

Under guard, Anne is escorted to the mayor's mansion in Lombard Street. My lord mayor, Martin Bowes, has been forewarned of her coming, it seems, for he has with him to aid in his questioning the bishop's chancellor, Dr Standish, who is tall and imposing, with fading beard and small eyes. The mayor is his opposite: short and round, pink-cheeked, with many rings on his fingers buried in the flesh of his hands. He wears his chain of office, Dr Standish a cleric's robe. The room where they question her is at the rear of the house. Through the small window behind, the scent of sewage drifts.

The lord mayor begins with a silken ruffling of his great sleeves and clearing of his throat. 'I am told you asked evil questions of Master Dare!'

'No, my lord.'

'Did you not demand he resolve this conundrum: If consecrated bread fall from the pyx and a mouse eat it, does that mouse ingest the very body of God?'

'I did not ask it, sir. He asked this of me.'

'And what was your answer?'

'I made none.'

'And what is your answer now?'

Anne smiles.

Dr Standish paces the room, a lion prowling. Her eyes follow him. She is outwardly calm, but the muscles in her jaws cramp. He stops suddenly, whirls to face her. 'You read lies aloud from heretical translations!'

'I am no heretic, sir.'

'You are much to blame for uttering Scripture. Saint Paul forbids women to speak of such things!'

'I know Paul's meaning so well as you, sir, which is that a woman ought not speak in the congregation by way of teaching. How many women have you seen go into the pulpit and preach?'

'None! God willing, I never shall!'

'I ask you, then, not to find fault in poor women, unless they have offended the law.'

The lord mayor bears down upon her. 'But you do offend, madam!'

'How so, my lord?'

'You, you, you—you are a sectary! Worse, madam,' he says, narrowing his eyes, 'I suspect you for an anabaptist.'

Anne looks blankly at him. Anabaptists are the most despised of all heretics. They are brought to the stake wherever they are found.

'Well?' the mayor growls. 'What say you?'

'I am not, sir.'

'Do you deny you consort with them?'

'I know some, sir. I do not consort with them.' This is true. In the teeming underground faith communities throughout the city, Anne has met more than a few of the outlawed sect, but she does not subscribe to their beliefs. She sees no need for a second baptism, nor to withdraw into separate communities, nor to deny that the king himself is the Supreme Head of the Church.

'Who are they, then?' Dr Standish demands. 'Name them! They'll be brought before the council!'

'I know none, sir.'

'You are a vain and deceitful woman,' Standish growls.

'I have sins enough, sir, but deceit is not one of them.'

'If you'll answer no questions,' the mayor says, 'you'll be taken in ward.'

'By what charge?'

'No charge is required, madam, but if you must have one, let it be this: you are an accused sectary and uncooperative witness. You'll remain in ward until your tongue is loosed and your heart changed.' He waves a dismissive hand. 'To the Compter with you.'

'Wait! Will not sureties release me? Allow me to send to my cousin Brittayne; he is a respected lawyer of Middle Temple—'

'I'll take no sureties, madam.' Impatiently, turning now to the wine pitcher on the sideboard, Bowes signals to the two escorts to remove her.

The sun has vanished behind St Paul's by the time they emerge from the lord mayor's mansion. The streets are crowded with home-goers, dim with shadow, cold with damp. The guards do not grip her arms now. They have quit their haste. 'Whose men are you?' Anne asks, but they do not answer; they are tight-lipped, serious, grim as reapers as they turn her onto Bread Street. Anne's heart clenches as they steer her towards a courtyard on the west side where the mottled edifice of an ancient brick house leers down: iron bars stripe the windows; smoke rises from one of the five chimneys. The Compter in Bread Street. The most pestilential of London's gaols. Anne had never thought to see beyond the courtyard wall, but her escorts conduct her through the gate, pound at the door, deposit her with the pit-scratching man who opens it, make haste to speed away. The stink when she enters near knocks her to the floor. The room is so dark she can make out very little—a fire flickering in the corner, the pale hulk of the man.

'Is it the sheriff or the mayor that sends ye?' the man says, still scratching.

'My lord mayor, I suppose.'

'Where are you to be lodged, then? On the third floor, I'll wager. But you'll have to pay up first. Quality lodgings always pays ahead.'

'I'll not lodge here, sir. The smell is abhorrent.'

The man laughs. 'You must take that up with the mayor, then. He'll send you straight home to your good family, I don't doubt.' His hair is greasy, his face slick. Anne stands glaring at him. Her eyes have adjusted to the dimness. She finds herself in a crude stone hall furnished with two benches, a table, a small desk. There's a fire-pit in the corner, three lit candles in sconces. The stink in the room is partly tallow, she knows, partly unemptied piss pots, partly the man himself—but there is another stench laced through which she cannot name. From below stairs, a good distance below and towards the back of the hall, she hears a faint, high-pitched keening. Overhead a rhythmic, incessant banging, as of someone beating an iron plate. For the first time on this day of days, Anne begins to be afraid.

'What's it to be, missus?' The man is eyeing the cut of her cloak, the faded grey velvet revealed underneath. He has the bulbous nose of a drinker, the sly eyes of a fox, and with them he skims her up and down. 'Your people will have to bring you your victuals, and money to rent your blankets and your wash water. So, have ye the shilling for the quality lodging?'

'Why am I here?'

'That'd be for the mayor to tell you. He's a stern one, is my lord mayor Sir Martin Bowes. Some's sterner than others. If you haven't the shilling, then you'll go to the commons floor.'

'But I'm a gentleman's daughter!'

'I don't take payment on promise, missus, not for the third floor. You can stay on the second on promise of the penny, and when your people comes to bring your supper, they can pay it. Else you're welcome to stay in the hole for free till your sentence is done, or your trial comes up, or your people comes to bail you. But I tell you, missus, I don't think you want to go down there.'

'They cannot come to bail me! They don't know I am here!'

The man shrugs. He goes to the desk and takes out an iron circle of keys. 'Follow me.'

'What? No! Who are you?

'Richard Husband, gaoler and sole proprietor.' He makes a mock little bow. 'At your service. What's it to be, missus? Third floor or second?'

Her voice sounds small in her own ears when she says, 'I've no money.'

'Second it is, then.' His eyes measure her. 'We'll sort the penny later.' He plucks a candle from a sconce, turns towards the stairs, but Anne does not follow. He stops, looks at her, considers a moment. Then he steps over and twists her satchel from her hand. He paws through the pamphlets and papers, plucks out the calfskin folio, runs his callused thumb over the leather. 'This'll do,' he says. 'For tonight's lodging.'

'No!' Anne cries. 'You may have the pamphlets. The paper can be sold for profit. And the satchel itself. But not my Bible, oh, please, sir!'

He looks long at her. 'One night's lodging,' he says. 'Tomorrow, we'll negotiate.' He sees by her face that she sees how it is. 'And to show there's no hard feelings, missus, I'll throw in tonight's bread and ale.'

– Chapter 42 –

For three days Beatrice does not know what's become of her mistress. Master Lascelles is searching all over London for her and has promised to send word the moment he knows. Beatrice is to wait in their lodgings in case Mistress Anne is released and makes her way home, in which event Beatrice is to hurry and find him straight away. Each hour that she waits, Beatrice's fear grows worse; it is a hot, knotted fist in her chest. This absence is not like when Anne was gone so long doing work for the queen. Beatrice knew where she was then, and that she would return. That was almost two years ago. The world was not so out of joint then, so upside down and full of danger. At last, on Friday afternoon, Lascelles' boy Jack knocks at her door. 'The Compter,' he says, panting. 'Hurry. Master John says hurry. He says if we bring money they'll let you in to serve her, maybe, he thinks. Come!'

They meet Lascelles at the corner of Watling and Bread Street. Without a word he sets off in his fast short-legged trot, and they hurry to keep pace. When Beatrice looks up and sees the ugly face of the building, the knot in her chest tightens. Master Lascelles pounds on the door. It opens, a horrid smell wafts out, and a man stands there, looking filthy and mean. They begin haggling, Master Lascelles and the gaoler, until the fellow growls, 'Pay the fee, sir, and the maid may go in, but not you, sir. She's not to have visitors, on the mayor's strictest orders. You'll have to take it up with him.'

'Go with him, Beatrice,' Lascelles says. At the gaoler's jerked head, Beatrice follows the man up the narrow stairs, stands aside while he unlocks a great iron-strapped door. When she enters the dark, reeking room, the knot in her chest twists tighter. The door closes behind her. She hears the key turn, *chink, chunk, chink.* The room is crowded with women, but Beatrice's eyes go straight to her mistress sitting on the side of a plank bed with her head in her hands. Anne glances up, then gets to her feet, reaching towards her as if she hardly believes what she is seeing. She takes Beatrice's hand, touching along the knuckles, the palms, then pulls her close and embraces her, weeping. Beatrice feels the knot softening in her chest, turning to something tender and warm. 'You've come,' Anne says. She wipes her face on her sleeve. 'Oh, I have prayed so hard! So hard, Beatrice. Bless you. Thank you. Thank you for coming. Oh, thank you, my good and gracious God!' She draws Beatrice to sit beside her on the bed, holds onto her hand as if she fears the girl might disappear. 'We must talk!' But then she says nothing, just sits gripping Beatrice's hand. Is she praying? Her lips do not move. Beatrice looks around the dim room.

There are eleven others here: she counts them. They sit on the floor with their backs to the wall or on the edges of the two beds in filthy smocks, unlaced bodices; she turns her eyes from their exposed bosoms. The youngest is no more than fourteen, Beatrice judges, the oldest past sixty—or perhaps she may be younger, but she has the collapsed mouth and greyed hair of an old woman. They stare at her. One says, 'Ain't we grand, to have a lady's maid come join us?' Another, half dressed, sitting cross-legged in the straw, eyes Beatrice carefully. 'Have you got a bit of bread about you?' Beatrice shakes her head. The old woman says from the corner, 'Leave her. She'll be gone in a quarter hour, and her mistress with her, if them that cares for her can grease Master Husband's palm.' Anne squeezes Beatrice's hand as if this is a sign. The only light is from a single iron-barred window, small, without shutters. It is open to the cold air, but even so, the stench in the room is overwhelming, reeking from the uncovered tub they use for a privy; it is a middling-sized wooden tub lined with tar, emptied only when it is too full to receive more waste. Anne tells Beatrice this later, after they have been moved upstairs: because indeed, in half an hour—not a quarter, as the old woman predicted—the gaoler returns, surly but subdued, and leads them up another flight to a gallery lined with four iron-clad doors. 'These is the quality quarters,' the man growls. 'You're paid for the week. After that, we'll see.'

Now they are locked inside a chamber alone. The bed here is also of planking, but it has a straw-filled tick, not loose straw strewn across it, and there is a blanket and a bolster—not clean, but at least, pray, without lice. Here is a fireplace, a wash bowl and ewer, a proper chamber pot. The window has shutters, no bars. The room is primitive, small, not pleasant, but Anne seems to think it a paradise. She sits down on the plank bed. Beatrice is alarmed at the change in her: she is bareheaded, dirty, pale as milk, thin as bone, and there is a kind of brittle desperation to her which Beatrice has never seen before. 'Please. If you'll stand up, miss?' With her hands—she has nothing else to work with—Beatrice brushes the dirt and straw from the mottled grey velvet. She pours water from the ewer, helps her mistress to wash, but the contamination of the women downstairs cannot be washed away; it's as if her mistress has taken some wretched part of them inside herself.

'You cannot imagine how terrible it is,' Anne whispers as Beatrice uses her fingers to comb and plait her hair. 'Every day. Every hour. They must pick oakum till their hands bleed, and at night they must fend off that evil man. Or else they haggle with him for privileges, a heel of bread, a few minutes in the sun. They pay with their bodies or their labour. Just to live, Beatrice. Just to live. Those that don't pay must go to the dungeon. But none of those are women, down below stairs. It is only men in the hole, they told me, for he causes the females, one way or another, to pay. But do men deserve to suffer so horribly, either? Would our Jesus say so? Oh, to think how often I have passed this way and never considered the misery behind these walls! But I shall, Beatrice! When I'm released, I shall come again and visit them. I'll not neglect to bring them God's Word!'

'What's become of your cloak, miss? And your cap?'

Anne goes rigid beneath her hands. After a moment, very quietly, she says, 'I gave them to him.'

Beatrice wants to ask further, but she is afraid. The chink of the key in the lock, they both jump, and the gaoler enters. Anne scuttles to the far side of the room, turns to face him with eyes fierce as a cornered cat's. The man tells Beatrice to come away now, or else she'll be locked in for the night. Beatrice looks in anguish to Anne.

'Go,' Anne says. 'Come again tomorrow.' Then, to the gaoler she announces, 'She'll come tomorrow.' She makes it a bold declaration, as if she is not afraid of him. As if she does not loathe and fear him like an adder. The man scowls, nods resentfully: this is part of what Master Lascelles' coins have paid for.

It is dusk already. In the courtyard two figures rush towards her: Master Lascelles and young Jack, herding her on either side, walking her quickly to the street, Master Lascelles' words tumbling: 'How is she? Is she well? Is she beaten? Oh, pray they do not beat her! You told her how we pray for her? How we pray with our whole hearts!' Yes and yes, and no, she is not beaten. Beatrice does not wish to say about the women, the filth, the naked bosoms. How her mistress scuttled away from the gaoler when he came. 'I think she'll be well now, sir. The accommodations are much improved. But we must come early tomorrow. Very early, sir.'

Beatrice arrives each morning as the church bells toll for matins, stands at the gate waiting to be admitted. She brings food, ale, candles, clean linens, a sliver of soap. The gaoler takes a portion of each basket, but this is accounted for, and so her mistress is fed well nevertheless. Lascelles does not come with her—he is working through channels, he says—but if the gaoler tries to keep her away, or cheat her, or extort more money, she is to come and find him straight away. 'She's to have a fire to warm her, and fresh water daily. If he does not provide these, you must tell me.' Every morning, the moment she arrives, Anne asks for news. Beatrice has little to tell—only that her mistress's friends are very worried for her, and that they are, with great diligence, doing all that they can. 'And what of my cousin Brittayne?' Anne says. 'And my brothers? They are working to help me?'

'Master Brittayne has been to Westminster many times, so his groom says. As to your brothers, I do not know, miss. It may be that word has not reached them yet.'

Anne nods, looks to the window. 'He has taken my Bible. All my pamphlets. I've nothing to read, no writing materials.' She turns. 'Can you bring me my Testament? The small one I keep behind the loose board—my Tyndale. It will fit beneath the cloth in your basket.'

Beatrice hesitates. What will the gaoler do if he discovers it while pawing through the victuals? Take it from her, at best. At worst—denounce her to the authorities? Lock her in with her mistress for good and all? 'I'll try, miss,' Beatrice says.

That evening she tells Master Lascelles. 'Not the Tyndale,' he answers. 'That would only put her in worse danger. Let me think on it.' This comment Beatrice relays back to her mistress, who at first appears angry, but immediately her brow smooths. 'Come look,' she says. 'I've fashioned a writing slate for us, from a bed slat and a charred stick.'

Days pass with no word, no visitors, no change, but that the money Lascelles paid has run out, the gaoler says, and the money Brittayne sends is not sufficient for the nasty man's greed. Beatrice fears what favours he may demand of her mistress—or of herself. And so she goes to Anne's friends among the evangelicals about the city: the merchants' wives, laundresses, drapers, the chandlers and tailors, the tanners and smiths, a number of young Jack's friends among the apprentices. She begs a penny here, a groat there, a shilling: it is enough. Just.

One morning a priest comes to see Mistress Anne. Beatrice retreats to her corner—she knows well how to make herself invisible—but she attends the conversation as keenly as a goshawk. The priest stands near the door with his hands crossed over his ample belly, explaining that he has been sent by my lord of London, Bishop Bonner, to examine the detainee, and also to give her good counsel. 'But first,' he says gently, 'can you tell me, daughter, by what cause are you shut up in the Compter?'

'I know not,' Anne says. 'Perhaps you can tell me.'

'It would be a great pity if you were here without cause.'

'It would. And yet here I am.'

'Then I am very sorry for you, Mistress Kyme.'

'I hope you'll relate your sorrow to my lord mayor, for he is the instigator of my injustice. And my name is not Kyme.'

Beatrice is surprised at her mistress's tone. This priest is the first visitor they've had in all these days; he is a man of God, his voice is gentle, his expression kind. Why is she so sharp with him?

'I am told,' the priest says, wagging his head sadly, 'that you have denied the Real Presence to the quest.'

'What I have said, I have said. If men tell lies about me, there is nothing I can do to stop them.'

This gives him pause. After a moment he continues in his sorrowful tone. 'I regret to see you in such straits, without spiritual guidance. Are you shriven, my child?'

Anne looks at him a long moment. 'No.'

'I will send someone,' he offers.

'I would be contented for that. So long as I might have one of these three: Dr Crome, Sir William Whitehead, or Father Huntington, for I know them to be men of wisdom. As for you, or another, I'll not dispraise, for I don't know you.'

The priest frowns. His voice is not so gentle when he continues. 'Answer me this, then, mistress. If the consecrated Host falls to the ground and a beast eats it, does that beast receive God or no?'

Anne laughs. 'That is an old duck, Father. I'm surprised you esteem it. But since you have taken such pains to ask the question, you must take further pains to resolve it yourself, for I will not do it.'

'It is against the order of schools that the one who asks the question should answer it!'

'Ah, well. I am but a poor woman and know nothing of the order of schools.'

'Do you intend to receive the Sacrament at Easter?' The anger in his face is now plain.

'Of course. Else I am no Christian woman. And I rejoice that the day of my Saviour's resurrection is so near at hand.'

'*Your* Saviour,' the priest sneers. 'Your own private alone-unto-yourself Saviour?'

'And so is He Saviour to us all, when we receive Him wholly in spirit and in faith.'

Beatrice watches the priest's face blanch with fury, then close smoothly as he seems to remember his instructions. His voice lowers into unctuous gentleness: 'Then must we send someone to shrive you, my child, that you may receive the Blessed Sacrament on that holy day.'

Anne will say nothing now, and so, at last, after many fair utterings, and making the sign of the cross to bless her, smiling benignantly, he goes out.

'How did you know, miss?' Beatrice says. 'That he'd not be so kind underneath?'

'I have seen his ilk before. God forgive them their ignorance. Come, let us practice.' And she sets Beatrice to copying her letters on a scrap of paper the girl has smuggled in.

Beatrice is leaving the Temple district very early next morning with the basket of supplies on her arm when she hears her name called. It is Master Brittayne, striding quickly to join her; he falls in step beside her, and they walk in awkward silence towards Bread Street. Her mistress's cousin is always awkward, this is his nature, but Beatrice feels acutely his discomfort today. It is very strange to be walking with a gentleman who is not her employer, and one whom she knows so little. Except she does know one thing: Master Brittayne is in love with her mistress. Both gentlemen are, in fact, both he and Master Lascelles. Neither will declare himself because Mistress Anne is, by law and by church, a married wife, and they are proper gentlemen. But mostly, Beatrice thinks, they'll not say because her mistress is entirely oblivious to their adoration and gives no hint of love in return.

At the Compter, Master Brittayne speaks to the gaoler with more politeness than does Master Lascelles: might his cousin the prisoner Mistress Anne be put to bail? 'No, sir, she's not allowed, sir.' 'But see here'—Brittayne shows his purse—'I've brought ready money: cannot the gaoler see his way to bail her?' 'Alas, no, sir, I've no authority to do it without I get permission under seal from my lord mayor. Howsoever, good sir'—the gaoler eyes Master Brittayne's purse—'should you wish to purchase amenities for the young lady, this could well be arranged.' Brittayne gives him a coin, turns to go, pausing beside Beatrice to say quietly in her ear: 'Tell my cousin your mistress that I . . . I . . . I'm on my way to see the lord mayor. Tell her to be of good cheer, we shall get it sorted. I'll return before night falls.' He goes out as the gaoler reaches for Beatrice's basket to see what victuals she has brought to share with him this day.

But in fact, Master Brittayne does not return before nightfall. In fact, it is two days later, as Anne and Beatrice are reading aloud from the queen's book on prayers and meditations—this is the reading material Master Lascelles has provided in lieu of Tyndale, in plain binding, along with sufficient coin to bribe the gaoler to let it pass—when the key clinks in the lock. They look at each other: what is this? The gaoler does not climb three flights except of necessity: to let Beatrice in at morning, and lock the door after her when she leaves at night; yet here he stands at midday, huffing with exertion. 'The gentleman that come with you the other morning is here,' he tells Beatrice. 'He wants you.' A slicing glare at her mistress, and he turns to lead the way back downstairs.

Master Brittayne waits in the courtyard. 'We have reason to hope,' he says. He does not appear hopeful—he appears mournful, angry, irritated, fatigued. There are puffy bags beneath his eyes. His words come out a long monotone: 'I requested my lord mayor to put her to bail, but he said he may not take sureties for one so accused without consent of a spiritual officer. "Accused how?" I said. "I have been to the king's council! I have been to the commissioners, the quest, Master Dare, I get no answers!" "Ah," says my lord mayor, "you must speak with the spiritual officer, then, the bishop's chancellor, Doctor Standish." "Oh, Christ help us," I spat, "that pompous priest!"'

He begins pacing the courtyard. Beatrice stares at him in wonder. She has never heard such a lengthy speech from him. 'And so I went to Doctor Standish, who said the matter is so heinous that he durst not do it himself, but that Bishop Bonner must be made privy to it!' Brittayne stops, stands peering at the top of the building as if he hopes to see Anne looking down from a window. 'I have made arrangements.' His voice cracks. 'They will send for her tomorrow at three of the clock. Bishop Bonner will examine her himself. He swears he'll take no advantage of her. You'll please tell her this.'

'Yes, sir.'

'The bishop is willing for her to have present such learned men as she is affectioned to. He wants witnesses, you see, to report that she is handled with no rigor. I told him that I, I . . .' He clears his throat. 'I know of no man that she is more affectioned to than another. But the bishop said he understood that she is affectioned to Doctor Crome, Friar Whitehead, and Father Huntington, for she knows them to be learned and of a godly judgement.'

'The priest told him that,' Beatrice says.

'What priest?'

'The one they sent four days since. My mistress says we mustn't trust him, though, for his kindness is sheep's wool.'

'Sent by whom?'

'Bishop Bonner, sir.'

'Oh, the devil!' Brittayne strides about the yard in increasing agitation. 'Bonner behaved as if this is news to him, as if he would hear the charges afresh, her testimony for the first time. He means to deceive us! Deceive Anne! Tell her to be aware. I shall meet her at the bishop's chambers, I'll bring friends. We'll be there at three o'clock, but tell your mistress not to be deceived by anything the bishop says.'

'Yes, sir. Will you bring Doctor Crome and the others, sir?'

'If she wants them.'

'I think . . . does it not seem strange, sir? That my mistress would mention these three, and the bishop did in turn name them to you? Is it a trick, sir?'

Master Brittayne stops his pacing. He stands gazing in hopeless longing at the empty windows along the top floor. 'Yes,' he says. 'Very possibly, it is.'

– Chapter 43 –

The guards came early to walk me to St Paul's. Bishop Bonner had told my cousin three o'clock—Beatrice was very certain about the hour—but the bells were pealing the first hour as they ushered me into my lord of London's chamber, so I perceived then Bishop Bonner intended to deceive me. He stood to greet me: a dog's face, heavy jowls, downturned mouth, hairy brows dark as coal, and a soft biretta like a fat black starfish on his head.

'I am very sorry for your trouble,' he said. Then he began at once to exhort me to tell him all the secrets of my heart. 'Anything you say, madam, I promise you, no man shall hurt you for it.'

'That is well to know,' I said. 'But as your lordship appointed three o'clock for my examination, and as my friends will not come till that hour, I desire you to pardon me from answering until then.'

'Ah, but you see,' said he, 'we have brought you early so that we might send for men to whom you are affectioned.'

'Which men might those be?'

'Why, the three you have mentioned: Crome, Whitehead, and Huntington.'

I looked on him a moment, his jowled face and piercing eyes. If he meant to surprise me, he did not. Beatrice had told me my cousin named to her these three. I knew if these faithful men came to stand for me, he would accuse them as well, or ensnare them in his specious arguments. Such tricks I would not be party to. 'I beg you not to put them to the pain,' I said. 'My friends, who will be here at three, are able enough to testify to all I should say.' This answer did not please him.

For two hours then my lord of London was in and out of the chamber, sometimes exhorting me, sometimes cajoling me, sometimes leaving me to his archdeacon, whom he charged to 'commune' with me: meaning deceive and trick me, until at last I was escorted to the large chamber where Bishop Bonner holds his court.

Here sat the bishop on his throne, and on his right hand, his chancellor, the stern Dr Standish, looking even more austere than in my lord mayor's mansion, and with him the scowling archdeacon, plus a dozen priests and prelates and gentlemen. As the bells of St Paul's rang the third hour, my cousin Brittayne arrived, and with him several others I know to be friends of the gospel. The bishop at once told my cousin he must persuade me to utter the very bottom of my heart. Brittayne looked hard at me, and with his lips said, 'It were well, cousin, for you to pour out to my lord bishop all he asks,' but his eyes told me: *Be wary, cousin. Be careful, alert, and aware.*

'Give heed to the counsel of your kinsman,' Bishop Bonner said, 'and tell us all things that burden your conscience. I assure you, there is no need to worry. No man here will take advantage of any word you speak.'

'I have nothing to say, my lord.'

'If a man has a suppurating wound, madam,' the bishop said, 'no wise surgeon will treat it before he has seen it uncovered. Just so, I cannot give you good counsel unless I know with what errors your conscience is burdened.'

'My conscience is clear in all things, sir. Therefore, to lay a plaster on healthy skin seems folly to me.'

'Not so! You have declared before the quest that a person receiving the Sacrament from an unworthy priest receives the devil, and not God!'

'I never said such words. What I said then, I say now: as to the Sacrament, the wickedness of a priest cannot hurt me, for in spirit and faith I receive the body and blood of Christ.'

'What saying is this? In *spirit*?' He met eyes with his chancellor. 'I'll not take advantage of you for that dissimulation, Mistress Kyme. Though it goes hard with me to let it pass.'

'My lord, without faith and spirit I cannot receive Him worthily. And my name is not Kyme.'

'What name would you have, then?'

'My name is Anne Askew.'

'Very well, Mistress Askew, I put it to you that you did say to Master Dare heretical words denying the Sacrament!'

'I quoted only Saint Paul's words in the Acts of the Apostles: God dwelleth not in temples made with hands.'

A light sparked in the bishop's eyes. 'And what is your faith and belief in that matter, madam?'

'I believe as the Scripture does teach me.'

'What if the Scripture says that it is the body of Christ?'

'I believe as the Scripture does teach me.'

'What if the Scripture says that it is *not* the body of Christ?'

'I believe as the Scripture informs me.'

Again he asked, and again, and again, till the whole room was wearied with the argument, and my friends grew restless, and some sniggered because I gave every time the same answer, but my lord of London was furious; he kept at his badgering, determined I should make an answer to suit him, until at last I said, 'I believe in this and all other things as Christ and his holy apostles did leave them,' and after that, I shut my mouth and answered his vain questions no more. This pleased him even less.

'Why have you so few words, madam?'

'God has given me the gift of knowledge but not of utterance, my lord. Wise Solomon did say that a woman of few words is a gift of God.'

'A woman with words enough, as I'm told, to avow that the Mass is superstitious and no better than idolatry!'

'Not so, my lord. Master Dare asked me whether private masses relieve souls departed. I merely answered, "What idolatry is this? That we should believe more in private masses than in the beneficial death of the dear Son of God."'

'What kind of answer is that?'

'A poor one, your lordship. But it was good enough for the question.'

Then Dr Standish leaned to the bishop's ear, murmured a few words. Bishop Bonner nodded, frowning. He turned to me. 'And what are your thoughts concerning the text you quoted of Saint Paul? You may speak openly.'

'Ah, forgive me, my lord, but it is against Saint Paul's learning that I, being a woman, should interpret the Scriptures. Especially'—I looked around the chamber—'where so many learned men are.'

A low chuckle came from my friends. The bishop glared. 'I am informed, Mistress Askew, that when a priest asked if you would receive the Sacrament at Easter, you made a mock of it.'

'Which priest? I would have you bring my accuser to face me.'

'I sent one to give you good counsel, and at his first words you called him a papist! You mock the priesthood at every turn, woman, the holy fathers and prelates! You have boasted to your friends that there were once bent against you three score priests at Lincoln!'

'I may have said so, my lord, for I was told if I went to the cathedral, the priests there would assault me and put me to great trouble. I went there indeed, not being afraid, and remained in the minster six days reading the Bible—in silence, my lord, as the law does allow me. The priests came by two and by two, by five and by six, and stood looking as if minded to speak to me, yet they went their ways without saying a word.'

'There was one who spoke to you, was there not?

'Yes, there was one, at the last.'

'And what did he say?'

'His words were of so small effect, my lord, that I do not now remember them.'

'There are many who read Scripture, madam, and yet do not live by it.' His voice was greasy with insinuation. 'They consort with one another most lewdly and keep not their own chastity nor God's laws!'

I gazed at him without blinking, for I understood his meaning. 'I would wish that all men knew my living in all points, sir. For I am so sure of myself this hour, I know there is none able to prove any unchastity by me. If you know any that can do it, I pray you bring them forth.'

He glared at me in silence. 'I shall retire to my chamber,' he growled, 'to make notes as to your testimony.' Then he stormed away, and his chancellor and clerk and priests with him.

I looked to my cousin and my supporters at the back of the room. Their brows were furled, their faces worried. I wanted to speak with them, but I was not permitted. The clerk came for me and took me to Bishop Bonner's inner chamber, where the bishop set before me a piece of writing.

'You are able to read this?' he said.

'I am.'

'Read it, then,' he said.

I did so, silently: *Be it known to all men that I, Anne Askew, alias Kyme, do confess this to be my faith and belief.*

The paper went on to say all manner of falsehoods, the most damnable one being this:

I do believe that after consecration, the Sacrament is no less than the very body and blood of Christ in substance, really.

The bishop demanded to know if I did agree to it.

'I believe so much here as the Holy Scripture agrees to,' I said. 'You will please add that to it, my lord.'

'You'll not teach me what I should write!' he shouted, and with that, he went out again to the great chamber, where all the others were, and I was made to follow. The bishop read the bill aloud to them, then stood waiting. My supporters came to me, by pairs and singly, urging me to set my hand to it, my cousin Brittayne being the last: 'Please. Just sign it,' he whispered. 'You've had much favour shown you.'

The bishop said loudly that I might thank others and not myself for the favour I found at his hand. 'You have worthy friends, madam, and are of good family, to which I give just consideration. Now, sign your confession of faith, and let's be done with this!' He laid the paper before me, inked the quill, and held it out.

I took the pen and at the bottom of his writings, I wrote: 'I, Anne Askew, do believe all manner of things contained in the faith of the catholic church.'

When he turned the paper and saw what I had written, his face reddened in fury, and he flung into his chamber. My cousin leaned over to look. 'Oh, Anne,' he said, and hurried after him. We all could hear my cousin within, pleading with the bishop to be good lord unto me, but the bishop was not appeased: 'She is a woman, and I am in nothing deceived by her!'

'Take her as a woman, then,' my cousin said, 'and set not her weak woman's wit to your lordship's great wisdom. She wrote catholic church only because she understands not the true meaning!'

Which is an entirely false saying. I know as well as he that the true catholic church is not the false church in Rome and its Romish bishop, but the universal apostolic invisible church of Jesus Christ. It is we who congregate in brewery backrooms and private cellars to study His Holy Word: *we* are the true universal apostolic catholic church! I would have said so aloud to the court, but I had no opportunity.

Rather, after much ado, the bishop was persuaded to come out again. He directed his clerk to take my name and the names of my sureties—my cousin and his friends. This being done, I should have been put to bail immediately. But Bishop Bonner would not have it. 'Tomorrow morning, at ten of the clock, you are to appear in the Guildhall. Your sureties may join you there. In the meantime, madam, you are remanded to the Compter.'

'But why, my lord? Have they not agreed to pay my bond, sir? Have we not done all you ask?'

'Ten o'clock, Mistress Askew. Without fail. I shall see you there.'

– Chapter 44 –

At the Compter, Master Husband says he's received no shilling for this night's lodging, so it is to the common floor he takes her, very late, the women's scant suppers already eaten, sleeping spaces for the night already claimed. They grumble and squint at the gaoler's rushlight, kick at Anne and curse her when she enters: get yonder, get out of the way! She lies on the floor beside the reeking waste tub, praying. By dawn she has not slept. By eight of the clock in the morning, Beatrice has not arrived. By the tolling bells of nine, Anne knows that Beatrice is not coming. She startles—they all do—when the gaoler unlocks the door. But it is only his boy, scratching and yawning; he motions Anne to come with him. In the dim downstairs hall, two guardsmen are waiting. She walks towards Guildhall between them with bits of straw stuck to her skirt, her hair tucked roughly beneath her cap. The morning is dank. The fog from the river has not yet lifted. The streets are filled with Londoners going about their business. Some turn to glance at her curiously. Most simply hurry past.

But inside the vast hall, a crowd is gathered. The people have come to see Mistress Anne Askew interrogated by Bishop Bonner. She must be a very obstinate heretic, they whisper, a worthy prize for the fire, if my lord of London will examine her himself! Others are here because they know her, or know of her, because they believe the same gospel doctrine she believes. Anne recognizes faces from her meetings about London, merchants and prentices, fishwives and tradesmen, but where is her cousin? Where is John Lascelles? The great hall is murky. No sunlight streams through the great windows. No candles have been lit. Has Edward come? Beatrice? Anne cannot see them among the crowd.

She is brought to stand on the flagstones below the dais. The clerk calls for silence, and Bishop Bonner rises from his chair. Several men are rowed beside him: his chancellor, his scowling archdeacon, the lord mayor of London, and, elegant and unsmiling in his russet robe and gold chain of office, my lord chancellor of all England, Sir

Thomas Wriothesley. These are her accusers, Anne knows, and her judges, and her jury. Bishop Bonner peers down from his place high above. He wears not his soft black cap today but a brilliant white mitre, shining bright even in the dimness, as if this were a Mass of holy solemnity. Anne waits for the same tedious round of questions. She is fatigued, her mind blurred with lack of sleep. She prays for strength, discernment, a nimble tongue. But Bishop Bonner does not ask questions; rather he unrolls a scrolled parchment and in a loud, booming voice begins to read:

'Be it known to all men that I, Anne Askew, alias Kyme, do confess this to be my faith and belief! that as touching the Blessed Sacrament, I do fervently and undoubtedly believe! that after the words of consecration be spoken by the priest! according to the common usage in this church of England! there is present, really, the body and blood of our saviour Jesu Christ!'

These are near the same words he wrote out for her yesterday, but they have been amended, they are not entirely the same—and this is not the same document. That was ordinary rag paper, this is parchment. Anne feels the shift of people around her, their low murmurs: What is this? A confession of faith by the famed gospeller? A declaration that Anne Askew 'fervently' and 'undoubtedly' believes in the Real Presence?

No, please, Anne thinks. I did not sign this! Or, yes, she signed, but with equivocation, with her own amendment, and it was not this same writing! She wrote the truth with her name: *I, Anne Askew, believe all manner of things contained in the faith of the catholic church:* the holy apostolic invisible church! Not superstition! Not idolatry!

'. . . and all things else touching the Christian belief,' the bishop reads loudly, 'which are taught and declared in the King's Majesty's Book! lately set forth for the erudition of the Christian people! I do truly and perfectly believe! and so here presently confess! In witness whereof, I have subscribed my name unto these presents . . .' Bishop Bonner pauses, gathering tension, before he sings out the ending: 'By me, Anne Askew, otherwise called Anne Kyme!'

'No!' Anne cries out. 'I do not call myself that! I have not read the King's Book! Never under God's Heaven would I sign that false name!'

But her voice is drowned in the rumblings and gruntlements of the crowd. The bishop motions his men to bring her closer. Here at last, to the side of the dais, she finds her cousin Brittayne and his co-lawyers, and her dear friend John Lascelles. Anne's face lights up when she sees him, she opens her mouth, but the bishop makes a slicing gesture, and the guards grip her arms: she is silenced. She looks to her cousin, but he is turned away, arguing with the bishop's clerk. She looks to John Lascelles, who is slowly shaking his head. His eyes are red-rimmed and wet, his face anguished. Oh, surely he does not think she signed that false declaration? She tells him with her eyes, do not believe them! But Lascelles' shocked and grieving face does not change.

Lord Chancellor Wriothesley rises from his chair, bends his lithe frame, leans his handsome face towards her: 'You were ordered to return to your husband, Mistress Kyme, when your vulgar plea for divorcement was dismissed months ago. How is it that we find you here?'

'I am called to be here, my lord. It is not of my will.'

'If you were at home in your husband's house, you would not be in this difficulty.'

'Nor would I be about my Father's work—' She breaks off, staring at the badge on his velvet cap: azure background, yellow cross between four hawks argent. The same emblem sewn onto the sleeves of the men who took her into custody in front of St Mary Aldermary. So, it was Wriothesley who'd had her arrested and brought before the quest? Why? Did she make such an enemy of him in the scant ten minutes she was before him in Chancery? She'd scarcely spoken. Indeed, her cousin Brittayne had barely uttered his own first words to plead her case when the lord chancellor dismissed them with a barked order that this unseemly woman be returned to her husband. She'd been neither surprised nor angry. She had said only,

'He is not my husband. The laws of man do not supersede God's law, my lord, as even you must know.'

The lord chancellor straightens now to his lean height, looking down on her. 'You have disobeyed our order, madam, in open defiance of the law.' He pauses, smiles faintly, an amused tuck to one side of his mouth. 'The laws of this court *are* God's law, madam. As even you must know.' With slow elegance, he returns to his place and sits. Anne stares at him, comprehending in a single heartbeat that his enmity towards her is personal: she had defied his peremptory order. Her cousin Brittayne is arguing with Bishop Bonner as the crowd grumbles: they are ready to see the next course of action. They have come here to see a show.

The bishop snaps at Brittayne, 'It matters not, sir! I know you have signed for her, you needn't keep saying it! We'll bail her tomorrow, provided she says no more unworthy sayings. Come before us on the morrow in Paul's church! And do not bring all these rousers you've called here!'

'I did not call them, your lordship! This proceeding was broadly noised about!'

'She'll not be bailed today! Not under these circumstances!'

'But these circumstances are *your* circumstances, my lord!'

'Return her to the Compter!' the bishop barks to his guards. And in an instant, she is being propelled towards the door through the crowd of people. Some back away from her. Others reach towards her as if to snatch her clothing, or else take a blessing. She hears voices whispering, cursing, spitting, the accusations contradictory, confusing: *Traitor. Papist. Apostate. Wanton. Strumpet. Heretic.*

'So, you're to lodge with us a while longer, are ye?' The gaoler leers, bids the guards leave her, leads the way up the stairs. At the women's door he turns, presses himself into her, his foul breath in her ear: 'A pity your friends have sent nothing for your keep, missus. You'll have to pay us your penny tomorrow. Or make other arrangements.' He unlocks the door, shoves her inside.

'Well, well. Look who's here to grace us.' This from the lank-haired woman who sits always with her bodice unlaced, her back to the wall.

'Our lady of last night, ain't it?' the ginger-haired slattern says.

'Our lady of last night's *airs*,' the old one sniffs. The women laugh. They are the same women as grumbled and cursed at her last night: the same as were here when she arrived thirteen days ago, except that the youngest girl is missing and a thin, sallow, coughing woman has taken her place. Anne picks her way between their sprawled legs to the space next to the waste tub where she'd lain in last night's misery. She lowers herself to the floor, sits with eyes closed, the back of her head against the wall, listening to the women snipe and gossip, argue over the gambling game they've devised using buttons and straws. Why have her friends sent no money? Why has Beatrice not brought it? And why, oh *why*, do her brothers not help her? Anne's breast heaves. She pulls herself straight, inhales a deep breath—through her mouth, not her nose—opens her eyes.

Upon the far bed, four women sit with their skirts twisted, rolling their homemade die, cursing and yelling. One is pregnant; her small-mounded belly swells over her lap. On the near bed the new woman is coughing as if her lungs might be spat from their cavern. She is dying, surely, Anne thinks, without feeling. And surely she will infect us all. A bony woman lies next to her, sleeping, the sticks of her legs bent weirdly beneath her. A third sits scraping bloody crevices into her bare arm with a wedge of sharpened pewter. Where did she get it? They are not allowed pewter spoons, only wooden. In the narrow space between Anne and the door, four others sit idly staring into space, or watching the gambling game on the bed. The lank-haired woman sees Anne looking. 'What are you gaping at?' Anne closes her eyes again, tries to pray for the woman. For all the women here. They are God's daughters, too, are they not? Why does she feel no tenderness towards them?

Because they stink, her mind whispers. Because they trade their bodies for favours. They curse and spit and gamble and gouge crevices in their arms: they are not properly women! Not so much as even the rag-pickers and beggars with whom Anne shares the gospel in the streets. A foot kicks her leg as one of the women steps over her to the privy. Anne hears the splashing rivulets, smells the reek of the tub's disturbed contents. Her throat works, her mouth fills, she retches several times, but she does not vomit. We are made to live like animals, she thinks. She remains sitting this way through the cold afternoon, mouth shut, eyes closed, until the evening bread is brought; she hears the women curse and scramble for their pieces. The door shuts, the key clinks; all is dark behind her lids now. She hears the women settling for their long night's horrors. Anne stretches out on the floor.

The oak planking is hard, the straw alive with fleas, roaches, the faint scufflings of mice. The woman beside her is moaning. The one on the bed above coughs and coughs. Anne turns this way and that, drapes her sleeve over her nose, scratches the bites on her legs and ankles till they bleed. She cannot reach the bites on her belly, where her bodice is still tight. The itching there is a small agony. She knows now why the lank-haired woman keeps her bodice unlaced.

Anne's mind echoes with the whispers she'd heard in the vast cavern of Guildhall: *Traitor. Papist. Apostate. Strumpet. Heretic.* Strumpet. Dear God, I am not! Not like these here! Traitor. Papist. In her mind's eye she sees the accusing, tear-stained face of her dear friend, her brother in Christ, John Lascelles. Did he really believe them, then? The false words of the bishop?

Of course he believed them. Everyone did.

In a great wash of shame and grief, Anne realizes her name will be used to the old religionists' purpose. They will say that the famed gospeller Anne Askew professes her belief in their superstitions, their idolatries, which would make a god of mere bread and put it in a box for people to worship. To all who doubt, they will show her signed 'confession': *I do fervently and undoubtedly believe.* Oh, how evilly she has been tricked! She never meant anything less than to recant her faith! But who now will believe her? O, Christ my Lord, my blessed Redeemer, she prays, give me courage, Lord. Grant me peace. Again and again, she asks, but she does not receive. The peace of the spirit cannot find her. What? she thinks in her misery. Is this place so wretched that even the Holy Ghost will not enter?

Late in the night, the woman beside her rolls close to her, facing her. It is the ginger-haired slattern who wears only her filthy chemise, no bodice, no overskirt. She is deeply asleep. The woman's chest rises and falls slowly; she moans, blows her rank breath in Anne's face. Her diseased breath. Her rotted breath. Anne shoves her away. The woman curls in on herself, whimpering, but she does not turn to her other side. In a moment, she softly snores again. I shall scream! Anne thinks. I shall jump up and claw the door! Oh, dear God, I must get out of here! I must! Why do you place me here, Father? These horrors, these whores—they are hardly human! I am not like them! Release me! Oh, pray God, release me!

Unto the least of these.

No, Father! Release me!

When ye have done it unto one of the least of these, you have done it unto Me.

Not this, Christ my Lord! Not here among these! Not this way!

On through the night, Anne prays; she begins in this desperate pleading. Release me! Help me! Take this cup from me! But as she prays, in tiny increments at first, and then more fully, she begins to yield: Forgive me, Father. Thy will, not mine. I cannot see, Lord. I cannot hear! Show me!

At last, as grey light seeps through the barred window, Anne lies on her side, weeping. The nearby woman rolls towards her again. This time Anne does not push her away. In a great deflation of breath and spirit, she surrenders: If my work is here, Lord, in this terrible place, I am willing. If I'm to go back to live as Kyme's wife, show me. As I am shown, Lord, so will I do. But please, God. Give me a worldly sign, that I might not mistake my will for Thine. If I have not Thy Spirit within me, show me. For I cannot tell.

And so, hours later, inside the bishop's court at St Paul's, when a letter from her brother Edward is laid surreptitiously in her hand by her cousin, Anne believes that these are not her brother's words but God's own, giving her instructions:

> You'll be released on bond today, my sister, for so we have arranged. But you must go home at once to Lincolnshire. You are in danger here, and you put us all in the same—your friends at court, your fellows in London, both your living brothers, our wives and estates. Go home to your sons, Anne. Do you not miss them? Do you not long to see their dear little faces? We shall tend to Master Kyme, something will be done to relieve you. But you must not remain in London.

II

If They Would Tend to Master Kyme

South Kelsey

May

1546

– Chapter 45 –

If they would 'tend to Master Kyme,' as Edward said in his letter, why did they not do so before? I have asked myself this, asked God, asked Beatrice. I have not asked my brothers. What good would it do? They would say they have tried. It matters not, now, anyway. By means of that very yoke, that bondage, that greatest misfortune of my life, did my Heavenly Father carry me to London to do His work there. Just as surely, in humiliation and suffering, has He brought me back home. Not to Kyme's household, I thank God for it, but to Francis's new manor house in Kelsey. Edward paid the escort to ride us to Friskney, but Beatrice refused to go there, and I would not leave her to walk to South Kelsey alone. So we came here. It was strange to come along the road in drizzling rain and see rising before us not familiar stone towers and moat and drawbridge but this new-built brick structure, flat and vast and square, sprawling across the land where my father's ancient fortress once stood. The afternoon was dark, dismal; it was the first day of April. We arrived road-weary, saddle-sore, drenched, famished. My Beatrice was crying. Francis came out in his furred robe to greet us; he bundled me quickly into the house, sent me to this small bedchamber in the east wing.

'Why were you crying?' I asked Beatrice as she reached to loosen my cloak. She shook her head, her eyes on her fingers. 'Is it because it is so ugly?'

'It is not ugly,' she said.

'No? Well, I suppose it is very modern, at least.' I scanned the room: oak wainscoting, tiled floors, glazed windows. 'We have stayed in uglier.' Our eyes met, and in our fatigue and sorrow, we laughed. She removed my soaked cloak and spread it before the fire, and we set ourselves to get warm. She did not cry again, and most certainly I did not, though I had seen how little pleased my brother was to see me. Beatrice's sadness is like mine, I think: to come home to a home that is not the home you have known.

Six weeks now. I have not yet seen my sons. I walk through each day expecting nothing. I'm forbidden to have pamphlets or 'dangerous writings,' as my brother calls them. He is willing to be my protector, he says, but I must not put his family in threat. Thanks be I have my Tyndale, at least. I almost did not. We were already mounted in front of the widow's house, our panniers stuffed for the journey, my trunk packed and stowed in her cellar to be sent for later, when I remembered it. My cousin Brittayne was pacing back and forth, looking about, restless. He'd come to see me off. I had hoped John would come, too, and some of our gospel friends, but it was only Brittayne. Even Mistress Hobbes did not come outside to say farewell. Edward's servant had taken up his reins and turned his mount towards the road when I called to him to stop. I whispered to Beatrice to run back upstairs and fetch the book from the cupboard, behind the loose board. She jumped down and ran, her face tight with urgency, and my cousin Brittayne's face was the same. This was but a few days after my release; he was afraid I would be arrested again. 'You needn't worry, cousin,' I told him. 'They'll not come for me now.'

'We don't know that.'

'I do,' I said. And I did. I had seen God's plan quite clear. Beatrice came down, flushed with running, and we started again. I turned in the saddle and called to him. 'You were there, cousin. You saw what I wrote. You must tell John I did not betray my faith! Please. You must tell everyone.'

He looked at me, then slid his gaze away. 'I shall tell Master Lascelles,' he said. 'Master Lascelles may tell whomever he wishes.'

But I have written three letters to my dearest friend in Christ and have received no reply. What small news we hear from London is not good. Dr Crome has been arrested; they say he will recant from the pulpit at St Paul's, but I do not believe that. The same sorts of false rumours were said about me. I try not to think of London so much, anyway, but I cannot help myself. Each time Beatrice returns from the village, I'm at once after her: What news of London? And whether there is small news or none at all, I am disappointed. In truth, I long for my life there as I long for my father, my dead brothers, my dear lost Maddie—as I long even for the old discomforts of South Kelsey Hall. I miss that vast, miserable, cold, ancient stone hall, perhaps all the more because it is razed to dust now.

Why does God give us this? This yearning for a tenderly remembered past that was never tender at all but filled with earthly strivings? It is our longing for Heaven, I think. My soul has been yearning since ever I can remember. I knew the ache all my life, but not its source, which is, which *must* be, that blessed union with our Blessed Saviour, which we who die in Christ may rejoice in after our earthly deaths. Why, then, do we fear? And why do I ache for that which is unattainable? Yet I do. This day, this hour, as I look out at the greening meadow, the dark woods beyond, even now I yearn for London.

Late afternoon. Beatrice came running, panting, wholly distressed. 'We're to move, mistress! To a tenant's cottage on the far side of the meadow. Master Francis says so. At once.' She was already gathering my clothing, my comb, my papers and pen.

'Why?' I said. 'What's happened?'

But here was my brother's great frowning hulk in the doorway, his broad face, shaggy head. 'A message has come from Edward. The privy council has sent yeomen in search of you.'

'They needn't search, Francis. I'm right here.'

'Forget nothing!' he directed Beatrice, who was hurriedly placing my possessions in a pile on the bed. 'Leave no trace behind!'

'I am not afraid of the council, Francis.'

'I know,' he snapped, glaring at me. 'That's the trouble. That is the very thing.' He handed me the letter. I recognized Edward's hurried scrawl: two yeomen of the chamber have been sent north with letters summoning one Kyme and his wife to appear before the council. 'I don't understand this,' I said.

'It is what it says. You're summoned before the king's council. You and Kyme together.'

'Why?'

'You know why.'

My eyes skimmed the page: *It was only with greatest difficulty she was released before, and circumstances surrounding the queen are worse now. You must send her into hiding, else, knowing Anne—and you do know Anne—she'll be condemned before we can help her.* 'Circumstances surrounding the queen,' I said. 'What does he mean?'

'You'd have to ask Edward. Hurry, now. We've no time to send you any distance; the messenger saw the king's men in Lincoln. It'll not be long before they reach here.'

'But why must I hide? I shall gladly go before the council and—'

Francis whirled on me in fury. 'By the blood of Christ, I have risked everything for you! Everything!' He came near, trying to hold his voice quiet, but he could not. 'You are ordered back to your husband, but will you go? No! You are accused as a sectary, you have been brought before the very Bishop of London, we have paid a great deal of money for your release, but will you be humbled? Will you be circumscribed? No! I have put myself and my family in danger for you, Anne. I do so this hour, this instant! If they find you here, they will say I have defied the courts' orders! I could be greatly harmed, I could—' He halted, his throat working. 'I could lose everything.' His face was mottled with fear. 'Do as I say, Anne. This is not a request. Quickly, Beatrice. Take your mistress and go 'round by the wood's edge; you must not be seen crossing the lea.'

– Chapter 46 –

When the king's men come, Sir Francis is watching from a high window: six horsemen cantering along the road from Market Rasen, two and two and two, a small force in formation, without haste. Two men wear the king's livery, two are in ecclesiastical garb, another is the high sheriff of Lincolnshire, and in the last figure Francis recognizes the round head and sloped shoulders of Master Thomas Kyme. Francis waits in his chamber until the groom comes to announce them. He descends to the receiving hall in his shirt, as if to say he has been casually at home, expecting no visitors. He opens his arms to greet Kyme. 'How are you, my brother? What brings you? And your good company? Welcome, sirs! How do you, Master Sheriff? Johnathan, bring more wine!' The servant bows out, and Francis turns to the wine table. His hands are shaking as he pours. He has recognized the apparitor from the bishop's court in Lincoln, Hugh Goodrick, that skinny, officious man whose lone word can condemn one to charges. How has it come to this? The king's men here to seize his sister, and with them her churl of a husband, a priest, the high sheriff, the bishop's very summoner himself. Sir Francis takes a steadying breath. He turns, smiling, two filled goblets in hand. 'Will you, sirs? Thomas? And how fare my young nephews your sons? You must bring them for the hunt soon!'

He looks hard at Kyme, and his heart stutters. His brother-in-law is not the instigator of this party, Francis sees now, but its unwilling participant. Its hostage, even. Kyme's pale, wary eyes dart about the room in fear. One of the king's messengers pulls a scroll from his satchel and brings it to Francis. He reads the words slowly, carefully, as if they are new to his knowledge, though of course they are not: *Master Thomas Kyme of Friskney, Lincs, and his wf., Anne, are hereby summoned to appear before His Majesty's Privy Council at Greenwich no later than 14 days from issuance of this letter*. It is dated 24 May. Three weeks ago. No matter what, Francis thinks, they will be in violation. 'Yes?' he says, looking up. 'And how am I to be of service?'

'You are to deliver to us your sister!' the apparitor snaps.

'If I knew her whereabouts,' Francis says, 'I would gladly. But I've had no word since she left London.'

'Liar,' the apparitor says.

'With apologies, Sir Francis,' the sheriff says, 'but under the council's summons I'm obliged to search for her.' He is deferential, embarrassed. 'Will you send in your wife and servants so that Master Goodrick may interview them? This will not take long, I trust. Good masters'—he means Kyme, the priest, and the king's yeomen—'you'll please join me?'

There follows a long hour, then two, then three, as Sir Francis and his household are interrogated. The servants hold fast. Even when Goodrick takes them aside one by one to question them, they are closed-mouthed, unrevealing. Sir Francis watches the summoner's growing frustration at their feigned stupidity. Silently he blesses his good servants: he'll reward them well when this turmoil is past. One by one they're released. Nurse takes the three squabbling children to the nursery. Sir Francis stands with gritted teeth. His wife Lisbeth sits, staring, her face blank with fear. The manor house is large, many-roomed, with numerous outbuildings, sheds and stables; it is perhaps two hours before the searchers return, saying they find no sign of Kyme's wife. Francis breathes. This should finish it.

But no. Master Goodrick bids the men go back and search again—every crevice! he orders, every chest and cupboard! Look for signs! In Francis's mind an image flashes: his sister emerging stone-faced and haughty from the consistory court inside the cathedral at Lincoln, and this same short, bony man marching officiously behind her, his heavy mace held high in swaggering authority as if he'd love to crash the great thing down on Anne's skull. Ah God, had he not tried to save her? With all his might and brotherly love, he had tried! *Do not go to the cathedral, Anne! Do not stand and read the Bible! The priests will put you to great trouble*—is this not what he said? And look now. Yes. Look.

The yeomen of the chamber and the priest go out to search again, with Goodrick at their heels, but Thomas Kyme remains; he strides the room scowling, hands clasped at his back Suddenly he whirls and demands of Francis: 'And how do you imagine it was for me? To receive a summons from the council and have no wife to produce for them? Had I known she was here, I'd have come for her months ago!'

'Indeed? You knew she was in London these two years past and did not go to fetch her. In truth, sir, you do not want your wife back.'

'I had no choice but to go to the priests!' Kyme cries out. He turns and begins pacing again. Francis watches him, a slow recognition dawning: it is true that Kyme does not want his wife returned, but nor does he want her free from him and living on her own. Every accusation against her reflects on him. He will scramble to distance himself from her. It was Kyme, Francis perceives now, who told the king's men they would find Anne at South Kelsey, Kyme who suggested they bring the bishop's minions with them. He is not the instigator of the search, no, but he looks to shape its unfolding. Anne has said he will kill her. Francis sees now by what means: rather than have returned to him a disobedient wife or be yoked in absentia to one who brings him ever into danger, Thomas Kyme will denounce her to the priests, and see her burnt.

Loathing swells in Sir Francis, a dark, sickening hatred, and yet he is paralyzed with fear. He stands gripping Lisbeth's shoulder; she is rigid beneath his touch, trembling. Inside his chest, his heart is pounding. Master Goodrick returns and renews his interrogations: You saw her last, when? You received her letters last, when? You knew she was ordered back to her husband, yes? And yet you aided and abetted her to defy the court's order, you have supported her heady opinions and obstinacy; do you deny that you defied a summons from the king's own privy council? And what is this, sir, but treachery, perfidy, the very scent of betrayal to His Majesty the king?

'I served His Majesty at Boulogne!' Francis protests. 'And was there knighted at his own hand! I am the king's loyal and devoted subject!'

'Yet you defy his summons!' Goodrick brings his bony face near. 'I shall have you brought up on charges of contumacy!'

'You have no authority for that, sir!'

'Oh, indeed I have!'

And of course he has. Authority is precisely what this official of the bishop's court has. And power. Here, now, this waning twilight hour, in Sir Francis's modern new receiving hall within his raw new manor house constructed from the very bones of suppressed monasteries, the three great forces of the age are come together: clerical, civil, monarchical, uniting as one to threaten his very existence, and his family's. A charge of contumacy, that is, refusal to comply with a summons or court order, may be a civil offence—thus the presence of the high sheriff. Or it may be an ecclesiastical offence—thus the bishop's summoner. One may be imprisoned for contumacy, heavily fined. But to defy the privy council's order, and thus, in effect, the king's own directive, oh, this can be named treason! That crime of all crimes, that condemnation of all condemnations: the cruel penalty for which Francis has seen with his own eyes at the execution of Thomas Moigne. And it is already too late, he thinks miserably. The king's men are here.

'I do not refuse to comply, sir,' Francis answers, but his voice is weak. 'I simply cannot. How can I, when I know nothing of her whereabouts?' He is losing his strength, he is losing his wits. His wife's head is drooping; he can see her fatigue. The hour is late, the room close and warm; they are all famished. His servants skulk outside the door, waiting for instructions. One of the king's men enters holding a piece of writing. The others crowd the room behind him. Francis feels his blood drain, the dread pouring through.

'We had seen books in one of the chambers,' the yeoman says, 'but as they appeared orthodox and without blame, upon the first search we passed them by. This time we fiercely shook them. From between the pages of a breviary this fell to the floor.'

Goodrick takes the small folded paper; he reads silently at first and then, triumphantly, aloud: '"Oh friend most dearly beloved in the Lord, I weep to think that you judge in me so slender a faith as to renounce those truths which we know from Holy Scripture to be beyond doubt. Since I came here to my brother's house . . ."' He pauses, glares at Sir Francis, repeats: '"Since I came *here* to my *brother's house,* I have writ down all I can remember of my examination, that the world may know I did not deny my faith, nor shall I ever, I pray, as long as life endures. Write to me, friend. I shall continue to pray for you, and for all our friends in London. By me, your devoted friend in Christ, Anne Askew."'

There is silence in the room. After a moment Lisbeth begins weeping. The sheriff clears his throat. Sir Francis sits with his great head in his hands. In his mind's eye he sees his brother-in-law Thomas Moigne standing on a scaffold in cold March light, shivering in his white shirt. His body is soon to be opened, his entrails pulled out and tossed on the brazier, his remains chunked into four bloody pieces and spread about the shire: but his body does not know this. His body shivers to keep warm. In the space of a heartbeat, for perhaps the ten thousandth time, Francis sees again the great gushes of blood, he smells the burnt entrails, hears Thomas's screams, his screams, his pitiful dying whimpers. Every moment of Francis Ayscough's life since that day nine years ago has led him to this moment now, when he uncovers his face, looks up, and says, 'Yes, all right. I'll tell you where she is.'

– Chapter 47 –

It is well dusk. Beatrice stands at the window looking out across the meadow. The manor house is a great long turretless rectangle on the horizon. Along the lower floors, wan light glows in a few of the windows. Behind her, Mistress Anne sits reading. Though she'll not read for long now, Beatrice thinks. The light is failing, and Beatrice did not think to bring candles. The cottage is cold, dark, sour: an ancient wattle-and-daub hovel, thatch worn thin in places, no shutter to the window. The tenants moved away long ago. Nothing within but cobwebs, dust, mouse droppings, the broken joint stool where her mistress sits reading, the permeating cold. It is as if winter seeped in and found a stronghold and will not be burned away even by June's early warmth. 'I should have gathered firewood while the light held,' she says.

'We're not to be seen,' Anne says. 'I suppose smoke from the chimney is not to be seen neither.'

Beatrice looks at her. 'What are we to do, then? Sit here all night in the cold and dark?'

'I suppose.' Anne does not lift her gaze from her book, though Beatrice cannot imagine how she can decipher anything in this dimness. The book is the small banished Testament, which the girl knows to be a danger to any person found with it in her possession—not just Mistress Anne alone, Beatrice thinks, but also herself.

'You'll ruin your eyes, miss,' she says.

Anne shrugs, still reading. 'I am the light of the world, Jesus said. He that followeth me shall not walk in darkness. John eight.'

Beatrice turns back to the window. At first, she's not certain what she is seeing, and then she is: the bounce and stumble of torchlights bobbing slowly across the meadow, one two three four five six seven. 'They're coming,' she says.

Anne looks up. 'Are you certain?'

'I see lights moving this way.'

'Are they meandering? As if searching? Or are they coming directly here?'

'Directly here.'

Anne closes the book, holds her finger in place between the pages. 'Then Francis has told them. Or Lisbeth has, or one of the servants.'

'It is no great distance to the woods. Shall we run?'

'To what purpose? If they are coming, let them come.'

'We must hide that,' Beatrice says, pointing to the Testament. Anne instinctively pulls the book to her breast. 'You are not alone in your danger, miss.'

'Yes,' Anne says after a moment. 'All right.'

Beatrice goes to her and gently tugs the book from her; she looks around the room, but the place is so empty. No cupboard. No loose board behind which to hide it. Only their piled soft goods tied in a sheet in the corner; that is not a good place. The fireplace has not been swept. Beatrice goes to the filthy hearth and kneels. The ashes are inches thick, clumped, greyish, littered with bones and old charcoal. With one hand she scrapes a depression, lays the Tyndale within, covers the book with ashes.

'We should have wrapped it,' Anne says. 'To protect it.'

'With what? Any cloth here would be identified as yours, miss. Or mine. This way, if they find it, we can say someone else buried it there.' Beatrice stands, looks around. She has nothing with which to clean her hand. She goes to a far corner and wipes as much ash off against the wall as she can. 'It smells better than pig dung, at least.' For a moment they are both smiling, remembering the Bible Beatrice buried in the pigsty years ago. Maddie's book, Anne used to call it. 'I wrapped that one,' Beatrice says.

'Indeed you did. Wrapped it and wrapped it.'

Beatrice shakes her head as if to say, why are we still burying Bibles? It has been explained to her, the different translations, why some are acceptable, some heretical, but Beatrice does not care about the reasonings, only the consequences—which are very terrible for anyone found with this one. Her mistress would for certain be imprisoned again. The torchlights are drawing nearer; it is hard to tell distance in the dusk, but she thinks there is still time. 'We can make it to the woods, miss—the dark will protect us.'

'It will serve Francis no good if they know I've been here and fled. He faces trouble enough. If they arrest me, Beatrice, you're not to come. You are home now. You must stay here.'

'But who will serve you in gaol?'

Who indeed? Anne has no answer. She swallows deeply. 'For my brother's sake would I have kept myself hidden, but if he has told them where to find me, why, there's no need for that now, do you see? I thank God for it—oh, I have wept bitter tears! As bitter as Saint Peter when the cock crew. But I'm to be given another opportunity! I'll not deny my faith again, Beatrice. I'll not sign their false confessions—shh!' Anne lifts her hand.

Just outside, men's voices, the flicker of torchlight. The women freeze: Anne in the centre of the room, her eyes on the door; Beatrice near the window, her eyes upon Anne. The men burst into the room, a rush of noise and confusion, barked orders, eye-stabbing light. Beatrice shrinks into herself. She recognizes the scarlet coats of the king's livery, Sir Francis's servant Johnathan, and there at the back of the pack, barking loudest, leaping and scowling fiercest, the master she has not seen since he knocked her to the ground in the castle square five years ago. A short, bony man with a face like a skull swoops towards Anne, spitting as he shouts: 'You are a known wanton and heretic! We'll see you to the council ourselves, you'll not escape again!'

'She is my wife, sir!' Kyme pushes forwards. 'She'll come with me!'

'Your wife if you can keep her! Which seems not likely, as you've never done so yet!'

'Madam.' One of the king's men holds up a scrolled document. 'You are herewith summoned before His Majesty's Privy Council, *sub peona,* that is to say, under penalty, no later than ten days from issuance of this letter.' He extends the document, not to Anne but to Master Kyme, who snatches it, brandishes it as if the thing itself were his triumph. 'See?' he chokes out. 'See what comes of your rebellions? This! This!'

Having accomplished their purpose, the two yeomen of the chamber take their torches and go out. The servant Johnathan stands by the door as empty of expression as if he were serving wine or holding coats. Kyme shoves his torch into Johnathan's hand and goes to seize his wife's arm. 'Do not touch me,' she says, without heat. She meets his gaze. Kyme releases her, and immediately looks to cover the moment with bluster: 'See here, Master Goodrick, what are you doing?' The skull-faced man has untied their bundle and is searching their belongings, his bony fingers sifting Mistress Anne's smocks and stockings, her veils. 'She is a heretic,' the man says, 'and I mean to find proof! Ah, now. What's this?' He lifts a small ill-shaped bundle like a tiny swaddled poppet: it is her mistress's capped inkhorn and quill and several tightly folded letters, all wrapped in linen like a winding-sheet. Beatrice knows, for she rolled and wrapped them herself.

'Letters to my sons, sir,' Anne says.

'*Your* sons!' Kyme sneers.

'I doubt that!' The skull-faced man peels one of the letters open, scans the writing. Beatrice realizes she has seen him before, she cannot think where. The man frowns; he looks from the page, to Anne, to the page again, reads aloud: '"Thirdly he asked me wherefore I said that I had rather to read five lines in the Bible than to hear five masses in the temple, I confessed that I said no less." What is this, madam? No letter to your sons, methinks.' He reads on a moment, then tosses the page onto the pile of soft goods, opens another. '"And he said it was against the order of schools that he which asked the question should answer it. I told him I was but a woman and knew not the course of schools." Did you now? Told whom?' He looks the page up and down, turns it over. Seemingly he does not see the answer. 'Bishop Longland, perhaps?' The contempt in his voice is like mercury, glowing, fluid, poisonous.

Beatrice recognizes him now, and her heart catches. The official from the bishop's court in Lincoln—the man who followed Mistress Anne through the cathedral with his mace raised like a club. He drops the paper, reaches for another. The stink of burning pitch chokes the room. Beatrice feels she cannot breathe; she is faint with fear, and thirst. They've had nothing to eat or drink for hours. She allows her gaze to drift about the room, anywhere but the cold ashes where the banned Testament lies. Her mistress's writings are troublesome, yes, but not so dangerous as the Tyndale, surely. They'll not get a person burnt. Would they? She glances at Anne, who stares boldly at the skull-faced man as if she dares him to misread a single word—as if she dares him to read them at all. His scanning grows swifter, more cursory, as he unfolds the pages, tossing each onto the pile when he's finished.

'The king's council will be most interested to read these,' he says, and scoops them into a loose handful, distastefully, as if they contain matter so foul he is loath to touch them. He starts to put them into his purse, but Kyme stops him.

'*I* shall carry those to the council!' Master Kyme holds out his hand, his face haughty with the wilful contempt of the coward; he thinks to save himself by surrendering Anne. 'She is *my* wife, sir! Therefore, these pages are *my* property!'

A moment of contested wills as the men glare at each other. Then the skull-faced man concedes with a scathing smile. 'This is what comes of teaching women to read, sir,' he says scornfully. 'And, perforce, because it surely follows as night dogs the day, to write.'

III

This Is What Comes of Teaching Women

London

June

1546

– Chapter 48 –

This is what comes of teaching women. Beatrice thinks of the man's words as the barge glides slowly downriver towards Greenwich. Her mistress spent many days writing for the queen. But this is good, surely, to have been in service to Queen Katheryn? Surely this will help her mistress when she goes before the council? But the words linger. They repeat themselves in rhythm with the clunk-creak-plash of oars: *This is what comes. Of teaching women. This is what comes.*

The sun advances. It is late morning. The barge is crowded. The river stinks. Beatrice does not like being on the water: if they should crash into another barge and be tossed out, she would sink like a stone. Her mistress and Master Kyme sit opposite her, between a white-faced merchant and a gentleman in a russet coat, facing downriver, towards Greenwich. Beatrice sits with the rowers and servants facing upriver, towards the receding quays, the wide bridge with its gruesome black-knobbed bouquets of spikes spearing skyward, topped with traitors' heads. She holds her mistress's soft travelling bag and a cloth sack with their dinner; it will be hours before they make their way back to the inn. Master Kyme had wanted to ride all the way to Greenwich, but Anne told him it is too far, the bridge crossing too slow, the stables near the water too few and too dear, and so they'd taken lodgings near Bishopsgate, walked the long mile to the river, put in at Fish Wharf. Master Kyme gave in to his wife's greater knowledge of the city, but his scowl tells how he seethes at every intimacy she knows about London which he does not.

It has been a miserable journey. Nights, in the inns where they've stayed, Beatrice has lain on a pallet outside their door listening to the muffled grunts and smacks and yelps within. Days, she has ridden behind them watching their rigid shoulders, their mute battles: Master Kyme's increasing fury, her mistress's growing ice. Kyme had refused to let Beatrice come with them; therefore, Anne had insisted. But Beatrice had wanted to come. What life for her alone in South Kelsey? And her mistress needs her.

On the second morning, when they stopped beside a stream to take their dinner and Master Kyme went behind a tree to relieve himself, Anne leaned near and whispered: 'You must retrieve my writings from his satchel.'

'But how can I, miss, without he sees me? He'll smash me sure!'

'I'll distract him. Or something. We'll make a plan.'

But they'd had no time to plan, for Kyme had returned then, retying his codpiece, and soon they were mounted again, travelling, travelling, and for all the days of the journey he never set his satchel aside. Even now, on the barge, it rests on his thighs. He holds one hand on the leather flap, the other grips the strap across his chest.

Mistress Anne, meanwhile, stares straight ahead with flat expression. This is how it has been: each day of the journey her face has grown harder, her expression more fixed. Beatrice has not retrieved her writings, and guilt for that failure presses upon her. But when might she have? Master Kyme never takes his hand off the satchel, nor his eyes off his wife! She fears the writings will bring her mistress into danger, like the Tyndale. She thinks of the little book buried in ashes, resting there even now—a condemnation to be discovered someday. Oh, pray not! *This is what comes. Of teaching women.*

A sudden stirring among the passengers, a gathering of parcels, a repositioning of doublets and coats. Beatrice turns to look. The great Palace of Placentia rises on the south bank, ruddy in the sunlight, white-toothed along the battlements, turreted, magnificent. She turns again to her mistress. Anne meets her gaze now, and together they glance at Master Kyme, who is gawking at the palace; they lower their eyes to the square leather satchel unattended in his lap, then meet eyes again. Anne makes a slight *no* gesture with her head. Is this a warning? A never mind? There are shouts now as they near the landing stairs. The rivermen work to steer the barge closer, and soon they are tied at the dock and the passengers are disembarking, gentry first, with their servants, followed by the merchants with theirs, Kyme and Anne near the last, and Beatrice with them. They are forced to pause, backed up on the plank, some slow movement ahead. She does not decide to do it, she simply does it, an impulse as reflexive as taking the next breath: when the line begins to move again, Beatrice juts her foot in front of Kyme's boot so that he stumbles, whirling his arms backwards, losing balance, and he tumbles into the muddy Thames. The bargemen shout; one jumps over the side and drags Master Kyme sputtering to the bank. The tide is, alas, at low ebb, and Master Kyme is not drowned. But he is gloriously wet. And so, too, his satchel.

Anne and Beatrice meet eyes again, their faces still as marble, inexpressive as slate. They quickly look away, else the laughter in their bellies might burble to their lips.

'Oh, sir! Let me help you!' Beatrice jumps to the bank, where Kyme is struggling to his feet; she loosens the ties on her mistress's bag she carries and pulls out a clean smock and two kerchiefs to use for towels. Kyme seizes them from her, lifts his leather strap over his head, drops the satchel to the ground, turns away to dry himself, cursing. His fury for the indignity he suffers, to be standing soaked in foul water, coughing, the gentlemen on the bank staring, their servants sniggering, is increased because he has no manservant to help. This was Sir Francis's final insult: to pretend he could spare no servant to attend him. Kyme must return to Friskney for one of his own, Sir Francis said. But they were too long past the summons deadline and in danger of severe penalty, and so, to further Kyme's resentment and ill will, they'd set out on the four-day journey with his wife tended by her maidservant, and he on his own, without. 'What are you gawking at?' he shouts at the sniggering servants. They and their masters begin to drift away, going towards the palace gate.

'Here you are, sir.' She extends the leather satchel towards him. He snatches it, holds it away from his dripping coat, strides after the others. Anne turns briefly to smile at Beatrice, then follows him, and the girl bends to gather the soiled smock and kerchiefs. They are too filthy and wet to be stuffed into her mistress's bag on top of the clutch of retrieved letters, so she crams them into the food sack atop the rye loaves and cheese.

In the antechamber they are ordered to wait. There is one strange revelation to Beatrice, and that is how she is not awed by the opulence around them, but Master Kyme is. She takes a secret glance at his tilted face, his flushed forehead, roving eyes, gaping mouth. He has lost his hat in the water. His thin hair is pasted in dull strings to his forehead. Mistress Anne appears as natural as if she were resting in her own solar. Her face holds its same stillness, but the look is placid now, not harsh. With them are passengers from the barge, the gentleman in the russet coat, the white-faced merchant, others in livery gowns or black broadcloth. One by one, they are called before the council; one by one, they come out again, frowning—their purses lighter for their fines, quite likely, Beatrice thinks. The food sack is damp on the floor at her feet; the bread will be spoiled, but the cheese is in rind, so perhaps it will be edible. She holds Mistress Anne's travelling bag on her lap, soft goatskin, leather ties: she had needed deft fingers to open it, pluck out the kerchiefs, and stuff in the folded pages. She's not certain she got them all, she'd had to grasp them from the satchel so quickly. She ponders what Master Kyme will do when he paws through his satchel and does not find them. She pushes the thought away. That moment will come when it comes.

An officer emerges from the inner chamber and calls for Master Thomas Kyme of Lincolnshire! and his wife! Beatrice rises to go with them but is looked back to her seat by the clerk. She resumes her place and waits. Her fingers pick at the drawstrings, but she is afraid to open the bag to look at the letters, to count them; she does not know how many to account for, anyway.

Then, far sooner than she'd expected, Master Kyme returns, alone. He strides towards her in such fury she cringes. He looks a wild man, a demon, but he does not raise his hand to her; rather, he spits at her, grinding out the words in mincing feminine imitation: 'Oh, but it will be the king's *pleasure* to hear me, says she! Oh, the king is as wise as *Solomon,* says she, and *I,* a meek and mild woman, his *obedient subject*: why would His Majesty *not* trouble himself with the likes of *me*!' Kyme kicks hard at the sodden food sack on the floor, turns and stomps away. The girl stares after him as he strides the length of the gallery, disappears around a far turn. The yeoman guardsmen stand with their same blank faces. The waiting servants show no reaction. Beatrice could almost believe she has not seen and heard what she has seen and heard, but that the food sack has been kicked yards away and Kyme's muddy boot print is plainly visible on its side. She retrieves it, returns to sit.

The guards do not flicker a muscle, do not lower their halberds or blink. The officer of the council does not come out again, and the few remaining petitioners, or defendants, or whatever they are, leave one by one. The sunlit squares on the flagstones lengthen, shift eastward, their amber colour bleeding to rose, then crimson, then ruby, then lavender; then it darkens and fades. And still Mistress Anne does not come.

– Chapter 49 –

My lords kept me standing before them many hours, asking the same questions again and again—those same questions which have been asked of me by so many for so long, it comes tedious to relate them. At the least, Master Kyme is sent home now, and I needn't watch him preen and swagger. How he did puff up at the sound of his name called! 'Master Thomas Kyme of Friskney, Lincolnshire!' the clerk sang out, 'and Anne Kyme, his wife!' Thomas strutted forwards as if he'd been bragged upon: he liked mighty much to be in the presence of such great personages—especially when he saw that I was to be their quarry, not he.

A fact which my lord bishop of Winchester, Stephen Gardiner, made evident straight away: 'Mistress Kyme,' he barked, 'you were ordered by Chancery to return to your husband, were you not? Some nine months past!' Bishop Gardiner hunched forwards with intensity. In the chair beside him, Lord Chancellor Thomas Wriothesley lounged casually, looking bored and triumphant, arranging his cuffs. I recognized two other gentlemen from court, Sir Richard Rich and William Paget, but who the others were, I could not say. The room was not large, and it was filled with men: the twelve privy councillors behind tables, the guardsmen at the doors, and, scattered about the room, several lawyers, as I took them to be, and scribes and clerks. Thomas Kyme was awed by their power and flattered at their attention. He preened like a peacock—although, truthfully, he looked pitiable, soaked and matted as he was, like a drowned cat. Bishop Gardiner's eyes were cold and hooded. 'Were you not so ordered, madam?'

'She was, sir!' Kyme piped.

'This man is not my husband,' I said.

'See her for a liar!' Kyme shouted. 'Before God and the church, I am her husband! And she my wedded wife!'

'Master Kyme!' barked Paget. 'Contain yourself!'

Bishop Gardiner held up his hand; the room quieted. 'How is it, madam, that you refuse this man to be your husband without honest allegation!' By his tone it was not a question, and so I made no answer. He leaned back in his chair then, fingers laced over his surplice as if he required a great distance from which to take me in. The black Canterbury cap he wears shows him to no advantage, I promise you. The tight band and square points serve to accentuate his thick, girlish lips and the peculiar length of his snout. If Bishop Bonner is a bulldog, Bishop Gardiner is a bloodhound, who would track to the death the blood-scent of any person he deems heretic. 'Speak, madam!' he ordered.

I turned my gaze then to the lounging gentleman beside him. 'My lord chancellor knows already my mind in that matter.'

Lord Chancellor Wriothesley stirred at last. He thrust his bearded jaw forwards, his light eyes sparkling. Though it is early summer, he wears the tawny browns and rusts and ochres of autumn to show off his fine auburn colouring. He knows himself a handsome man. 'What am I, a soothsayer, madam, that I would read a woman's mind?'

'You needn't read, sir, for I have told you.'

'The question before the court is how dare you refuse your husband without allegation!'

Kyme's anger was rising. I felt the near heat of him beside me, his stuttered breaths.

'You must make us a satisfactory answer,' Wriothesley said. 'It is the king's pleasure that you open this matter to us.'

'If it is the king's pleasure, I should be glad to show him the truth. Please bring me to him.'

'Why should the king be troubled with the likes of you?' Master Rich sneered.

I smiled at him with what sweetness I could muster. 'King Solomon was reckoned the wisest king that ever lived,' I said, 'yet he misliked not to hear two poor common women who entreated him. How much more kindly might His Grace hear the words of a simple woman like me? Therefore, sirs, I'll make no other answer in this petty matter.'

Master Kyme turned with an oath to cuff me, for he hated that I called the matter petty, but his hands could not help themselves:

they went straight for my throat. At once the councillors shouted, the guards swooped in; one grasped him by the arms while he cursed me: 'Wretched wench! Devil's dam! Whore!' He tried to get loose to strike me, and Master Paget's voice lifted above the others: 'You may go, sir! Return to your own country! We'll send for you if your assistance is needed! Go, sir!' And in an incredible fury, Kyme wrenched himself free and stormed out.

A brief silence. The councillors turned then to their primary business, to interrogate me regarding the Six Articles, as I'd known that they would.

'What is your opinion of the Sacrament?' Wriothesley demanded at once. This, and this, and this again. I know not the precise wording of the First Article in the same degree I know Scripture, for they are of man's making, and not God's, but I know that, in essence, the terms are this: that if a person hold the opinion that, in the Sacrament of the Altar, there is not present really the natural body and blood of our Saviour Jesu Christ, such person shall be deemed heretic and condemned to pain of death by way of burning. And yet, by the Word of God, I am persuaded that the living Christ dwells within, in truth and in spirit, and may not be eaten with teeth.

'Speak, woman!'

From the first this is how they have meant to intimidate me and bend me to their purpose. What purpose that be, I know not, but I am not deceived.

'I believe, my lord, that when I, in a Christian congregation, receive the bread in remembrance of Christ's death, I receive with it also the fruits of his most glorious passion.'

'Answer straight, woman!' Bishop Gardiner snarled.

'I'll not sing a new song to the Lord in a strange land.'

'And what is that supposed to mean? You speak in riddles and parables!'

'It is best for you that I do so, for if I show you the open truth, you'll not accept it.'

'Parrot! You recite meaningless cant you've heard from others!'

’s meaning is there, certainly,’ I said. ‘As also in these verses:
door, John ten. I am the vine, John fifteen. Behold the Lamb
John one. The rock stone was Christ, First Corinthians ten.
Master Paget, do you take Christ for the material thing He
ied by in these verses? If so, then you make of our Redeemer
door, a vine, a lamb, and a stone—clean contrary to the Holy
meaning. All these do signify Christ, as the bread signifies
dy. Take, eat this in remembrance of Me, He said. But He did
them hang up that bread in a box and make it a God or bow

ster Paget bumbled around incomprehensibly, offering such
erly conceived fancies that at last I told him it was a shame that
uld make no better understanding of God’s Word. In a huff he
out again, and in a short while there appeared the guardsmen
cort me to the home of my lady Garneys once more. Beatrice
n step behind us, the guards walked fore and aft with halberds
ed, and I thought: What think ye, gentlemen? That my mild
nds in Christ will attack from all sides to free me? They will not.
ey would not even if they knew I were here. For our Lord admon-
es us to resist not evil. Whosoever gives us a blow to the right
eek, we are to turn to him the other also.

And so out into the hot sunlight to walk guarded like the most
ngerous of prisoners to the home of that plump lady Joan Gar-
eys, whose kind, baffled eyes tell me she is not one of us. And yet
her heart I believe she is, for she has the love of Christ in her. She
ed me herself to the clean, small bedchamber, just as she’d done the
evening before, saying she’d send up a warm supper and a cool basin
of water, not only for me but for my maid also, and I thought then,
the fierce pounding beginning already behind my eyes: with what
temperance and care doth my lady keep our Lord’s commandment.
Whatsoever ye would that men should do to you, even so do ye to them.

And what might I have said to that? The Bishop of Winchester, one of the highest churchmen in the land, and yet he recognized not the words of the Psalmist.

‘Speak up, madam!’ he cried. ‘What is your belief concerning the Sacrament? State your opinion clearly, or we’ll have you to Newgate! Do you understand?’

‘I am ready to suffer all things at your hands, my lord. Your rebukes do not frighten me.’ I drew silent then and would not speak again, though they went on questioning me, badgering and badgering, until the ninth hour, when the guards were called, and I was taken in ward. I was not surprised to be taken up, nor especially fatigued then, though it did seem to me that my lords were tired, for they sighed and frowned and fanned themselves with papers. They ordered the clerk of the council to remand me to the nearby home of my lady Garneys, who sometimes houses witnesses for the council, to await their summons next day. When the guard escorted me through the gallery where we’d first entered, I glanced about, half fearful that Kyme might still be lurking, but I saw only my faithful Beatrice scrabbling to gather her bundles and hurry after us.

On the morrow, in the pale light of morning, once more I was brought before the privy council. Beatrice waited without, as before, and Bishop Gardiner led the inquisition, as before, whilst my lord chancellor sat back in his chair, sly and bored, and Sir William Paget kept order, and Sir Richard Rich intruded from time to time with his lawyerly sneer. As before, my lord bishop asked what had I to say to the Sacrament. I answered that I had already said what I would say. They harangued me a long while, then sent me to a small antechamber to wait while they conferred.

It was perhaps three quarters of an hour later that the queen’s brother, William Parr, Earl of Essex, entered, and behind him John Dudley, Lord Lisle, and for a moment my heart warmed, for I know them to be believers in the true gospel. I thought that Her Highness had sent her brother to stand for me. I have not seen Queen

Katheryn or her ladies or my good friend the queen's cousin Maud Lane for a long while. Even before my return to Lincolnshire, I'd not been called to their studies for many months, and so to see the queen's brother brought in to meet with me was at first a great pleasure—quickly dimmed.

For behind the two of them strolled Bishop Gardiner, his eyes hooded, his black-capped forehead tipped in artificial concern. He stood next the wall, hands folded, as Essex and Dudley began with soft words and earnest looks to entreat me to confess that the Sacrament is flesh, blood, and bone.

'It is a great shame, my lords,' I said, 'for you to counsel contrary to your own knowledge.'

Tut-tut, they said, harrumph, yes, well. They muttered and dissembled, their eyes scanning the ceiling, the tapestries, the carved mouldings, everywhere but my face. How strange it was to see two lords so wonderfully discomfited. They hoped gladly, they said, that all things are well. At that, Bishop Gardiner came forward. 'May I speak as your friend?' he began gently, his false smile sliding over his face like a leer.

'My friend?' said I. 'And so declared Judas when he unfriendly betrayed Christ.'

His leer turned to a scowl. He glanced at my lords standing splay-legged in their rich finery, and with effort, Bishop Gardiner smiled again. 'I would have a word alone with you, madam.'

'No, sir,' I said. 'You'll not.'

'What?'

'In the mouths of two or three witnesses every matter should stand. This is both Christ's doctrine and Saint Paul's.'

He liked not my answer nor my attitude; he turned and stormed out of the chamber, my lords Lisle and Essex following close upon his heels, and in a while the clerk came to fetch me before the whole council again. I saw how their distemper had grown. Now it was Lord Chancellor Wriothesley who leaned towards me—a different

voice, a different demeanour, but e

'What say you to the Sacrament, M

I met the lord chancellor's gaze

friend of the gospel in the time of

Now Thomas Wriothesley is as ruthl

ers as any man living, save Stephen

will you halt on both sides, sir?' I aske

'Halt on both—Where do you find s

'In Scripture, my lord. Book of Kings,

The lord chancellor held my gaze for t

abruptly he stood and walked out of the

is how it is: they cannot abide my presen

go, and so they dart in and out like small f

Bishop Gardiner, who seemed to have gat

wards across the table. His teeth were tight-

lipped and sleek. 'You are to state clearly, ma

in plain English, that the Real Presence of C

body is in the Sacrament. Else you shall burn.

'Whose law? Christ's law? I have searched a

beginning to end, and never can I find that eith

tles put any creature to death. Well, well,' I said,

smile faded. 'God will laugh your threatenings t

'Bailiff! Take her out!'

Then was I removed to the antechamber again.

voices through the wall, rising and falling, now hea

ing, now conspiring. At length the king's secreta

came in, as falsely sincere as any of them. He bad

mind to him alone, openly and honestly. 'You mig

later, if need be.'

'I'll not deny the truth, sir.'

'But you deny the very words of Christ! "Take, e

body, which shall be broken for you." These are His

madam! How can you avoid them?'

– Chapter 50 –

It is deep in the night this night, at the home of Lady Garneys, that Beatrice realizes her mistress is very ill. The signs do not come in dry coughs and little cat sneezes but in terrible, low-in-the-gut groanings. At first, from her pallet, Beatrice thinks her mistress is dreaming, but the groans endure too long for a dream, and so the girl, exhausted, drawn hard from a hard sleep, rises from her pallet, reaches a hand to Anne's brow. The skin is dry and hot as a baking stone. Beatrice draws the stool to the bed and sits. After a while, Anne curls onto her side, crying out as she turns—the movement seems to stab her—and then quietens. When her mistress makes no further sound, Beatrice goes to lie down again, just for a moment, she tells herself, just to rest her eyes. But it is morning, a wash of thin, watery light seeping in, when she startles awake; she scrambles up from the floor.

Her mistress lies atop the tumbled sheets staring at the ceiling, glassy-eyed, pale, breathing shallowly, but the fever is broken. It is Sunday. The bells of Greenwich are ringing. Her mistress reaches a groping hand towards her. What does she want? Something to drink? Beatrice puts her hand in Anne's palm, but Anne bats it away. Her fingers knead the air.

'What is it, miss?'

Anne shakes her head, allows her hand to drop.

'We ought to send for a doctor, miss. Should I ask the lady?'

Anne shakes her head no again. Her eyelids are twitching. Her breaths come small. Watching her now, the fine sheen of sweat on her brow, her eyelids trembling, Beatrice realizes that her mistress was already, last evening, becoming ill. She recalls how Anne suddenly sat down on the bed, her hand to her forehead as if shading her eyes. How she'd refused the warmed supper Lady Garneys sent up. 'Take mine, Beatrice,' she'd said. 'Eat it. Let it not go to waste.' Beatrice had quickly downed her own porridge and her mistress's mutton besides, while Anne lay on the bed, dozing, until the boy came for the dishes. She'd been limp as a kitten when Beatrice undressed her for bed.

'Help me sit up, Beatrice,' she says now. 'Ask my lady for ink and writing paper.'

'Oh, mistress, should you?'

'I must.'

But she has written very little by late morning when the clerk arrives to tell her the privy council would speak with her again. 'No,' Anne says simply. She is sitting in a chair, wrapped in a warm blanket. 'I cannot.'

'But, madam,' the man says, 'you will.'

And indeed she does. Beatrice is furious as she dresses Anne while the guards wait downstairs, more furious still, watching her mistress's thin back as she follows her through the narrow sun-washed streets, across the green sweep of lawn, through the gardens, winding down into the dim undercroft, and then up the steep stairs to the long gallery. There are no other petitioners or examinees waiting. The clerk stands at the door to the inner chamber. He gestures Anne to come in. Beatrice prepares for another long wait, but within half an hour her mistress emerges from the council chamber, the clerk walking beside her. Beatrice can see with what effort her mistress is moving. The guardsmen fall in step, moving together along the gallery towards the far end, and of course Beatrice follows. At the landing stair, a wherry and boatman are waiting. Mistress Anne turns, swaying slightly, her voice weak but calm. 'You mustn't come now. They are sending me to Newgate.'

'Oh!' Beatrice feels her blood drop. *Newgate!* That most terrible of prisons! Where the bloodiest of criminals await their executions and others die daily from pestilence and lack of light; it is a horrifying place, worse by reputation than any gaol in England—how can they send her mistress there? And she so ill she is near to drop! Can they not see this? Anne is trembling. She lays a hand on Beatrice's arm, looks at her with meaning: 'You must return to my lady's home and retrieve my things. The Lord strengthen you, Beatrice. Go quickly.

And pray.' Then Anne is being steered roughly onto the gently rocking wherry. The council clerk and guardsmen turn back towards the palace, and Beatrice is left standing in the lovely June warmth, sparks of sunlight glinting on the water, a faint breeze bringing the feculent stink to her nostrils as she watches her mistress being rowed away. How will she ever find her way back to the lady's home?

But good fortune, clean wits, and her own excellent sense of direction see her there: she finds her way to the half-timbered house within half an hour, knocks timidly, and the instant she is brought into the lady's presence, she pours out the tale, her words tumbling. The lady calms her, offers an escort to see her to Newgate to join her mistress and a bit of money for Anne's keep. 'But you mustn't tell anyone,' Lady Garneys says. 'Do you understand? My lords mustn't know! I'm contracted to keep female prisoners from time to time, but I'll not have them think I abet heretics.'

Beatrice nods. She holds the coins in her open palm. Seven shillings. They are debased now since the war, the silver so thin the king's nose is worn away. They'll not buy much. 'Thank you, my lady.' She slips the coins into her pocket. Quickly she goes upstairs to gather Anne's things: the laundered smock and kerchiefs spread yesterday to dry at the window, the soft goatskin travelling bag with its clean coif and veil, mended stockings, the clutch of letters . . . The letters. Of course. This was Anne's meaning at the dock: *Retrieve my things*. Meaning: *Retrieve my writings.* And just so, Beatrice does. She takes everything from the bag, wraps the clean smock around the letters, places the bundle gently in the bottom of the bag, stuffs everything else on top of it. The letters are a danger, Beatrice knows, but she is charged to bring them; she cannot discard them. Nor burn them. Nor let them be found.

The next days and nights are wretched. Beatrice believes at any moment her mistress will die. They have put her in a basement cell—it takes three of the precious coins even to learn where they've put her—and the darkness and damp serve no good for Mistress

Anne. The fever comes and goes, but the stabbing pains remain constant. Never in her life, Anne moans, has she felt such pain. Beatrice purchases cheese and ale, but her mistress will take only small sips of the ale, so Beatrice eats the cheese before the rats get it, and then the money is gone. Without money for food, prisoners receive only one mouldy piece of bread per day and water from the cistern, which their servants must pump into urns they bring to the central hall for the purpose. Beatrice would never give her mistress that tainted water.

And then, on the third morning, Anne grows worse; she rolls about on the filthy mattress, cries out in her sleep—or it is not sleep but delirium, for she calls Beatrice by her dead sister's name. She reaches for Beatrice's hand, pleads for something to drink, *Maddie, help me, I thirst.* Oh, her mistress must have a doctor! But they've no means, no money. She must go to Anne's cousin Brittayne to plead for money. She looks at her mistress shivering on the straw bed on the floor. If I leave her, Beatrice thinks, she may die. But if I do not leave her, she will die surely. Beatrice hides the travelling bag beneath the damp mattress, calls for the gaoler to come let her out.

But Master Brittayne is strangely changed. He draws her quickly away from his lodging when she knocks at his door to ask for him, walks her well south of the Temple district, steers her into an empty courtyard. He says nothing when she tells him Mistress Anne is imprisoned at Newgate. 'She is ill, sir. I must have some money for her.'

Master Brittayne shifts his eyes around the walls, to the street beyond the courtyard gate. 'Francis has been called before the council,' he says.

'Sir Francis? But why? When?'

'They say it is to do with certain debts.' Clearly Master Brittayne does not think this is the reason. 'He's travelling from Lincolnshire even now.'

'Oh, tell him I must speak with him! My mistress is in need of a doctor! And food, and money to move her upstairs.'

'If I see him, I'll tell him,' Master Brittayne answers vaguely. 'And in turn you may tell her that her friend John Lascelles is imprisoned in the Tower, and Bishop Latimer with him.'

'What, sir?'

'And not they two alone,' Brittayne mutters, 'but many others of their persuasion. You will please tell her.'

'Yes, sir,' Beatrice says, even as she thinks, but how can I? It will cause too grave a shock. It might kill her. 'My mistress is very ill, sir.'

'These are woeful times,' Master Brittayne says. 'Doctor Crome has lost his pulpit at Saint Mary Aldermary. He'll recant at Paul's Cross on Sunday.'

'When will Master Francis go before the council, sir? Perhaps I can catch him there.'

Master Brittayne continues as if he has not heard her. 'This is to be Crome's second recantation. The one he gave at Lent was, according to the law and Stephen Gardiner, insufficient.'

Beatrice cannot understand why he is so uninterested in her mistress's fate. 'I must have money for her, sir! She is like to die, truly. It is so much worse than the Compter, you cannot believe—'

But Brittayne is already digging in his purse. He fishes out a half-crown and lays it in her palm. 'You'll find Lascelles' boy Jack in Basing Lane.' His worried eyes glance about. 'Tell her I pray for her,' he whispers, and turns to make his way back to Middle Temple.

And so it is to Lascelles' young servant Jack she must turn. The boy knows exacting details about all the arrests and imprisonments and summonses of evangelicals: he has an ear to the ground and connections among the apprentices, and he helps her make moan among them for money for her mistress. 'This all come by Doctor Crome,' he says, and spits in the gutter; they are hurrying along Poultry Street. 'It was him named your mistress for a heretic, and my master, too, and others besides. My friend Dick Wilmot don't believe it, he don't want to hear a bad word about Doctor Crome, but *I* know.'

The money from the prentices allows her to have Mistress Anne moved to a room on the ground floor—it has no privy or wash basin, as some of the gentlemen's do, but it is drier, at least. Every day, in slow and small ways, Anne's health improves. Though not her mind, Beatrice thinks. She still calls Beatrice by her dead sister's name and seems not to know it. She asks for ink and paper. 'No, madam,' Beatrice whispers, 'please.' But it is her mistress's wish, and so Beatrice uses a bit of the money to buy ink instead of food.

Anne sits below the slit of window and writes and writes, and then reads her words aloud to Beatrice, and sometimes they make sense, and sometimes they seem like ravings: 'O, king, be not deceived! Daniel fourteen. For God will be in nothing made with hands of men, Acts seven. What stiff-necked people are these that will always resist the Holy Ghost! Truth is laid in prison! Luke twenty-one. The law is turned to wormwood, Amos six.' The verses are all smudged and smushed together, as if her mistress must write out every verse she remembers against the day all the Bibles in the world are taken away and burned. Or at other times, when she is more herself, it is as if she must prove she knows God's Word back to front—but to whom? No person reads her writings. It is as if she believes there is someone out there who will see, someone who'll hear all the Bible verses.

Beatrice says nothing, only takes the pages when her mistress is finished and hides them away with the others.

– Chapter 51 –

It is the last week of June 1546, the thirty-eighth year of Henry Tudor's reign: the last June of Henry's life. So believe all who attend him, although none will say this aloud, for even to think it is treason. The privy council is meeting at Greenwich again, as they have done for weeks. Henry moves his court less and less often now: it is too hard to be hoisted, too painful to be carried. Increasingly he withdraws to his privy chambers, roars and grumbles and complains, sometimes whimpers; he sees only his closest advisors now, upon rare occasion his queen. The business of the kingdom he leaves to his councillors, having first charged them to call in all the debts owed to him. The kingdom is bankrupt. Henry's vain war with France, his continual assaults upon Scotland, the debased coinage, the extravagances of his long reign: all have taken their toll. The vast wealth from the suppressed monasteries is gone, the great monies raised in taxes, the myriad lands and goods from attainted traitors: all vanished into the gaping maw of Henry's vanity.

Nevertheless, there are turnips yet from which blood may be wrung, those who can be persuaded to exchange good lands for poor, riches for pittance: there are always those in the kingdom who fear Henry's wrath more than the loss of their own fortunes. Find them. Wring them. This, according to word from the privy chamber, is His Majesty's manifest will, to be duly executed by his privy councillors.

Thus do we find Sir Francis Ayscough in the council chamber at Greenwich, standing in a cruel slash of sunlight—the same place, in fact, his sister stood a week past, though he cannot know this—with black cap in hand, fear bold on his features. They have brought him here, he believes, to answer for the heresies of his sister, and his own complicity in the same. The councillors are rowed up sternly before him, Lord Chancellor Thomas Wriothesley in the centre, flanked by the Bishop of Winchester on one side, the Duke of Norfolk on the other. Here, too, Essex, Durham, Gage, Sadler, the king's secretary, William Paget. Francis served with Durham and Gage at Boulogne;

he tries to catch their eyes, call on that fraternity, but they gaze placidly at him as if they do not know him.

Master Paget begins: 'Our late audits reveal discrepancies, sir. The king is owed monies from your father, Sir William.'

'I beg your pardon?' Francis says. He has ridden four days from Lincoln with black fear swelling his belly, which he drank into submission last night with his brother at the sign of the Dolphin, only to awaken this morning in Edward's rooms with raging thirst, a killing throb to his forehead, and the fear liquefying his vitals again. 'How's that again, sir?'

'Three hundred pounds,' Paget says, shuffling papers, 'owed by Sir William Ayscough, knight, as surety for one Geoffrey Chamber, late receiver of certain lands.'

'I don't—' Francis is at first confused, and then aghast. Three hundred pounds! It is a shocking sum. It is also, Francis thinks, a lie. He wants to demand to see the documents, examine his father's signature, but he knows he will not. Whatever the king will have of him, he will have.

Because of Anne.

Because of his troublesome, troubling, high-stomached sister. Since the moment he told the king's men where to find her, Francis has suffered a torment of guilt and fear—guilt for his betrayal of her, fear for his own safety. Now, half in relief, half in fury, he sees how his penance is to be made. He closes his aching eyes against the sunlight. Three hundred pounds. Where will he get such a sum?

As if listening to his thoughts, Master Paget continues: 'We have consented, by the king's command, to receive part payment in lands, and to forestall the rest for a certain number of days.'

Payment in lands, Francis thinks. Certain number of days. And how long is a certain number? Ah. Suddenly he understands. He is not here to answer with his life for the crime of harbouring a heretic, as he'd feared, nor to answer for his father's debt, as he has just been told. He is here to persuade his sister. Francis knows what has happened. Edward told him last night at the tavern: how Anne defied the privy council with her silences and her smiles; how she is held now at Newgate and will be brought to Guildhall the day after tomorrow to be tried—there to make a public recantation to save her life. If she'll do it, Edward said. He looked at his brother. In silence, in despair, holding one another's gaze, they agreed: she will not. Now, in the bright heat of the council chamber, Francis rubs his throbbing temples. He licks his dry lips. 'It will require time, sirs, to survey my lands.'

'Clerk, draw up a letter!' Wriothesley takes up the business. 'To Sir Edward North, Chancellor of Augmentations: Sir Francis Ayscough being before us for three hundred pounds due by his father to His Majesty the king,' he rattles off the words, at once bored and impatient, 'we remit him unto you, with a survey of the lands and tenements offered, to wit: Bishop Burton, Lockington, and Kilham.'

Francis blinks in surprise—his fallow Yorkshire lands? Is he to be let off so easy?

'Further, you shall draw up an indenture,' Wriothesley orders the scribbling clerk, 'between the king and Sir Francis Ayscough, whereby the latter delivers said parcels in the East Riding, surveyed by Sir Michael Stanhope, appointed thereto by commission from the lords of the king's privy council, etcetera.' He waves his hand impatiently: you know what to write, the gesture says.

His Yorkshire lands have been surveyed? This makes no sense. Francis scans the row of councillors. None seem interested in the proceedings, save three: Norfolk, Gardiner, and Wriothesley. Even Master Paget appears ready to move on to other business. But the three lords of the conservative faction glare at him in silent expectation. They'll not say the words, will they? They'll only threaten with this invisible sword, three hundred pounds—and more, oh, yes, they'll find papers for other debts, sufficient to drive Francis to utter ruin. He has ridden from Lincoln in fear for his life. Now he knows it is not to be his life but his fortune—unless, as these three lords declare with their glaring expectation: unless Sir Francis turns his sister to their purpose.

A great despair falls upon him. He cannot. It is not just that he hasn't the powers of persuasion to turn Anne to their calculations. It is that he cannot see her. He cannot bear to face her, look in her eyes, see her in prison and know that his betrayal placed her there. Francis says nothing. He sets his hand to the paper the clerk proffers, bows deeply, and goes out, squinting, his head pounding, retreating along the gallery to find his way to the stables, so that he may mount his weary stallion and ride home.

– Chapter 52 –

'This is the efficacy of prayer,' Mistress Anne says, and Beatrice believes her—for hasn't she herself prayed with fervour that her mistress would live? And here she is, sitting up beside the window, reading. 'The fervent prayers of a righteous man availeth much.' Anne smiles at Beatrice, lifts a brow. 'Also, a righteous woman.'

Beatrice smiles back. It is indeed miraculous how quickly her mistress has healed. She tires easily still, and her eyes are not what they were, but by all other signs, Mistress Anne is near herself again. It is the power of prayer, yes, Beatrice thinks, but also the strengthening letters of encouragement she receives from her friends.

Word has gone out among believers, Jack says—making clear he is part of the cause for that—and Mistress Anne has many supporters. Every day he brings two or three letters to Beatrice to smuggle into Newgate with the day's rations. The one her mistress is holding now did not come from Jack, however, but from a man in a blue coat, who asked for Beatrice by name. He gave her the letter and ten shillings and said they were from Lady Lane. Anne has read the letter many times in silence, as if committing it to memory. She hands the page to Beatrice, who holds it over the candle, and when it lights, drops it to the stone floor, where it flares and browns and curls in on itself. Glancing towards the door, Beatrice grinds the ashes under foot. This they do with all the letters. 'Thank you, Beatrice,' Anne says. 'We daren't keep evidence that could implicate others in my suffering.'

'What of your own writings, miss?' Beatrice ventures carefully. This has long worried her, that her mistress's words might be used against her.

'My writings endanger no one, Beatrice. When Master Lascelles comes, which pray God will be soon, we shall give them to him. Then he and our friends may read how cruelly I am handled and know I have withstood.'

Beatrice looks away. She should have told her by now that Master Lascelles is imprisoned in the Tower. But her mistress is not strong enough yet. And indeed, when the letter from Lady Lane is a black smear on the floor, Anne passes a hand over her eyes, sinks down on the bed. 'I should like to answer her, Beatrice. How many sheets have we left?'

'Two, miss. I can buy more, but there'll be no bread for supper.'

'Man does not live by bread alone.'

'Nor woman, neither.'

Anne cuts her a glance, then laughs. 'Well. My eyes are tired. You must take down my words.'

'I can't write like you, miss. The lady won't ever know what I'm saying.'

'You must practice, then. Oh, for pity's sake, Beatrice. Maud Lane is as astute a lady as lives on this earth; she'll decipher your scribblings.' Anne massages her fingertips against her eyelids. 'Bring the inkpot. I'll spell out the hard words.' She lies back on the mattress, dictates the words with her eyes closed. 'I do perceive, p-e-r-c-e-i-v-e, my dear friend in the Lord, that you are not yet persuaded—what? Persuaded. P-e-r-s-w-a-d-e-d . . .'

It takes a long while.

When the letter is finished Beatrice asks, 'How shall I deliver it, miss?'

Anne frowns. Well, here is a conundrum. The man in the blue coat is gone, of course, and Beatrice dare not carry it directly to the palace where my lady is at court, for the danger it would be both to herself and to Lady Lane. 'Let me think on it a while,' Anne says. Beatrice folds the letter, frowning at her own clumsy markings, hides it away with Anne's others. Her mistress remains on the bed, eyes closed. After a long while, Anne begins to murmur. '"Behold, I send ye forth as sheep among wolves." Yes, I know. I know. This is as my Lord promised.' It is as if she is talking to someone—not Beatrice, the other someone. The invisible listener. 'I have more enemies than hairs on my head.'

– Chapter 53 –

I woke in the night and saw her there, not falling and burning, as before, but standing at the door in her bridal clothes with that sweet smile on her face, her hair golden. I called out to her, *Maddie! My dear sister!* Her smile became all the more tender, more loving, beatific, but she did not come to me. I beckoned, I pleaded, but there was the gulf fixed, that great chasm between the quick and the dead; she could not come to me, nor I to her. Not before my work is done. O, Father, let me not stumble! Let me not fear. And as for these bodily sufferings, they will not endure. Only Christ endures, and I in Him. On the far side of the gulf, my sister said nothing, only smiled sorrowfully as she faded back into the darkness. I knew then I must prevaricate no longer. I began writing my confession of faith to the council when dawn's light came.

But see the hand of God here? Beatrice has already brought the materials required: inkpot and paper, quill and fresh ink. I have no penknife to sharpen the quill, but my Lord gave me good teeth. He will provide if we bind our will to His—just as He provided the ram caught by its horns in the thicket, so that Abraham might slaughter the ram and not his son Isaac. I have sacrificed my sons already. I pray God He will allow me to see them again. Daily, hourly, I pray. But I am not afraid.

I think this is the one thing my enemies cannot understand. Even when they threaten me. Even when they came for me on Sunday and brought me under guard to Paul's Cross to hear Doctor Crome recant. Did they think that sad man's false recantation would persuade me? I felt only sorrow, standing in fine June mist to hear that good man stumble out words he knew were not of Christ: he read them aloud in a flat, dull voice, all the fire and fury of his sermons vanished, as if they'd never been. Hugh Latimer would not do so. Hugh Latimer will endure, I doubt not, to the very end. As I pray that I shall.

The people stood in silence at Paul's Cross, the misting rain turning to drizzle, and when Doctor Crome, in his misery and fear, had finished, Bishop Bonner sent to me a messenger with this word: 'Turn from your heretical opinion, madam, as the good Doctor Crome has turned. Else you shall be summoned to Guildhall tomorrow to answer to the law.'

Here is the message I sent back to Bishop Bonner: 'Though I walk in the valley of the shadow of death, I will fear no evil, for the Father is with me. Psalms 23.'

And so, early next morning, I was brought before the council at Guildhall. With me in the antechamber were John Hadley the tailor, a merchant named White, and Nicholas Shaxton, the former Bishop of Salisbury, all brought to answer to the Six Articles. I saw how Bishop Shaxton's hands trembled; his face was ashen. I tried to comfort them all with the sixth chapter of Matthew: 'When you are brought before the council, concern yourself not with what you will say, for the words will be given unto you.' Whether this proved to be true for them, I cannot say, because we were brought singly before the council, each alone, and I the last.

They were all present, of course, all the men of the king's privy council and the church and the city, whom I have faced time and again: the mayor, the Bishop of London, the Duke of Norfolk, the chief justices of the king's bench and common pleas, my lord chancellor Thomas Wriothesley, the Bishop of Winchester . . . oh, yes. The Bishop of Winchester. Stephen Gardiner. He began without prelude as soon as I stood in the dock: 'This woman is a heretic and condemned by the law if she will stand in her opinion!'

'I am no heretic, sir,' I said. 'Neither do I deserve death by the law of God. If the laws of man say so, then these laws cannot be of God. And as for my faith, which I have written to the council, as you have it in your hand, I'll not deny it.'

'You would deny the Sacrament to be the very flesh, blood, and bone of our Saviour?' He wanted me to say it aloud, before all these witnesses, that there be no uncertainty of my condemnation.

'The Son of God, Christ Jesus, that was born of the Virgin Mary, is now glorious in Heaven. As for that which you call God, it is a piece of bread. If you wish proof, my lord, leave the bread in the box but three months, and it will be mouldy and so can turn to nothing good. Therefore, I am convinced it cannot be God.'

'Bring forward a priest!' one of the council called out. 'Let him bless the bread and break it and see will she receive it with these blasphemies in her mouth! Let him hear her confession!'

'Will you have a priest, woman?'

I smiled.

'What? You think it not good to confess to a priest, when the very law of God demands it?'

'Show me in Scripture where such law is writ. Ye cannot, for it is not. I shall confess my faults to God, for I am sure He will hear me with favour.'

Then another of the council said, 'Is the consecrated bread in the pyx God or no? Answer plainly, woman!'

'God is a spirit, my lord, and will be worshipped in spirit and in truth. John three.'

And from another: 'Will you plainly deny Christ to be in the Sacrament?'

'How does communion bread come into the world, sir? Is it manna come down from Heaven? No, it is material flour and water, moulded by the hands of mortal men and placed in men's ovens, and the wine also, ground of grapes by men's hands and placed in vessels to ferment. The Son of God does not dwell in anything made of man.'

'Hear it!' Bishop Gardner waved in the air my confession of faith. 'She has written these very heresies in her own hand!'

' "Woe unto you, scribes and Pharisees, hypocrites!" ' I quoted our Saviour. ' "Which build the tombs of the prophets and garnish the sepulchres of the righteous and say, if we had been in our fathers' time, we would not have been partakers with them in the blood of the prophets." ' I scanned their faces. 'I say to you, sirs, ye *all* have blood of prophets on your hands! And their names be John Lambert, John Frith, Thomas Bilney, Robert Barnes, Thomas Garrett—'

'Burn her!' Stephen Gardiner cried as he rose to his feet, and the wrath in his face was marvellous to see. 'Burn her for a heretic!' Lord Chancellor Thomas Wriothesley stood also. 'Burn her!' he called out, and the Duke of Norfolk got to his gouty feet. 'Aye!' he said, and one by one, Sir Richard Rich, Master Paget, Bishop Bonner, all the lords and the gentlemen of the council stood in agreement: Aye, aye, aye, aye.

– Chapter 54 –

Early the next morning following her condemnation at Guildhall, four guardsmen arrive at Newgate to take Anne away. They will not say where they are taking her, and they'll not allow Beatrice to follow. As they turn with Anne towards the river, they shout at Beatrice: 'Go back! You must wait for your mistress here!' But when Beatrice returns to Newgate, the gaoler says she has no mistress within now, and she may not enter. That night she sleeps on a chandler's floor amid the stink of rendered lard and tallow, protected by Jack and the apprentices. At first light she hurries back to the prison. But Anne is not there. Her chest tight with worry, Beatrice returns to Basing Lane and asks until she finds Jack again. He knows nothing more than Beatrice knows, but his apprentice friends have eyes and ears everywhere; they know more than all the council's spies together. The apprentices will bring word.

And surely it is true, Beatrice thinks that evening as Jack guides her through the dark streets: it has taken him not even until full night to find out where they've taken her mistress. He leads her to a merchant's home in the narrow, crowded streets near the Tower. The man answers Jack's knock, glances over their heads, up and down the street, allows them to enter. He does not call for a servant but rather leads them himself along the dim hall to a low door in the back, beside the kitchen. He extends to Beatrice his stub of candle, says to Jack gruffly, 'Come away.' And the merchant, Master Mildmay, and Jack leave her.

The room is small, dark, lit only by the candle Beatrice carries, but she can see Anne lying on the bed in her smock, uncovered, her arms above her head at an awkward angle, her legs splayed. 'The light,' Anne whispers. 'Put it out.'

Beatrice snuffs the candle. The room is black now. 'Oh, mistress,' she says, stepping nearer, 'what have they done to you?'

'Don't touch me.'

The girl stops. She hears Anne panting lightly.

'Don't come nearer. I cannot be touched.'

'Yes. No. I won't.' Silence again, but for the sound of her mistress's harsh breathing. 'Can I bring you something? Ale? I can ask—'

'No.' The word is faint. 'There is nothing.' Anne shifts slightly on the bed, and the movement makes her cry out.

'Oh, what is it, miss? Let me light the candle.'

'No! I'm sorry. The light is too harsh. I think . . . the strings of my eyes are burst.'

'Your eyes!'

Her mistress swallows. 'I am racked, Beatrice.'

'Oh, Mother of God, oh, please, oh, surely they would not!' But yes. Of course they would. They have. She had seen by the candle's light the strange way her mistress lies, how her body seems near elongated, her arms and legs spread. And she is wearing only her smock; dear God, did they carry her through the streets like that? 'What can I do, miss?' she whispers.

'You can—' Anne stops, swallows, a choked gulping sound. 'You can take a letter for me.' She swallows deep again. 'Tomorrow when I can bear the light. Not tonight.' After a little while she whispers, 'They said I should be burnt. If my Lord wills, so I shall be.'

Beatrice begins to cry quietly.

'Please. Do not cry, Beatrice. See me here, I am not weeping, I am as merry'—she halts again, panting lightly—'as merry as one bound towards Heaven.'

'You mustn't talk, miss. Rest now.' She starts to feel her way towards the door. 'I'll fetch some ale, we'll send for a doctor.'

'No, please,' Anne says. 'Just stay with me.'

Through the night the girl sits on the floor in the dark beside the bed. Sometimes she thinks her mistress is sleeping, but other times feels her awake, praying. The straw bed rustles when Anne tries to move; then she'll cry out, and Beatrice will scramble up from the floor. 'Don't touch me!' As if to be touched is her greatest terror.

'No. I won't. I won't,' Beatrice whispers. 'What can I do for you?'

'Pray.'

Near daylight, Beatrice hears the slow, rhythmic sound of Anne's breathing: she is sleeping at last. The girl gets wearily to her feet. By the grey light from the window, she sees now what they have done to her: the cruel gashes around her wrists and ankles, the flesh puckered and swollen, her arms awkwardly crooked above her head. It looks so painful a position, and her hands, too, are in strange positions, one twisted backwards at the wrist at an impossible angle, the other curled in on itself, not as a fist but dropped loosely forward as if it is barely hanging to her bones, the fingers limp. Her mistress's smock is wadded at her waist, exposing her legs. Beatrice wants to pull the linen down, for modesty's sake, but she is afraid to touch her. She traces with her eyes the bruises along her mistress's thighs, her swollen knees, her elbows. Her neck is discoloured also, her eyelids white and puffy. The welts where the cords were lashed to her wrists and ankles are red and angry now, but these will turn blue-black, Beatrice knows, then purple, then yellow, the slow phases of healing, at every stage a new colour to give testament to their tortures. What is ruined on Anne's insides does not show: the muscles torn, bones broken, joints separated. The sinews of her arms stretched. The sinews of her eyes perished in her head. Even in sleep, Anne's face shows the ravages of pain.

Later that afternoon: a knock at the door. The merchant's wife stands in the dim hall, speaks apologetically to Beatrice: 'My lord chancellor has ordered his servant to deliver a message to the gentlewoman from his own hand. He insists he must bring it in himself. He'll not allow me to bring it to you. I'm sorry.' Beatrice glares.

'It's all right, Beatrice.' Anne's voice is faint, but that she can speak at all gives the girl hope. 'Tell him to wait. Close the door.'

The girl turns. Her mistress is grimacing. 'Help me, Beatrice. Bring my arms down.'

'Oh, miss, can you?'

'I cannot. You must move them for me.'

'Oh, no, I can't!'

'You can. Slowly, now. Easy.'

Beatrice leans over her mistress; timidly, gently, she slides one hand beneath Anne's forearm, the other beneath the soft flesh above her elbow. Supporting the length of it as best she can, she moves the limp arm a tiny increment. Anne cries out. Beatrice stops. 'Tomorrow, miss. We can try tomorrow.'

'Tomorrow will be worse. My shoulders are wrenched, Beatrice. We cannot let them set this way.'

The girl begins again. Anne's face is white, the sweat slick on her forehead, running down the sides of her face. She issues small, muffled cries, bites her lip, groans. In twenty minutes' time, Beatrice has brought both arms from above her head to her sides. They lie at odd angles, her crippled hands limp on the counterpane. 'Cover me,' Anne says. Beatrice looks around. Her mistress's kirtle is tumbled in the corner. It is not clean, but it is the only thing she has. Tenderly, as gently as she can, she spreads it over her mistress.

The lord chancellor's man turns out to be a stripling boy in ill-fitting livery, short and wiry, full of himself. He charges into the chamber, flourishing his sealed letter. Seeing Anne on the bed, he stops, averts his eyes. 'My lord chancellor sends greetings, madam. I've a letter to deliver, to your own hand and none else.'

'My hand is indisposed to receive my lord chancellor's letter. As you can see. Read it to me, please, Beatrice.'

Beatrice can feel the boy's gaping stare as she takes the letter, breaks the seal, bites the silk thread with her teeth. The message is, thankfully, very short. She reads haltingly, puzzling out the words, spelling many of them aloud for her mistress to pronounce:

'Madam,' she reads aloud, 'herein is my final offer of clemency. If you will leave your obstinate opinion, you shall want for nothing. If you will not, you shall forth this day to Newgate, and so be burned.'

'You would think,' Anne says, 'that my lord would tire of repeating the same useless entreaties.' Beatrice looks at her. How can she? Where does she get strength, not merely to withstand, or endure, but to keep the sharpness to her tongue?

The boy shifts his feet, his satchel. 'I'm to wait for an answer, miss.' This is directed to Beatrice, not Anne, but it is Anne who answers.

'Tell your master that I would rather die than break my faith.'

The boy's eyes dart to her face, then quickly back to Beatrice. 'Can I have it in writing, miss? I don't know that my master will believe me.'

'Write it down, please, Beatrice. Ask Master Mildmay for utensils.' It takes only a few moments. The flustered merchant provides not only ink and quill but sand also, and Beatrice writes on the reverse side of the lord chancellor's letter, sands the page before she folds it, seals it with a blob of wax from the candle. When the boy is gone, Anne says, 'That is not what he wants. Thomas Wriothesley. Or yes, that too. But my opinion in the Sacrament'—she pauses to breathe—'is not what caused him such fury. That he must throw off his cloak and turn the rack himself.'

'Oh, mistress, he is the highest official—oh, surely, he did not!'

Anne closes her eyes in lieu of a nod. After a moment she says, 'And Master Rich with him.' Then, after a long while, she says, 'I see that even you do not believe me.' Her voice is raspy as a file on cold iron. 'This is why you must write it for me. My handlings since Newgate. Carry my letters to Master Lascelles, that he might—no, don't cry. You mustn't cry. Why are you crying?'

The words pour forth now: 'Master Lascelles is in the Tower, and not him alone, miss, but also Bishop Latimer, and others, a dozen or more, Jack says, and Master Brittayne has gone strange, he won't help us now, and Master Francis your brother was here—he was *here*, miss! in London! And he did not come to see you in prison. I do not know if he knows, but he must know, for all London knows, it is, oh, mistress.' She buries her face in her hands and sobs and sobs. Anne whispers soothing words, but the girl cannot stop weeping. For the first time, she has understood that there will be no reprieve. Master Brittayne, Master Edward, Sir Francis, they will not intervene. No one will be seen to ally themselves with her mistress. She has no help, no hope, from any direction. And so Beatrice knows now it is true. Her mistress will burn.

– Chapter 55 –

Late at night the guards came to the merchant's house to return me to Newgate, as I had known that they would. Two guards carried me from the bed to the street, where other men and torchbearers stood in a tight murmuring knot. Four of them hoisted me onto the litter, while Master Mildmay stood in the doorway yelping, 'Take care! Watch yourselves! Gently, now!' They were not gentle. They lifted me and started towards the river, and I could not keep from making sounds—the litter was not a chair but more a sling or hammock that swayed and bounced as they walked. Beatrice ran after us uttering her sharp cries: 'Stop! Stop, you are hurting my mistress!' At the landing stage, the Tower guardsmen and one of the torchbearers left us, so then it was one torchbearer, the four litter bearers, one halberdier, two bargemen, and a black-cloaked gentleman who directed everything. And Beatrice. Her tears were dried now, her attentions bent on seeing they did not hurt me—an impossible task. The return journey to Newgate was more painful than almost anything that had gone before, but for the racking itself.

The Thames is a ghost river at night, did you know? And we a ghost barge gliding silently upriver. We docked in a short while, then there was the painful lift and climb, the rough jostle through the night streets. I begged Beatrice to hush; I was afraid they would banish her, or beat her. At the door of the prison, the gaoler stood with rushlight, waiting. The man in the black cloak passed something to the gaoler's hand, coins, I suppose, and they brought me in and laid me in the bed. It is not the cell I inhabited before but a larger one, somewhat drier, with even a small window. This is so they may claim I have not been poorly used. They are not pleased that word has gone out I was racked. Well, God forgive them their cruelties. I cannot. Though I pray I shall be able to do so when my hour comes.

Oh, it is such a brutal intimacy! You cannot imagine what it is to have men force you to unclothe before them and climb onto stained and stinking planks, to lie in your bare smock, spread open on the wood like a hind to be gutted. By his face, even the lieutenant of the Tower could not believe what they were doing. He did not argue, but nor did he work the lever very hard—he at my feet and his attendant behind me at the head. I cannot think this is a common task the lieutenant performs. He fumbled with the cords as he wrapped them 'round and around my joints. Or perhaps he was simply loath to touch me.

Not so Rich and Wriothesley: their anger was so great that, when the lieutenant stepped back and would have released me, they swooped in and clamped their hands around my wrists to wrap the lashes tighter. The lieutenant protested: 'She is condemned already, my lords. And a gentlewoman! His Majesty the king will not countenance this!'

'You are commanded!' Master Rich said.

'I am at the king's commandment, sir,' the lieutenant answered. He went out and took his attendant with him. Then did Wriothesley and Rich proceed to rack me with their own hands. I cannot describe it. It cannot be described. Only to tell you this: my lord chancellor's languid boredom had surely disappeared. His face was red and frowning, great gobs of sweat pouring into his beard, his cap and cloak cast aside. It was night then, and hot, the cellar room reeking of must and sweat, the torches stinking in the sconces. Not only the cloak of his body did my lord chancellor cast off, but the cloak of his boredom and disdain, the impassive face he wears at the public quests, or, as he wears in private, the cloak of sincerity, his glossing words. In private he speaks in a voice falsely tender, reasonable, loving. As if this would move me. As if I do not see through his lies. How he loathes me! He cannot direct me. He cannot cause me to deny my faith, cannot force me to live with Thomas Kyme, cannot persuade me to name my friends or cause me to cry out, though he stood at my feet and pulled the great lever towards himself with both hands, grunting. Above all, he hates me for this reason: he can neither trick me nor torture me into betraying the queen.

Oh, yes, this is their true purpose. Wriothesley has ever despised Queen Katheryn, so Maud Lane said years ago, and why this is so and why he will commit such sins to his soul to condemn her, only the Master can tell. He sends word now: recant, recant, you shall want for nothing; but that night in the Tower, as I lay upon the rack, the lord chancellor did not ask of my opinion in the Sacrament—rather, he demanded I speak of the queen's ladies. My lady of Suffolk! he growled through gritted teeth. My lady Hertford! The queen's cousin, Lady Lane! I heard my bones crack, my sinews pop, felt my joints torn asunder. The agony was so great I did not know how I should endure, but the merciful Lord took pity upon me, He sent His balm upon me, gave me strength, not to endure, but to yield: it is finished, I thought in my agony. I shall die now, I shall fly to be with Him. I surrendered to that mercy.

But the Lieutenant of the Tower returned—I know not how much later; very long it seemed—and it was he who caused them to release me. When they lifted me off the rack, I immediately swooned. They revived me with salts of ammonia and a splash of water. After that I sat two long hours reasoning with my lord chancellor upon the bare floor. With many flattering words, he tried to persuade me to leave my opinion. But my Lord God, I thank His everlasting goodness, gave me grace to persevere. And will do, I hope, to the very end.

Now, though, are they desperate. My lord chancellor wishes that no man should know of their uncomely doings, but it is too late for that. Word has gone out, though I talk to no one, only Beatrice. I try to comfort her. 'You shall return home to South Kelsey,' I tell her. 'Sir Francis will see to you, he will take care of you.' But she only looks away, her face like a stone. Forgiveness comes easier blood to blood, I think. Or so it is for me, perhaps not others. But how can I blame our brother and refuse to forgive him, Maddie, when I have all my life begged for forgiveness from thee?

IV

Flesh, Blood, and Bone

London

16 July

1546

– Chapter 56 –

With one hand Beatrice holds a thatch of her mistress's dark hair close to her skull; with the other she tugs the comb gently through to the loose ends. 'Will they . . .' Beatrice does not like to say it, but Jack says this is how it is done, and she cannot bear to think it. 'Must you be drawn through the streets on a hurdle, miss?'

Anne looks up at her from the bed. It is almost a smile. 'They do not tell me their plans.' She closes her eyes again. Her face, in this moment, is smooth, without pain—a momentary release for which the girl is deeply grateful. It will not last long. Beatrice gently spreads the thatch of combed hair on the mattress, reaches for a new handful. She does not want to dress her mistress any sooner than she must—when the pain is waked up, it will not lie quiet again—but she has to make sure Anne is ready, the pouch placed, before they come for her. Which could happen, Beatrice thinks, glancing at the window, any time now. She picks up the small cloth bag, weighs it in her palm: a coarse linen kerchief filled with gunpowder, knotted and tied with a leather thong at one end. It weighs no more than the breast of a songbird. 'Is it enough?' she whispers. Well, and if it isn't? she answers herself. What then? It is all we have. 'I pray it is enough,' she says.

'It will be enough,' Anne says. She opens her eyes. This time it is truly a smile. 'Only traitors are drawn on hurdles, Beatrice. I do not think His Majesty will cause us to be moved that way.'

'Will the king be there?'

'No. Of course not. Come now, don't start. Dress me.'

Beatrice has promised not to cry, and she is not crying. Not really. It requires all her strength to help Anne to a sitting position; she is leaden weight from the waist up. Beatrice removes her soiled smock, guiding one useless arm at a time through the armholes, lifting the linen over her head. Anne sits patiently, trembling a little with the effort, her head hanging down, her hair covering her face. The sharp bones in her back show beneath her skin like knobs and wings. Beatrice bathes her, drops the clean smock over her head, again the excruciating guiding of hands and arms. She reaches for the pouch. 'What if they see the cord at your throat, miss? Maybe we should tie it at your waist like a girdle.'

'You yourself said it is small.'

'But if they see it and take it away?'

'And if the explosion is small, I want it at my heart, not my bowels.'

'Yes. I see.'

'You said you would not cry.'

'I'm not. I am not crying.' She parts the back of Anne's hair with her fingers, ties the leather thong at the nape. Now she puts on her the simple linen gown Anne's supporters have sewn for her. They have sent also a new coif and veil, but Anne says she will go to the fire in her hair, as a bride to the altar.

'Do you want to lie back down till they come?'

Anne nods. Beatrice helps her, though the down-lying seems more painful than the rising-up. It is over a fortnight since she was racked, and still she cannot walk or use her hands, though her eyesight is better; she can read the letters Beatrice brings, if the girl holds them. She cannot write her answers, so she speaks them. Beatrice takes down her words. Each morning for a week, Beatrice has awakened in greater dread. Each day Mistress Anne seems more peaceful.

Since yesterday the workers have been knocking together wooden stands in front of St Bartholomew's church, where the dignitaries will sit to watch the burning. So Jack tells her. He is her informant for all things outside the prison—as she is his informant for what happens within. Master Lascelles is here at Newgate now: he was moved from the Tower after his condemnation, and also two others who are to be burnt with them—the tailor named Hadley, who was condemned on the same day as her mistress, and an Observant friar, a defrocked one, Nicholas Belenian. Master Lascelles and Mistress Anne have not seen each other, nor are they allowed visitors. But their servants may come and go. And they do.

Jack, however, spends more time outside the prison than in—his master prefers it, so that communications with their supporters may come and go more easily. Beatrice thinks again of what Jack told her: that their masters will be tied on a wooden sled back to back, as Barnes and Garret were, and dragged behind horses, bumping and thumping on the harsh road and the crowds jeering, to the execution place at Smithfield. She cannot bear to think of this indignity for her mistress, the pain of the thumping and bumping, and yet—

'If you are not drawn, miss, how will you go?'

Anne doesn't answer. She lies on her back, eyes closed, as she does so often. Beatrice thinks she is praying, but then she says, 'You needn't come, Beatrice, if you don't wish.' It sounds a statement but is meant as a question. Or perhaps it is only that, for Beatrice, it is a question—one she has asked in the night of herself and of the Holy Mother of God, time and again. Of course she will go. She must. But how can she? She has never seen a person burnt. She has never seen any sort of execution, only their black and bloody aftermaths, rotting limbs, boiled skulls. How can she watch her mistress suffer?

'What is the weather like today?'

Beatrice turns to look at her. It is so strange a question. She steps to the window; it is only a small square, too high to see the street, though she hears the gathering crowd's murmur. 'It's quite grey, miss. The sky is dull white.'

'A good day for us to meet our Lord, then.' Anne has said more than once how grateful she is that she and John Lascelles are to be burnt together. 'We shall comfort and strengthen one another,' she says, and Beatrice grits her teeth, turns away, picks up her mistress's comb. She has lived through the days and nights this way: doing only what is next, not thinking of what is to come. Sometimes, in the night, she awakens to her heart stuttering in terror. Then she does as her mistress does: she prays, as she was taught in the old days, for this is what gives her comfort: *Sancta Maria, Mater Dei, ora pro nobis peccatoribus, nunc et in hor mortis nostrai* . . . Push it away, push it away, she will not think on it.

When the men at arms come, Anne is sitting up again. The indignity of the awkward rising is saved, at least. The captain reads from a scroll: she is hereby condemned by the law, etcetera. He tells her she must come. Anne looks at him. 'I cannot walk, sir.' He nods to two of his men, who take Anne beneath her armpits and lift her. She does not cry out, but Beatrice sees her face blanch. 'She cannot! Please, sirs!' The men carry Anne through the cell door. Beatrice scrambles to gather her mistress's things—as if, what? she will need them afterwards?—and hurries to follow. These days, all these hours, have been so interminable, so slow—and now the unfolding is so swift!

Outside, she squints at the daylight; the sky is overcast, but she has been inside for so long. The crowd is an unfathomable mix of street urchins and apprentices and merchants, and very many of her mistress's supporters. In their midst, surrounded by guards, she spies the debased friar and the tailor and Master Lascelles. They are in their shirts. Their hands are not bound. They are bareheaded. Master Lascelles has grown drawn and thin; he is nearly unrecognizable, but for his red complexion and bald pate, and he is turning, straining, to see behind him. Beatrice follows his gaze, and sees the chair sitting on the ground, four liveried men beside it, and the two men at arms tying Anne by the waist to the seat back. Anne is not looking to meet Master Lascelles' gaze; she is not looking at Beatrice; she seems to be staring at a blank inner space, swaying side to side now as the men hoist the chair strapped to two long poles carried between them. The captain calls out the order, and then they are all moving forwards on the cobbled street, her mistress lifted high above the rest as they move in unison, like a wave, the crowd closing like the sea behind them, washing like the tide towards Smithfield. And Beatrice follows.

It is no great distance, but the press of the crowd is so close she has to struggle to make her way; she's afraid she'll not be there in time. She clutches Anne's filthy travelling bag tight to her chest, squeezing between the pressed bodies. The narrow street opens at last to the sky, the great open field, but the crowd thins only a little as it spreads to the left and right around the circle. In front of the church of St Bartholomew are all the lords and councillors seated high on their scaffold. She cannot see Anne, cannot see any of the prisoners, until she worms through, pushing and shoving, to the thick ropes that hold back the crowd.

There, in the centre of the circle, a wooden platform is raised, perhaps a yard off the ground, with three great wooden stakes driven through holes in the platform into the ground, and stacked all around the base, the faggots tied in their bundles, while workers bring more, and more, stacking them in neat rows. Tied to the three stakes: the priest and tailor together, Lascelles alone, and Anne tied to the third—but how is she standing? She cannot! Then Beatrice sees it is an illusion. Her mistress is not standing but half seated; they have made a saddle for her, a type of wooden seat nailed to the stake at hip height. Anne is bound 'round her middle with a thick chain holding her upright against the stake. Beatrice is weeping fully now, great ragged sobs shaking her chest. She tries to catch Anne's eye to tell her she is here, but her own white-coifed head, she knows, is but one of hundreds gathered at the edge of the field. She lifts her arm and waves, but Anne is not looking at the crowd; her eyes are on the clergyman climbing the steps now to stand in the wooden pulpit, which must have been dragged here from a church, Beatrice thinks, for it is ancient carved oak and does not look raw and new, as do the platform and scaffolding. Her mistress watches the man with rapt attention. Beatrice knows who he is: the former Bishop of Salisbury, Nicholas Shaxton. She knows this because Bishop Shaxton, like the tailor praying and sweating on the platform, was condemned on the same day as her mistress at Guildhall, and the next day recanted. How furious her mistress must be to see him in the pulpit to preach at her burning!

But Anne does not appear furious; she appears, rather, intently interested as the bishop begins. He does not thunder and shout, as Dr Crome used to do in his sermons, but seems to be mumbling. Beatrice cannot hear what he says, but clearly Anne hears him. At times she nods in agreement; at other times she frowns, shakes her head. She speaks in a low voice throughout, as if offering commentary to her companions, and once she calls out sharply: 'There he misses! Hear him? He speaks without the Book!' Master Lascelles joins voice: 'Hear, hear!' And the others murmur agreement as the crowd all around her mutters. But Bishop Shaxton goes on. And on. And on. The people grow restless; children whine and pull away from their mothers' hands. Beatrice can feel and hear the wash of people behind her, teeming this way and that, slipping away to go for food or drink or a piss, and even on the distant scaffold there is movement among the dignitaries, this or that lord rising to descend the skeleton steps, and later coming back again. But those, like Beatrice, with a clear view from the front of the rope line stay where they're standing. They'll not take a chance on losing their good place from which to see the burning.

The sky has changed. It is not solidly overcast now, but mottled, separating into patches of light blue and dark rolling clouds. At last the bishop is praying a benediction, it seems, his one hand raised, the monotone words flowing. He makes the sign of the cross, turns to descend from the pulpit. A long, breathless wait. The crowd is quiet. A page walks down the steps from the dignitaries' platform, walks slowly across the empty field with a large scroll in his hand. He must have been chosen, Beatrice thinks, not for his speed but for the strength of his lungs. He sings out in a voice loud enough to crack Heaven: 'My lord chancellor offers to you all the king's pardon! Turn from your ungodly opinions and you shall have mercy! Recant not, and the laws of justice will prevail! Here, in my lord chancellor's own hand, is your pardon!' The page starts towards them with the scroll, but Anne stops him with a voice equally piercing and loud: 'I came not hither to deny my Lord and Master!'

A pause. Lascelles calls out, 'Nor I!'

'Nor I!' cries the debased friar.

'Nor I!' calls the tailor John Hadley.

Beatrice sees now that two black-masked men are standing on either side of the platform with flaming torches. No, please, she prays. No, please. On the scaffold in front of the church, the lord mayor rises from his seat. He steps forwards to the edge of the platform, raises his arm. No, please, Beatrice prays. '*Fiat Justitia*!' the mayor cries, and there is a satisfied gasp from the crowd as the two executioners bend with their torches towards the base. A spume of smoke rises at once as the wood ignites. Oh, pray God it is dry! Pray God it is well cured, that it will burn hot and fast and her mistress will not suffer! A thin light of fire shows weak in the daylight. Her mistress and the three men are praying aloud, the men's hands raised towards Heaven.

'Mistress!' Beatrice calls. 'I am here!'

It is not possible, she knows, that her mistress can hear her over the roar of the fire and the exhorting crowd, but Anne turns her eyes towards her—her ruined eyes that can scarcely see. It is not possible, Beatrice knows, but still: Anne matches her cloudy gaze to her maid's, and smiles. For all the remainder of her days, Beatrice will hold in her heart this moment. Her mistress's eyes looking to see her. The smoke is roiling black now, the flames lick higher. Her mistress turns her gaze away, looks upward now, and now comes the miracle, the absolute miracle, which Beatrice sees with her own eyes and will never disbelieve for the rest of her living life forever: her maimed mistress, who cannot grip or move or stand, folds her two hands together in prayer, lifts her arms over her head, holds her hands high towards Heaven, and is holding them just so when the flames reach her breast, where the pouch is hidden. A flicker of lightning in the dark sky, a great crack of thunder sounds, at just the same moment as the small, merciful explosion.

– Chapter 57 –

The girl wanders the streets carrying her mistress's bundle. It reeks of the stench of Newgate, but she cannot discard it. And who will want her mistress's filthy smock? Her dingy veil and torn stockings. Her broken quill. And what must she do with Anne's writings? They are folded small, buried in the heart of the bundle. Beatrice cannot think what she must do now, where she must go. Her home since June has been the rancid prison cell. Before that, South Kelsey. Before that, Mistress Hobbes' house. She'll not return to any of these places. Her home, truly, is with her mistress. But her mistress is charred bone and ash, a smouldering pile in the centre of the market square, guarded by halberdiers. And so Beatrice wanders. She is well east now, she thinks, though she recognizes none of these shops, these inns and taverns. She comes to a city gate, sees the spire of a church rising beyond the city wall. She turns back. Evening is near, she senses the failing light, but she keeps her gaze trained on the muck of the street. She doesn't realize where her feet are carrying her until she looks up and finds herself in Watling Street. As if she'd intended it all along, she makes her way directly to the narrow alley off Basing Lane.

Jack is sitting on a stone step with his arms on his knees and his head on his arms; his cap is off, his lank hair hanging down. She says his name, and he jerks up. His eyes are red-rimmed but dry. He looks empty, numb, shocked to his very soul. Beatrice goes to sit beside him. His rough, reddened skin and bent nose are so familiar, a comfort.

'What will you do now?' she says.

Jack shrugs. After a long while he asks, 'You?'

Beatrice doesn't answer. They have both known for so long this day was coming, and yet neither could know what it would be like, not truly. Beatrice had never let herself think that there would be no funeral Mass, no sacrament, no ritual with which to lay away her mistress. No hallowed ground to receive her. No dark, tangled hair to comb. No body to bathe or wrap or bury. Behind her eyes, again

Beatrice sees her mistress flung back like a poppet as the red burst from white linen, the flames swooshing up, the swirling, fiery halo. She scrambles to her feet, takes a few steps, stops. Where? Where shall she go? She returns to the stone ledge, sits, bends her head over the bundle.

'You'll have to find you a new mistress.' Jack's voice is flat, dull. The statement is so obvious, he might have said the sky is up, the earth down. After a moment he adds, 'I don't want one, m'self.' This time his voice catches. He works his throat, clears it. 'I been thinking I might try for making a prentice. I'm a good hand with a scraping knife. Dick Wilmot would speak for me.' The sun is gone now, the alley closed in shadow. 'You could sleep at the chandler's tonight,' he offers.

'No,' Beatrice says. Jack's pale eyes flick towards her. 'I could not bear it,' she says.

And he knows. Jack knows. The stink of rendered fat at the chandler's house, the boiling tallow: the smell would be unendurable. 'I keep seeing it,' he whispers. 'Master John—'

'Hush!' She grips his shoulder. 'Do not say it. Please.'

Jack wipes his nose on his sleeve. Lays his head on his arms again. They sit together while the sky darkens, the curfew bells toll. And here again, behind her eyes, Beatrice sees, as she's seen it all this day, over and over while she wandered: the burst of red on white linen, her mistress flung back, the flames leaping. It was only an instant, she'd shut her eyes, tight, tight; she had not looked up again. The whole time after, she'd stood with her head down, her eyes trained on the trampled earth. But she could not stop her other senses: her ears heard the hungry, crackling fire, the roaring crowd, the curses and yells, the wailing and prayers, a lone man's voice crying out, *Woe unto you that burn Christ's members!* and in her nostrils, the smells: burning hair, roasting meat, wood smoke and ash, the stench of burning organs, and later the rendered stink of grease and bone. Jack says, his voice muffled, his head still on his arms, 'You might find you a new mistress among the believers.'

'I do not wish a new mistress.'

He lifts his head. 'What will you do, then?'

It is the very question. Beatrice hesitates an instant, answers as her mistress would answer: 'Pray.'

Jack puts his head down again. In a moment she hears him softly snoring.

What she means is that she'll go to a church to pray. She'll light a candle for Anne. She does not know which church. Not St Mary Aldermary. Not St Mary-le-Bow. She would like to go to the cathedral of St Paul, but she fears to see her mistress's tormentors there. This is what they had always intended, she thinks. To rob Mistress Anne of Christian burial. That is the heretics' curse, their condemnation, their doom. But Mistress Anne is not condemned. Beatrice knows this. She remembers the moment their eyes met, how Anne gave her the old familiar look that said she had something important to discuss when they're alone together again.

Oh, but they'll never be alone together no more.

In the dark alley, as the night cools and Jack snores gently beside her, Beatrice holds her mistress's soft travelling bag in her arms, and weeps.

In the morning, the path, to Beatrice, seems clear. She shoves Jack's arm to wake him. It is very early. The sky is just turning light. 'Where is the king's court now?'

Jack is rubbing his sleep-matted eyes. 'What? How should I know? Whitehall, I think.'

'You must find out for me. And can you get us something to eat? Have you any money?'

He shakes his head, blinking around the empty alley as if dazed, half asleep. 'I can beg us some bread, maybe. Or the believers will feed us. Master John said they will.'

'Well, go to them, then. And bring me word of the court.'

The boy yawns, scratches his scalp. He nods vaguely, dons his cap, sets out in the ruddy light.

It will be good, Beatrice thinks, if the court is indeed at Whitehall; she'll not have to travel by water then, she can walk there. She has no money to pay a wherryman. No money to live on whatsoever. But the Lord will provide. Mistress Anne says this all the time, quoting from Scripture, her old familiar ways, *upon the mountain shall the Lord provide.* Beatrice aches in every bone of her body. She aches in her heart. The sky is coming lighter, but it will be a muddy day, she thinks; the swaths of grey she can see above her are dull as pewter. How will she get word to Lady Lane past the guards once she reaches Whitehall? She doesn't know, but surely the path will be made straight. This is something else her mistress often says. Said.

Beatrice sits down again on the stone step. The first letter she'd laboured over was to Lady Lane. Never delivered but kept folded and secret with her mistress's writings in the depths of the dark cell. Now she must bring Lady Lane's letter to her. This is what Anne's eyes were saying: I have something to discuss with you. When next we are alone: Deliver my letters, Beatrice, each unto each.

All around her, London is waking. She hears the rumble of carts in the distance, the cries of the fishmongers, the bread-sellers' voices. She opens her mistress's bundle, pulls out the soiled clothes, and lays them on the cobbles; she reaches in deep and withdraws, in several handfuls, the tightly folded pages. One by one, she unfolds them. Most are in Anne's hand, the script beautiful but tiny, crimped small, so as to squeeze as many words as possible onto the precious paper. Beatrice places each missive in order; it requires some time to sort them. The later ones are in Beatrice's own crabbed, ugly hand. She is ashamed how the letters look, like crippled children, but she is not ashamed of the words. Mistress Anne told each one to her, spelled each word, letter by letter. She pages through, finds the first one she wrote, to Lady Lane: *I do perceive, dere frend in the Lord, that thou art not yet perswaded thoroughly in the truth . . .*

Beatrice breathes hard; she smooths the last page open. The very last one she wrote. The words are scarcely legible, so ill-formed and blotched are they, but there is a great wash of familiarity as she looks at them. The words are alive in two ways. They live here, as these ugly scratches on crinkled paper, this July morning in this shadowed alley. And they live in Beatrice's ear, in the voice of her mistress, speaking quietly from her small, hard bed in the dark prison cell: 'For my God will not be eaten with teeth, neither yet dieth he again. And upon these words that I have now spoken, will I suffer death.'

Flesh, blood, and bone.

This was all Mistress Anne needed to say to her tormentors. The bread of the sacrament is flesh, blood, and bone. She need not believe, as Beatrice believes. She had only to say it: At the blessing of the priest, the bread is transformed into the very body of Christ, really.

But it is the miracle of the Mass! Beatrice thinks. It is God's holy miracle. If God could make the entire world in seven days and create Adam of dust and Eve of his rib, why may He not make of the Blessed Sacrament the very body and blood of His precious Son? Why would Mistress Anne not say so? Beatrice's chest is heaving. Her throat is dry. She reads the words of her mistress, written in her own square, clumsy blotches, but she hears them in Anne's voice, as if sifting in the dust of the air, as if drifted like ash on the wind from Smithfield.

O Lord, I have more enemies now than there be hairs on my head.

They burned her. Flesh, blood, and bone.

The morning light slants into the alley. The bells of St Mary-le-Bow are ringing, calling the faithful to Mass. Beatrice crosses herself. She yearns to go. And she will go. Later. After she has finished her work. From South Kelsey to Greenwich to Newgate to Smithfield, her mistress charged her to keep her writings, to care for them, not let them be taken. Now she is charged to deliver them where Mistress Anne would have them go. 'My friends ask of my handlings,' she'd said—this in the dark cell after she'd been returned from the Tower. 'You must write it for me, Beatrice, for I cannot do it now. I would have my friends in Christ know the truth. I never surrendered, I never named others. I never denied my faith.'

And so, word by word, Beatrice wrote as Anne told her, to the very last, until the very morning the guards came for her—can it be only yesterday? Yes. Just yesterday. Praying the Lord to forgive them, her enemies, *that violence which they do, and have done, unto me.* Beatrice looks down. The page blurs before her eyes.

. . . and to set forth thy verity aright, the blotched letters say, *without all vain fantasies of sinful men.*

'And sinful women,' Beatrice whispers. Alone in the alley, the cathedral bells ringing, the task before her weighing like a crushing stone, she reads aloud the last words her mistress gave her. In the bright echoing sunlight, she hears Anne's voice murmuring inside the dark cell:

'So be it. O Lord so be it.'

Acknowledgments

Many sources have gone into the making of this book. I am particularly indebted to Derek Wilson for his excellent histories *A Tudor Tapestry* and *The Queen and the Heretic* and to Hilary Mantel for the guiding inspiration of her magnificent Cromwell trilogy. This research was supported in part by a grant from the Research Council of the University of Oklahoma Norman Campus. Additional support was provided through a National Humanities Center Summer Residential Fellowship sponsored by the OU Arts & Humanities Forum. Special thanks to Sue Addison of Goodlane B&B, Lincoln, UK, who took me to South Kelsey, North Willingham, the Rambler's Church in Walesby, and on so many wonderful walks in the Lincolnshire Wolds. My gratitude, always, to those who've supported this work over many years, especially my husband, Paul Austin, my sister Ruth Askew Brelsford, and my friend Anne Masters. The most important source for this book has been Anne Askew herself and the invaluable record she left behind in her writings. First published in 1546 by John Bale in the months after her death; later collected in John Foxe's *Actes and Monuments*, also known as *Foxe's Book of Martyrs*; reprinted many times over the centuries and reissued in the late twentieth century in a volume effectively edited by Elaine V. Beilin, the account stands as one of the most important early works by a woman writer in English: *The Examinations of Anne Askew*.

Author's Note

Ayscough was the traditional spelling of Anne's surname, as used by her father, Sir William, and her brothers, Francis, Christopher, and Edward. In her own writings, Anne signed her name Askew, sometimes spelled *Askewe*. I've chosen to have her adopt the latter spelling only after she moves to London.

Some sources cite the year of Anne's first examination at Saddlers Hall as 1545, but this dating relies on sixteenth-century records that used the medieval calendar, wherein the new year began on March 25, Lady Day. In his footnotes in *The Queen and the Heretic* (pp. 110–11), historian Derek Wilson makes an excellent argument for dating Anne's first examination to March 10, 1546, according to the modern calendar. I agree with his assessment and have used his dating of Anne's trials, as well as his birth order for the Ayscough siblings, throughout. Some repetitive elements of Anne's trials have been elided in the interest of narrative tension. As we know from her autobiographical writings, she was asked the same questions again, and again, and again . . .